T0333004

PENGUIN BOOKS

THE GRANDEST GAME

Also by Jennifer Lynn Barnes

The Inheritance Games Saga

The Inheritance Games

The Inheritance Games

The Hawthorne Legacy

The Final Gambit

The Brothers Hawthorne

The Grandest Game

The Grandest Game

Coming next: *Glorious Rivals*

Games Untold

The Debutantes

Little White Lies

Deadly Little Scandals

THE GRANDEST GAME

JENNIFER LYNN BARNES

PENGUIN BOOKS

PENGUIN BOOKS

UK | USA | Canada | Ireland | Australia
India | New Zealand | South Africa

Penguin Books is part of the Penguin Random House group of companies
whose addresses can be found at global.penguinrandomhouse.com

www.penguin.co.uk
www.puffin.co.uk
www.ladybird.co.uk

First published in the USA by Little, Brown and Company, a division of
Hachette Book Group, Inc., and in Great Britain by Penguin Books 2024

001

Cover design by Karina Granda
Interior design by Carla Weise
Printed and bound in Great Britain by Clays Ltd, Elcograf S.p.A.

The authorized representative in the EEA is Penguin Random House Ireland,
Morrison Chambers, 32 Nassau Street, Dublin D02 YH68

A CIP catalogue record for this book is available from the British Library

Hardback
ISBN: 978–0–241–67205–1

International Paperback
ISBN: 978–0–241–67204–4

All correspondence to:
Penguin Books
Penguin Random House Children's
One Embassy Gardens, 8 Viaduct Gardens,
London SW11 7BW

For Rose

Prologue

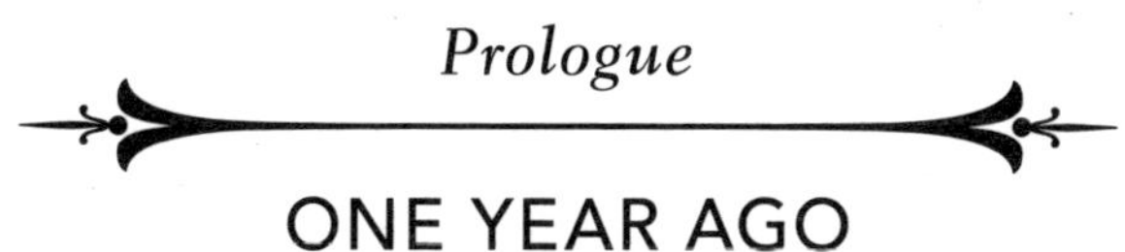

ONE YEAR AGO

There was a price to be paid for power, always. The only question was how steep that price was—and who was going to pay it.

Rohan knew that better than most. He also knew better than to get his knickers in a twist about it. What was a little blood loss or the occasional broken heart or finger among friends?

Not that Rohan had *friends*, per se.

"Ask me why you're here." The Proprietor's quiet command slashed through the air like a sword.

The Proprietor of the Devil's Mercy *was* power, and he'd raised Rohan like a son—a Machiavellian, amoral, *useful* son. Even as a child, Rohan had understood that in this hidden, underground palace, knowledge was currency, and ignorance was weakness.

He knew better than to *ask* a damn thing.

Instead, he smiled, a rogue's smile, as much a weapon in his arsenal as any blade or secret he'd collected. "Asking is for those without other ways of obtaining answers."

"And you are a master of those other ways," the Proprietor acknowledged. "Observation, manipulation, the ability to go unseen or command a room at will."

"I am also quite easy on the eyes." Rohan was playing a dangerous game, but then, that was the only kind of game he'd ever played.

"If you will not *ask*..." The Proprietor's hand curved around the handle of his ornate silver cane. "Then tell me, Rohan: Why have I summoned you here?"

This was it. Certainty thrummed through Rohan's veins as he answered. "The succession."

The Devil's Mercy was, on its surface, a luxurious gambling club, hidden and known only to its members: the ultra-wealthy, the aristocratic, the influential. In truth, the Mercy was so much more. A historic legacy. A shadow force. A place where deals were struck and fortunes set.

"The succession," the Proprietor confirmed. "I am in need of an heir. I've been given two years to live, three at the outside. By December thirty-first of next year, I will pass the crown."

A different person might have focused on the prospect of death, but Rohan did not. In two hundred years, control of the Mercy had passed only four times before. The heir was always young, the appointment for life.

This was and had always been Rohan's endgame. "I am not your only option for heir."

"Why should you be?" Coming from the Proprietor, that was not a rhetorical question. *Make your case, boy.*

I know every inch of the Mercy, Rohan thought. *Every shadow, every trick. The membership knows me. They know not to cross me. You've already spoken of my skills—the more palatable ones, at least.*

Out loud, Rohan opted for a different tactic. "We both know I'm a magnificent bastard."

"You are everything I made you to be. But some things must be won."

"I'm ready." Rohan felt the way he did every time he stepped into the ring to fight, knowing that pain was inevitable—and irrelevant.

"There's a buy-in." The Proprietor cut to the chase. "To take control of the Mercy, you must first purchase your stake. Ten million pounds should suffice."

Automatically, Rohan's mind began charting paths to the crown. The fact that he *could* see options set off his sixth sense. "What's the catch?"

"The catch, my boy, is what it ever was—for me, for all who came before us, all the way back to the first Proprietor's heir. You cannot make your fortune within the walls of the Mercy, nor use any leverage obtained while in her employ. You cannot so much as enter these halls, use the Mercy's name, or approach or accept favor from any member."

Outside of the Mercy, Rohan had nothing—not even a last name.

"You will leave London within twenty-four hours, and you will not return unless and until you have the buy-in."

Ten million pounds. This wasn't just a challenge. This was exile.

"In your absence," the Proprietor continued, "the duchess will act as Factotum in your stead. If you fail to obtain the buy-in, *she* will be my heir."

There it was: the game, the stakes, the threat.

"Go," the Proprietor said, blocking the way back to Rohan's rooms. "*Now.*"

Rohan knew London. He could move through any part of the city, high society or low, like a ghost. But for the first time since he was five years old, he didn't have the Mercy to go back to.

Look for an opening. Look for a loophole. Look for a weakness. His mind churning, Rohan looked for a pint.

Outside his pub of choice, two dogs fought. The smaller of the two had the look of a wolf about her. She was losing the fight. Stepping into the middle of it probably wasn't the wisest course of action, but Rohan was a little beyond *wisdom* at the moment.

When the larger dog had been sent on its way, Rohan wiped the blood off his forearm and knelt in front of the smaller one. She snarled. He smiled.

The pub door opened. Inside, a television blared—an anchor's voice. "We're hearing reports that the first annual Grandest Game, the sprawling, mind-twisting competition designed and funded by Hawthorne heiress Avery Grambs, has reportedly reached its conclusion. A winner of the seventeen-million-dollar prize is expected to be announced via livestream any—"

The door slammed shut.

Rohan met the dog's wolfish gaze. "Annual," he murmured. Meaning that next year, there would be another. He would have a year to plan. A year to arrange things just so. Fortunately, Avery Grambs had never been a *member* of the Devil's Mercy.

Hello, loophole. Rohan stood. He reached for the pub door and glanced down. "Coming?" he asked the dog.

Inside, the owner of the pub recognized Rohan immediately. "What'll it be?"

Even without the backing of the Mercy, a man of Rohan's skills and reputation still had a card or two to play. "A pint for me," he said. "A steak for her." Rohan's lips curved, more on one side than the other. "And transportation out of London. Tonight."

Chapter 1

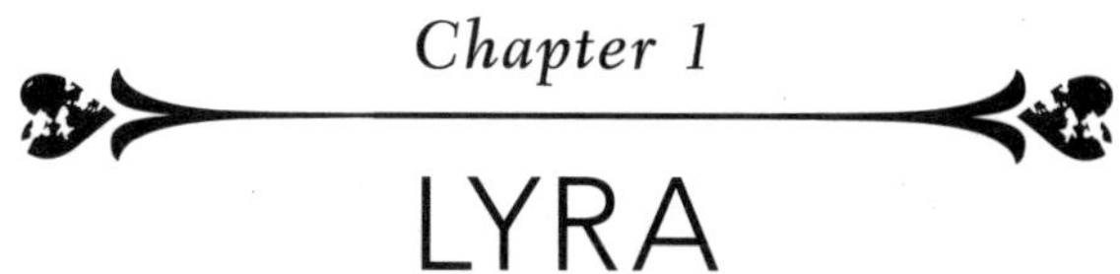

LYRA

The dream started the way it always did, with the flower. Seeing the calla lily in her hand filled Lyra with sickly sweet dread. She looked to her other hand—and the sad remains of a candy necklace. It held only three pieces of candy.

No.

On some level, Lyra knew she was nineteen, but in the dream, her hands were small—a child's hands. The shadow looming over her was large.

And then came the whisper: *"A Hawthorne did this."*

The shadow—her biological father—turned and walked away. Lyra couldn't see his face. She heard footsteps going up the stairs.

He has a gun. Lyra woke with a start, a breath trapped in her chest, her body rigid, and her head . . . on a desk. In the time it took for her vision to clear and the real world to slide firmly back into place in front of her, Lyra remembered that she was in class.

Except the lecture hall was almost empty.

“You have ten minutes left on the test.” The only other person in the room was a fifty-year-old man wearing a blazer.

Test? Lyra’s gaze darted to a clock on the wall. As she registered the time, her panic began to ebb.

“Might as well just take the zero at this point.” The professor scowled at her. “The rest of the class is already done. I suspect *they* didn’t spend last night partying.”

Because the only reason a girl who looks like me could be tired enough to fall asleep in class is because she was partying. Annoyance flared inside Lyra, banishing the last remnants of the dream’s dread. She looked down at the test. Multiple choice.

“I’ll see what I can get done in ten minutes.” Lyra fished a pen out of her backpack and began to read.

Most people could see images in their minds. For Lyra, there were only words and concepts and feelings. The only time she *saw* anything in her mind’s eye was when she dreamed. Luckily, not getting bogged down in mental imagery made her a very fast reader. And just as luckily, whoever had written this test had fallen into a predictable pattern, a familiar one.

To find the right answer, all a person had to do was decode the relationships between the options offered. Were two of them opposites? Did one of those opposites vary from the remaining choices only by nuance? Or were there two answers that *sounded* the same? Or one or more answers that *seemed* true but probably weren’t?

That was the thing about multiple-choice tests. You didn’t need to know anything about the material if you could break the code.

Lyra answered five questions in the first minute. Four the next. The more test bubbles she filled in, the more palpable the professor’s irritation with her grew.

“You’re wasting my time,” he said. “And yours.”

The old Lyra might have taken a tone like that to heart. Instead, she read faster. *Spot the pattern, spot the answer.* She finished with one minute to spare and handed the test in, knowing exactly what the professor saw when he looked at her: a girl with a body that said *party* to some people more than it had ever said *dancer.*

Not that she was a dancer, anymore.

Lyra grabbed her bag and turned to leave, and the professor stopped her. "Wait," he ordered tersely. "I'll grade it for you." *Teach you a lesson* was what he meant.

Turning slowly back to face him gave Lyra time to school her features into a neutral expression.

After grading the first ten questions, the professor had marked only one of her answers incorrect. His eyebrows drew closer together as he continued grading, and that percentage held—then improved.

"Ninety-four." He looked up from the test. "Not bad."

Wait for it, Lyra thought.

"Just imagine what you could do if you put in a little more effort."

"How would you know what kind of effort I put in?" Lyra asked. Her voice was quiet, but she met his eyes head-on.

"You're wearing pajamas, you haven't brushed your hair, and you slept through most of the test." He'd recast her, then, from the party girl to the sloth. "I've never even seen you in lecture," the professor continued sternly.

Lyra shrugged. "That's because I'm not in this class."

"You—" He stopped. He stared. "You're..."

"I'm not in this class," Lyra repeated. "I fell asleep in the prior lecture." Without waiting for a reply, she turned and started up the aisle toward the exit. Her stride was long. Maybe it was graceful. Maybe *she* was, still.

The professor called after her. “How did you get a ninety-four percent on a test for a class you’re not even taking?”

Lyra kept walking, her back to the man, as she answered. “Trying to write trick questions backfires if the person taking the test knows how to look for tricks.”

Chapter 2

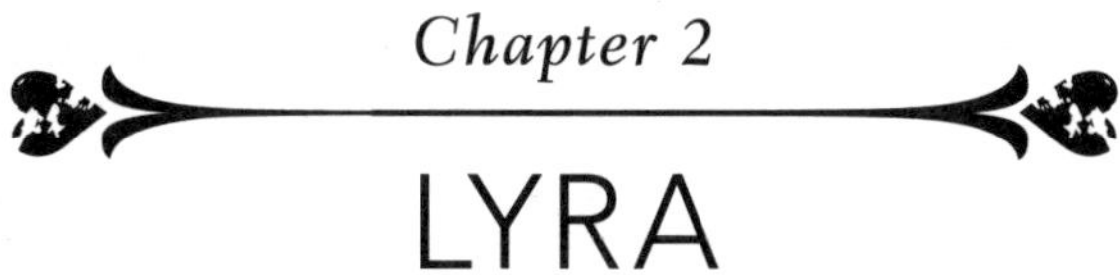

LYRA

The email came in that afternoon: from the Registrar's Office, CC-ed to the Bursar's Office, subject line *Enrollment Hold*. Reading it three times didn't change its contents.

Lyra's phone rang halfway through her fourth read. *You're fine*, she reminded herself, as much out of habit as anything. *Everything is fine.*

Bracing herself for impact, she answered. "Hi, Mom."

"So you *do* remember me! And your phone *does* work! And you *haven't* been kidnapped by a mathematically minded serial killer intent on adding you to his incredibly sinister equation."

"New book?" Lyra guessed. Her mother was a writer.

"New book! She likes numbers more than people. He's a cop who trusts his instincts more than her calculations. They *hate* each other."

"In a good way?"

"A *very* good way. And speaking of mind-blowing chemistry and sizzling romantic tension... how are you?"

Lyra made a face. "Bad segue, Mom."

"Answer the question, you avoider! I am going into daughter withdrawal. Your dad thinks the first week in November is too early for Christmas decorations, your brother is four and has no appreciation whatsoever for dark chocolate, and if I want anyone to watch rom-coms with me, I'm going to need zip ties."

For the past three years, Lyra had done everything she could to seem normal, to *be* normal—the Lyra who loved Christmas and chocolate and rom-coms. And every day, pretending had killed her a little more.

That was how she'd ended up at a college a thousand miles from home.

"So. How are you?" Her mom really was going to just keep asking, indefinitely.

Lyra offered up three words in response. "Single. Petty. Armed."

Her mother laughed. "You are not."

"Not petty or not armed?" Lyra asked. She didn't even touch on *single*.

"Petty," her mom replied. "You are a kind and generous soul, Lyra Catalina Kane, and we both know that anything can be a weapon if you believe in your heart that you can maim or kill someone with it."

The conversation felt so normal, so *them*, that Lyra could hardly bear it. "Mom? I got an email from the Bursar's Office."

Silence fell like a thousand-year-old tree.

"It's possible my last check from my publisher was late," her mom said finally. "And lower than I expected. But I'll figure this out, baby. Everything's going to be fine."

Everything is fine. That was Lyra's line, had been her line for three years, ever since the name *Hawthorne* had started dominating the news cycle and memories she'd repressed with good reason had come flooding back. One in particular.

"Forget about tuition, Mom." Lyra needed to get off the phone. It was easier to project *normal* at a distance, but it still came with a cost. "I can take next semester off, get a job, apply for loans for the fall."

"Absolutely not." The voice that issued those words wasn't her mom's.

"Hi, Dad."

Keith Kane had married her mother when she was three and adopted her when she was five. He was the only *dad* she'd ever known. Until the dreams had started, she hadn't even remembered her biological father.

"Your mom and I will handle this, Lyra." There was no arguing with her dad's tone.

The old Lyra wouldn't have even tried. "Handle it how?" she pressed.

"We have options."

Lyra knew, just from the way he said the word *options*, what he was thinking. "Mile's End," she said. He couldn't mean it. Mile's End was more than just a house. It was the attic gables and the front porch swing and the woods and the creek and generations of Kanes carving their names into the same tree.

Lyra had grown up at Mile's End. She'd carved her name into that tree when she was nine years old. Her baby brother deserved to do the same. *I can't be the reason they sell.*

"We've been talking about downsizing for a while now." Her dad was calm, matter-of-fact. "The upkeep on this old place is killing us. If I let Mile's End go, we could get a little house in town, put you through school, start a college fund for your brother. There's a developer—"

"There's always a developer." Lyra didn't even let him finish. "And you always tell them to go to hell."

This time, the silence on the other end of the line spoke volumes.

Chapter 3

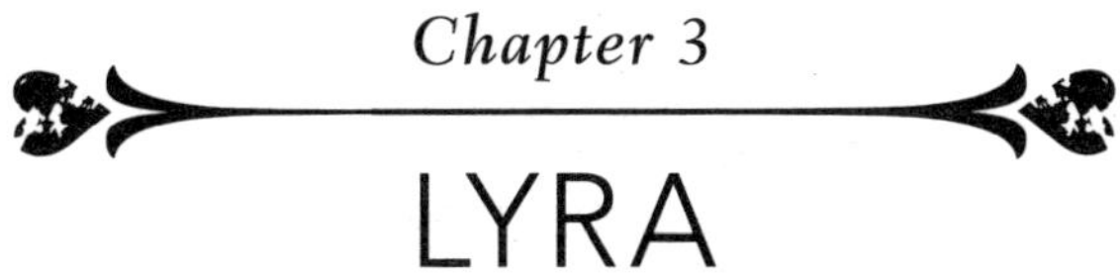

LYRA

Running hurt. Maybe that was why she liked it. The old Lyra had hated running. Now, she could go distances. The problem was that, over time, it started hurting a little less. So every day, she pushed herself further.

And further.

And further.

Her parents and friends had been bewildered when she'd given up dancing for this. She'd held out until November of her senior year of high school, a year ago, nearly to the day. She'd faked it as long as she could. But even she wasn't a good enough actress to fake the kind of dancer she'd been. *Before.*

It seemed wrong that her whole life had been derailed by a dream. A single memory. Lyra had known that her biological father was dead—but not that he'd committed suicide, not that she'd *been there*. She'd repressed the trauma so thoroughly, it hadn't even existed for her. One day she'd been a normal, happy teenager, and the next—literally overnight—she wasn't.

Wasn't normal. Wasn't okay, let alone *happy*.

Her parents knew—not what had changed but that something had. She'd fled to a faraway college, but look where that had gotten her. Scholarships only covered so much. Her parents had told her that the remainder of her out-of-state tuition wasn't an issue, but clearly, they'd lied, which probably meant Lyra hadn't done nearly as good a job at pretending to be normal as she'd thought.

As she ran—no matter how far she ran—Lyra's brain kept cycling back to the same conclusion: *I have to drop out*. That would buy some time at least, take one bill off her parents' plate. The prospect of quitting college shouldn't have hurt. It wasn't like Lyra had made friends this semester or even tried to. She'd coasted through her classes like an academically inclined zombie. She was just treading water.

But that was better than drowning.

Gritting her teeth, Lyra picked up her speed. This far into a run, that shouldn't have been feasible. But sometimes, all you could do was *push*.

By the time she stopped, she could barely breathe. The track blurring in front of her, Lyra bent over, her hands on her knees, sucking in oxygen. And some asshole chose that moment to catcall her. Like she'd bent over *just* for him.

A moment later, a soccer ball rolled to a stop by her side.

Lyra glanced up, spotted a group of guys waiting to see how she would react, and spent a few seconds wondering what the collective noun for *asshole* was.

A bevy?

A clutch?

No, Lyra thought, picking up the ball. *A circus.* The circus of assholes probably wasn't expecting her to punt the ball over their heads toward the goal, but her dad was a high school soccer coach, and once her body knew how to do something, it never forgot.

"Missed!" one of the guys yelled, cackling. The ball hit the crossbar at an angle, ricocheted off, and smacked the jerk who'd catcalled her in the back of his head.

"No," Lyra called out. "I didn't."

Dropping out was the right move. The only move. But when Lyra tried to walk up the steps to the Registrar's Office, she ended up a block away at the campus post office instead.

I'm going to do it. I just need a minute. Lyra walked mechanically to her PO box. She wasn't expecting mail. This was pure procrastination, but that didn't stop her from turning the key and opening the box.

Inside, there was an envelope made of thick linen paper. *No return address.* She reached for it. The envelope was heavier than it looked. *No postage.* Lyra froze. This envelope—whatever it was—hadn't been mailed.

Looking back over her shoulder, feeling suddenly like she was being watched, Lyra ripped the envelope open. There were two items inside.

The first was a thin sheet of paper with a message scrawled across it in dark-blue ink. *YOU DESERVE THIS.* As she read the words, the paper began crumbling in her hands. Seconds later, there was nothing left but dust.

Acutely aware of the way her heart was beating in her chest—pounding against the inside of her rib cage with brutal, repetitive force—Lyra reached for the second item in the envelope. It was the size of a folded letter, but the instant her fingers brushed its golden edge, she realized that it was made of metal—very thin metal.

Removing it from the envelope, Lyra saw that the metal was engraved: three words, plus a symbol. *Not a symbol*, she realized. *A QR code, just waiting to be scanned.* Reading the words told Lyra exactly what she held in her hand.

This was a ticket, an invitation, a summons. The words engraved above the code were instantly recognizable—to her, to anyone on the planet with access to media of any kind.

The Grandest Game.

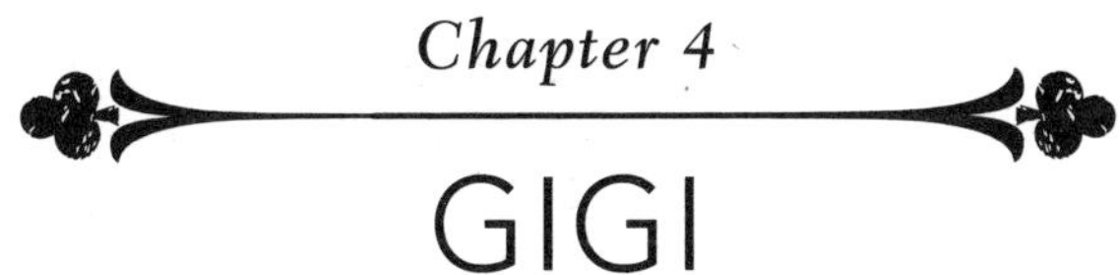

Chapter 4
GIGI

Gigi Grayson was not obsessed! She was not over-caffeinated! She certainly wasn't about to fall off the roof! But try telling a Hawthorne that.

A steady hand caught her elbow. A suit-clad arm encircled her waist.

The next thing Gigi knew, she was safe in her bedroom. That was the way it was with her Hawthorne half brother: He made things happen in *an instant*. Grayson Hawthorne bled power. He won arguments with a single arch of his sharply angled blond brows!

And there was a teeny, tiny chance that Gigi *had* been about to fall off the roof.

"Grayson! I've missed your face! Here, have a cat!" Gigi swooped up Katara—her large Bengal cat, practically a leopard, really—and dumped the cat in Grayson's arms.

Cats were an excellent way of disarming people.

Grayson, however, was impossible to take off guard. He stroked a hand firmly over Katara's head. "Explain." As the second-eldest of the four grandsons of deceased billionaire Tobias Hawthorne, Grayson was prone to issuing orders.

He also had a bad habit of forgetting that he was three and a half years older than she was, not thirty.

"Why I was on the roof, why I haven't been returning your calls, or why I just handed you a cat?" Gigi asked cheerfully.

Grayson's pale gray eyes roved over her room, taking in the hundreds of pieces of scratch paper that littered every surface: her mattress, her floor, even the walls. Then his gaze returned to Gigi. Without a word, Grayson gently pushed up her left sleeve. Notes danced across her skin, freshly inked in Gigi's loopy, haphazard scrawl.

"I ran out of paper. But I think I'm getting close!" Gigi grinned. "I just needed a little change in perspective."

Grayson gave her a look. "Hence, the roof."

"Hence, the roof."

Grayson set Katara gently down. "I thought you were going to use your gap year to travel."

And *that* was why she'd been avoiding his calls. "I'll have plenty of time to go all Gigi Without Borders later," she promised.

"After the Grandest Game." Grayson did not phrase that as a question.

Gigi didn't deny it. What was the point? "Seven players," she said, her eyes alight. "Seven golden tickets—three to players of Avery's choosing and four wild cards."

Those wild card tickets had been hidden in secret locations across the United States. A single clue had been released to the public less than twenty-four hours earlier. Gigi Grayson, puzzle solver, was on the case!

"Gigi," Grayson said calmly.

"Don't say anything!" Gigi blurted out. "It's already going to look iffy enough that I'm your sister, when everyone knows the Grandest Game is a group effort."

A group effort between the Hawthorne brothers and the Hawthorne heiress, between Tobias Hawthorne's four grandsons and the seemingly random teenager who'd inherited the eccentric billionaire's entire fortune.

"As it happens," Grayson said, "I've had no involvement whatsoever in designing this year's game. Avery and Jamie requested I be boots on the ground. I'll be running things; thus, to protect the integrity of the puzzles, I'm going in with no foreknowledge whatsoever."

Can't tip your hand if you don't know the cards, Gigi thought. "I love that for you," she told Grayson. "But still! Shush." She gave him her firmest look. "I have to do this on my own."

Grayson responded to Gigi's attempt at firmness with exactly two seconds of silence, followed by a single question: "Where is your bed?"

Gigi hadn't been expecting the subject change. *Very tricky, Grayson.* Offering him her sunniest grin, Gigi gestured to the mattress on her floor. "Voilà!"

"That," Grayson told her, "is a mattress. Where is your *bed*?"

The bed in question had been mahogany, an antique. Before Gigi could summon up a suitably chaotic distraction to deflect the question, Grayson strode toward her closet and opened it.

"You're probably wondering where the rest of my clothes are," Gigi said brightly. "And I would be happy to tell you—after the game."

"In five words or less, Juliet."

The use of her given name was probably a sign that he wasn't going to let this go. In the year and a half since she'd met her brother, Gigi had gathered—through her powers of inference and also snooping—that Grayson was the grandson that billionaire Tobias Hawthorne had molded from childhood to be the perfect heir: formidable, commanding, always in control.

With a roll of her eyes, Gigi gave in to his demand, ticking the words off on her fingers as she went: "Reverse heist." She grinned. "I did it in two!"

Grayson responded to that with another dreaded arch of his brow.

"Reverse heist," Gigi clarified helpfully, "all the breaking, all the entering—but you leave something behind instead of stealing."

"Am I to take it that your mahogany bedframe is now residing in someone else's home?"

"Don't be ridiculous!" Gigi said. "I sold it for cash and reverse-heisted *that*." Making an executive decision, Gigi squatted and called Katara toward her.

Anticipating—correctly—that he was about to have a very large cat placed on his head, Grayson knelt and laid a light hand on Gigi's shoulder. "Is this about our father?"

Gigi kept right on breathing. She kept right on smiling. The trick to pretending that THE SECRET was just a secret and that she excelled at keeping them was never to even *think* about Sheffield Grayson.

Besides, smiling made you happier. That was just science.

"This is about *me*," Gigi said. She gave Katara some neck scritchies and used one of the cat's paws to gesture to the door. "Vamoose."

Grayson did not vamoose. "I have something for you." He reached inside the jacket of his Armani suit and produced a black gift box: an inch tall and maybe twice the length of a Pop-Tart. "From Avery."

Gigi stared at the box. As Grayson removed the lid, all she

could think, over the sound of the roaring beat of her own heart, was: *Seven golden tickets—three to players of Avery's choosing.*

"It's yours if you want it." Grayson's voice was softer now. He wasn't a soft person, and that told Gigi that this gift wasn't just a lark. This was Avery trying to make up for—

Don't think about it. Just keep smiling.

"I'm not going to tell anyone," Gigi said, a traitorous lump rising in her throat. "Avery knows that, right?"

Grayson brought his eyes to hers. "She knows."

Gigi took a deep breath and a step back. "Tell Avery thank you—but no." Gigi didn't want anyone's guilt. She didn't want their pity. She didn't want Grayson to think for even a second that she wasn't strong enough. That she was worth pitying.

"If you don't take it," Grayson said, "I have instructions to give this ticket to Savannah."

"Savannah's busy," Gigi replied immediately. "With college. And basketball. And world domination." Gigi's twin didn't know THE SECRET. Savannah was the smart twin, the pretty twin, the strong one. She was focused, determined, thriving in college.

And Gigi was . . . here.

She looked back to the writing on her arm, banishing Grayson's presence from her mind. She could do this—all of it.

Keep THE SECRET.

Protect Savannah.

Break the code and obtain a ticket of her own.

And prove, for once in her life, that she had what it took to win.

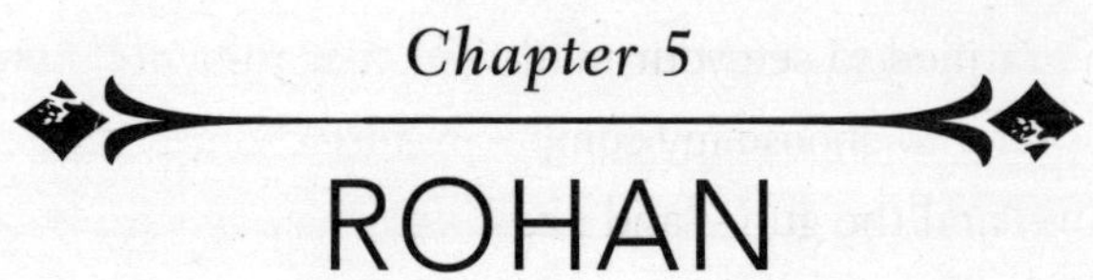

Chapter 5
ROHAN

If I had a tenner, Rohan thought, *for every time someone pointed a gun at the back of my head*...

"Hand it over." The fool with the gun had no idea how much his voice betrayed him.

"Hand what over?" Rohan turned, displaying his empty hands. Granted, they hadn't been empty the second before.

"The ticket." The man shook his gun in Rohan's face. "Give it to me! There are only two wild cards left in the game."

"Point of fact," Rohan said lazily, "there are none."

"You couldn't possibly know that."

Rohan smiled. "My mistake." He saw the exact instant his opponent realized: Rohan didn't make mistakes. He'd found his first wild card ticket in Las Vegas and a second one here in Atlanta, at which point, he'd moved on to the next phase of his plan.

This rooftop provided an excellent vantage point from which to observe the courtyard below.

"You have the last two tickets? Both of them?" The man lowered his gun and took a step forward—mistakes, both. "Give me one. *Please.*"

"I'm gratified to see your manners are improving, but as it happens, I prefer to choose my competition." Rohan turned his back on the man—and the gun—and angled his gaze toward the courtyard below. "She'll do."

Four stories down, a young woman with hair the color of chocolate and a gravity-defying bounce in her step was investigating a statue.

"It's possible," Rohan said, a pleasant hum in his voice, "that the ticket I found up here is now residing down there."

After a split second, the man with the gun bolted for the stairs—for the courtyard below. *For the girl.*

"Hurt her, and you'll regret it." Rohan didn't put any heat in those words. He didn't have to.

Most people had enough sense to recognize the moment he'd flipped the switch.

"That's it, folks! A press release from Hawthorne heiress Avery Grambs has confirmed that, less than forty-eight hours in, all seven slots in this year's Grandest Game have been claimed."

Sitting on the edge of a bed that was not his, wearing nothing but a lush Turkish cotton robe, Rohan twirled a knife slowly through his fingers. There were advantages to being a ghost. In the past year, he'd slipped in and out of luxury hotels like this one with ease. He'd spent that year obtaining funds, contacts, intelligence—not enough, in and of itself, to win him the Mercy, but enough that nothing about his current plan had been left to chance.

"Last year's game was a free-for-all," the reporter continued onscreen, "as people from around the world raced through a series of elaborate clues that took them from Mozambique to Alaska to Dubai. This year's affair looks to be more intimate, with the identities of the seven lucky players currently a closely guarded secret."

Not that closely guarded. Not against someone with Rohan's skill set.

"The location of the game is also being kept tightly under wraps."

"For some values of the word *tightly*," Rohan quipped. He turned off the television. Upon claiming his ticket, he'd been given a pickup location and a time. Now that it was drawing close, he made his way to the luxury suite's massive shower.

He lost the robe but kept the knife.

As the glass walls of the shower steamed up around him, Rohan brought the tip of his blade to the glass. He'd always had a light hand, always known exactly how hard—or soft—to push. Lightly, he skimmed the knife through the steam, drawing six symbols in the moisture on the surface of the glass.

A bishop, a rook, a knight, two pawns, and a queen.

Already, Rohan had begun to classify his competition. *Odette Morales. Brady Daniels. Knox Landry.* He dragged the tip of his blade through the bishop, the rook, and the knight. That just left the three players nearest to Rohan's own age of not quite twenty. Gigi Grayson he'd observed from the rooftop. The other two he knew only on paper.

A game such as this one would require the cultivation of certain assets. Those three were…possibilities.

Gigi Grayson. Savannah Grayson. Lyra Kane. Only time would tell which of the three would prove of the most use to Rohan—and if any of them had the versatility of the queen.

Chapter 6

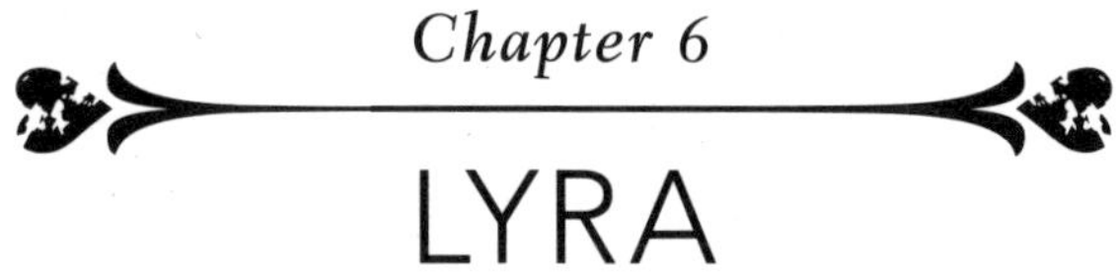

LYRA

A chauffeured car picked Lyra up at the designated meeting spot. A private jet flew her from one secured airstrip to another. There, she found a helicopter.

"Welcome aboard." A voice spoke from the far side of the aircraft, and a moment later, a long, lean form strolled around it to join her.

Lyra recognized him immediately. Of course she did. Jameson Hawthorne was very recognizable. "Technically, I'm not on board yet," Lyra said.

Was that petty? Maybe. But he was a Hawthorne, and seeing him brought back the dream—and the only three things Lyra could remember her dead father ever saying to her.

Happy birthday, Lyra.

A Hawthorne did this.

And then, a riddle: *What begins a bet? Not that.*

"When I said *aboard*, I wasn't talking about the chopper." Jameson Hawthorne was apparently the kind of person who could roll a smirk right into a smile in the blink of an eye. "Welcome to the Grandest Game, Lyra Catalina Kane."

There was something in the way he said those words, an unholy energy, an invitation.

"You're Jameson Hawthorne," Lyra said. She didn't allow an ounce of awe in her tone. She didn't want him to think she was affected by his presence, by his looks, by the way he leaned up against a helicopter as casually as he would have a wall.

"Guilty," Jameson replied. "Of most things, really." And then he looked over her shoulder. "You're late," he called.

"If by *late*, you mean *early*."

Lyra froze. She knew that voice, knew it the way her body knew choreography she'd practiced a thousand times, like decades from now, she'd still ache with the memory of it the second she heard the music. She *knew* that voice.

Grayson Hawthorne.

"Definitely late," Jameson called.

"I am never late."

"It's almost as if," Jameson said innocently, "someone told you the wrong time."

Lyra barely heard Jameson, because the only sound her brain could process was footsteps on the pavement behind her. She told herself that she was being ridiculous, that she couldn't *feel* Grayson Hawthorne coming closer.

He was nothing to her.

A Hawthorne did this. That memory gave way to another, her father's voice replaced by Grayson's: *Stop calling.* That was the imperious, dismissive order he'd issued the third and final time she'd dialed his number looking for answers, looking for *something.*

To this day, Grayson Hawthorne was the only person she'd ever told about the memory, the dreams, her father's suicide, the fact that she'd been there.

And Grayson Hawthorne hadn't cared.

Of course he hadn't. She was a stranger to him, a nobody, and he was a Hawthorne, an arrogant, cold, above-it-all, *asshole* Hawthorne who didn't care how many lives his billionaire grandfather had ruined—or whose.

Grayson stopped a few feet shy of Lyra. "I assume, Jamie, that you're aware that you're being watched."

"Oh, I assure you, he most definitely is." That reply hadn't come from Jameson.

Lyra finally managed to turn around. Beyond Grayson—who she did *not* look at—she could see a figure strolling toward them, far enough away that he shouldn't have been able to hear or respond to the conversation.

And yet... Lyra studied the new arrival. He was tall, broad through the shoulders but lean everywhere else, and he moved with a grace that she recognized, like to like. His accent was British, his skin light brown, his cheekbones sharp.

And his smile was nothing short of dangerous.

His black, thick hair curled slightly on the ends, but there was nothing *messy* about it. About him. "Though, as a point of clarification," the newcomer said, his eyes locking on to Lyra's, "*Jameson* wasn't the one I was watching."

Me, Lyra thought. *He was watching me. Scoping out the competition.*

"Rohan," Jameson greeted, his tone half-accusing and half-amused.

"Pleasure to see you, too, Hawthorne." The guy's accent sounded less aristocratic than it had a moment before, and Lyra was hit with the sudden sense that this *Rohan* could be whoever he wanted to be.

If only it were that easy for her.

"Take a step back," Grayson ordered. Lyra wasn't sure if he was talking to Jameson or Rohan. The only thing that was clear was that *her* presence didn't even register.

"My uptight and somewhat less charismatic brother here is going to be the one making sure everybody plays by the rules this year," Jameson warned Rohan. "Yourself included."

"Personally," Rohan said, his gaze going back to Lyra's, his lips slowly curving into *that* smile again, "I find that playing by the rules is *exactly* half the fun."

Chapter 7
LYRA

Jameson flew the helicopter, which surprised Lyra less than the fact that Grayson deigned to ride in back with the players—four of them in total. The introductions had already been made.

Focus on the competition, Lyra told herself. *Not on Grayson Hawthorne.*

Rohan was to her right, conveniently blocking—or mostly blocking—Grayson from view. The British competitor sat with his long legs stretched out slightly, his posture casual—deliberately so. Opposite Rohan was a guy in his mid-twenties who Jameson had introduced as Knox Landry. Lyra turned her attention to him.

Knox had frat-boy hair, gelled and combed back except where it fell artfully into his face. He was white, lightly tanned, and brunette with shrewd eyes, dark eyebrows, and a sharp jawline, and he wore an expensive fleece sports vest over a collared shirt. The combined effect of his outfit and his hair should have screamed *country club* or *finance bro*, but a nose that had been broken one time too many whispered *bar fight* instead.

As Lyra studied him, Knox openly returned the favor. Whatever he saw in her, the guy clearly wasn't impressed.

Underestimate me. Please. Lyra was used to it. There were worse things in the world than being handed a strategic advantage, right off the bat.

Her temper fully in check, Lyra turned her attention to the old woman seated beside Knox. Odette Morales had thick, silvery-gray hair that she wore long and loose. The tips—and only the tips—had been dyed jet black. Lyra wondered how old she was.

"Eighty-one, darling." Odette read Lyra like a book, then smiled. "I like to think I've mellowed with age."

Not mellow, Lyra registered. Something about Odette—her aging beauty, her smile—reminded Lyra of an eagle on the hunt.

The helicopter took a sudden, sharp turn, trapping a breath in Lyra's throat as the view out her window banished every other thought from her mind. The Pacific Ocean was vast and blue—a rich, dark blue woven through with shades of green just as deep. Along the coastline, large rock formations jutted out above the water, like monuments to another time and a more ancient earth. There was something magical about the way the waves broke against the rocks.

As the helicopter peeled off the coast and soared out over the water, Lyra wondered how far they had to go. What kind of range did this helicopter have? A hundred miles? Five hundred miles?

Take it all in. Breathe. For an instant, as the chopper continued zinging along its path, all Lyra could see was ocean—fathomless, limitless.

And then, she saw the island.

It wasn't large, but as the helicopter drew closer, it became clear to Lyra that the splotch of land wasn't as small as it had first appeared, either. The view from above was mostly beige and green—except where it was black.

That was when Lyra knew: where they were, where they were going. *Hawthorne Island.*

The helicopter dipped suddenly, diving downward, then straightening just in time to skim inches above the tree line. In the span of a heartbeat, the chopper crossed from healthy forest to the charred remains of long-dead trees, a reminder that this wasn't just a private island, a holiday getaway, a billionaire's indulgence, one of many.

This place was haunted.

Lyra knew better than most: Tragedy couldn't just be wiped away. Loss left marks. The deeper the scar, the longer it lasted. *There was a fire here, decades ago.* She tried to remember everything she'd read about the fire on Hawthorne Island. *People died. Blame fell on a local girl, not the Hawthornes.*

Convenient, that.

Lyra leaned forward in her seat and inadvertently caught sight of Grayson. He had the kind of face that looked like it had been carved from ice or stone—sharp angles, hard jaw, lips full enough that they should have softened his face but didn't. His hair was pale, his eyes a piercing, silvery gray. Grayson Hawthorne looked, in Lyra's opinion, exactly like he sounded, like weaponized perfection: inhuman, in control, without mercy.

To whom am I speaking? his voice said in her memory. *Or would you prefer I rephrase the question: On whom am I about to hang up?*

Lyra slammed herself back in her seat. Luckily, no one noticed. They were landing.

A circular target marked the helipad, and thanks to Jameson

Hawthorne, they touched down dead center in a landing so smooth that Lyra barely felt it.

It was less than a minute until the helicopter doors opened, but even that felt like too long. Lyra couldn't escape the enclosed space fast enough.

"In some senses," Jameson announced once the players had deboarded, "the game starts tonight. But in another very real sense… it starts right now."

Right now. Lyra's heart rate ticked up. Forget Grayson. Forget the Hawthornes. They'd been children when her stranger of a father had died with the Hawthorne name on his lips. Maybe they could have found something out about the truth, if they'd cared to—if *he* had cared to—but that wasn't why she'd come. Lyra was here for her family. For Mile's End.

"You'll have until sunset to explore the island," Jameson told the players, leaning back against the helicopter once more. "It's within the realm of possibility that we've hidden a few things out there. Hints about what you can expect in this year's game. Objects that will prove of use, somewhere down the line." Jameson pushed off the helicopter, prowling around the lot of them as he continued. "There's a newly built house on the north point. Do whatever you like between now and sundown, but anyone who fails to make it inside the house by the time the sun fully disappears from the horizon is out the game."

Explore the island. Make it in by sundown. Lyra's body was ready, her muscles primed to move, her senses heightened. She walked straight past Grayson Hawthorne to the edge of the landing pad.

"Watch your step," his crisp, self-assured voice ordered behind her. "There's a drop-off."

"I don't fall," Lyra said flatly. "Good balance." There was no reply, and despite herself, she glanced back. Her gaze landed first on Jameson, who was looking at Grayson with the oddest expression on his face. And Grayson . . .

Grayson was looking at *her.* He stared at Lyra—not just like he was noticing her for the first time, but like her very existence had smacked him in the jaw.

Was he really so unused to anyone pushing back?

Lyra didn't need this. She needed to *move.* Knox and Rohan were already gone. Odette stood facing the ocean, the wind blowing her long, black-tipped hair behind her like a flag.

Jameson looked from Grayson to Lyra and smiled a smile that could only be described as wicked. "This should be fun."

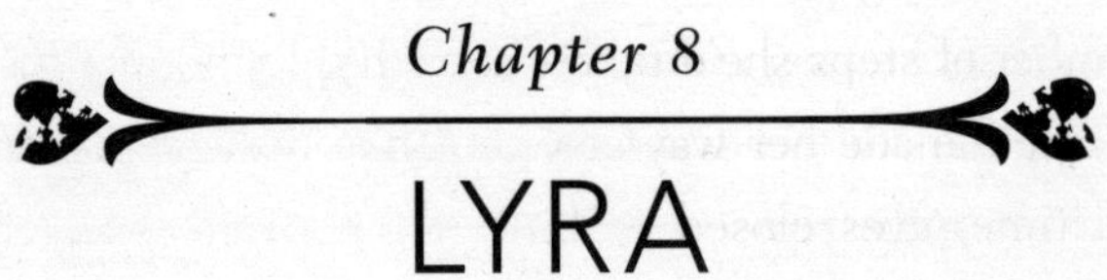

Chapter 8
LYRA

Lyra went straight for the burned side of the island—and the ruins of the house where the fire had started all those years ago. As she stared at what was left, an eerie feeling settled over her body. There were parts of the old mansion that had burned to the ground and parts where its tattered frame still stood, stripped to the bones by the flames. The floors were blackened, the ceilings nonexistent. A stone fireplace still stood, its base overgrown with plants.

Leaves crunched beneath Lyra's feet as she crossed the threshold into the ruins. All around her, whips of green had grown through cracks in the foundation, latching themselves around chunks of concrete. The ground was uneven. There were no remnants of furniture or belongings—just the leaves, the first few to turn color and fall in an unusually warm autumn.

For a full minute, Lyra took it all in, looking for anything that might qualify as a hint or an object to be used in the game. Seeing nothing, she began walking the perimeter of the ruins, giving her body a visceral sense of their size. Later, she wouldn't be able to call to mind a single image, but her body would remember the slight wind coming off the ocean, the cracks in the ground, the exact number of steps she'd taken in each direction.

After she'd made her way around, Lyra walked the same path a second time, eyes closed, willing her body to *sense* the world around her. She made a full circuit, then turned into the wind, toward the back of the house.

Toward the ocean.

Eyes still closed, Lyra paced forward, lifting her hand when she passed by the stone fireplace. Her fingers trailed along its surface—and she felt something in the stone. *Writing.*

Lyra opened her eyes. The letters were small, the carving shallow. It would have been so easy to miss. She dug her fingers into the grooves as she read, feeling the letters.

You cannot Escape the reality of tomorrow by evading it today. —Abraham Lincoln

That had to have been a hint of some sort, but the words felt oddly like a warning: There was no escaping now.

Lyra spent the next ten minutes running her fingers over the rest of the fireplace, looking for more, but there was nothing. Closing her eyes again, she resumed walking. As she passed like a ghost through what had, at one point, been an exterior wall, she lifted her chin. The wind was stronger without even the skeleton of a house to protect her.

She stepped forward again—and a hand locked around her arm.

Lyra's eyes flew open. Grayson Hawthorne stared back at her. Where had he come from? There was nothing painful about the way he held her arm, but there was nothing particularly gentle about his grip, either.

The two of them were standing far too close.

“You are aware that there is a cliff here?” Grayson didn’t let go of her arm, his tone making obvious his belief that she’d somehow failed to realize how near she was to the edge of what probably used to be an expansive patio with a spectacular view.

“Well aware.” Lyra looked down at his hand on her arm, and he dropped it, as suddenly as if her skin had scalded his fingers through her shirt. “Going forward,” Lyra said tersely, “you should probably just assume that I know what I’m doing. And while you’re at it, assume that you should keep your hands to yourself.”

“My apologies.” Grayson Hawthorne did not sound sorry. “Your eyes were closed.”

“I hadn’t noticed,” Lyra said in a scathing deadpan.

Grayson gave her *a look*. “Going forward”—he echoed her own words back at her—“if you intend to make your recklessness my problem, you should expect that problem to be solved.”

He spoke like someone used to making all the rules—his own and everyone else’s.

“I can take care of myself.” Lyra brushed past him, back into the ruins, away from the cliff.

Just when she thought he would let her go, Grayson spoke. “I know you.”

Lyra stopped walking. Something about the way he said the word *know* ripped through her. “Yeah, asshole. We’ve met. Helicopter? Literally less than an hour ago?”

“No.” Grayson Hawthorne said *no* like an absolute, like it didn’t matter if he was giving an order or informing you that you were wrong—either way, all you needed to understand was *no*.

“Yes.” Lyra didn’t mean to turn back toward him, didn’t intend to lock her eyes on to his, but once the two of them were caught in a staring contest, she refused to look away first.

Grayson's silvery stare never wavered. "I know you. Your *voice*." The word got caught in his throat. "I recognize your voice."

It hadn't occurred to Lyra that there was even a chance he would recognize anything about her. They'd talked all of three times a year and a half earlier. Less than three minutes, total. She'd never given him her name. The calls she'd made had been placed from a disposable phone.

"You must be mistaken." Lyra looked away first. She turned and walked away. Again.

"I am rarely, if ever, mistaken." Grayson employed a tone that seemed made for stopping people in their tracks. Lyra didn't stop. "*You* called *me*." Grayson emphasized the first word in that sentence and the last, equally, pointedly. *You. Me.*

And you told me to stop calling. Lyra bit back those words. "So what if I did?" She managed not to turn back around this time, but it didn't matter, because a moment later, Grayson was somehow in front of her, blocking her path.

She hadn't even heard him move.

Lyra swallowed. "You're in my way."

Grayson looked at her like he was standing above a pool of dark water looking for something beneath the surface, like she was a mystery—and his to solve. The barest hint of emotion flickered in his pale eyes, and for an instant, Grayson Hawthorne looked almost human.

Then he stepped abruptly to the side, clearing Lyra's path. There was something gallant about the motion, a match for the finely tailored black suit he wore like a second skin.

Lyra hadn't asked for his gallantry. "Stay out of my way," she said, stalking past him.

Grayson called after her, countering her order with an ironclad command of his own: "Stay away from the cliffs."

Chapter 9
GIGI

Gigi's hair was a little too excited about being on a boat—specifically, a speedboat, and even more specifically, an Outerlimits SL-52.

In a game like this one, details mattered. Gigi clocked it all. The fire-engine-red detailing on the boat. Its impressive, fifty-one-foot length. The island toward which they were hurtling.

The Hawthorne driving the boat.

Gigi's always-wild, two-inches-below-chin-length waves danced madly in the wind, flying in every direction at once, like they were trying to make a break for it.

"You didn't bring a hair tie," Savannah said beside her, not a question but a statement of fact. Based on experience, Gigi expected her twin to slip an extra hair tie off her own long, pale braid, but Savannah made no move to do so.

Things between them had changed since Savannah had left for college.

Since before that.

Gigi hated lying to her twin, and everything short of blurting out the whole sordid truth always felt like a lie. *Dad isn't in the Maldives—he's dead! He died trying to kill Avery Grambs! There was a cover-up! He also blew up a plane! Two men were killed.*

A chunk of hair thwapped Gigi in the face.

"Here." A quiet, baritone voice broke through the wind. Gigi turned to look at the remaining passenger on the boat—the remaining *player.* He held out a hair tie identical to the one that held back his own shoulder-length dreadlocks.

"Thanks," Gigi said. After she'd put his gift to use, she beamed at him. "I'm Gigi," she declared. "And you're my new best friend."

That got her a slight smile, as her new friend (and also: opponent) fixed his gaze on the island in the distance. He had deep ebony skin and wore thick-rimmed glasses, and there was stubble along his rather remarkable jawline.

Okay, his *totally* remarkable jawline.

Gigi waited for him to say something else, but he didn't. *The strong and silent type?* Luckily, she excelled at filling silences. "I love islands. Private islands. Deserted islands. Peculiar island towns full of quirky people."

Next to her, Savannah sat with perfect posture, not a hair out of place, as poised on a boat as she would have been on a throne. She didn't say a word.

"Take any book or movie and set it on an island," Gigi continued, stubbornly cheerful, "and it gets about a thousand times better, no idea why."

"Closed system," that quiet voice said.

Gigi looked again to her new friend/opponent. "Closed system?"

"In quantum physics, it's a system that doesn't exchange energy or matter with any other system. There are equivalent concepts in thermodynamics and classic mechanics. Chemistry and engineering, too." He gave a little shrug. "Under those definitions, an island wouldn't qualify, but the same concept applies. Nothing in, nothing out."

"A closed system," Gigi repeated. She amended her previous assessment: *strong, not always silent, and nerdy!* "Are you a physicist?" she asked.

Figuring out the competition would make it easier to beat him. And also: She wanted to know.

"Recovering."

"A recovering physicist?" Gigi grinned.

"Currently I'm a third-year doctoral student in cultural anthropology."

The boat began to slow, closing in on the island—and a dock. "Hypothetically speaking," Gigi said to the recovering physicist, "how old are you and what is your name?"

That got her another *very* slight grin. "Twenty-one. And Brady Daniels."

"He's not your friend." Savannah didn't bother looking at Gigi. "He's your competition. And if he's a third-year graduate student at twenty-one, he finished his undergraduate degree at seventeen or eighteen at the latest."

A prodigy. Gigi's gaze cheated back toward Brady as the boat slid into the dock.

The boat's driver, Xander Hawthorne, pumped a hand into the air. "Nothing but net!"

"It would be a mistake to trust anyone in this game," Savannah told Gigi, climbing effortlessly out of the boat before Xander could even tie it to the dock. "Your new best friend here will take you out the first chance he gets."

To anyone else, Savannah's expression probably would have looked icy, standoffish, equal parts cool and calm, but Gigi recognized Savannah's game face. That face was as good as an announcement: Savannah had come here to *play*, and Gigi knew better than most that the only way her taller, blonder, perfectly self-possessed, probably smarter, definitely more driven twin ever *played*...

Was to win.

Chapter 10

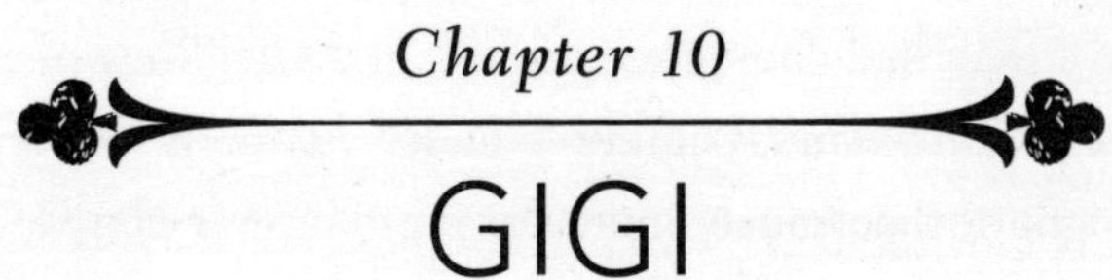

GIGI

In her entire life, Gigi had beaten Savannah exactly three times: once at Monopoly, once at hangman, and once in a dance battle that Savannah had insisted they weren't actually waging.

Gigi told herself that the Grandest Game was going to be number four. She had big reverse-heisting plans for her winnings. Maybe then it would feel like enough.

"In some senses," Xander Hawthorne announced with no small amount of dramatic flair, "the game starts tonight. In another very real sense, it starts right now..."

The instant Xander finished imparting instructions, Savannah took off, full speed. Recovering physicist Brady Daniels slipped quietly away, and Gigi...

Gigi tilted her head back to take in the view of the island from the dock. *A rocky beach. A soaring cliff. A mansion straight out of* Architectural Digest. The house was five stories tall, widest at the base, narrowing with every floor, giving it an almost triangular shape.

The entire ocean-side wall of the house looked to be made of glass.

Nothing but windows, Gigi thought, awe washing over her. Even just the sight of that house built into those cliffs made this all feel real. She was here. She was playing the Grandest Game. She'd *won* her ticket, one of only four wild cards in the world.

"I can do this," Gigi said, forgetting for a second that she wasn't alone on the dock.

"You can do this," Xander Hawthorne echoed encouragingly. "And when you do, Viking-style epics will be composed in your honor." He paused. "By me," he clarified. "They will be composed by me."

Gigi hadn't spent *that* much time with her half brother's half brothers, but Xander was an easy person to know. He liked to describe himself as a human Rube Goldberg machine. In Gigi's experience, Xander was an innovative, baked-goods-loving, big-hearted chaos factory who was always designing or building *something*.

And that gave Gigi an idea. "Our instructions were to search the island," she noted. "The dock is attached the island. The boat is in the dock. Ergo, by the transitive property, I am totally allowed to search this boat."

"There's nothing on the boat," Xander told her, but Gigi was already scrambling back over the side of the SL-52.

"Your obligatory hidden Twinkie supply begs to differ," she called back. It didn't take her long to find a locked compartment. A little recreational lock-picking, and . . . "Voilà."

Inside, Gigi found what was, essentially, a Xander Hawthorne survival kit: two scones wrapped in paper towels, a box of Twinkies, an energy drink, a puzzle cube, a roll of leopard-print duct tape, and a permanent marker.

"I'll be taking this." Gigi claimed the energy drink. "And these." She slipped the roll of duct tape onto her wrist and grabbed the marker. Given that the players hadn't been allowed to bring any supplies with them to the island, having obtained anything potentially useful could give her an advantage. Turning back to face the massive cliffs and *that house*, she uncapped the marker and started drawing on the back of her hand.

"I have been sternly warned against ever giving you caffeine," Xander said solemnly.

Gigi opened and downed the energy drink. "Have I ever mentioned that I love maps almost as much as I love islands?" She turned her hand so Xander could see the symbols she'd drawn there: a *T* for the T-shaped dock, a triangle for the house, some squiggly lines for the cliffs.

"Gigi Grayson, lay cartographer," Xander declared.

Explore the island. Map it. Search for hints and Objects with a capital O, *to be used in the game.* Her brain buzzing and her plan solidified, Gigi bid Xander adieu. "For the record," she told him, "I'm going to hold you to the promise of Viking epics, plural."

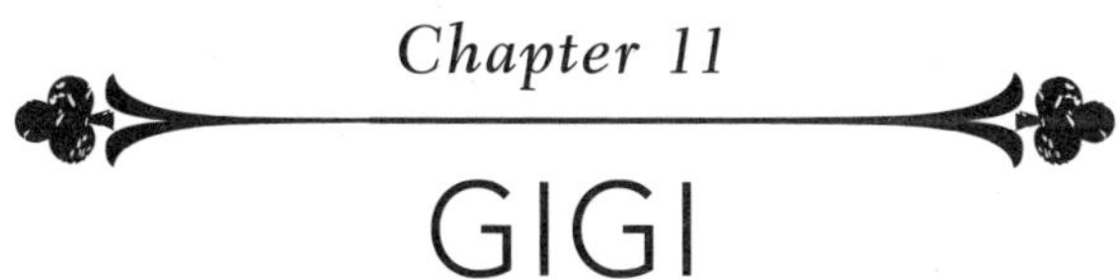

Chapter 11
GIGI

Two hours later, Gigi's left hand and arm were getting crowded, and she was starting to think that maybe she should have done some cardio in the lead-up to the game. But who was she kidding? Gigi didn't do cardio.

Wherever her twin was, *Savannah* definitely wasn't out of breath.

"I'm not wheezing." Gigi gave herself a little pep talk. "I'm breathing in an almost musical manner."

Regardless, she kept going. *More cliffs. Ruins. The forest—half-burned, half-alive.* She came out of the forest on the south side of the island to find a staircase carved in stone that stretched all the way down to the rocky shore below.

Standing at the top of that staircase made Gigi feel small. Not in a bad way—in a Stonehenge, Grand Canyon, Wonder of the World kind of way.

She managed to squeeze a staircase symbol onto her arm, and then she descended the stone steps. The last three were covered with moss. The back of Gigi's neck tingled. *There wasn't moss on any of the others.*

Gigi knelt to swipe at the step beneath her feet. She'd cleared an inch of moss off the stone when she saw the edge of the first letter. *Chalk.* It was smeared, but only a little.

Two minutes and one carefully cleared step later, she had a word. *MANGA.*

There was nothing under the moss on the next step. But on the final step, there was another word: *RA.*

"Manga," Gigi said. "As in, a Japanese graphic novel. Ra, the ancient Egyptian god of the sun." She paused. "The sun." Gigi looked to its position in the sky, a reminder that she was racing the clock. *I've only got until sunset.*

Not willing to waste precious time puzzling over a clue she could work to decode later, Gigi lifted her shirt, grabbed her pen, and scrawled the clues across her midriff. *MANGA. RA.*

She looked back down at the chalk writing on the steps and hesitated. This *was* a competition. Catching her bottom lip between her teeth, Gigi scuffed the chalk off with the heel of her hand.

Down the shoreline, around the bend, on the southeast side of the island, Gigi found a building rising out of the water. It looked like the kind of thing she would have expected to see in medieval Europe, possibly on a canal, all archways and heavy stone. It wasn't until Gigi got closer that she realized that underneath all that stone, out on the water, was another dock.

"Boathouse," she concluded. "Creepy, somewhat gothic boathouse." Out of canvas on her left arm, she switched her pen to the other hand and began sketching a trio of arches on the back of her right.

Further exploration revealed that the dock beneath the archways contained two smaller boat slips perpendicular to a very large one, with a sizable platform in between. Gigi sketched a series of rectangles beneath the arches. "Who's feeling triumphantly ambidextrous? *This girl.*"

That was when she saw the ladder built into the boathouse wall.

"When in doubt, go up." Gigi went up—and immediately discovered she wasn't alone.

Standing on top of the archway was an old woman. She had gray hair that had been dyed black at the ends and held herself like a person used to walking through hurricanes. In her hand, she held... *something.*

Gigi took a cautious step forward. The old woman didn't so much as turn. Instead, she lifted the object in her hand to her eyes.

Binoculars? As Gigi got closer, she realized: *Not binoculars. Opera glasses.* They were ornate, encrusted with jewels, and aimed at something—or *someone*—on the island below.

Gigi turned her head. From the top of the boathouse, you could see the entire eastern coast of the island, a long stretch of unmarked shore broken only by the helipad in the distance. A ways down, Gigi saw a familiar figure. *Brady.* He wasn't alone.

Another player? Gigi couldn't make out the other guy's features, but something about the way he was standing reminded her of a honey badger or possibly a wolverine.

"They know each other," the old woman said. "Quite well, I would wager."

Gigi wondered just how good the magnification on those opera glasses was—and where the old woman had found them. They *had* to be an Object, capital O, a part of the game.

"How can you tell?" Gigi said.

"How can I tell that they know each other?" The woman continued peering through the opera glasses. "Body language, mostly."

In the silence that followed, Gigi clocked the slightest move of the woman's lips. *Mostly*, Gigi thought. *Body language, mostly.*

"You're reading their lips," she realized. "What are they saying?"

"The one on the left likes ponies. The one on the right likes to eat ponies." The old woman's voice was dry. "Timeless tale, really."

The one on the left was Brady. "Ponies?" Gigi repeated. "You don't actually expect me to believe that?"

"Oh, let an old lady have her fun." The woman lowered her opera glasses and turned to look at Gigi head-on. "I'm Odette, and you, darling young thing, are observant."

"I'm Gigi," Gigi said. "And I try."

"You do, don't you?" Odette replied. "Try. The world just loves women who try." Odette caught Gigi's gaze and held it. "Unless and until we try too hard."

With that, the old woman began to make her way slowly back to the ladder. Right before she descended, she spoke again. "I'll tell you this much, from one woman who tries too hard to another: They were talking about a girl, and, from what I gather, she's dead."

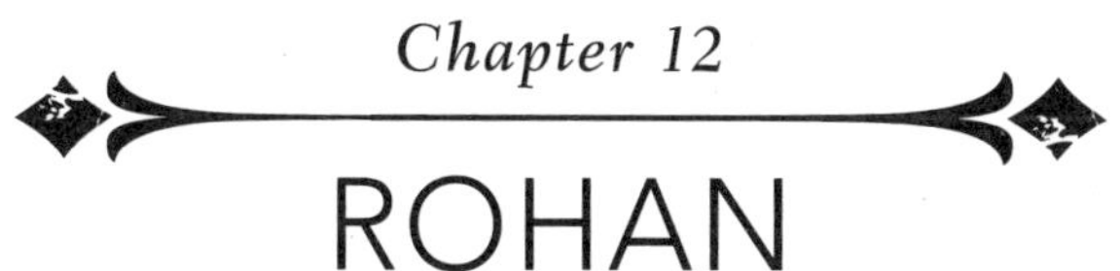

Chapter 12 ROHAN

Rohan examined the hint he'd uncovered. Around the base of a flagpole on the western point of the island, he'd found a thick metal chain fixed in place with a padlock made of a gleaming platinum. The lock had no keyhole, no combination pad, nothing to allow it to be opened. A sentence had been engraved into the surface of the platinum in elaborate script.

No man is an island, entire of itself. Rohan recognized the words, the start of a famous poem. So what was the clue, the hint, the advantage meant to be obtained by the player who found this? His brain sorted mercilessly through possibilities: the poet's name, *John Donne*; the poem itself, focused on the idea that mankind is inherently connected to one another.

Never send to know for whom the bell tolls. Rohan allowed himself to jump to the ending of the poem. *It tolls for thee.*

Deep in Rohan's mind, a warning sounded: *Someone's coming.* He'd long since trained his senses to operate exactly as he needed them to. Even when his mind was elsewhere, his ears were always listening, his body always alert. Footsteps were never just footsteps. They were tells—and Rohan was an expert at reading people.

Soft-soled shoes, aggressive stride, weight skewed toward the balls of the feet. He set the lock down and silently faded into the shadows. He already had the clue memorized, and observing another player's reaction to it would tell him more than fighting over it possibly could.

Within seconds, the owner of the soft-soled shoes and that aggressive stride appeared. *Tall and powerfully built.* Her long, silvery-blond hair was pulled into two tight braids that wreathed her head on either side like a crown of laurels, joining together in a thicker braid that hung down her back like a gilded rope.

Savannah Grayson. Rohan knew the basics about her already: eighteen years old, college basketball player, a reputation as an ice queen, Grayson Hawthorne's half sister.

Tell me, Savannah, Rohan said silently. *Who are you really?*

As he watched, Savannah zeroed in on the lock with remarkable speed. She read the clue. Most people would have paused to ponder, but the slightest shift of her weight tipped Rohan off to the fact that she wasn't *most people*.

He saw her next move right before she made it.

She slid her arm under the chain, looping it over her shoulder, and began to climb. There was no flag at the top of the pole. Nothing for Savannah Grayson to find there. *You're not looking for anything, are you, love?* She was getting the lock—and the chain—off the pole.

The fifty-foot-tall pole.

Savannah climbed the way she walked—with purpose. *With fury,* Rohan thought. Her arms were strong, her endurance impressive. Drawn by that purpose, that fury, that endurance, Rohan stepped out of the shadows. The pole was solid enough and large enough to support his weight as well as hers.

Rohan could think of worse ways to make a person's acquaintance.

Savannah was halfway to the top when she realized she had company. Her gaze didn't linger on his. She climbed harder, faster, but Rohan had four inches, half an arm's length, and a lifetime at the Devil's Mercy on her.

Soon enough, his hands grabbed the pole just above her ankles, the backs of his fingers brushing the front of her leg. A second later, the two of them were neck and neck. Something in Rohan wanted to push past her to see how hard she would push back, but in Rohan's world, strategy was never subject to *want*. He paced her, hand for hand and foot for foot, never taking the advantage and never giving it up.

As they neared the apex, Savannah Grayson's eyes met his.

"Nice day for a climb," Rohan said.

Savannah raked her gaze over him, from head to toe, and arched a brow. "I've seen nicer."

Oh, he liked her. Rohan had a certain appreciation for being put in his place. And for the set of her lips as she did it.

"Need any help with that?" Rohan nodded toward the chain looped around Savannah's shoulder. *I've already seen the clue, but you don't know that. Let's see how far you'll go to protect what you perceive as yours.*

"Does it look like I need help?" Savannah's tone was completely unperturbed, like they weren't fifty feet off the ground, like her body wasn't inches from Rohan's, their legs practically intertwined. She let go with one hand and lifted the chain off her shoulder and up over the top of the flagpole.

Nice to meet you, Savannah Grayson. Rohan had wanted to know who she was. She'd shown him.

By the time they'd made it back down the pole, the two of them were no longer alone.

Savannah favored her right leg as she landed on the ground beside the interloper.

"Your knee, Savannah." Grayson Hawthorne bore a striking resemblance to his half sister. Both of them kept their emotions tightly locked away—or tried to, at least.

Physical locks weren't the only ones that Rohan had taught himself to pick.

"I'm fine." There was a note of tension in Savannah—not in her voice or in her face, but in the long, graceful lines of her neck.

Someone did not appreciate being reminded of her weaknesses.

And someone else didn't appear to appreciate how close to his sister Rohan was standing.

"Elsewhere." Grayson let that word stand on its own for a second. "That," he clarified for Rohan, "is where you want to be right now."

The brother was overprotective. The sister didn't want to be protected. Whether or not he knew it, Grayson had just done Rohan a favor.

"Is this the 'stay away from my sister' speech?" Rohan smirked in Savannah's direction. "He's right, love. I'm a very, very bad idea—unless you're a hedonist, and then I'm a very good one."

Grayson took a single step forward.

"Don't," Savannah ordered her brother. "I can take care of myself."

"I can see that." Rohan lingered on that statement. "Though, in your brother's defense, there is some chance he's carrying a grudge about that whole business with the ribs."

"Ribs?" Savannah said.

"Jameson's," Rohan clarified. The incident in question had happened in the ring of the Devil's Mercy. "It was amicable," he continued lightly, "as far as rib-breakings go."

Contrary to his tone, Rohan hadn't enjoyed it. Jameson Hawthorne was one of those people who didn't know when to stay down.

Grayson Hawthorne appeared to have more restraint. He didn't respond to Rohan's bait, choosing instead to refocus his laser-like attention on Savannah. "You had surgery barely three months ago. Your knee can't be at more than eighty percent."

There was a flash of *something* in Savannah's eyes, and for a moment, Rohan saw a tension in her body that went far beyond her neck.

The body never lies, Rohan thought.

"We both know I don't do eighty percent," Savannah told Grayson.

"As luck would have it," Rohan said, "neither do I."

Savannah shifted her gaze to his for a full three seconds, which felt tantalizingly like a challenge, and then she took off into the forest like an Olympic runner exploding off the block.

Rohan rather enjoyed watching her go.

"It would be prudent," Grayson said, his tone calm but his elocution blade-sharp, "for you to stay away from my sister."

Rohan considered allowing Grayson the final word. He was, after all, the Hawthorne tasked with the enforcement of rules in this game, whatever those rules turned out to be. Backing off was the safer play here. But Rohan had a theory to test, and he hadn't gotten where he was in life by playing *safe*.

"I'd be happy to stay away from your sister," Rohan said. "Both of them, actually." He locked his eyes on to Grayson's and ran a little experiment. "But that would require turning all of my attentions to Lyra Kane."

Chapter 13
LYRA

A perverse part of Lyra wanted to get up close and personal with every cliff on the island just to prove that Grayson Hawthorne didn't get to give her orders. Instead, she ran—through burnt trees and healthy ones, down the center of the island, then along the coast.

Push harder. Go further. Miss nothing. Lyra let the rhythm of her feet beating against dirt and rock and grass fill her, its own kind of song. She *felt* the island. In the space between the ruins and the new house, between the dock and the boathouse and the helipad, this place had been left in its natural state: wild and free and real. *Beautiful.*

She made it back to the ruins and cut across the island again—a different path, and this time, she stopped at every structure she found, eschewing only the house on the north point. When she finished, she circled back to the ruins again, via the perimeter this time.

Keep pushing. Her lungs started burning before the muscles in her thighs did, and when her entire body was on fire? *Then* she climbed, exploring the cliffs and the rocky shore below.

As sundown drew nearer, Lyra found herself back in the fire-ravaged part of the forest one last time. Breathing hard, she placed her hand flat on a blackened tree and closed her eyes.

A Hawthorne did this. For all Lyra's brain couldn't produce mental images, it made up the difference with sounds. She never just thought those words; she *heard* them—the way her biological father had said them, the depth in his voice, his accent shifting, impossible to place.

Happy birthday, Lyra. He'd pronounced her name wrong: Lie-ra instead of Leer-a, a reminder that she was only his daughter by blood.

A Hawthorne did this.

What begins a bet? Not that.

A sound snapped Lyra back to the present. *Something flapping in the wind?* She whipped around, her eyes scanning the charred trees. And then she saw it—paper taped to blackened bark.

Another hint? Lyra jogged to the tree in question. Gingerly, she loosened the tape from the bark. *White paper. Dark-blue ink.* A surge of adrenaline hit her immediately. Processing the single word written on the page took longer.

Not a word, she thought. *A name.* All the paper said was *THOMAS.*

A breath froze like cracking ice in Lyra's throat, and she heard another sound and another. More papers in the wind, more flecks of white among the blackened trees.

More pages.

She bolted from one tree to the next, less gentle in removing the notes, the words burning themselves into her mind. *THOMAS* again. *TOMMASO. TOMÁS.*

"Thomas, Thomas, Tommaso, Tomás." Lyra could only manage a whisper. Her fingers curled into a fist, crumpling the pages, which sparked.

Sparks turned to flame. *Fire.* Lyra yelped and dropped the notes. She watched as her biological father's name—*all* of his names, variations on a theme—burned to ash on the ground.

Lyra had no idea how much time she lost to staring at those ashes. *Thomas, Thomas, Tommaso, Tomás.* Jameson Hawthorne had said the island bore hints about what was to come. Was that what this was? Just another part of the game?

Did you tell your brothers about our phone calls, Grayson? Did you tell Avery Grambs everything that I told you? Lyra didn't want to be addressing Grayson in her mind, and she didn't want to think the obvious, the one thing that she'd been avoiding thinking since she opened her golden ticket: *This is why I'm here. This is why they chose me.*

A chance at unfathomable riches had been handed to her. *A gift.* But in reality, she'd always known on some level that it was probably more like blood money, somewhere between damage control, a payoff, and amends.

And yet, Lyra would have sworn that Grayson Hawthorne hadn't known who she was—that he'd had *no idea* who she was—until the moment he'd heard her voice. And on those phone calls, she'd never told him her father's name. Or hers.

I know you. Grayson's words echoed in her mind. *Your* voice. *I recognize your voice.*

"Are you unwell?"

Blinking, Lyra managed to pry her gaze away from the ashes and dirt to look at the person who'd spoken. The first thing Lyra noticed about her was her hair, long, braided, and so pale a blond it looked almost silver, a match for the girl's fair and practically luminescent skin. The next thing Lyra noticed was the thick chain wound around the stranger's arm from shoulder to wrist.

The last thing Lyra noticed was the girl's eyes. *Grayson Hawthorne's eyes.*

He was everywhere. *Am I unwell? Unwell?* The girl in front of Lyra even sounded like him. "This game is sick," Lyra bit out. "*They* are."

"*They* as in the Hawthornes and the Hawthorne heiress?" A familiar, British voice came out of nowhere. "Doubtful."

Lyra scanned the forest for Rohan, and he appeared in the clearing as if by magic. His long legs made short work of the stretch of burnt forest between them.

"Self-aggrandizing, overly angsty, and prone toward mythologizing an old man who seems like he was a right bastard?" Rohan continued. "Yes. But cruel? Avery Grambs and the Hawthornes four? I think not. And whatever it is that put that look on your face..." Rohan openly studied Lyra, the feel of his attention like a silk glove against her skin. "Was cruel."

Thomas, Thomas, Tommaso, Tomás. Lyra swallowed. Thankfully, her apparently poorly masked turmoil didn't capture Rohan's attention for long. His gaze traveled languidly to the girl with *those* eyes.

"Savannah Grayson," Rohan said, "meet Lyra Kane."

Grayson. They have to be related. Lyra didn't let herself dwell on that.

"What, precisely, upset you?" Savannah aimed that question squarely at Lyra. "Did you find something?" Savannah took a single step forward. "A hint?"

She even *walked* like him. Lyra had no intention whatsoever of answering Savannah's question. And yet... "Notes. With my father's name on them." *His names.* "He's dead." Lyra's voice sounded flat even to her own ears. "What the hell kind of hint is that?"

"I suppose it depends." Savannah clearly didn't consider Lyra's question to be rhetorical. "Who was your father, and how did he die?"

Right for the jugular, Lyra thought.

"Not a hint," Rohan said airily.

"I don't want to talk about my father," Lyra told Savannah.

"I sympathize." Savannah didn't sound all that sympathetic.

"Not a hint," Rohan coughed.

"Ignore him," Savannah advised. "It's good for the soul."

"Easier said than done, love," Rohan replied. "And..." He smirked. "Not a hint."

"A dead man's name didn't just write itself." Lyra focused all her frustration on Rohan. "The notes *burst into flame.* You really expect me to believe this isn't the game makers' idea of being clever? That it's not some twisted part of the game?"

"I never said it wasn't a part of the game," Rohan replied. "Now did I?"

Savannah swiveled her gaze toward him. "You said it wasn't a hint."

"I also said that the *makers* of this game aren't cruel. I don't believe I made any such assessment of the other players—though I would wager, Lyra, that whoever smuggled in the supplies to set up this little display was hoping you would come across it a bit closer to sunset."

Sunset. Lyra saw the meaning there. *The curfew.* "Distraction," Lyra said. *Sabotage.* Rohan was suggesting that she'd been targeted by another player.

A player who somehow knew her father's name. *His names, plural.*

"And just like that," Rohan said, his fathomless brown eyes angling back toward Savannah's once more, "the gloves come off."

Chapter 14

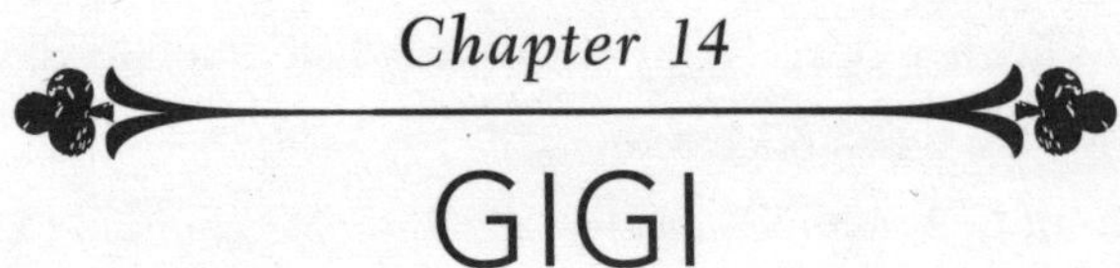

GIGI

With maybe twenty-five minutes left until sundown, Gigi looped around the eastern shore of Hawthorne Island, where there were no cliffs, no trees, just island and ocean and thick, thorn-ridden brush separating the two. She jogged—by a generous definition of the word *jog*—along the interior side of the brush, her brain sorting through everything that had happened in the past few hours: *Manga. Ra. Odette with her opera glasses. Brady and another player... and a dead girl.*

That was assuming, of course, that Odette hadn't been lying. Savannah's warning still rung in Gigi's mind: *It would be a mistake to trust anyone in this game.*

Gigi slowed—then backtracked, her eyes on the ground. There was something beneath the brush. A *glint of metal.* Gigi knelt for a better look. "A buckle?"

Reaching for it, she pulled on what looked to be some kind of strap, but whatever she'd found, it was really lodged back there under the brush. Gigi pulled harder. When that didn't work, she pushed her hands elbow-deep into the brambles, thorns catching at the map on her skin. Gigi ignored the pain, her mind going to Odette's opera glasses once more.

This could be it. My chance at an Object with a capital O. Finally, Gigi's strength and persistence (but mostly persistence) prevailed, as a large black bag came loose from the brush. She unzipped it. Inside, the first thing she saw was more metal.

"An oxygen tank?" And beneath it, something dark. *And damp.* "A wetsuit," Gigi breathed. She could picture one of the Hawthorne brothers donning it to hide a key part of the game to come somewhere beneath the ocean's surface, then stashing the diving supplies for one lucky player to find.

Me, Gigi thought fiercely. She pushed the wetsuit to the side, digging beneath it to reveal two more objects.

A necklace, Gigi marveled. *And a knife.*

She picked the necklace up first. A delicate gold chain held a stone the exact deep blue-green as the ocean. The pendant was the size of a quarter, thin and curved. Gold wiring wrapped the jewel, attaching it to the chain and visually bisecting it down the middle.

Unlatching the clasp and fixing the gold chain around her neck, Gigi turned her attention to the knife. It was sheathed. She unsheathed it.

The knife's blade was silver and slightly curved, its handle short. The sheath was made of battered leather and marked with a series of scratches that looked almost like claw marks.

Thirteen of them, Gigi counted. Her brain organized the details of her bounty. Eventually, there *would* be a payoff to everything she'd found. That was how Hawthorne games worked. Everything mattered. *The number thirteen. The knife blade. The handle. The sheath. The gold chain. The jewel. The diving equipment. Manga. Ra.*

Did Gigi have even the faintest idea what any of it meant or how the Grandest Game was going to play out? No. No, she did not. But one thing was clear: This was *the* find of the game. The motherlode of all motherlodes.

This. Was. *Everything.*

Among her many and varied talents, Gigi was a rather innovative victory dancer—and then she heard footsteps behind her. With the knife in one hand, she zipped up the bag with the other.

"What have we here?" The voice that posed that not-really-a-question was unmistakably male and a little flat.

Gigi slung the bag over her shoulder, stood, and turned. "Hi," she said. "I'm Gigi. I like your eyebrows."

In her defense, they were impressive eyebrows, dark and thick and angled, a key part of an equally impressive scowl on the stranger's face.

"Knox." His introduction was curt. So was that scowl. Almost…

Honey-badger-esque, Gigi thought. She remembered Odette's assessment of the man Brady had been talking to earlier: *The one on the right likes to eat ponies.* And then there was the other thing that Odette had said.

About the dead girl.

"I'll be taking that." Knox nodded toward the bag on Gigi's shoulder. He looked a few years older than Brady, far enough into his twenties that Gigi didn't feel quite so compelled to assess his jawline.

Besides, right now, she had bigger issues.

Gigi's hand tightened around the strap on her shoulder. "Over my cold, dead body," she said cheerfully. And yes, given the context, that was probably not the most prudent or appropriate statement, but that didn't stop Gigi from continuing, "And not just like an *I've been dead a couple of days, so I'm not warm anymore* kind of cold. I'm talking *drawer in the morgue, I've been refrigerated, and steps have been taken to prevent me from resurrecting myself* cold, dead body."

Knox was not impressed. "I don't like your chances here, half-pint."

"No one ever does," Gigi replied. Her heart was beating like a bongo drum in her chest, but luckily, Gigi was an expert at ignoring both her hindbrain animal instincts and her frontal lobe common sense. "Granted, this would be easier if I had a cat. But, as you can see, I'm armed with both duct tape and a knife." Gigi smiled hopefully. "And you don't want to hurt me?"

Gigi hadn't meant to make that a question per se. Deep down, she didn't believe Avery and the Hawthornes would have let anyone truly dangerous into the Grandest Game. *But they didn't choose the wild cards*, her good sense whispered. Gigi dismissed it. Besides, when Odette had mentioned the dead girl, she hadn't said anything to suggest that it was a particularly *nefarious* death. More likely, it was tragic, and Gigi had a soft spot for *tragic*.

"I'm not going to hurt you, pipsqueak." Knox's voice was still flat. "I'm not going to lay a finger on you, because I'm smart enough to know that this isn't that kind of game. What I will do, however, is get in your way." Knox let that sink in. "Until you hand over that bag—and the knife and duct tape, for good measure—anywhere you try to go, there I'll be, blocking your path. *Step. By step. By step.*"

Given that he hadn't mentioned the necklace, Gigi could only assume that Knox either hadn't noticed it or had assumed it was hers and that she'd worn it to the island. Summoning up an impressive Death Glare, Gigi folded her arms over her chest. "I take back my appreciation of your eyebrows."

"Tick-tock, little girl." Knox stared her down. "Sunset's coming, and you're on the wrong side of the island. I run a five-minute mile. I'm betting you don't, which means that I have time to waste right now..."

And Gigi didn't.

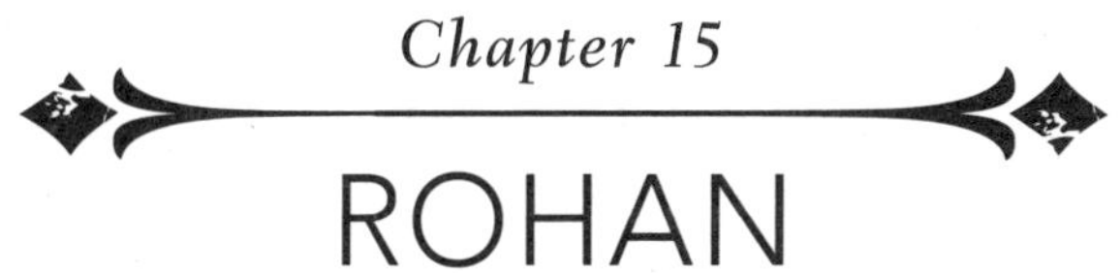

Chapter 15
ROHAN

N*ine minutes until sundown.* Rohan seldom entered locations of interest through their front doors. Windows were much more his style, and of the dozens and dozens of windows on the house on the north point, there was a grand total of one that was penetrable.

Ocean side. Four stories up.

Rohan made it in with no one the wiser. He slipped through the shadows, committing the fourth-floor layout to memory. *Seven doors with seven locks.*

Then came the footsteps. *Heavy boots, worn soles. A languid stride.* The person in question made no attempt to mask his approach, but he was lighter on his feet than he should have been.

How very Hawthorne of him.

"Fancy meeting you here." The eldest Hawthorne brother's pronounced Texas drawl matched his boots—and the cowboy hat he was wearing. “Nash Hawthorne.” He introduced himself, then leaned back against the wall, crossing one foot over the other.

“Handsome bugger,” Rohan said. He let Nash think that was a compliment, then clarified. “Nash Hawthorne,” he said, nodding to Nash, and then he gestured toward himself. “Handsome bugger. Pleasure to make your acquaintance.”

Nash snorted. “You got a last name? I already know your first.”

Rohan somehow doubted that all the players in the Grandest Game were getting personal welcomes from Nash Hawthorne. He sighed. “If this is about your brother’s ribs...”

“I’ve never begrudged a man a fair fight.” Nash removed his cowboy hat and ran his thumb along the rim. “This is just me, making a prediction: It’s not gonna be you.”

Nash was talking about the game. He was saying that Rohan was going to lose.

“Behold my devastation.” Rohan held a hand to his heart.

Nash pushed off the wall and strolled toward Rohan. The fact that the cowboy kept eye contact should have felt like a challenge, just like Nash’s *prediction* should have, but Rohan couldn’t sense even the slightest hint of a dominance maneuver in the man’s words or actions.

Nash Hawthorne simply *was*.

“Our games have heart,” Nash said, and then he squatted to place something on the floor in front of Rohan and straightened back to his full height. “It ain’t gonna be you, kid.”

This time, the words felt less like a prediction than an admonition. In other circumstances, Rohan might have even considered the delivery...brotherly. But Nash Hawthorne wasn’t looking for another little brother, and Rohan wasn’t looking for anything but the monetary resources he needed to win to claim the Mercy.

He looked to the object Nash had placed on the floor: a bronze key, large and ornate.

"Find the room that opens," Nash advised. "You'll know what to do once you do." With that, Nash turned to saunter away.

You think you know what I'm capable of, do you, Hawthorne? Rohan did love to make people think again. "Congratulations, by the way," he called after Nash. "On the babies."

Chapter 16

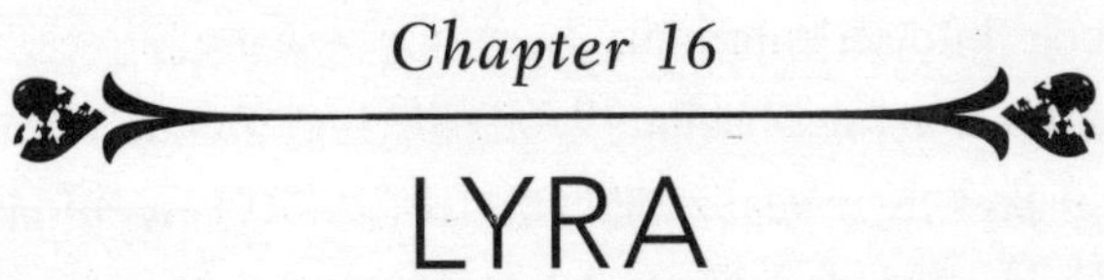

LYRA

Someone was playing mind games. As Lyra stepped onto a stone porch framed by enormous wooden pillars on either side, she looked to the western horizon, where the setting sun dyed the ocean in shades of stormy purple and a deep, burnt orange.

Sundown couldn't have been more than three minutes away.

Lyra had resisted the urge to *run* to the house on the north point. Her dancer's body could focus even when her mind was elsewhere, but she'd very pointedly taken her time, because if the person responsible for those notes had hoped to throw her off her game, if they'd hoped to either make her miss the deadline or make her rash, they were going to be sorely disappointed.

Lyra was not that easily manipulated.

The enormous house in front of her was made of brown stone and natural wood that might have looked rustic if the structure's design—the angles, the pillars, the height—hadn't called to mind something more like a church with a soaring steeple. The front door looked like it was made of solid silver, its surface etched with a geometric design.

Lyra ran her hand over the silver door, then opened it. Crossing the threshold into an enormous foyer, she saw a white spiral staircase rising up from an obsidian floor. Moving toward the staircase, light on her feet, Lyra realized: The stairs didn't just spiral *up*.

What had appeared from the front of the house to be the ground floor was actually the *third* story. The stairs spiraled up; the stairs spiraled down. Lyra saw now what would have been obvious if she'd explored the north point in detail earlier: This house hadn't just been built on a cliff, at the tallest elevation on the island.

It had been built *into* the cliff.

On either side of the sprawling entryway were identical doors, with a third visible beyond the staircase. All three doors were made of dark, gleaming wood, each standing ten feet tall, each closed. In the foyer, there was a black granite table bearing seven silver trays, each marked by a card on which a name had been written in extravagant calligraphy.

The entryway was eerily silent as Lyra read through the names, one by one.

Odette.

Brady.

Knox.

Lyra.

Savannah.

Rohan.

Gigi.

Six players besides me, Lyra thought. *Six suspects.* As far as Lyra was concerned, neither Rohan nor Savannah was in the clear on the mind games front. Either one of them could have planted those notes then circled back. But at the end of the day, Lyra hadn't come to Hawthorne Island to solve a mystery—not about notes on a tree and not about a man with more than his share of names who hadn't even known how to pronounce hers.

Instead, she focused on the object sitting on the tray marked with her name. *A key.* It was large and bronze. Elaborate swirls of metal met to form a complicated shape at the head of the key. In the center of that shape, there was a symbol.

An infinity sign. That felt significant to Lyra—but significant how?

She looked back to the silver trays. All the others, except for one, were empty. The lone remaining key—on the tray labeled *Gigi*—appeared nearly identical to Lyra's, the only visible difference the pattern in the keys' teeth.

They unlock different doors, Lyra thought. *And I'm the second-to-last player in.* She looked down at her key once more and noticed words engraved along its stem.

EVERY STORY HAS ITS BEGINNING... Lyra rotated the key in her hand, reading the words on the reverse side. **TAKE ONLY YOUR OWN KEY.**

Lyra thought about Jameson's welcome to the island. *In some senses, the game starts tonight. But in another very real sense...it starts right now.*

The front door flew inward. A petite, brown-haired blur barreled in. Not two seconds later, the heavy silver door swung shut of its own accord, followed by a sound like a gunshot. *The deadbolt.*

The front door had just slammed and locked itself.

"Sunset," wheezed the new arrival, bending over, her hands on her knees.

Lyra studied her for a moment. "I'm guessing you're Gigi?"

Hers was the only key left on the table.

"I am indeed!" Gigi replied, and then she straightened. "Question," she huffed. "Human wolverine, eyebrows like *this*." Gigi placed her index fingers on her forehead at opposite angles, so that they met in a V just over her nose. "Conceited vest, darkened soul. Seen him?"

It was the mention of the vest that told Lyra exactly who Gigi was looking for. "Knox Landry?" *Conceited vest, darkened soul.* Lyra had to hand it to Gigi: That was descriptive. "I haven't seen him recently, but his key was already gone when I got here."

Gigi followed Lyra's gaze to the trays on the table. Within seconds, the other girl had claimed her own key. *"Every story has its beginning..."* Gigi zeroed in on the tiny script faster than Lyra had. After reading the reverse side, Gigi looked up, thought for a moment, then reached for her name card and flipped it over.

A poem stared back at them from the reverse side. Lyra turned her own card over and found the exact same thing. Instructions.

> FIND YOUR ROOM. USE THE KEY.
> LEAVE THIS CARD FOR ALL TO SEE.
> DON YOUR COSTUME AND YOUR MASK.
> THE BALL BEGINS AT QUARTER PAST.

Chapter 17

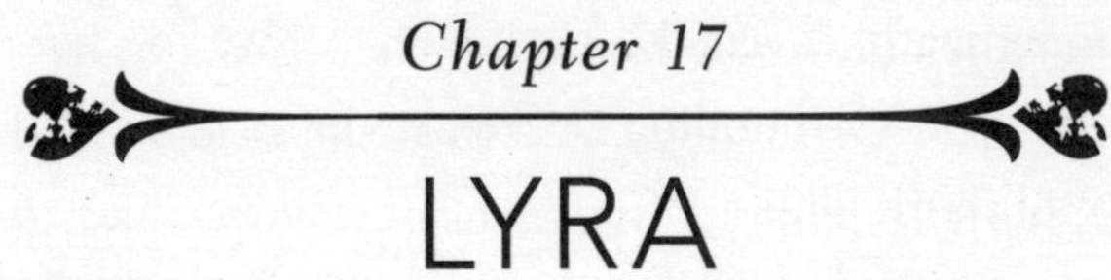

LYRA

On the fourth floor of the grand house, Lyra found seven doors, each bearing an ornate bronze lock. On the wall, there was an enormous clock, roman numerals marking the time.

Five o'clock, almost exactly.

Lyra stepped up to the first door and tried her key. It slid into the lock but wouldn't turn. Moving on to the next, Lyra heard Gigi behind her, trying out her luck with one of the other doors. Lyra's second attempt was unsuccessful, but on her third, the key turned in the lock.

The door opened.

The room beyond was startlingly simple, a king-sized bed the only piece of furniture in the room. Laying across the pristine white bedspread was a ball gown.

Lyra walked forward, the door closing behind her as she forgot everything but the gown on the bed. Its bodice was a dark navy blue, almost black, like the ocean at midnight. The skirt was long and made of layers of tulle.

Don your costume and your mask, Lyra thought. *The ball begins at quarter past.*

She lifted the gown off the bed, revealing a mask, delicate and jeweled, underneath. It was the kind of mask that covered only the region of the face surrounding the eyes, the kind a person might have worn to Mardi Gras.

Or to a masquerade ball, Lyra thought. Bewitched despite herself, she laid the gown over her arm and ran her fingers lightly over the jewels on the mask. Surely those were rhinestones. *Surely* those weren't diamonds, arranged in elaborate, hypnotic swirls, each individual jewel small but flawless.

Surely.

Lyra forcibly turned her attention from the mask back to the gown. Guarding herself against the urge to get carried away in the magic of the moment, she did as she'd been instructed and donned her costume, shedding her own clothes and slipping on the gown.

It's just a dress, Lyra told herself—but it wasn't *just* anything.

The bodice gripped her curves, the fit uncanny. *Perfection.* At the smallest part of her waist, the tulle skirt was the same dark blue as the bodice, but the fabric lightened, inch by inch, to a brilliant blue that gave way to a light, frothy one, that melded into the lightest pastel. The bottom of the skirt was completely white. The color didn't change evenly across the skirt; it changed in waves.

Lyra felt like she was wearing a waterfall.

She reached for the mask. Long, velvety black ribbons hung from either side. Lyra wasn't sure what she'd expected from the Grandest Game—but not this. She hadn't expected it to feel like this. Like *magic.*

Glittering mask in hand, Lyra made her way from the bedroom into the attached bathroom, drawn to the mirror. She studied her own features as if they belonged to a stranger: dark hair, amber eyes in a heart-shaped face, golden-tan skin.

She stepped back, taking in the look, the feel, the damn *aura* of the dress, trying to remember that this wasn't a fairy tale.

This was a competition.

Her gaze caught on the bathroom drawers—two of them, built into the vanity. Inside one, Lyra found a pair of ballet flats. She put them on.

Inside the other drawer, she found a pair of dice.

They're made of glass, Lyra realized. The glass dice were positioned off-kilter from each other, like they'd been rolled. *A three and a five.* Lyra picked them up, and the instant she did, words appeared on the bathroom mirror, transposed over her reflection.

PLAYER NUMBER 4, LYRA KANE. Lyra stared at herself, and then the words on the mirror changed. *GAME ON.*

She put on the mask.

Chapter 18

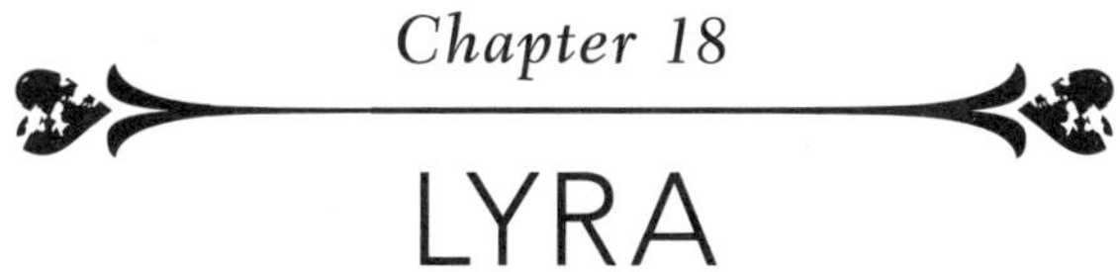

LYRA

As Lyra stepped into the hallway, she saw a flash of someone else headed down the spiral staircase. She went to follow, but as she hit the stairs, she paused, glancing back at the clock.

5:13.

The stairs spiraled down. The stairs spiraled up.

They'd been given hours to explore the island, but what about the house? Giving in to instinct, Lyra ran up the steps, light on her feet, surprised at how comfortable the ballet flats she'd been given were, how sturdy they felt beneath her feet as she came to the very last step of that grand spiral staircase and—

Lyra came to a complete and utter stop. The staircase let out in a circular room, the *only* room on the top floor of the house.

A library. Lyra took three steps forward—and spun. She couldn't help it. Fifteen-foot shelves ringed the room, filled with thousands of books. The ceiling was made of thick stained glass that, in daylight, would have cast colored light across the gleaming wood floors.

Like the dress and the mask and all the rest of it, this room was magic.

"I'm a sucker for libraries." The voice came from behind her. "Circular ones in particular."

Lyra turned to come face-to-face with the speaker—or, more accurately, mask-to-mask.

If she'd thought her own mask was breathtaking, this one was a sight to behold, and so was the gown that went with it, the fabric a deep, midnight purple, richer somehow than Lyra's blue, the skirt full and covered in breathtaking stitching in a shade of silver like moonlight on water.

The matching mask was lined with delicate black gemstones, with deep purple ones framing the eyes, but the most remarkable thing was the metalwork. Was there such a thing as black gold? If so, some artisan had cajoled it into delicate, interlocking tendrils that resembled nothing so much as lace.

Stop staring, Lyra told herself. She looked back to the shelves circling the room. "It's beautiful," she said, but what she was thinking was *There's only one player I haven't met.*

"And you don't trust beautiful things?" There was something in the masked girl's tone, an audible spark, like Lyra had just tipped her hand more than she'd intended to. Belatedly, Lyra recognized that voice, and she knew suddenly who the girl in that moon-kissed dress, behind that dark, glittering mask, was.

Not a player. "You're Avery Grambs." The Hawthorne heiress, here, right in front of her.

"I was you once." The heiress smiled, but because of the mask, Lyra had no idea if that smile reached Avery's eyes. "Trusting people wasn't exactly my forte, either. But if I could give you a little advice, going into this game?"

Everything about this interaction felt surreal. Lyra exhaled. "Like I'm going to turn down advice from the person who masterminded all of this?"

The one pulling the strings. The one at the center of this game. The billionaire. The philanthropist. *The* Avery Kylie Grambs.

"Sometimes," Avery said, "in the games that matter most, the only way to really play is to *live*."

Lyra's throat tightened, and she looked away. She wasn't even sure why. When she'd gathered herself, when she glanced back—

The Hawthorne heiress was gone.

Chapter 19

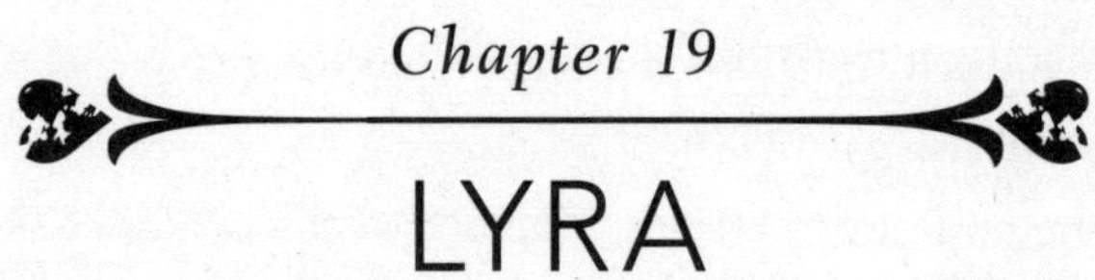

LYRA

Instrumental music floated up from the ground floor as Lyra descended the spiral staircase. Avery Grambs was nowhere in sight. It was like the heiress had disappeared into thin air.

When Lyra made it to the foyer, she discovered that it had been transformed. Towering chocolate and white chocolate fountains sat opposite Greek columns the height of her waist. Each column boasted a platter piled high with meat or fruits. The three massive doors Lyra had seen earlier were now open, revealing the rooms beyond.

A dining room. A study. The music was coming from beyond the third door, on the far side of the staircase. Lyra followed the sound of it into what was, unmistakably, a Great Room. Soaring ceilings boasted an elaborate crystal chandelier, but Lyra barely even noticed the sparkling crystals. Her brain couldn't process anything but *the view.*

The entire back wall of the Great Room was made of glass.

Floor-to-ceiling windows offered an unvarnished panorama of

the Pacific Ocean at twilight. Thousands of fairy lights dotted the rocky shore. Lyra paced forward, pulled to the windows like a moth to a flame, and it was only once she'd crossed the room that she was able to turn back and shift her attention to what was happening inside the Great Room.

To the ball.

Lyra still didn't see Avery anywhere, but based on the number of tuxedo-clad masked men present, at least some of the Hawthorne brothers *had* to be there.

Not Grayson. Lyra couldn't shake the feeling—the very annoying feeling—that she would have recognized him instantly, no matter the mask he wore.

Forget him. Focus on your competition. Odette was easy to pick out, with her long, thick, black-tipped hair. The old woman wore a black velvet gown complemented by matching gloves that covered her from elbow to fingertip. Her mask was white. *Feathered.* On the outside edge of each catlike eye, there was a single, deep-red gem.

Rubies, Lyra thought—and not small ones.

Savannah was just as recognizable. Her platinum blond hair was pulled into an even more elaborate braid now than it had been before. From behind, Lyra couldn't see Savannah's mask, but that did nothing to lessen how striking the other girl looked draped in ice-blue silk, a vintage-style gown that seemed like it had been plucked straight from the 1930s.

The heavy chain Savannah had worn around her arm before encircled her hips now.

"You're staring, pet."

Lyra hadn't heard Rohan approach, hadn't so much as seen him out of the corner of her eyes. His mask was a light and shining silver, the metalwork more befitting a crown. It covered the entire left side of his face but for his eye and extended above his brow and down the temple on his right. The startling asymmetry of the mask made Rohan look, if not broken, then just a little bit twisted.

In a good way.

"I wasn't staring," Lyra said.

"Let me guess," Rohan murmured. "You were looking at the walls."

The walls? For the first time, Lyra looked to the perimeter of the Great Room. Wood panels lined the walls. A raised design in the wood was reminiscent of Art Deco, but the longer Lyra stared at it, the more the design called to mind a maze.

This is the Grandest Game. What are the chances that it is *a maze?*

"Are we talking about walls? I *love* walls." Another masked gentleman slid in between Lyra and Rohan with an impressive shimmy. The newcomer was tall and wore a golden mask. He held out a hand to Lyra. "This is the part where I humbly admit to being the boldest and most dashing Hawthorne—or, at a minimum, the least wary of explosions and social rejection—and ask if I can have this dance."

This, Lyra realized, was the youngest Hawthorne brother. *Xander Hawthorne.*

Dance? Lyra looked beyond Xander's outstretched hand to the center of the Great Room, where two others had indeed begun to dance. One of them was Avery Grambs, which made her masked partner Jameson Hawthorne.

Avery and Jameson each held a hand up, their palms touching as they walked in a slow, seductive circle around each other. The dance looked like it had been lifted from another era, one where men and women could barely touch, and yet, watching the two of them circle each other, Lyra found it hard to breathe.

Snap out of it, she told herself, tearing her gaze away from them and taking Xander's outstretched hand. She was here to do a job. *Anything it takes to win.*

"I don't suppose you have a clue to dispense?" Lyra asked Xander. She and the other players still hadn't been told anything concrete about what was to come—other than the fact that, *in some senses*, the game would start tonight.

Xander spun her out, then in, then solemnly raised his right hand and waited for her to lift hers before responding to her request for a clue. "The stork flies at half past ten," he said dramatically. "The hummingbird eats a cookie. My dog is named Tiramisu."

Lyra snorted. "Oddly enough, I think you're telling the truth about that last one."

After their third clockwise circle, Xander put his right hand down and raised his left. Lyra mirrored the motion, and they began circling each other counterclockwise.

"Muffins or scones?" Xander said seriously.

"Excuse me?"

The Hawthorne across from her somehow managed to raise an eyebrow so high it shot up above the top of his mask. "If you had to choose: Muffins or scones?"

Lyra considered her options. "Chocolate."

"They can be chocolate." Xander was clearly the most agreeable Hawthorne.

"No," Lyra told him as they danced. "I choose chocolate. Just chocolate."

"I see." Xander grinned. "A small enough piece to melt on your tongue or a bunny the size of your fist?"

"Both." Lyra realized right after she'd answered that she hadn't spoken that word to *Xander*, who was no longer standing where he'd been a moment before.

Grayson had displaced him. "May I cut in?"

She'd known that she would recognize him, no matter the mask. His was black. No adornments. Just... black. "You already have."

They were circling each other now, their hands barely touching. Lyra had never felt so aware of every inch of skin on her fingers and palms. It felt less like they were dancing than like they'd been pulled into each other's orbit. *Gravity* was nothing compared to the force that kept Lyra from stepping away—no matter how much she wanted to, no matter how vehemently she reminded herself that he was a Hawthorne.

That Hawthorne.

The music changed, and with it, the dance. Grayson effortlessly took Lyra's hand, as his other arm curved with utmost efficiency around her back. There was still space between them, a respectable amount of space.

Too much—and not nearly enough.

"Last year, when you called me," Grayson said, his mask doing nothing to shield Lyra from *those eyes*, "you had questions about my grandfather's presumed role in your father's death."

A Hawthorne did this. Lyra steeled herself against the feel of Grayson's hand on her back, against the interweaving of their fingers. "I didn't *presume* anything except that your grandfather was the Hawthorne most likely to ruin a man." Lyra raised her chin. "And I didn't come here—to this island, to this game—to talk about my father with you."

Grayson stared at her from behind that mask. "You wanted to know the truth before."

Lyra had wanted a lot of things back then. "If you'd discovered that you'd spent your entire life living a lie, you would have wanted answers, too." She kept her voice perfectly even, perfectly controlled. "But I don't need them now, the way I did when I called you."

Despite her best attempts to the contrary, emphasis crept into the last word of that sentence: *you*.

"My grandfather had a list," Grayson said after a moment. "The List, capital L. Enemies. People he'd taken advantage of or wronged. There was a Thomas Thomas on it, the last name the same as the first."

Thomas, Thomas. Lyra's thoughts went to the notes on the trees. Rohan had been so sure they hadn't been the work of the Hawthornes or the Hawthorne heiress, but what if he'd been wrong?

"I see," Grayson said, not specifying *what* he saw in her expression.

"My father's last name wasn't Thomas." Lyra just couldn't keep from pushing back.

"The file in question was scant," Grayson told her. "But the details, such as they were, matched your description of your father's death."

Lyra felt the room begin to spin. The sound of a gunshot echoed through her mind. She fixed her eyes on Grayson's, like a dancer spotting by keeping her gaze locked on one point for pirouette after pirouette.

"Why are you telling me this?" Lyra demanded. *Now,* she added silently. *Why are you telling me this* now? She'd gone to him for help when she was seventeen, at a time when it had felt like she had no one. She'd tricked herself into believing that Grayson Hawthorne had some shred of honor, that he might actually help her, that she wasn't alone.

And what she'd gotten from him was: *Stop calling*.

"I am telling you this," Grayson stated, his tone far too gentle for her liking, "because that file led nowhere. Every detail in it, besides the description of your father's death, was artificial. A lie." There was a slight pause. "I had no way of finding you to tell you that."

The warmth of his hand on her back was getting harder and harder to ignore.

"But you tried," Lyra said cuttingly. "To find me." Her withering tone made her skepticism clear, because if Grayson had *actually* tried to find her, he would have—the way Avery Grambs apparently had for the Grandest Game.

You told the heiress something, and she *found me—or your brothers did. Or maybe they chose players from that capital-L List of Tobias Hawthorne's. Either way,* they *didn't have any problem tracking me down.* Lyra didn't think for a second that Avery or the rest of the Hawthorne family was somehow more capable of moving mountains than Grayson was.

Grayson Hawthorne could damn well move mountains with a flick of his wrist. *If you'd really wanted to find me, you would have.*

For the longest time, Grayson was silent, and then his expression shifted, the angles of his face becoming more pronounced. "If you are here as part of some vendetta against my family—"

"I'm here for the money." Lyra cut him off. If she'd been capable of it, she would have cut him down, but he was Grayson Hawthorne, not easily felled. "And you don't get to act like I'm a threat because of some *list* made by your soulless, life-ruining billionaire grandfather. I am here because"—Lyra almost said *because I was invited,* but she thought about what that invitation had said, and the words burned true—"because I *deserve* this."

Now was not the time for her to go hoarse.

"I don't have a vendetta against your family," she continued, her voice low. "I'm not a threat, and I am not asking for anything from *you.*"

"Except," Grayson said, the oddest undercurrent in his tone, "for me to stay out of your way."

Lyra wanted so badly to look away from him. Her anger smoldered, then burned. "That's the only thing I could ever want from you, Hawthorne boy."

Grayson dropped her hand. He pulled back, ending their dance. "Consider it done."

The music stopped, and the next thing Lyra knew, Avery and Jameson were making their way to the front of the room.

Focus on them. Not him. Never him.

"Hello, everyone." The Hawthorne heiress took off her mask, and for a moment, her gaze lingered on Lyra. "And welcome to the second annual Grandest Game."

Chapter 20

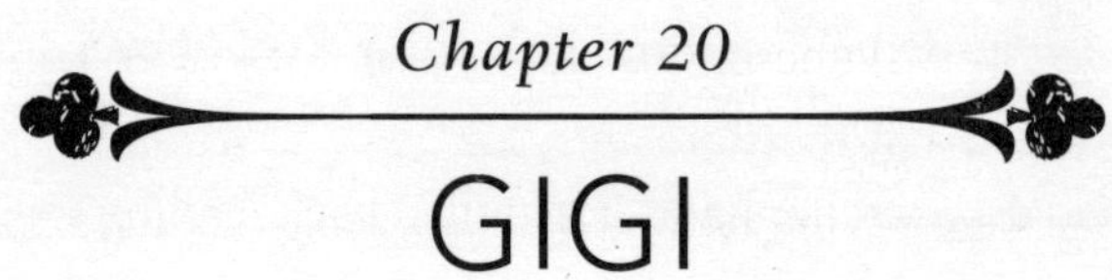

GIGI

Here we go. Gigi tried to clear her mind. Did she have a knife strapped to her thigh with leopard-print duct tape beneath her ball gown, where no one could see it? Yes. Yes, she did. Did anyone in this room realize that? No. No, they did not. Was she carrying a grudge the size of Pangaea about what she'd had to sacrifice to keep said knife and said duct tape? Also yes.

But right now, *none* of that mattered. The only thing that mattered was that Avery was addressing the room. "The seven of you are here because three years ago, I went from living in my car to having the world. I became an extremely unlikely heiress."

At the front of the room, the remaining Hawthorne brothers took up position around Jameson and Avery in a way that made it hard for Gigi to think of the five of them as anything other than a unit: Nash-and-Xander-and-Grayson-and-Jameson-and-Avery against the world.

All four Hawthornes removed their masks.

"Anything I could imagine," Avery continued, "was suddenly within my grasp, and I was thrown into the middle of a game I can't even describe."

Beside Avery, Jameson was looking at her like she was the sun and the moon and the stars and eternity, all rolled into one.

In Gigi's entire life, no one had ever looked at her like *that.*

"I was given the chance of a lifetime," Avery said, her voice echoing through the Great Room. "And now, I'm giving it to you. Not the fortune—not all of it anyway. But the experience? The ultimate puzzle, the most incredible game, the kind of challenge that will show you who you are and what you're capable of, all with life-changing riches in the balance? That, I can give you." She paused. "This year's prize is twenty-six million dollars."

Twenty-six million. And unlike Gigi's trust fund, that money would be unrestricted.

"Although only one of you will walk away the winner of this year's game..." Avery cheated her gaze to Jameson. "None of you will be leaving this island empty-handed."

"The masks you're wearing tonight," Jameson said, "are yours to keep."

Gigi brought her hand up to her own mask. Its edges were lined with tiny, perfect pearls. Diamond chips encircled her eyes, and the trio of peacock feathers on the side of the mask was held in place by an aquamarine the size of her smallest knuckle. Gigi wondered how much money she could get for it—and how many reverse heists she could pull off with the proceeds.

"And then, there's *these.*" Jameson produced a long, velvet box, seemingly out of nowhere. Avery flipped the box open. Gigi pressed forward to get a better look. All around the room, the other players were doing the same.

Inside the box, there were seven pins. *Small gold keys.*

Avery removed one from the box. "However this shakes out, I want you to remember: The people in this room with you tonight are the only ones who will ever know what it was like to play this year's game. From now through the ends of your lives, that's something you'll share."

"Growing up," Jameson said, looking at each of his brothers in turn, "it was something of a rite of passage in Hawthorne House to receive a pin a bit like these. Consider them a symbol: Win or lose, you're all a part of something now."

Avery smiled. "You are not alone."

Not alone. Gigi's heart managed to twist and leap in her chest at the same time. She looked instinctively to Savannah, but her twin's gaze was locked on Avery and only Avery, as the heiress and the Hawthorne brothers began distributing the pins.

"For the record," Jameson announced, as he affixed Savannah's pin in place, "you should all know that our beloved, if somewhat emotionally constipated, brother Grayson had no part in designing this year's game. He might be the one ensuring things run smoothly, but he's every bit as in the dark as the seven of you."

Nash appeared in front of Gigi. With gentle hands, he pinned the gold key to her ball gown. "Here you go, kid." He winked. "Nice necklace. Color suits you."

"Enough already," Knox cut in. "Enough with the masks and the formal wear and the speeches." He spoke precisely but with almost no pauses between his words, like he considered the ebb and flow of speech a waste of time.

That bag-stealing scum-basket.

"What's the game?" Knox demanded.

You just wait, Eyebrows of Doom, Gigi thought. *Just. Wait.*

"Every story has its beginning, Knox." Avery's voice took on an almost musical lilt as she spoke the familiar words. "Your story—all of yours—starts when the sands of time run out."

With no small amount of dramatic flair, Xander knelt and bopped the wood floor with the heel of his hand. A panel popped up. *A hidden compartment.* Xander withdrew an object from it.

"An hourglass." Gigi hadn't meant to say that out loud.

The hourglass was about a foot and a half tall and filled with sparkling black sand. Xander strolled forward and set it on one of two identical marble coffee tables.

Gigi watched, mesmerized, as black sand began to fall.

"Until then..." Avery held out an arm out for Jameson, who took it. "Follow us."

Chapter 21

GIGI

Through the foyer, out the front door, around the side of the house. Gigi tracked their progress as she and the other players followed Jameson and Avery. *Down the cliff.* Once they hit the rocks below, Gigi suddenly knew: *They're taking us out to the ocean.*

It was darker now than it had been even ten minutes earlier, but hundreds of strings of tiny lights illuminated the way across the rocks to the shore.

"You made it in by sunset." Even in a silk gown, Savannah moved through the night like a knife through butter. That she slowed her pace, even a little, Gigi took as an expression of love.

"I'm going to pretend that you don't sound surprised about that," Gigi told her twin.

"I'm guessing something happened during your exploration of the island?" Savannah raised an eyebrow. "Did one of the other players actually manage to get on your bad side?"

"I don't have a bad side," Gigi said pertly. "I believe in rehabilitation."

"I sincerely hope that is as terrifying as it sounds," a voice said behind them. *Male. British.*

And, Gigi realized, as he fell in next to them, *tall. Very tall.* "You think I'm terrifying." Gigi was delighted.

"Don't," Savannah ordered. Which one of them was the intended recipient of that order was anyone's guess.

"Is it your turn for the *stay away from my sister* speech now?" the masked stranger quipped. "It was so very effective for your brother when he told me to stay away from you."

Gigi's eyes widened as she swiveled her head to look at her twin. *Do tell.*

In the moonlight, the swirling, silvery-blue mask Savannah wore made her look fairy-tale beautiful, like a Snow Queen come down from the icy north to turn the world white. On either side of her face, a trio of teardrop diamonds hung down from the mask, resting on Savannah's high, sharp cheekbones like actual tears.

Gigi couldn't help thinking that she hadn't seen her sister cry in years. *Dad's not in the Maldives!* The dreaded mental chorus was back with a vengeance. *He's dead! He died trying to kill—*

"And here we are." Jameson Hawthorne's voice cut through the night air.

As Gigi took a final step forward toward the ocean's edge, she realized that she'd just stepped from rocks to sand. *Black sand.*

"Shoes off," Jameson called out. Clearly, he was enjoying this.

Gigi didn't even hesitate. She kicked off her flats and sank her toes into the sand. As chilly as the night air was, the grains of sand beneath her feet were warm.

There hadn't been black sand on this beach earlier.

"Everyone should dance barefoot on the beach at night at least once in their life," Avery said, sounding for all the world like a Hawthorne, magnetic and sure. "But first..."

"Masks off," Jameson finished, moving forward to collect them, one by one. "Don't worry. We'll keep these safe for you. And the keys to your rooms, if you please."

Safe from what? Gigi wondered, and her gaze was pulled out to the velvety black water. Waves lapped at the shore.

"Some of you have already found hidden treasure of a sort," Avery said. "Objects that were hidden on the island that will be of use to you at some point over the next few days." The Hawthorne heiress's gaze went first to Savannah, then to Odette.

Gigi lifted a hand to her necklace and thought about the knife duct-taped to her thigh. *The next few days.* That was the first time any mention had been made of the length of the game.

"There's just one such piece of treasure left," Jameson declared. "One more Object that could give you an advantage in the game you'll be playing very shortly. You'll have a little less than an hour to find that Object. We won't steal too much of your time, but allow me to share a piece of advice that someone once shared with me: *Leave no stone unturned.*"

Jameson cast his gaze back up toward the rocks. Within seconds, Gigi was the only competitor still standing on the black sand beach. All the others had darted for the rocks.

Leave no stone unturned. Gigi looked back to Jameson, but he and Avery were dancing. *Barefoot on the beach,* Gigi thought. And then she thought about misdirection. About distractions. About *hidden treasure* and the fact that the black sand on this beach matched the sand in the hourglass inside.

Gigi dropped to her knees and began raking her fingers through the sand. Maybe she was wrong. Maybe everyone else was right. But she kept going. And going. And going. For twenty minutes. Thirty. Until—

"Back. Off."

Gigi jerked her head up, toward the sound of that voice—not a quiet voice this time and not all that calm, but recognizable all the same. *Brady Daniels.* Gigi scanned the rocks, but the fairy lights only did so much. Then she saw movement. *Definitely Brady.* And the person he'd just told to back off—the person he was striding away from—was definitely Knox.

They were talking about a girl. Odette's voice echoed in Gigi's mind. *And, from what I gather, she's dead.*

Gigi tracked Brady's movements as best she could through the dark, all the way back up to the house.

Who was she—and how did she die? Gigi curled her fingers into the sand beneath her, and she was suddenly struck, as she often was, by a rogue idea, the way another person might be struck by a bus.

What if, instead of spending any more time competing to look for the last Object, she took advantage of the fact that Knox was out here to steal back the ones he'd taken from her?

The bag. The oxygen tank. The wetsuit.

Gigi stood and brushed black sand off her palms. *I am not,* she told herself sternly, *looking for an excuse to follow Brady Daniels back to the house.*

Chapter 22

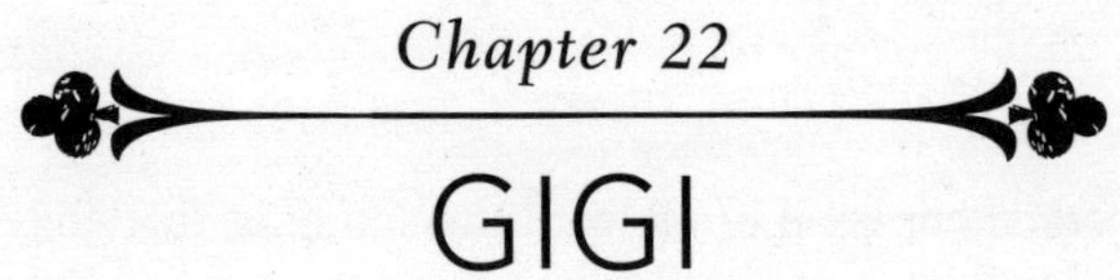

GIGI

A little breaking and entering never hurt anyone. It took Gigi three tries to find Knox's room, but the second she saw the vest, she knew she'd hit paydirt. A systematic search of the room didn't yield anything other than Knox's clothes.

A less systematic search also yielded nothing.

Either Knox had hidden the bag—and its contents—somewhere on the island after she'd finally given it up or . . .

Actually, Gigi couldn't come up with an *or*. When Knox had made good on his threat to block her path—and block it and block it and block it—Gigi had eventually responded by flinging the bag out into the ocean like she was some kind of demented Olympic discus thrower. Knox had cursed her out and gone after the bag, giving Gigi a chance to make a break for it with the duct tape and the knife.

She'd barely made it back to the house by sundown, but Mr. Five-Minute Mile definitely would have had time to hide the bag after he'd retrieved it.

That didn't stop Gigi from searching the room and attached bathroom a third time. Through the bathroom wall, she heard someone in the next room turn on the shower.

Brady? Why would he be showering now? Gigi told herself very sternly that (1) that was none of her business, and (2) she had no real reason to break into *his* room. She had no basis on which to think that Brady and Knox were in cahoots. *None.* But Brady *had* made it up to the house several minutes before Gigi had.

What if he'd beat her to going through Knox's room? What if he was, even now, washing away his sins and the very specific sin of *theft*?

This is a very bad idea. Gigi's mind-voice was chipper. *But am I doing it anyway?*

Yes. Yes, she was.

Soon enough, she'd ascertained that the bag wasn't in Brady's room, either. Gigi eyed the bathroom door, but even she had more common sense than that. Instead, she looked to the floor, where Brady's tuxedo was strewn next to the clothes he'd worn earlier.

In for a penny, in for a bad-idea pound. Gigi checked the pockets of Brady's clothes. All she found was a worn photograph of a teenage girl with mismatched eyes—one blue, one brown—notching an arrow in an oversized bow.

Gigi knew immediately with incredible certainty that this picture wasn't part of the Grandest Game. It wasn't an Object.

From what I gather, she's dead.

The shower turned off. Gigi put the photograph back and fled as silently and stealthily as she'd come, and she didn't stop when she hit the hallway or the spiral staircase or even the ground floor. She kept going, down another story to the second.

Pausing to take what might have been her first breath since the shower had turned off, Gigi blinked when she registered what she saw.

The second floor. To her right, there was a long, flat wall—no doors at all and barely any space between the wall and the staircase. Moving counterclockwise, she found another blank wall, then another.

The fourth and final wall boasted two doors, both closed. The first door was covered—*entirely covered*—in gears. Gigi had never seen anything like it. She reached out to lightly touch a golden gear, and then a bronze one. *No doorknob,* Gigi thought. She latched her hand around the biggest gear. It wouldn't turn, so she pulled, then pushed.

The door didn't move. She tried the rest of the gears one by one with the same result.

The second door didn't have a knob, either. It was made of marble—swirling, golden marble. In the middle of the door, there was a complicated, multitiered dial, like something you would expect to see on a bank vault.

Nothing Gigi tried opened either door, which made it pretty obvious: They were part of the game to come.

Turning her attention back to the three blank walls, Gigi remembered the way the house had looked from the shore. There had been five stories, and the bottom two had been the largest. *Hidden rooms?*

Gigi suddenly *needed* to see what the final floor—the lowest floor, the biggest—held. She took to the spiral staircase and made her way down. On the landing, where there should have been doors, where there should have been *something,* all Gigi saw was four white walls.

"Will you at least look at me?" That question, demanding and sharp, floated down from the staircase above. *Knox.*

"You never give up, do you?" *Brady.* "This is me looking at you and knowing exactly what I am looking at."

From where Gigi was standing, she couldn't see anything but their feet—which meant that they couldn't see her.

"You want to blame me for the way last year's game went down, Daniels? Fine."

Last year's game? Gigi's mind raced. It had never occurred to her that any of her competitors might be return players in the Grandest Game.

"I do blame you for last year, Knox. Just like I blame you for Calla."

Something about the way Brady said *Calla* made it clear that it was a name.

"Calla *left*," Knox bit out.

"Calla didn't just leave, and you damn well know it. She disappeared. Someone *took* her."

Neither one of them was talking like Calla was dead. They were talking like she was *missing*. Gigi wondered: Had Odette been mistaken or had she lied? *Or maybe Calla is missing... and dead.*

"How the hell would you know what Calla would or wouldn't do, Brady? She was with *me*. You were just a kid."

A kid? Gigi mentally scrambled to keep up. It didn't sound like they were still talking about the previous year's game, and in the picture, Calla had clearly been a teenager. *Sixteen? Seventeen?* And if she'd been with Knox... He had to have been at least twenty-four or twenty-five now.

"I was never just a *kid* to Calla." Brady's voice went even deeper. "And at least I haven't forgotten her. Like a coward. Like she was nothing."

"Screw you, Daniels. You won't make it two seconds in this game without me on your side. You're soft. Weak. You don't have the stomach for doing what it takes to win."

The next sound Gigi heard was Knox storming *up* the stairs. Before she could breathe a sigh of relief about the direction of those footsteps, there was a second set. Quieter. *Coming down.*

All Gigi could do as Brady stepped out onto the landing was desperately hope that he had *absolutely no idea* she'd broken into his room—and that he was particularly forgiving of semi-accidental eavesdropping.

Brady, once again clad in the tux she'd last seen on the floor, stared at her. Gigi prepared herself to be yelled at. But instead, Brady Daniels studied her for a moment, then nodded to the drawings on her bare arms. "Is that a map?"

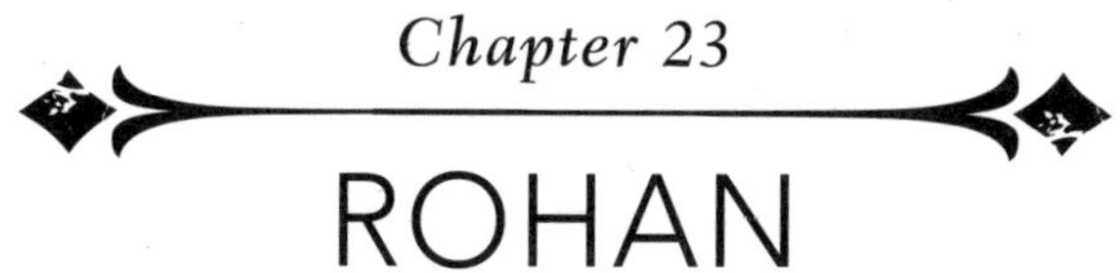

Chapter 23
ROHAN

Leave no stone unturned. It had not escaped Rohan's attention that Jameson Hawthorne had borrowed that line from him, from a game of Rohan's design, one that Jameson had won. *Cheeky bastard.*

As Rohan searched the rocks, he kept tabs on his competition while they did the same. He knew the instant Odette Morales found something. By the time the old woman had pried it—whatever *it* was—loose, Rohan was already halfway to her. Automatically, he reviewed the positions of the other players. Gigi, Brady, and Knox had already gone back to the house—and wasn't *that* interesting?—leaving only Lyra and Savannah, the latter of whom…

Had just spotted Rohan moving toward Odette.

"I don't like your chances with that one, young man," Odette called as Rohan approached. "But if I were sixty years younger, you might have stood a chance with me."

The old woman wanted Rohan to know: He wasn't the only one who could read people.

"You flatter me, Ms. Mora." Rohan closed the last of the space between them.

Odette registered Rohan's use of *Mora* instead of *Morales* and snorted. "If I was flattering you, you'd know it."

Rohan looked to her gloved hands. In one, Odette held the opera glasses he'd clocked the moment he'd first seen her tonight. In the other, there was what appeared to be a glass box with a luminescent button inside.

Odette flipped open the box and pressed the button.

For a second, maybe two, it seemed like nothing had happened, and then Rohan realized: *the house.* An enormous shade was descending, covering the massive Great Room windows on the third floor. Beams of concentrated light from the ground illuminated the shade.

Just for a moment.

Just long enough for Rohan to read the words written on it: *IN CASE OF EMERGENCY, BREAK GLASS.*

The shade began rising once more. The beams went dark. Beside Rohan, Odette hurled the glass box to the ground. It shattered, shards raining down into the crevices of the rocks. In an instant, Savannah was there, on the ground next to Odette, sorting through the carnage.

Rohan made no move to join them. *Break glass.* If he'd been the one to design this game, that wouldn't have been a reference to the glass box—too obvious. *And what is glass*, he thought intently, *but melted sand?*

Gigi had already spent a good chunk of time searching the black sand beach. Lyra was headed that way now. Rohan replayed the moment Jameson had issued their clue. *We won't steal too much of your time . . .*

And there it was.

Rohan made for the house. He slipped away unnoticed—for a time. He knew the exact instant Savannah realized where he was heading. She burst after him. Rohan picked up his own pace, shedding stealth for speed. He only allowed himself to look back over his shoulder once, as he began to scale the cliff. There was something almost Amazonian about the way the thick metal links of that chain hugged Savannah's hipbones, a sharp contrast with the ice-blue silk over which she wore it.

Neither the gown nor the chain seemed to slow her down. They should have. They *damn well* should have, especially on the cliff. *You're fast, love. I'll give you that.*

But Rohan was faster. He made it to the house first, to the Great Room first, to the *hourglass* first. Their time was almost up. There was little enough sand left in the top half of the hourglass that Rohan could clearly see the object that resided inside, the one that had been masked by all that black sand before.

A metal disk two-thirds the size of his palm.

Rohan didn't bother picking up the hourglass or trying to smash it. Savannah was incoming, so he held the hourglass with one hand and smashed his other fist straight through the glass, locking his fingers around the disk.

I win.

"You're bleeding." Savannah said those words the way another person might say *you have mud on your shoes.*

Oh, he really did like her. Rohan pulled a shard of glass from his knuckles. "Price of victory."

Savannah took a step toward him, her eyes on the disk. *Woe be,* her expression seemed to say, *to the person who stands in the way of Savannah Grayson.*

Rohan made the disk disappear in a flash, and then he gave himself a moment to read her. *The rise and fall of her chest. The slightest clench of her throat. Fury in her silvery gray eyes.*

Something clicked into place for Rohan then, something that had as much to do with the punishing pace she'd managed as it did the myriad of ways her body was giving her away now.

"You want this," Rohan murmured.

"Do you make a habit of telling women what they want?"

"The game," Rohan clarified. "You want to win. Badly."

Savannah straightened, standing taller than her nearly six feet. "I do not do anything badly, and I am not in the habit of *wanting* things. I set goals. I achieve them." *End of story.*

Rohan took a handkerchief out of the pocket of his tuxedo, wiped the blood off his knuckles, and captured her gaze with his own. "Fair warning, love: I want it more."

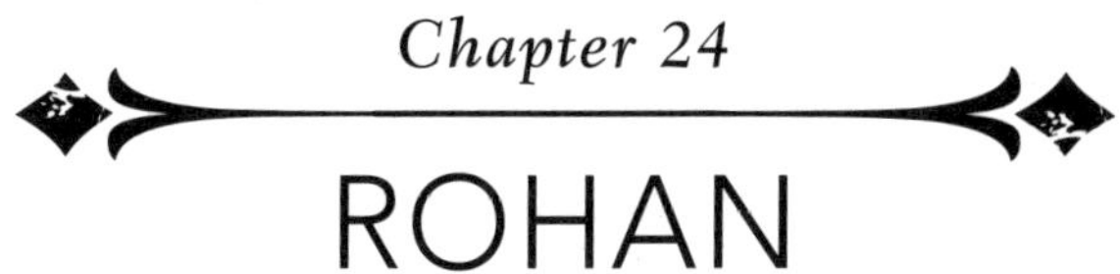

Chapter 24
ROHAN

One by one, the remaining players returned to the Great Room. Rohan was guessing they'd been summoned. Even without the hourglass to mark the passing of the final minutes, it was clear: *It's time.*

Grayson Hawthorne stepped into the room unaccompanied. *No Avery Grambs. No Jameson, Nash, or Xander.*

A sound, high and clear, broke through the air. *A chime.* Then another—from the foyer. Rohan moved liquidly in that direction. The second he stepped out of the Great Room, there was a cacophony of notes, coming from all around him. Chimes—and bells.

Rohan tracked each individual sound back to the location from which it had originated. *The dining room. The study. That one—it came from back in the Great Room.* Rohan wasn't the only player in the foyer now, not by a long shot.

He tuned out the chimes and listened only for the bells. *Never send to know for whom the bell tolls*... He turned sharply toward the dining room. *There.*

A tall blond blur tried to cut him off, but Rohan didn't let her. He squeezed through the door to the dining room half a second before Savannah crossed the threshold.

An instant later, the door slammed shut behind them.

Savannah tried the knob. It didn't turn. Through the thick, wooden door, Rohan heard a flurry of movement in the foyer, and then another slam. And another. *Three total—for three doors.*

Dining room. Study. Great Room.

"Locked in." Rohan leaned back against the wall next to the door. "That's one way to start a game."

A screen descended from the ceiling. An image filled the screen: *Avery Grambs. Three Hawthornes.* Rohan wondered if the four of them had made use of strategically placed cameras and remote triggers for the doors, or if they'd used motion sensors to track the locations of the players and the number of people in each room.

Had this game been one of Rohan's design, he would have opted for cameras.

"Good evening, players." Xander Hawthorne appeared to be channeling his inner James Bond, accent and all. "And behold: *the Grandest Escape Room.* Your mission: Get out of the house before sunrise."

Twelve hours, Rohan thought. *Give or take.*

"The good news," Avery announced on the screen, "is that you won't be working alone. Look around the room, whatever room you're in now. The people you see? From now until sunrise, they're your teammates."

The previous year's Grandest Game had been individual. There had been alliances, of course, players who had chosen to work together—right up until they didn't. But official teams? That was new.

"No man is an island, entire of itself," Rohan murmured. "In other words: No one is doing this alone. Clever."

Savannah's hand went to the chain encircling her hips, but her face didn't betray any surprise she felt that he'd already read the words on the lock. Rohan wondered idly what it would take to bring down those walls of hers.

Or scale them.

"Either your entire team makes it out and down to the north dock by sunrise," Jameson Hawthorne declared on-screen, "or none of you moves on to the next phase of the competition."

"Vincit simul, amittere simul." That was Xander again—and Latin.

"Win together," Savannah translated out loud. "Lose together."

"Almost." Rohan flicked his gaze to her. "The second part is closer to *give up together*, technically." He was playing with her—a bit *too* much, perhaps. But Rohan did love to play.

And glowering was an excellent look for her.

"If, at any point, your team finds itself stuck," Avery announced on-screen, "you may request a hint. In each room, you will find two buttons: one red, one black."

Right on cue, the dining room table parted on one end to reveal a hidden panel with the promised buttons.

"Push red to request your team's one and only hint," Jameson instructed. "But be warned: That hint won't be free. Everything comes at a cost." Now Jameson Hawthorne was speaking Rohan's language. "Hints in this game," Jameson continued, "must be earned."

One hint. Twelve hours. Rohan's brain cataloged the situation with a certain amount of dispassion, and then: *No one in this room except Savannah Grayson and me.*

On a completely objective level, Rohan could see the benefits to that.

"And now for the rules." Xander was enjoying this way too much. "Don't break the windows. Don't break the doors, walls, or furniture. Don't break any of the other players."

"Except by mutual consent." Jameson flashed a wicked little grin at the camera.

That earned Jameson a warning look from Nash. "Your team can't strong-arm or lock-pick your way out of this," the oldest Hawthorne brother summarized in his characteristic, laid-back drawl. "Solve the puzzle, unlock the door. More puzzles, more doors."

Rohan thought back to Nash's prediction: *It ain't gonna be you.*

"We won't be able to see or hear any of you while you're locked in." Avery took back over. "What happens in the Grandest Escape Room stays in the Grandest Escape Room. If there's an emergency, we can be contacted by pressing the black button."

Red button, hint. Black button, emergency.

And just like that, the screen went black. Three blinking white cursors appeared, each on its own line.

"To solve the first puzzle, insert your answers here." Jameson's disembodied voice rang through the room. "And no, we're not going to tell you the question. Also, you should be aware…"

An image flashed across the screen. Rohan recognized it as the symbol from the head of their keys.

"There are three teams," Jameson said, a self-satisfied lilt in his tone.

On-screen, the swirls on the head of the key were pulled apart into three directions, dividing them into distinct shapes, the patterns that had been masked before suddenly unmistakable now: a heart, a diamond, a club.

Three symbols. Three teams. Rohan turned his attention to the lone remaining image on the screen: the infinity symbol. As he watched, it rotated ninety degrees clockwise.

"Not infinity," Savannah said suddenly. *"Eight."*

Rohan suddenly knew *exactly* what the game's architects had been hinting at by building that image into the key. *Damn it all to hell.*

"There are three teams," Avery reiterated, her voice coming from all around them. "And eight players."

Chapter 25

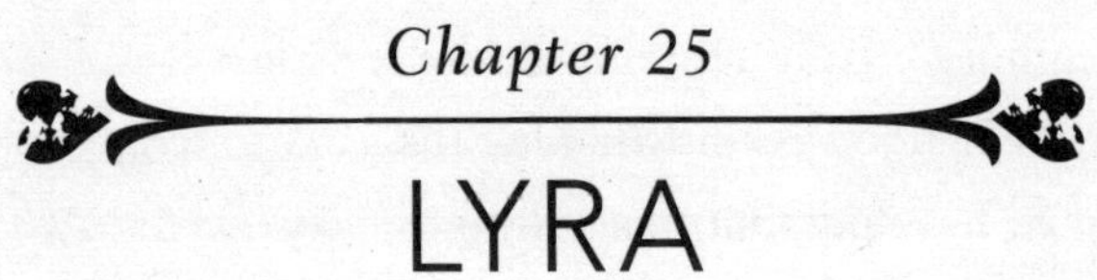

LYRA

In the Great Room, Lyra stared at the numeral 8 on the screen. Then the screen went black, and the cursors—three of them—reappeared and began to blink.

Eight players. Lyra's heart pounded in her throat.

"You do realize who the eighth player in this game is?" Odette aimed that question squarely at the last occupant of the Great Room.

You-Know-Who.

Why had Lyra come back to the Great Room? She'd made it into the foyer before backtracking. Why couldn't she have followed the chimes into *any other room*?

"Your brother Jameson made it a point to tell all of us that you were just as in the dark about this game as we are," Odette continued. "Search that tuxedo, Mr. Hawthorne. I wager you'll find one of these."

Lyra turned just in time to see Odette bring a gloved hand to the high neck of her black gown—and her player pin. Ten feet away from Lyra, Grayson executed an efficient search of his tuxedo and found a pin, just as Odette had predicted.

He's not running the game. He's a player. We're a team. Something in Lyra rebelled against that thought. Hard. *Odette. Me. Him.*

She could still hear Grayson saying *consider it done* in the exact same tone with which he'd once ordered her to *stop calling.*

"I am not in the habit," Grayson informed Odette, "of allowing myself to be manipulated. My brothers and Avery know that."

"You must admit that your inclusion does add a certain level of challenge," Odette said. "We may be a team at the moment, but in the end, to win it all, one must best a Hawthorne."

Something about the way Odette talked about *winning* and *besting* reminded Lyra that the gloves in this competition were already off. *Mind games. Those notes.* Lyra studied Odette Morales more closely. The old woman held something in her left hand, a jeweled object that reflected the chandelier's light, preventing Lyra from seeing exactly what it was.

"It is well within my power," Grayson said, directing his words to Odette and only Odette, "to refuse to play."

Refuse to play? Lyra felt that like a slap to the face. She whirled on Grayson. "You can't refuse without taking us down with you." She took a step toward him, every muscle in her body taut. "Either the whole team makes it out before sunrise or all of us are out of the game."

She didn't know why she expected him to care. Lyra knew what came of expecting things of Grayson Hawthorne. But that didn't change the fact that right now, she needed him. Regardless of what her masquerade mask was worth, Lyra knew her parents—her dad, especially—wouldn't take a penny of that money from her.

To save Mile's End—long term, with any kind of certainty—she had to win it all.

"You'll play," Lyra told Grayson fiercely. "And you'll hold nothing back."

He owed this to her. For whatever role his grandfather had played in her father's suicide; for giving her hope and taking it away; for talking to her and then *not* talking to her; for that dance and the way she could still feel his hand on her back—Grayson Hawthorne *owed* her.

"You are not going to ruin this for me." Lyra's voice tipped over the line from low to husky. *"I need this."* She hadn't meant to admit any kind of weakness to him.

"If it's money you need," Grayson said, "there are other ways."

"Spoken like a Hawthorne," Lyra retorted.

"It's funny." Odette walked slowly over to the wall of windows and stared out into the night. "Until just now I hadn't seen the resemblance." She turned her head sideways, her profile striking. "To Tobias."

"You knew my grandfather." Grayson did not phrase that as a question, but he did follow it up with one. "How?"

Lyra thought again about the notes—and her father's names. How *had* Odette Morales known Tobias Hawthorne?

"Help us get to the dock by sunrise, young man," Odette said, "and perhaps I'll tell you."

There was a beat of silence and then: "There's a lever," Grayson stated. "Underside of the screen."

Lyra turned and saw it. She crossed the room. *I should pull the lever.* She didn't. Not yet. "Is that a *yes*?" she demanded, twisting back to face the last person on the planet she wanted to be locked in a room with. "You'll play?"

Grayson stared back at Lyra, his pupils expanding, inky black against irises that walked the icy line between blue and gray. "It hardly seems I have a choice," he said. "I value my life, and you appear to have a temper." Muscles shifted over his granite jaw, like he'd entertained the idea of smiling—and decided against it.

Locked in. With Grayson Hawthorne. Lyra's mind went to the quote in the ruins—her hint about the nature of the game. *Escape.* All she had to do was survive the next twelve hours and beat what was probably the world's most complicated escape room. With *him.*

It's just one night, Lyra told herself. She pulled the lever. There was a mechanical whirring sound. The wall behind the screen opened to reveal a hidden compartment. Inside it was a chest made of gleaming mahogany, accented in gold.

Lyra walked toward it. Engraved on a gold plate on the front of the chest was a phrase that she deeply suspected was Latin. *Et sic incipit.*

Grayson walked to stand directly behind her and translated: "And so it begins."

Chapter 26

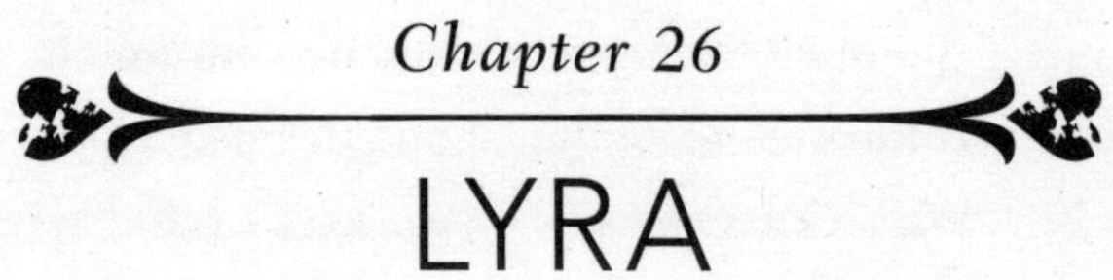

LYRA

Inside the chest was a collection of six objects:

A Styrofoam cup from Sonic.

A box of magnet poetry.

A roll of quarters.

A mirrored dinner plate.

A black velvet pouch of Scrabble tiles.

A single red rose petal.

And that was it. No further instructions. Not even the barest hint of a suggestion about what they were supposed to *do* with those items.

"My grandfather was fond of games and fonder of giving his grandsons ways to test and prove ourselves." Grayson's voice was neither quiet nor loud. He put no particular emphasis on the words, but there was an intensity to *him* that could not be ignored. "Every Saturday morning, the old man would call us into his study and lay out an assortment of objects, just like this one. We were given, at best, minimal instructions or a cryptic prompt. Part of the game was figuring out the game. By its end, every single one of the objects would have proved itself necessary at one point or another, their purposes obscured until the exact moment in the game when a part of the grand plan revealed itself. One clue led to another to another, puzzle after puzzle, riddle after riddle, always a competition."

Lyra flashed back to the way Grayson had spoken about his billionaire grandfather on their phone calls. *Whatever Tobias Hawthorne did or didn't do, it's none of my concern.* That had been on their first call. On their second: *Probabilities being what they are, whatever Tobias Hawthorne did or did not do, it likely ruined your father financially.*

And later, after she'd recited her father's cryptic last words—*What begins a bet? Not that*—Grayson had interpreted those words as a riddle and parted with one final piece of almost humanizing information: *My grandfather was very big into riddles.*

For a brief moment in time, she'd let herself entertain the idea that they might solve that riddle together.

Lyra slammed a door on the memories. "We've got the cryptic prompt," she said evenly. "*To solve the first puzzle, insert your answers here. And no, we're not going to tell you the question.* Those were Jameson's exact words. There are three cursors, which suggests the answer has three parts."

Three answers, no question. Just the objects and the room we're locked in. Lyra took a moment to survey the Great Room: the wall of windows facing the fairy-lit rocks and the black ocean beyond; the mazelike design of the cherrywood walls; a granite fireplace; the adjacent seating area where an enormous leather couch was framed by two smaller but otherwise identical pieces. *Three-seater, two-seater, one-seater.* The asymmetry of that arrangement should have felt unbalanced but didn't. The only other furniture in the room was a pair of marble coffee tables, one of which was covered in the remains of the hourglass. *Shards.*

A crystal chandelier hung from the ceiling.

"Among the objects we have just been given, there will be one that starts us off." Grayson was all business. "One object is the initial clue that will point us to the next step of the puzzle. The trick is identifying which object that is and decoding its meaning."

"You sound pretty sure about that," Lyra said, halfway under her breath.

"Ask me how often I won my grandfather's games," Grayson suggested silkily.

Lyra did not. Instead, she lined their objects up on the floor, letting her mind linger briefly on each one as she did. *A Styrofoam cup. A box of magnet poetry. A roll of quarters. A mirrored dinner plate. A black velvet pouch of Scrabble tiles. A single petal from a red rose.*

"Six objects," Lyra said out loud.

"Eight." The correction came from Odette. "The bag and the box." The old woman sank to the floor beside the objects with surprising ease. She poured the Scrabble tiles out of the velvet bag and dumped the poetry magnets out of the box. "I have an eye for technicalities and loopholes. Indulge me."

"Eight objects," Lyra said, coming to kneel next to Odette.

Grayson reached forward and unwrapped the roll of quarters, setting the paper to one side and the coins to the other. "Nine—and that's assuming the coins, the magnets, and the Scrabble tiles all function as units."

Nine objects, Lyra thought. *A piece of paper. A small box. A black velvet pouch. Quarters. Scrabble tiles. Poetry magnets. A mirrored plate. A disposable cup. A single petal from a red rose.*

Lyra reached for the poetry magnets. Grayson did the same. Her fingers brushed the back of his hand, and Lyra's body was taken back—to the cliffs, to their dance. There were downsides to having the kind of memory where you saw nothing in your mind's eye and felt *everything*.

Lyra jerked her hand back. She turned her attention to the Scrabble tiles. He could have the damn poetry.

"By my count, there are twenty-two Scrabble tiles," Grayson said brusquely. "Unless there are fewer than five vowels total, you'll want to start by finding a way to eliminate some of the letters. Look for patterns, repetition, anything that will let you get it down to a smaller pool, otherwise the number of possible combinations will render the tiles virtually useless to us on the puzzle front—until or unless we uncover a clue that sheds light on which ones to use."

"I don't recall her asking you for advice, Mr. Hawthorne," Odette commented austerely, but she was smiling like a cat that had just eaten the proverbial canary.

"You take the Scrabble tiles, then," Lyra told Grayson, clipping the words.

"No." Grayson's gaze settled on hers, like a laser locking on its target. He arched a brow. "Are we going to have a problem here, Lyra?" He said her name the way her father did in the dream: *Lie-ra*.

"It's Lyra," she corrected. *Leer-a*.

"Rest assured, Lyra." Grayson's voice was low and smooth. "For the duration of this game, I'll be keeping my hands to myself."

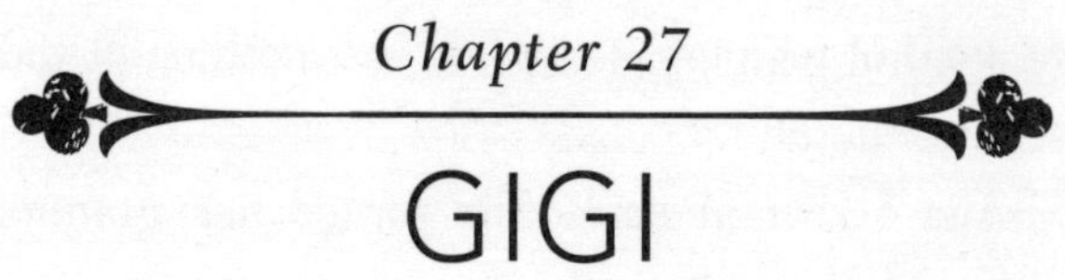

Chapter 27
GIGI

Rehabilitation took time. So did examining the chest of items Gigi's team had liberated from a compartment built into the desk in the study in which they were now locked—*they* being Gigi, Brady, and the jerk formerly known as *Eyebrows of Doom*, who Gigi was currently mentally referring to as *Grumpy Pants Tuxedo Abs*, because hey, the man was built.

He was also going to rue the day he'd stolen that bag, but she was pacing herself.

Grabbing the mirrored plate off the desk, Gigi took up position dead center in the study, then slowly turned three hundred and sixty degrees, angling her makeshift mirror up and down as she did, taking in the room's reflection, drinking in every last detail.

When it came to puzzles, the minutiae mattered.

The study was rectangular, half as wide as it was deep with soaring ceilings. Built-in shelves ringed the top of the room, well out of reach. Gigi angled her mirror to pay special attention to the moldings on the shelves, hand-carved pieces that looked like they belonged in a cathedral.

The shelves themselves, to all appearances, were empty.

Gigi kept turning and angled her mirror toward the desk. Knox was seated in a throne-like chair behind it, taking apart the wood chest, board by board. *With his bare hands.* Gigi ignored him in favor of the recovering physicist standing over the desk, looking down at the items spread across its surface.

Brady stood so still that Gigi could make out every rise and fall of his chest beneath his tuxedo jacket. *Deep breaths. Slow ones.*

"Don't just stand there, Daniels," Knox snapped, ripping another board off the chest. "Do something."

Just for that, Grumpy Pants, Gigi thought, *I am demoting you to Grumpy Knickers.*

"I am doing something," Brady said, his tone meditative. "Have a little faith, Knox."

The way Brady said those words made Gigi think that *have faith* was a criticism Knox Landry had heard before. It was tempting to chew on that, to go down the rabbit hole of thinking about everything she'd overheard. About the photograph. About *Calla*.

But Gigi was a Gigi on a mission. "I'm sensing some tension here." She lowered the mirrored plate. Since they were stuck as a team until sunrise, Gigi figured it was better to poke at the elephants in the room than to ignore them. "Luckily," she continued, "I am an expert mediator and a pleasure to have in class."

Disarming people with cheerful goodwill was an art form, and Gigi was an artist.

"*You* are a liability," Knox said.

"Hey." Brady put a little heat behind his tone. "Knock it off. She's just a kid."

That stung more than Gigi wanted to admit. *Just a kid. A liability.*

"She's a kid who happens to be Grayson Hawthorne's half sister," Knox told Brady, his tone equal parts intense and smug and just *intensely smug.* "Happy-go-lucky little rich girl here had her ticket to this game handed to her, just like she's probably had everything handed to her for her entire life."

There was a type of person—a lot of types of people, really—who took Gigi's bubbly demeanor and determined optimism as faults, a combination of vacuousness and naivete, when really, happiness was a choice Gigi made every day.

Gigi didn't *get* to fall apart. "As it so happens," she said pertly, "I won one of the four wild card tickets all on my own. And, if it weren't for me"—she smiled a thousand-watt smile—"you wouldn't have even found that bag, *you grumpy-knickered smirk-face.*" Gigi gave a happy little shrug. "I forgive you, by the way, and you should find that very frightening."

"What bag?" Brady said.

Knox replied with two words: "Mine, now."

"Yours?" Brady retorted. "Or your sponsor's? It's not like you're your own man anymore."

"Sponsor?" Gigi wrinkled her forehead.

"There are a handful of wealthy families that have taken an interest in the Grandest Game," Brady informed her. "They hire players, stack the deck where they can, bet on the outcome. Last I checked, Knox was on the Thorp family payroll."

Well, that sounded... ominous. *Stack the deck how?*

"I play to win." An utterly unapologetic Knox tore another board off the chest. "And Brady here has always had a soft spot for spoiled little girls."

Spoiled. Little. Girls. Clearly, for the sake of Knox's rehabilitation and the good of his soul, a little demonstration was going to be necessary. *I'll show you* little girl, *you misogynistic smugweasel.*

Gigi smiled beatifically. "This room is eight feet two inches by sixteen feet six inches," she began. "The painting on the back wall shows four paths converging to one, and the artist signed in the upper right corner instead of one of the lower corners, as one would more commonly expect. There are a total of nine moldings carved into the shelves ringing the top third of the room, among them carvings of a lyre, a scroll, a laurel wreath, and a compass."

Brady turned his head slowly toward her. "Muses," he said. "The symbology matches up, and in Greek mythology, there are nine."

"Maybe there's some significance to that," Gigi replied. "Or maybe it's just the game makers' way of suggesting that to solve this puzzle, we're going to have to get a little creative."

Gigi turned to Knox. "How many uses can you think of for this?" Gigi held up the mirrored plate. "Because off the top of my head, I've got at least nine. Want to hear a few? It could work as a mirror, obviously, which means that it could be particularly useful in decoding anything written or drawn backward. Mirrors are also good for redirecting light, which could help with revealing certain kinds of invisible ink. And speaking of invisible ink..." She breathed on the plate, causing the glass to fog up. "Certain oils can leave behind traces on a mirror's surface." Gigi turned the mirror toward her audience. "Just smudges on this one, but it was worth a try."

She probably could have stopped there. But alas, moderation was not one of Gigi's strong suits; see also: *caffeine.* "The diameter or circumference of the plate could be a unit of measurement. Shatter it, and you could use the shards to cut something—though personally, if *I* needed to do a slice and dice, I would probably just use the knife strapped to my thigh." Gigi's most innocent voice was pretty darn innocent. "Then again, I could probably also use that knife to pick the locks on the three obvious desk drawers and the hidden one on this side, which I'm sure you've both already noticed, right? Alas, we were told we couldn't lock-pick our way out of this, and I am nothing if not a rule-abiding Gigi, so maybe I'll just keep *my* knife in reserve."

The knife, Gigi tried to telegraph, *that* you *failed to steal, Knox.*

Brady stared at Gigi for a moment. "Point taken," he said, a slight smile pulling at his lips. "Not a kid."

"Not a kid," Gigi agreed. She walked over to the desk and stared down at the items spread across its surface. "When most people look at those Scrabble tiles," she told Brady, "they probably see letters. I see the number of points each tile is worth. And when I look at the poetry magnets, I start to wonder if all of the words really *are* magnetic, or if there might be a few very significant outliers that look like magnets but aren't. Someone should try all of them on the metal chair Knox is sitting on. And speaking of, am I the only one who's noticed that chair is made of swords?"

Gigi could *see* the effort it took Knox not to look down.

"In your defense," she told him, "the workmanship really masks the swordiness of it all."

Brady shook his head wryly, his dreadlocks gently swaying. "You're a force of nature."

"I get that a lot," Gigi replied. "Hurricane metaphors, mostly, some tornadoes." She shrugged. "While we're in sharing mode, my other specialties include computers and code, breaking and entering, cutting my own hair, puzzle boxes, visual memorization, eating candy on rooftops, calligraphy, tying knots, untying knots, cat memes, rotating objects in my head, providing distractions, picking up on seemingly insignificant details, and making people like me, even when their whole personality is not liking anyone or anything."

She turned pointedly to Knox. "And you?" she said. "What are your specialties?"

Knox scowled, but he also—grudgingly—answered. "Logic puzzles. Identifying weaknesses. Finding shortcuts. I have a high tolerance for pain. I don't sleep much. And I always do what needs to be done." Knox shot Brady a pointed look, heavy on the eyebrows. "Doesn't always make me popular."

Hello, tension. Back again so soon? "Brady?" Gigi said. "Specialties?"

"Symbols and meanings." Brady had a way of taking his time with words. "Ancient civilizations. Material culture, especially anything involving rituals or tools."

That's right, Gigi thought. *Talk nerdy to me.*

"I speak nine languages," Brady continued quietly, "and can read seven more. I have an eidetic memory, and I tend to be pretty good at recognizing patterns."

"You forgot constellations," Knox said suddenly, and it was like that one word—*constellations*—sucked the oxygen out of the room. "He knows every damn one." Knox's jaw was hard, but something in his eyes definitely wasn't. "Musical puzzles are also a forte of his, and Brady here can hold his own in a fight." There was a very loaded pause. "We both can."

If Gigi hadn't been a twin, she might have missed the way that Knox said *we*, but she'd spent most of her life as part of a unit. She knew what it was like to be a part of that kind of *we*.

And then, suddenly, not to be.

However Brady and Knox knew each other, Gigi was pretty sure it went beyond the probably missing, possibly dead girl they'd both known. But right now? Gigi's teammates wouldn't even look at each other.

Pace yourself, Gigi reminded herself. She took a deep breath. "I'm going to compare the Scrabble tiles to that wonky signature on the painting and see what I can come up with," she said. "Someone should really try the poetry magnets on the sword chair."

Brady reached for the box of magnets and threw it—a bit harder than necessary—to Knox, who caught it with one hand. Making her way to the painting, Gigi did everything in her power not to turn around as Brady said something in a voice she had to strain to hear.

"If you want to walk down memory lane so much, Knox, how about this? Severin sends his regards."

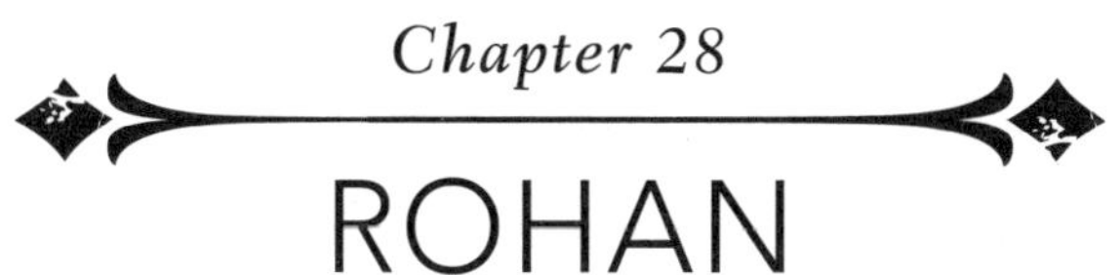

Chapter 28
ROHAN

Rohan put the odds at fifty-nine percent that Grayson Hawthorne's inclusion in this game had been a recent decision, a last-minute change. There were, after all, only *seven* player rooms. It would have been difficult but not impossible for Grayson's brothers to have had new keys to those rooms made to incorporate the number eight, once they'd seen what Rohan had.

Grayson Hawthorne and Lyra Kane. Hadn't Nash told Rohan that this game had *heart*?

"The eighth player is your brother." Rohan addressed Savannah, who was coolly examining the array of objects they'd just uncovered. "He has the advantage."

This was a Hawthorne game.

"Half brother." Savannah was the picture of calm—and a portrait of unimpressed. "And he only has the advantage until we take it back." Savannah nodded imperiously toward the objects. "Make yourself useful, British."

A locked room. A partner who didn't believe in *wanting* things, their goals aligned until dawn. Rohan could work with that.

He allowed his gaze to travel to the chain around Savannah's hips and the lock that hung on it. "Do you think that's served its one and only purpose?" Rohan asked. "A hint that we would be playing on teams?"

"You'd like me to believe it has no further value." Savannah gave a delicate arch of her brow. "Trying to get me to take it off?"

Take it off. Rohan had a certain appreciation for that turn of phrase, and he didn't doubt her usage of it was intentional. For all her ironclad control, Savannah Grayson apparently wasn't above playing with *him*.

"Wouldn't dream of it, love," Rohan told her.

He eyed the items they'd been given to work with for the first puzzle, then he reached into his tuxedo jacket and produced an object of his own. *The metal disk.*

Savannah's hand snaked out.

Rohan side-stepped. In the light, the markings etched into the metal were clear—broken lines, all around the edges of the disk on both sides, front and back.

"Was it worth it?" Savannah said. "Beating me to that, now that we're a *team*?" The slight edge of sarcasm in the way she said the word *team* did not go unnoticed.

"It's always worth it." Rohan looked to the dried blood on his knuckles. "If I second-guess one sacrifice, suddenly, there might be lines I'm not willing to cross."

Rohan didn't give her a chance to reply as he made his way to the dining room table and bent down, his eyes even with its surface. He placed the disk vertically on the table, holding the circular piece of metal between his middle finger and his thumb.

"What are you doing?" Savannah said, less question than demand.

Rohan snapped his fingers, spinning the disk. Savannah planted her hands on the table and lowered her upper body to Rohan's level, taking in the head-on view of the rapidly spinning disk. The markings on the front side blurred with the markings on the back. Broken lines became whole. Incomprehensible symbols became letters.

"*Use the room*," Savannah read out loud.

Rohan waited until the disk fell to its side, rattling against the dining room table. "Use the room," he echoed. "Tell me, Savannah Grayson . . ." He pitched his voice to surround her, a trick he'd picked up as Factotum of the Devil's Mercy, an occupation in which it was useful to project the idea that you were *everywhere*. "What do you see?"

Savannah didn't immediately respond, and Rohan turned his own discerning gaze to their surroundings. What *he* saw was this: a round dining room table with six chairs. The seats of the chairs were covered in a velvety fabric that matched two sets of heavy, golden drapes on the south wall. The drapes were closed. Positioned between them on the wall was a bar cart. *Antique*. The east wall held a silver hutch, likely also an antique. It was tall and wide but not more than a foot deep. The doors were wide open, the shelves empty.

The detailing on those cabinet doors matched the design inlaid into the table's top, a complicated swirl of flowers and vines. The center of the round table was raised, forming a smaller circle. The design on the raised circle's surface was striking.

"A compass." Savannah walked toward the table.

What do you see? He'd asked, and she'd provided only one answer. *The* answer, as far as she was concerned. Savannah placed a hand on the raised part of the table. Closing her fingers around the edge of the wheel, she turned it.

The center of the table spun. It made a complete rotation before Rohan caught Savannah's wrist, his touch feather-light. "Careful, love. What if it turns out we're meant to enter some sort of combination using that 'compass'?"

Savannah turned her head slowly toward him, her eyes even with his, her *lips* even with his. "Do you intend to keep that appendage?"

"My apologies." In one liquid movement, Rohan left her and crossed to the curtains on the front wall. Pulling the first set revealed no windows, just a painting on the wall where a window should have been.

"A mural." Savannah crossed the room and pulled the second set of curtains. "And another one here."

One of sunrise, one of sunset. Rohan pushed on, the rest of the world melting away as he executed a visual search of the room, scanning every inch of it, looking for—

That. Rohan's gaze landed on the bar cart between the windows. Sitting on top of it were three crystal decanters, each holding liquid of a different color. But Rohan had eyes only for the fourth bottle. It was the simplest, boxy in shape, made of plain glass. The liquid inside was a very distinct shade.

Sunrise orange. Rohan reached for it, and this time, Savannah caught *his* wrist.

"I assume that you are also attached to your appendages," Rohan quipped. Her thumb was on his pulse. He could feel her feel it.

The body never lies.

Savannah dropped her grip, allowing Rohan to lift the bottle in front of his face. The colored liquid served as a lens, filtering out light waves of the same frequency—and illuminating the writing hidden in the sunrise mural.

Rohan smiled—not a roguish smile but one that was sharp-edged, wolfish. His *real* smile.

He handed Savannah the bottle, and she read the hidden message for herself.

TO SOLVE THE PUZZLE, FOCUS ON THE WORDS.

Chapter 29

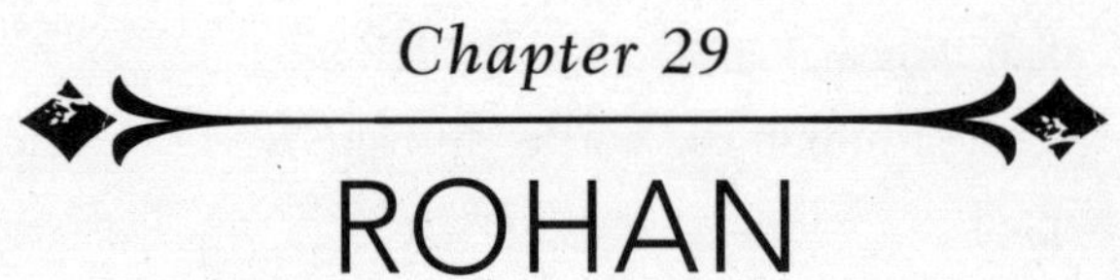

ROHAN

Rohan dumped the magnet poetry onto the table. Savannah took up position to his right. Without even a glance in his direction, she began laying the words out face up, efficient and precise, each word a half inch from the next. By the time Savannah had the entire magnet poetry kit laid out in three evenly spaced lines, Rohan had already finished his preliminary assessment of the set.

"Twenty-five words total," he commented.

"Only four verbs." Savannah's pale hair was braided back from her face in a complicated twist that reminded Rohan of a tiara, but there was nothing princess-like about the way she assessed the spread before them, her palms flat on the table, sinewy muscles visible in her arms. She looked like a general preparing for battle. "*Burned*, *is*, *will*, and *be*."

Rohan pulled three of the four, rearranging their order.

"It seems a poor strategy to use all of the verbs in one go," Savannah said intently.

"Are you suggesting we ration our verbs?" Rohan smirked.

She ignored him, scanned the word bank, and pulled three others. "These are the only ones that could even possibly go with your little combination there."

There was no hesitation in Savannah Grayson. It was like she was incapable of it.

She'd pulled the word *the* and two nouns. "*Skin*." Rohan allowed himself to linger on that word for a moment. There were benefits to letting yourself want someone if strategy called for making them want you. "And *rose*." Rohan drew a finger across the remaining word, then slid it and the word *the* into place.

"The rose petal." Savannah was already on the move.

Rohan was beside her in a flash. "Up for a little bonfire, winter girl?" The title suited her. *The hair. The eyes.* Though Rohan had to admit: She was far more *woman* than *girl*.

"Burning anything would be premature and rash." Savannah looked back to the bank of magnetic words. Rohan wondered which ones jumped out to her. *Danger? Cruel? Fast? Touch? Fair?* "And besides," she continued crisply, "to burn anything, we'd need matches or a lighter, which we do not have."

"Matches, a lighter, or..." Rohan waited until her eyes flicked toward his. "A beam of light and a concave mirror."

Chapter 30

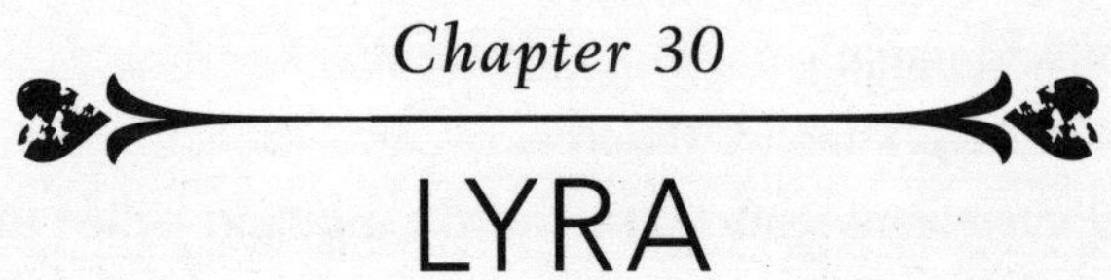

LYRA

Grayson flicked a button open on his tuxedo jacket with one hand as the other laid out quarters on the marble coffee table with an audible *click, click, click*. Lyra couldn't help noticing that he'd chosen to work on the coffee table that was half-covered in glass shards.

The one that was farther away from her.

Focus on the letters, Lyra told herself. *And only the letters.* She'd lined the Scrabble tiles up on the floor, the way she would have if she were actually playing Scrabble: vowels first, then consonants in alphabetical order.

A, A, E, E, E, O, O, U, U, B, C, D, G, H, N, P, R, R, T, T, W, Y.

Grayson's *suggestion* echoed in Lyra's mind: *Look for patterns, repetition, anything that will let you get it down to a smaller pool.*

I could *do that.* Lyra looked up to see a single strand of blond hair fall into that stone-carved face of his. *Or I could* play.

Grayson's logic had been that too many words could be made

from a pool of letters this large. But if the goal wasn't just making words or a sentence? If the goal was laying out the perfect Scrabble board, focusing on choosing the right plays to maximize your score?

That changed the game—and Lyra had never lost at Scrabble.

She settled on *UNPOWERED* as her opening play. *Fifteen points.* She went to the *D* and made *ADAGE*—another seven points—then doubled up, forming *YE* and *YACHT* in one go, crossing through the first *A* in *ADAGE* and allowing her to count the *Y* twice. *Eighteen points.*

Less than a minute later, Lyra had finished her board. She dragged a finger lightly over each tile, feeling the words, committing them to memory—and then she scrapped the whole thing and made another board from scratch. Then another. And another. Certain words cropped up again and again.

"Power, crown, adage," Lyra murmured.

"If only there were an adage about power."

Lyra realized with a start that Odette Morales was standing directly over her.

"One with explicit reference," the old woman continued, "to a crown."

Adage. Power. Crown. It took Lyra a moment, but she got there. *"Heavy is the head that wears the crown."*

"I prefer the original version myself." Odette walked toward the wall of windows, commanding the room as if she were on a stage and the audience was out there in the dark. *"Uneasy lies the head that wears a crown."*

"Shakespeare." Grayson stood. *"Henry IV, Part Two."* He crossed the room and took in Lyra's board. "You're not even trying to eliminate letters."

Lyra wasn't about to let him tower over her, so she stood.

"Maybe I don't need to eliminate anything." She walked briskly past him to the screen and its three blinking cursors. She tapped one, and a keyboard appeared. "Shakespeare." Lyra tried the word, then hit enter. The screen flashed red. "Henry. Henry4. Henry4P2. Henry4Part2."

Every combination Lyra tried ended with the same result: a red flash, a wrong answer.

"Try Roman numerals instead of numbers," Odette said, coming to stand behind her.

Lyra did as she'd been bidden, trying each of the combinations again. "No go."

"*Prince. Knight. Succession. King.*" Odette threw out one suggestion after another.

"It won't be that simple." Grayson strode toward Lyra. He stopped three feet away from her, but Grayson Hawthorne had the kind of presence that extended well past his body.

Lyra's own body clocked his position, no matter where he stood.

"If you've indeed found something—and I am not convinced you have, Ms. Kane—then it is almost certainly the case that what you have found is not an answer but a clue."

There was something about the overly formal, self-important way Grayson said *Ms. Kane* that made Lyra briefly entertain the idea of throwing something at him.

"And did *you* find anything, Mr. Hawthorne?" Odette asked pointedly.

"There are forty quarters in a roll." Grayson arched a brow. "All of ours were minted in the same year except two."

"I suppose you want us to ask about the year?" Odette said dryly.

"Thirty-eight of the quarters were minted in nineteen ninety-one." Grayson looked to Lyra, and she couldn't shake the feeling that he was testing her.

She just *loved* being tested. "Is this the part where you tell us about the other two quarters, or do we have to earn that information, your highness?"

"I'm feeling magnanimous." Grayson's lips twitched slightly. *Very* slightly. "One of the remaining two quarters was minted in twenty-twenty, the other in two thousand and two."

"Same digits in both numbers," Lyra noted. "Just rearranged."

"And nineteen ninety-one," Grayson replied, one-upping her, "is a palindrome."

The part of Lyra's brain that loved a good code latched on to the pattern, as that same damn strand of blond hair fell into Grayson's face a second time. He brushed it back.

"And the years on the quarters matter why?" Lyra said tartly.

"In a Hawthorne game, everything matters. The question is not *why* but *when*." Grayson looked at Lyra like the answer to that question might be buried somewhere behind her eyes. "Assume for the moment that the words *adage* and *crown* are indeed the clue that is meant to start us off." Grayson turned and stalked toward the fireplace on the far side of the room. "In that case, the pattern to the quarters will matter later, and what matters now..." He laid a hand flat on the black granite of the fireplace. "...is finding a crown."

Lyra watched as Grayson ran his hands over the granite, left to right, then down, his movements automatic, like systematically feeling every square inch of a massive fireplace was something he'd done ten thousand times before.

"Why a crown?" Lyra pressed. "Why not something heavy? *Heavy is the head that wears the crown.*"

"*Heavy* is vague, and vagueness makes for imprecise puzzles." Grayson Hawthorne said *imprecise* like it was a fighting word.

Lyra looked to Odette, who'd been suspiciously quiet, and found the old woman tracing a finger through the mazelike path on the wood-paneled walls. Rather than join her, Lyra turned her attention to the heaviest pieces of furniture in the room.

Imprecise, my ass. The coffee tables were made of what looked like solid white marble. Tiny hairline cracks marked the surface of the stone, each crack inlaid with gold.

"Like a crown," Lyra murmured, running her own hand over the first table, aware on some level that she'd adopted Grayson's exact pattern of movement as she searched. Within a minute, she'd turned her attention to the second table, the one covered in shards of glass.

"All things being equal, Ms. Kane, I would prefer you did not shred your hands to ribbons this evening." Grayson's tone took Lyra right back to the cliffs, to his hand on her arm.

"I have twenty-twenty vision and an above-average amount of common sense." Lyra plucked a shard off the table. "I can handle a little glass."

Grayson's eyes narrowed ever so slightly. "The number of scars my brothers have collectively obtained directly after uttering the statement *I can handle a little glass* means you will have to forgive my skepticism."

I don't have to forgive anything, Lyra thought. Out loud, she opted for a different message. "You don't need to worry about me, Hawthorne boy."

"I don't worry. I calculate probabilistic risk."

"As entertaining as it would be to let the two of you bicker," Odette interjected, "at my age, you only have so much time left, so I suggest the pair of you ask me what I found."

Lyra set down the shard of glass. "What did you find?"

"Nothing yet," Odette said, playing the contrarian. "But in the decades I spent cleaning other people's houses to scrape by, I learned how to read them—the people *and* the houses." The old woman pressed her palm to the wood. "There's a compartment hidden *here*." She slid down the wall four feet and rapped it with her fist. "And something larger over *here*."

"That hardly sounds like *nothing*," Grayson told her wryly.

"Until we figure out how to trigger the compartments, it is precisely nothing," Odette replied. She edged farther down. "*This*, on the other hand..."

Lyra joined the old woman at the wall.

"Look at the grain of the wood," Odette murmured. "See the shift? There's no visible seam—the work is *that* good—but feel the wood."

Lyra brought her fingers up and explored the area that Odette had indicated. The wood gave. Not much. Barely enough to notice.

Suddenly, Grayson's fingers were right next to hers. True to his vow, he didn't allow their hands to so much as brush as he pressed on the wood. *Hard*. An entire section of the wall depressed.

Somewhere, gears audibly turned, and the chandelier began to descend from the ceiling. It sank inch by inch, crystals vibrating with the movement, clinking against one another in a fragile melody that had Lyra holding her breath.

When the chandelier stopped moving, it was still well out of reach.

Odette gestured imperiously at Grayson. "Well? Don't just stand there, Mr. Hawthorne." The old woman extended her gesture to encompass Lyra. "You're going to have to lift her up."

Chapter 31

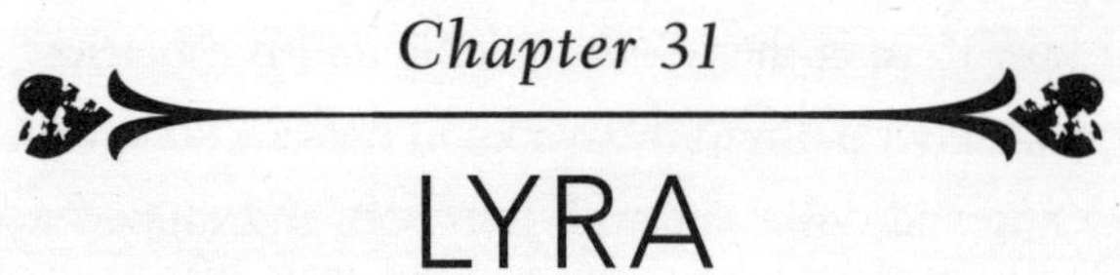

LYRA

Lyra's heart turned to stone in her chest. *Lift me up?* She knew already how Grayson's touch could linger, how its ghost refused to be exorcised. This could not happen.

There had to be another way.

Lyra looked up at the chandelier, which was still a good twelve feet out of reach. "The furniture—" she started to say.

"The furniture is fixed to the floor." Odette seemed to be enjoying this. "And I am neither as light nor as agile as I once was, so I am afraid this is up to the two of you."

There had to be three hundred crystals on the chandelier. *Any one of them could hold a clue.*

"It could be nothing," Lyra said, her voice tight. "A distraction."

"It is not," Grayson told her, "a distraction. There are patterns to this kind of game if you play enough of them. My grandfather's last game—the one he set to begin upon his death—started with adages and a girl."

The way he said *a girl* made Lyra remember an interview she'd seen, years earlier. *Grayson Hawthorne and Avery Grambs.* At sixteen, Lyra had watched and rewatched that interview more times than she wanted to admit. *That kiss.* In truth, the interview had been the reason that Grayson was the Hawthorne that Lyra had decided to approach, the reason she'd spent more than a year trying to track down *his* number.

Part of Lyra had hated Grayson and his entire overprivileged family, and part of her had thought—on some level—that anyone who could kiss a girl like that couldn't be all bad.

"That same game," Grayson continued evenly, "ended nearly a year later with a crystal chandelier. And now, in *this* game, which was designed by the very people who played my grandfather's last one, there is again an adage and a crystal chandelier."

"And there is, again," Odette added, "a girl."

Me. Lyra's mouth was dry. *Screw this.* Grayson Hawthorne didn't get to make her feel like this. He didn't get to make her feel a damn thing. "Go ahead," she told him curtly. "Lift me up. Let's get this over with."

"Over with?" Grayson repeated.

Lyra didn't feel a need to clarify herself.

"Your hands," Odette told Grayson imperiously, "her hips."

Bracing herself, Lyra walked to stand directly beneath the chandelier. She *felt* Grayson follow.

"I won't do anything unless you tell me to, Lyra." He said her name right this time—*exactly* right.

Lyra swallowed. "Go ahead."

Grayson's touch was gentle, but it wasn't light. His thumbs came to rest just above the place on her waist where her hips met her lower back. His fingers wrapped around the front of her body, spanning her hipbones, reaching inward.

The layers of fabric in her gown suddenly felt far too thin.

"On three." Grayson didn't phrase that as a question.

Lyra ripped the bandage off and beat him to counting. *"Three."*

Grayson lifted her up and over his head. Lyra stretched her arms, her eyes on the prize, feeling like an electric pulse had torn through her body. The tips of her fingers brushed the bottom of the chandelier, but it wasn't enough.

Grayson's hand moved upward to her back, which arched in response. *A reflex*, Lyra told herself. That was all.

With one hand on the small of her back, Grayson slid the other one down, gripping her thigh through the gown, the tulle compressing under his grip. Lyra's body responded, her other leg extending backward and her hand up as Grayson lifted her completely overhead.

The position should have felt precarious. It shouldn't have felt like a pas de deux. *Swan Lake.* She shouldn't have felt Grayson Hawthorne's touch like an invitation, a beckoning.

To him, it doubtlessly felt like nothing.

Her resolve hardening, Lyra stretched. Her hand soared into the bottom row of crystals.

"Feel for one that's loose." He just couldn't stop ordering her around.

Lyra forced herself to breathe and focused on her hand, on the cool crystals beneath her fingers. *Not on him. The gown, his hand, my thigh—*

She touched first one crystal, then another, and beneath her, Grayson began to rotate. Slowly. Delicately.

Crystal after crystal after crystal.

Lyra breathed, and she *felt* him with every damn breath. And then she felt *it*—a loose crystal. "I've got something." She tried grasping it between her finger and her thumb, and when that didn't work, between two fingers. "I can't—"

The next thing she knew, both of Grayson's hands were on her thighs. Lyra's legs split in a V, her back straightening as he lifted her straight overhead. Her hand closed over the crystal.

"Got it." The words came out guttural.

Grayson dropped her. Lyra snapped her legs together as her body fell. Grayson caught her around the waist an instant before she would have landed. Just like that, Lyra was standing on her own two feet.

Just like that, his touch was gone.

Lyra's body ached like she'd run a marathon. A tremor threatened to go through her. Gritting her teeth, she looked down at the crystal in her hand. Etched into its surface was an image.

"A sword." Lyra's voice came out low in volume, low in tone, a honey-whiskey whisper that sounded raw, even to her own ears.

"You, Ms. Kane," Odette said, coming to stand in front of Lyra, "are a dancer." The old woman turned her attention to Grayson. "And you are very much a Hawthorne."

Very much a Hawthorne. It was clear Odette meant that as a compliment, but Lyra took the words as a reminder of who and what she was dealing with.

Grayson didn't rise to the old woman's bait. He also didn't say a single word to Lyra as he turned and stalked away.

"A sword," Lyra said again. She lied and told herself that her voice sounded more normal this time. "We need to—"

"I need a moment." The muscles across Grayson's shoulder blades pulled visibly at the fabric of his tuxedo jacket. *Tense.* Just like his voice.

Lyra refused to read a thing—*a single damn thing*—into that. Instead, she walked to the screen and hit the blinking cursor with her right index finger.

"What are you doing?" Grayson's *moment* must have ended—either that, or he could multitask.

"I'm trying the word *sword*." Lyra did her best to project a calm she did not in any way feel.

"It won't be that simple." Grayson's voice was rough.

Lyra hit the letters harder than necessary. *S-W-O-R-D.* She pressed Enter, and the word flashed green. A familiar chiming sound filled the air. An image appeared on the screen.

A scoreboard.

At the top, there were three shapes: a heart, a diamond, and a club. Beneath the heart, a score appeared. *1.*

"You were saying?" Lyra resisted the urge to turn around. She wasn't gloating. Much.

"Simply that *sword* is not merely an answer." Grayson didn't even miss a beat. "It is, almost certainly, also our next clue."

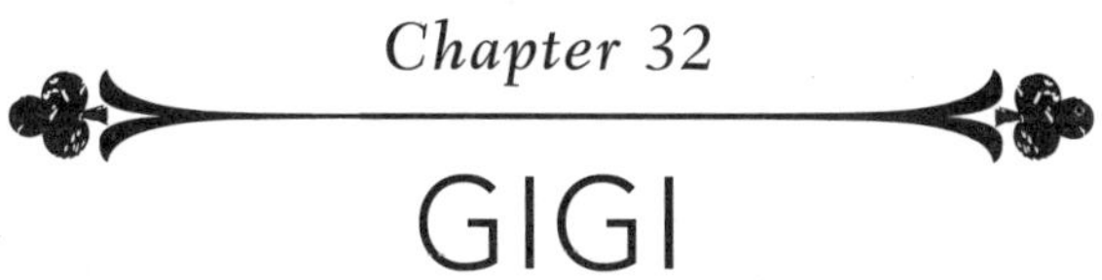

Chapter 32
GIGI

Gigi stared at the scoreboard. One of the other teams had just gotten an answer correct.

"Probably my sister's team," Gigi said, because Savannah was *Savannah*.

"Or your half brother's, assuming they ended up on different teams." Knox swiped his hand angrily through the magnetic words he'd been obsessing over and stood, finally vacating the throne of swords. "The Grandest Game is a real family affair this year, isn't it?" he said bitterly.

Gigi could feel another nepotism rant coming on. "Sure is," she said agreeably. "In more ways than one." Now was as good a time as any for poking elephants. "You two *are* brothers, aren't you? Or the closest thing to it." Gigi was going, almost entirely, on the way Knox had said *we*. "Either that or—"

Knox didn't let her finish. "Stop talking and hand over the knife, pipsqueak."

"*My* knife?" Gigi asked sweetly. "The one you already tried to steal from me once? No, thank you."

"We both know it's not *just* a knife." Knox walked toward her. "Objects in the Grandest Game have a use in the game. Where is it?" He raked his gaze dispassionately over her two-piece gown, which had a Cinderella silhouette with a thin strip of midriff separating the skirt from the bodice.

Gigi's hand came to rest on the band of delicate jewels that marked the top of the skirt. Directly underneath that band were the words she'd written on her stomach. *MANGA. RA.*

The knife was, of course, safely strapped to her thigh.

"Leave her alone, Knox," Brady said quietly.

Knox came to a standstill. "A real hero," he commented.

Gigi noted that neither of them had denied her earlier assessment. *Brothers—or the closest thing to it.*

"It's okay," Gigi assured Brady. "Knox might be surly now, but I'll grow on him." She beamed at the surly individual in question. "Give it a little time," she promised, "and I'll be like the annoyingly upbeat, brilliant, resourceful, better-than-you little sister you never had." With that, Gigi moseyed over to the desk, hoisted herself up on top of it, and stood.

Knox scowled. "What are you doing?"

"The top of this room is rimmed with bookshelves." Gigi looked up. "But no books. Is that suspicious to anyone else?" She bent her knees and pounced. Vertically! Her right hand skimmed the bottom of the shelf. She missed, but on the bright side, she bounced instead of falling flat when she landed.

If at first you don't succeed... Gigi climbed onto the sword-chair this time. She stood on its arms, then eyed the back of the chair. *If I can launch myself off its highest point...*

"You're going to fall," Knox gritted out.

Gigi shrugged. "I'm a solid B at parkour." *Arm, arm, back, up, leap, and—*

Gigi fell. Knox caught her. His rehabilitation had officially begun. "Almost made it that time," Gigi told him, wriggling out of his grasp. "Hold the chair."

"You're going to break your legs," Knox snapped. "Both of them. Possibly an arm."

Gigi was not deterred. "My bones are bendy. I'll be fine."

Knox picked Gigi bodily up off the chair and set her unceremoniously on the ground. "*You,*" he practically growled, as he stripped off his tuxedo jacket. "*Stay here.*" And then he climbed up on the desk and leapt, his fingers locking firmly around the bottom shelf.

Gigi watched as good old Grumpy Knickers pulled himself upward, every visible muscle tensed beneath his apparently thin dress shirt. Knox grabbed onto the next shelf up, and a moment later, he had his feet braced against the lowest shelf and a steady hold on the highest one.

"A-plus in parkour," Gigi called.

"Your bones aren't bendy," Brady told her, his deep voice mild.

Gigi turned to face him. "Metaphorically."

"You might have to explain that metaphor to me," Brady said.

"Sure thing," Gigi replied brightly. "But first, I was thinking we could try scratching the mirrored plate with the quarters and also, what if we compared the Scrabble letters to the words on the poetry magnets? And also-also—" Gigi cut herself off. "Sorry."

"Why are you apologizing?" Brady asked. Overhead, Knox was making his way around the shelves, bracing his feet against the wall and holding his body aloft like it was nothing.

"Habit?" Gigi replied. "I am, to use the clinical term, *A Lot*. And seriously, how are his muscles not on fire right now?"

"Training," Brady murmured. Behind his glasses, there was a faraway look in his brown eyes. He blinked, and it cleared. "I already tried scratching the mirror with the coins," he told Gigi. He smiled slightly. "And also? I triple-majored in undergraduate. My brain likes *A Lot*."

Gigi smiled—and not *slightly*.

There was a faint scraping sound above. Knox had found something on the shelves. Multiple somethings, it sounded like, which reminded Gigi that it was probably more useful to dwell on the first thing Brady had said, instead of his statement about what his brain liked.

Training. Gigi heard Knox drop to the ground behind her, and she lowered her voice to a whisper. "What kind of training?"

"All kinds. But, Gigi?" Brady leaned forward. "You aren't going to be the little sister he never had. Knox doesn't let people in."

Except for you? Gigi thought. *And Calla.* She wanted to ask about the girl, but even she had more of a filter than that, so she opted for a different question instead. "Who's Severin?"

Brady didn't so much as blink—but he also didn't answer.

"Here." Knox thrust a hand between the two of them. In his palm there were three tarnished dimes. "This do anything for either of you geniuses?"

Dimes. Gigi thought about the puzzle, the locked room, the rest of their objects, especially the quarters—but she didn't know where to go from there.

"Didn't think so." Knox fixed Gigi with a look. "If your idea about comparing the Scrabble tiles to the poetry magnets doesn't pan out, you're showing us that knife."

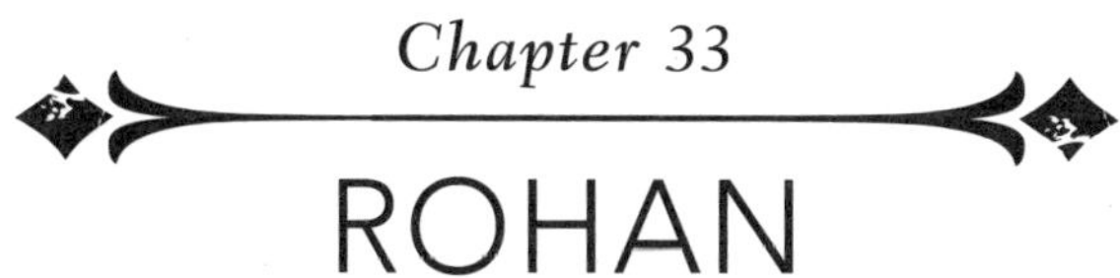

Chapter 33
ROHAN

The rose petal wouldn't burn—wrong kind of mirror, perhaps, or the wrong kind of light. *But not*, Rohan thought, *a total loss*. There had been a moment in the process when he and Savannah had both had hold of the plate, a moment when her breathing had fallen in sync with his.

Just a moment. But every plan was a collection of moments, and Rohan was no stranger to the long game. He was also becoming increasingly sure with each move she made that Savannah Grayson was a queen.

She returned the words *the*, *rose*, *will*, *be*, and *burned* to her neat little rows of magnets. "We tried this your way, British. Now we do it mine."

She looked down at the words, and Rohan obliged her by doing the same.

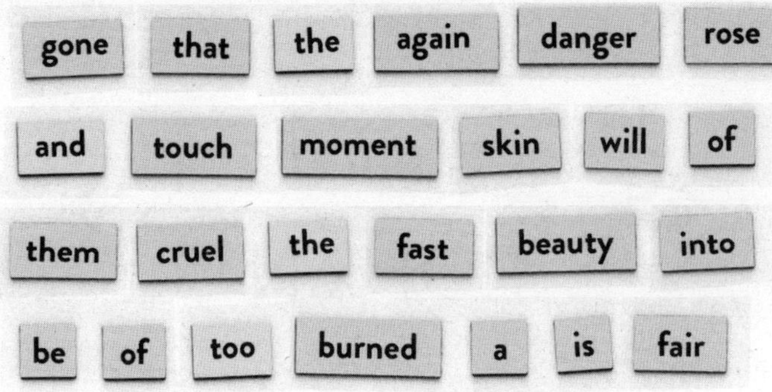

Rohan had a knack for zeroing in on possibilities. *Beauty. Danger. Skin. Touch. Cruel. Fast. Fair. Burned. Gone.* Those were the words with emotional resonance. The rest was noise.

"And what," he queried, "might your way be?"

Savannah reached across him—for the Scrabble tiles. The next thing Rohan knew, she'd pulled a word from the third row of magnets.

BEAUTY.

Rohan watched as she lined five tiles up beneath the word. *B-E-A-U-T-Y.*

"A little compare and contrast?" Rohan pulled a word of his own, then another. "Don't mind if I do, love." He kept the pace of his speech even, but his hands—a dealer's hands, a thief's—moved faster and faster, lining up Scrabble tiles beneath the magnetic words.

The result was two words, added to the one she'd made. *BEAUTY. DANGER. TOUCH.*

There were only five letters remaining.

Savannah swept the tiles into her hand, a power move. "Mine," she told him.

Rohan raked his gaze from her hand to her shoulder, from her shoulder to her neck, her mouth, her eyes. "By all means," he said, "have at it."

Lifting her chin, she placed the letters down, one after another. *P-O-W-E-R*. There really was no hesitation in Savannah Grayson.

Power. Rohan took the word as a reminder. *Power* was why he was here. *Power* was the Devil's Mercy, the Proprietorship. *Power* was winning the Grandest Game and winning the crown. And to do that, he had to remember: *Savannah Grayson, glorious though she might be, is an asset—a queen, perhaps, but a game piece nonetheless.*

In life, everyone was a piece to be moved around the board. Rohan was a player, and in an endeavor like this, the only true opponent was the game itself—and the people pulling the strings behind the scenes.

So Rohan directed his mind away from Savannah and concentrated for a moment on them. *Avery. The Hawthornes.* "We're complicating this." Rohan was certain of that. To clear his mind, he curled his right hand into a fist and watched the knuckles pull against the skin.

"You're going to bust that cut open," Savannah said dryly.

"Wouldn't be the first time," Rohan told her. He wasn't afraid of pain. He hadn't been, even as a child. By the time he'd come to the Devil's Mercy at the age of five, there had been no fear left in him.

A single bead of blood welled up on his knuckle, and Rohan lowered his hand, his mind sharp. "The best puzzles *aren't* complicated." He was certain that the makers of this game knew that. "Take a step back. We were told to focus on the words."

"And we did," Savannah countered.

"Did we?" Rohan challenged. *To solve the puzzle, focus on the words.* Her breathing fell in with his again, and suddenly, it clicked.

He *saw* it. The simplicity of the puzzle. The beauty of it. A clever architect built challenging games, yes, but there had to be objective answers, a clear path, one that, once recognized, was starkly, obviously correct.

Rohan moved the Styrofoam Sonic cup next to the quarters. And then he paired another two objects: the rose petal, the mirrored plate.

That just left the Scrabble tiles and the poetry magnets.

"Forget everything we've done," Rohan told Savannah, his voice charged. "Forget the letters on those tiles, forget the words in the poetry kit, forget any ideas you might have entertained about searching this room for more clues. All paths lead to Rome."

Who knew how many hints there were in this room—or any of the others? Who knew how many ways the puzzle makers had given them to realize that it really was *this simple*?

"Do you see it?" There was a low hum of anticipation in Rohan's voice. He wanted her to solve this, wanted her to see what he saw. *The cup, the coins, the petal, the plate.*

"Focus on the words," Rohan murmured.

He knew the exact second Savannah saw it.

Chapter 34
LYRA

Chimes sounded. The scoreboard reappeared on the screen. Beneath Lyra's team's symbol—the heart—the score remained the same. Beneath the diamond, the numeral 2 appeared.

"Two answers in one go," Lyra noted. "One of the other teams found the trick." There was always a trick, and Lyra and her team were missing it. They had *been* missing it.

Lyra looked down at the word magnets spread out on the floor in front of her. She'd had her way with it, her hands piecing together a poem that had led exactly nowhere, one she couldn't afford for anyone else to see.

She dashed her hand through the words.

"The only way another team gets two answers right at the same time," Lyra continued doggedly, pushing to her feet, "is if there's a pattern." She closed her eyes. "So what's the pattern?"

Silence, and then: "Persuasive, isn't she?" Odette said.

A full five seconds passed before Grayson replied. "Unexpectedly so."

He'd spoken those words from the floor. Lyra's eyes flew open. Grayson was kneeling, with one knee down and one raised, over the poetry magnets and the poem that he had—seemingly effortlessly—pieced back together.

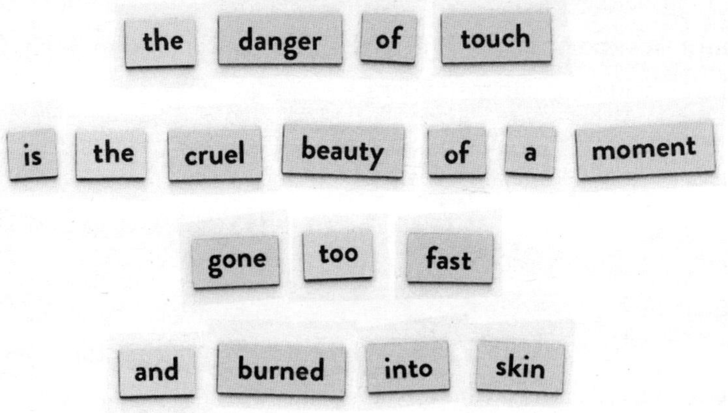

Lyra cursed herself. And the room they were locked in. And him. Mostly him.

Grayson stood. Lyra thought for one horrendous moment that he was going to look at her, but he turned his attention to the scoreboard instead. "For the past year or two," Grayson said, his cadence slow and deliberate, "there is something that I have been working on. Practicing."

"And what is that?" Lyra asked, doing what she thought was a pretty good impression of someone who *wasn't* burning with the profound desire to launch herself head-first into the sun.

"Being wrong," Grayson said.

"You have to *practice* being wrong?" Lyra considered the merits of launching *him* into the sun instead.

"Some people can make mistakes, make amends, and move on." Grayson kept right on looking at the scoreboard. "And some of us live with each and every mistake we make carved into us, into hollow places we don't know how to fill."

Lyra hadn't been expecting that. Not from him. She knew the hollow places all too well.

"Growing up," Grayson continued, "I was not allowed to make mistakes the way my brothers were. I was supposed to be his heir. I was held to a higher standard."

His. Grayson's meaning was very clear. *Tobias Hawthorne's.* Lyra managed to recover her voice. "Your grandfather left everything to a stranger."

"And now," Grayson replied evenly, "I practice being wrong." He took a step toward her. "I *was* wrong, Lyra."

She hadn't ever let herself even imagine him saying those words, not once in the year and a half since she'd heard the arctic chill in his voice. *Stop calling.*

"I was wrong," Grayson said again. He finally looked away from the scoreboard. His Adam's apple bobbed. "About the nature of this puzzle."

The puzzle. He was talking about the *puzzle.*

"I assumed that this challenge would unfold sequentially, one clue leading to the next, each object with its own use. *However.*" Grayson gave that one word the weight of a whole sentence. "Your logic is sound, Ms. Kane."

Was that his version of a compliment? *Your logic is sound?* He'd read that poem, and it had inspired in him the sudden realization that *her logic was sound*? Forget the sun. Lyra could think of better ways to end Grayson Hawthorne.

"Two correct answers in quick succession," he continued,

unaware that she was plotting his demise, "indeed suggests the answers are themselves connected. There *is* a pattern—or a code."

Odette looked from Lyra to Grayson then back again. "As I said earlier," the old woman told Lyra. "Very much a Hawthorne."

That sounded a lot less like a compliment than it had before. Lyra narrowed her eyes. "How did you say you knew Tobias Hawthorne again?"

"I didn't. And my earlier terms still stand." Odette lifted the jeweled object in her hands—*a pair of opera glasses*—to her face. "I won't answer that question unless and until all three of us make it out and down to the dock by sunrise." Odette peered through the opera glasses at their array of objects, then lowered the glasses. "Nothing. But it was worth a shot." The old woman cheated her gaze toward Lyra. "I don't suppose you found anything useful out on the island?"

If Odette had been the one to plant those notes, then she was still playing mind games. If she hadn't, then she was fishing.

"I found an Abraham Lincoln quote with the word *escape* in it." Lyra took in every aspect of Odette's expression, preparing to track even the most subtle shift. "And then there were the notes. *Thomas, Thomas, Tommaso, Tomás.*"

Odette had very few wrinkles for a woman her age. She also had an excellent poker face. "And the significance to those names..."

"Your father?" Grayson's tone called to mind the hardening of a jaw and the ticking of a rather foreboding muscle near the mouth, but Lyra kept her eyes focused on Odette.

"My biological father was a man of many names." Lyra kept her voice perfectly even, perfectly controlled. "My mother first knew him as Tomás."

Odette took in Lyra's features. "Puerto Rican? Cuban?"

"I don't know," Lyra said. "By the time my mom was pregnant with me, she'd heard him tell business associates a dozen different stories about his background. He'd claim to be Greek or Italian one day, Brazilian the next. He was always working a new hustle. *Big ideas*. That was how my mom described him." Lyra expelled a breath. "Not so big on telling the truth or keeping promises. She left him when I was three days old."

Lyra had no memories of the man, other than *the* memory.

"Am I to understand that someone on this island left you notes with a variety of your father's aliases written on them?" Grayson's voice was edged, each word precise and as sharp as the tip of a knife.

"Rohan seemed to think it wasn't your brothers or Avery." Lyra finally looked away from Odette but spared herself from looking directly at Grayson.

"I assure you," Grayson replied, "it was not."

"And I assure you both," Odette cut in, "that I am not a person who has to resort to parlor tricks or dramatics to win." She smiled like a cookie-baking grandmother. "Now, rather than assuming facts not in evidence about my intentions and character, perhaps you two could join me in looking for that elusive pattern?"

Pushing her long, gray hair back over her shoulder, Odette lined their objects up one by one. Lyra welcomed the distraction—and then she had to remind herself that the game *wasn't* the distraction.

The game was the point. It was why she was here.

Lyra picked up one of the quarters and studied it. *1991*. She thought back to her exchange with Grayson about the years. Numbers, at least, were safe. Numbers were predictable. And these numbers had a pattern.

1991. 2002. 2020.

Lyra looked to the Scrabble tiles, the poetry magnets, and all the rest of it. Taking another large mental step back from the Great Room and its occupants, she thought about multiple-choice tests and trick questions, about working backward, deriving clues from the answers.

Or in this case, the answer, singular, that they'd been given. *SWORD*.

If there *was* a pattern to all three answers, then maybe Grayson hadn't been *entirely* wrong about the puzzle. Maybe *SWORD* was indeed a clue, just not the linear kind he was used to. Lyra turned that over in her mind. *What if, having been given one of the answers, what we've really been given is a means of decoding the other two?*

"Sword." Lyra said it out loud as she pulled four letters from the Scrabble letter bank—*W*, *O*, *R*, and *D*. There was no *S*, so she drew it with her finger.

And then she realized...

SWORD. Lyra moved her hand from the beginning of the word to the end, drawing the *S* once more. And just like that, *SWORD* became *WORDS*.

"An anagram." Grayson was suddenly right there beside her. "Like the dates on the quarters."

"The magnets, Scrabble..." Lyra said, thinking out loud. "They're *words*."

This, she could do. This was so much easier than anything else having to do with Grayson Hawthorne.

"Our one and only correct answer," Lyra continued, "is an anagram of a word that describes two of the objects in our set."

Grayson swept the Scrabble tiles and magnet poetry to the side and focused wholly and completely on the remaining objects. "The plate," he said urgently.

Lightning tore through Lyra's brain. "And the petal."

“Two objects.” The intensity radiating off Grayson’s body came out in his tone. “Each an anagram of the other.”

“Is there another anagram?” Lyra matched that intensity. “Same five letters. *Plate. Petal.*”

Odette moved with impressive speed for a woman her age. She made it to the screen and began to type. “P-L-E-A-T.”

Pleat. The screen flashed green, and a chime sounded—another correct answer.

Lyra and Grayson looked back down at their remaining objects. The velvet *pouch*. The poetry *box*. The *quarters*—and the *paper* they’d been rolled in. The Sonic *cup*.

Lightning struck Lyra again. “*Sonic*,” she whispered.

“And *coins*,” Grayson finished.

Sonic and coins and . . .

“*Scion*,” Lyra breathed. Grayson said it, too, the same word at the same time, his voice low and clear, hers husky, their tones blending together in a moment so intense that Lyra could *feel* it, like a fire burning inside her, like a hollow place suddenly filled.

Odette entered the answer. There was a flash of green, a chime, and then bells, an entire melody’s worth.

They’d gotten all three answers. They’d solved the puzzle. And as much as Lyra tried to keep herself firmly grounded, she felt like she was standing on the peak of a mountain. She felt untouchable, like nothing could hurt her.

A section of the mazelike wall dropped, revealing a hidden compartment exactly where Odette had said there would be one. Inside that compartment, there was an object. Lyra reached for it before she’d even processed what it was.

A sword. The hilt was simple but beautifully made, gold at the ends, silver for the grip. Lyra closed her hand around the hilt and pulled the sword from the compartment. The action triggered something, and a larger section of the wall began to part, revealing…

A doorway.

"You know how to hold a sword." Grayson was looking at her in the oddest way—like she'd surprised him, and his highness wasn't quite sure how he felt about surprises.

"My mother's a writer," Lyra replied. "Her books can be kind of stabby. Sometimes she needs help blocking out fight scenes."

"You're close to her." There was something…not *soft*, exactly, but tender and deep about the way Grayson said that. "Your mother."

Another second passed, and he turned and gestured—gallantly, of course—toward the now-open passageway. For the first time, Lyra noticed how old-fashioned the tuxedo he was wearing was, like it had been lifted straight from another era, like *he* had.

"After you," Grayson said.

"No." Lyra gave the sword a test swing. "After you."

Chapter 35

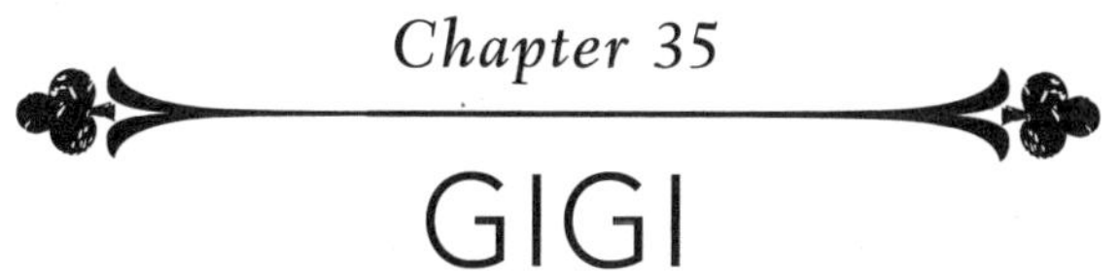

GIGI

"The Hearts just solved the whole damn puzzle." A pseudo-Southern accent snuck its way into Knox's voice, which Gigi guessed was probably a warning sign that the nickname *Grumpy Knickers* was getting ready to prove itself a total understatement.

She prepared herself for the shift to *Grumpy Pantaloons*.

"And all we have," Knox continued, narrowing his eyes at Gigi, "is that knife."

"Which I very generously showed to you," Gigi pointed out. "And sidenote: You should not be at all nervous about me holding it with the pointy end aimed vaguely in your overtly negative direction."

"We also have the sheath." Brady turned it over in his hand. He'd asked to see it. Gigi had given it to him, as much to annoy Knox as because something about trusting Brady felt right, no matter what Gigi's mental-Savannah had to say about it.

Brady ran his thumb over the surface of the sheath. "Thirteen."

"The number of notches carved into the leather," Gigi said, holding out her hand. Brady passed the sheath to her without a moment's hesitation or a word of complaint.

See? Gigi told the Savannah in her mind.

"So trustworthy," Knox said under his breath. He swiveled his head back toward Gigi. "Do you want to know what the real difference between Brady and me is, short stuff?"

"*Short stuff*?" Gigi repeated. "Really? You need a serious nickname tutorial."

"The difference," Brady told Knox, his voice quiet and low, "is that I loved her."

Calla. Every instinct Gigi had said this was going to get very ugly, very fast. "Dimes!" Gigi opted for the first distraction that came to mind. "Three dimes! What do they mean?"

It was a good question, but the distraction didn't stick.

"It's been six years, Brady." Knox's voice reminded Gigi of sandpaper. All traces of the accent she'd heard earlier were gone.

"I know exactly how long it's been." Brady took off his glasses and cleaned them on the end of his dress shirt. "And I already gave you your second chance." The glasses went back on. "Last year."

"If you would just—"

"Dimes." Brady cut off Knox and turned to Gigi. "Three dimes."

Gigi made the executive decision to step in between the two of them and prophylactically try for another distraction "What makes you happy?"

"What?" Knox looked like he'd just snorted milk out his nose and was trying to recover without anyone noticing. His nostrils flared. His eyes opened wider—but not in a good way.

"What is one thing," Gigi said, "that makes you happy? You might recall that one of my specialties is providing distractions.

Brains aren't built to be neutral. When you get stuck in a loop of confirmation biases and stale ideas, you have to take the bull by the horns and jar the hamster off the wheel."

"No hamster metaphors," Knox practically snarled.

Gigi sheathed her knife, pushed up her skirt, propped her foot up on the side of the desk, and used her duct tape to strap the blade back to her thigh. "What? Makes? You? Happy?"

Knox didn't know it yet, but he wasn't going to win this one.

Brady answered. "My mama's dog. His name is *That Dog.* That Dog is not a particularly small or sweet-smelling canine, but he sleeps on Mama's bed every night."

"I love him already," Gigi said. "Knox? What makes you—"

"Money," Knox said flatly. "Money makes me happy." Gigi stared at him, cheerfully waiting, and finally, Knox broke. "Fried chicken," he grumped. "Okay? Drumsticks that have been in the refrigerator overnight. Old cars. Expensive scotch." Knox looked away, his body wound tight. "And constellations."

Brady went very, very still.

Sufficiently distracted herself, Gigi forced a mental pivot. Her brain latched on to a new course of action, and she didn't question it. She just grabbed the jeweled band on her skirt and bent it down, baring the rest of her midriff—and the words she'd written there.

MANGA. RA. The knife hadn't been the only thing she'd found on the island.

Brady immediately crouched, his eyes level with her stomach. He studied her exposed skin from behind his thick-rimmed glasses, and Gigi thought suddenly of the way that Jameson Hawthorne had looked at Avery Grambs, about the fact that no one had ever looked at *her* like that—or with the kind of naked, raw fascination clear on Brady's face now.

"Manga." Brady brought his hand to hover just over Gigi's stomach. "Ra."

"Egyptian god of the sun," Gigi said, and if she had to remind herself to breathe a little, that was totally normal and probably, hopefully, maybe not *that* conspicuous.

"Knox?" Brady brought his hand to actually touch Gigi's skin, lightly tracing the word *RA*. "Do you see it?"

Warmth spread over Gigi's skin, radiating from every point of contact.

"She's eighteen," Knox snapped. "I'm twenty-five. I don't see a damn thing."

"The letters." Brady's touch was gentle, sure. "Rearrange them."

So nerdy, Gigi thought. *Such jaw! And he sounds so... so...*

She cut her imagination off before it could generate a vivid depiction of what it might be like to touch Brady's stomach the way he was touching hers.

The letters, Brady had said. *Rearrange them.*

Gigi's brain exploded—in a good way. "It's an anagram," she breathed. "For..." Gigi sorted through the possibilities at warp speed. "Anagram! *Manga ra* is an anagram for the word *anagram*. A little meta for my tastes, but totally useful."

Brady dropped his hand to his side. Her body buzzing for more than one reason, Gigi bounded toward their collection of objects. "Anagrams. We're looking for *anagrams*."

Anagrams. And the dimes and the quarters were both *coins*.

Just like that, Gigi Grayson, barer of hints and solver of puzzles, saw the answers, all three of them, all at once.

And just like that, she could fly.

Chapter 36

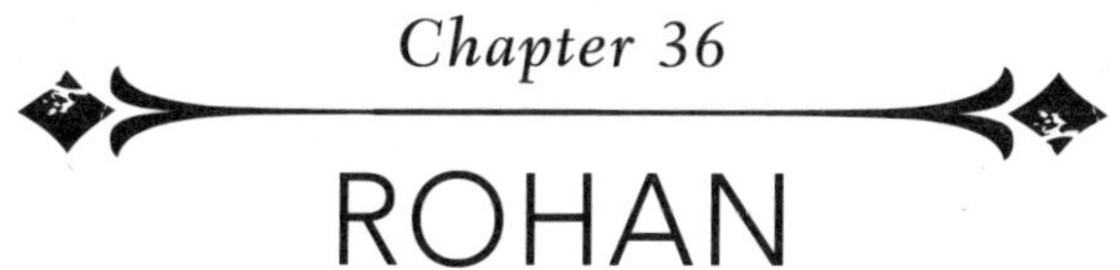

ROHAN

"Words." Savannah's silvery gaze locked on to the Scrabble tiles, then the poetry magnets. "They're just words."

Rohan's mind made quick work of the last anagram, but he let himself linger longer on *her*. "You say that as if it's a phrase you've said to yourself before." Rohan met her eyes. *"They're just words."*

He wondered what *words* people weaponized against someone like her.

"Not everyone shares my appreciation for unapologetically powerful women," Rohan noted. "How many times have you been told *you think you're so much better than us*?"

How many times had someone called her a *bitch*—or worse? And how many times had she believed it?

"You're in my way." Savannah held on to every ounce of her admirable control.

Rohan wasn't a stranger to refusing the empathy of others, so he could hardly blame her for doing the same. "Then by all means, love, go around me."

She took a threatening step forward. "Don't call me *love*."

"Does anyone call you *Savvy*?"

"No." Savannah pushed past him to the screen. Rohan didn't bother telling her the final answer. She knew it was *sword*.

Soon enough, there was a flash of green, then a chime, then bells. The melody wasn't familiar, but something about it took Rohan back to another time and place. To a nameless, faceless woman. To being small and warm, to a melody softly hummed.

To darkness.

To drowning.

Rohan didn't stay gone for long. He came back to himself to see the dining room wall separating in two, revealing a hidden compartment on the far side of the room—and a sword.

Savannah made a beeline for it. Rohan didn't even think. He went *over* the dining room table, sliding across its surface, beating her to the prize. He gave a twist of his wrist, swinging the blade in a half-circle that left him holding the sword vertically, both of his hands on its hilt.

"There's something therapeutic about winning." Rohan made that statement sound more cavalier than it was, lest she realize he'd just told her something true.

On the other side of the room, a section of the floor dropped. *A trapdoor.* Savannah walked toward it, then stopped, turned, and walked back toward him. *Long strides. Angry ones.*

He'd gotten a rise out of her, and he hadn't even been trying to. Much.

She stopped with her face mere inches from the blade of the

sword. "Save that wolfish smile for someone else. Save the quips and the charm and, while you're at it, save the rest."

"The rest?" Rohan stole one of her habitual facial expressions and arched a brow.

"The way you always angle your body toward mine," Savannah said. "The way you pitch your voice to surround me. Calling me *love*. Shortening my name. Pretending you *see* me, like I am a person desperate to be seen." Savannah's gaze flicked up and down the sword's blade. "I am not desperate. I see *you*: Rohan the charmer, Rohan the player, Rohan the great manipulator who thinks he knows the first thing about who I am and what I'm capable of."

She smiled, a cutting, socialite smile backed by all the poise in the world. "There's a message engraved on that blade, by the way." With that parting shot, she stalked back toward the trapdoor.

"Is there now?" Rohan twisted the sword in his hands. Words stared up at him from the blade's edge. "*From every trap be free*," he read. "*For every lock a key.*"

"For the record," Savannah said, standing with her back to him at the edge of the trapdoor, "this was the last time you will ever beat me to anything."

Those words were both promise and threat—and what a promise and a threat they were.

"And for your edification..." Savannah began lowering herself into the darkness, "I do not care what *words* other people use to describe me, because those people are beneath me." He knew what was coming. "And so are you."

Rohan should have taken the fact that she was lashing out as a sign that he'd read her a little too well, gotten a little too close to something raw, but for some reason, Savannah's statement took him back to the woman. To being small.

To *darkness*.

To *drowning*.

"Consider this *your* fair warning, British." Savannah's voice cut through the darkness. "I don't have any tender feelings for you to play on. I don't have any weaknesses for you to exploit. And when it comes to winning this game? I promise you: *I* want it more."

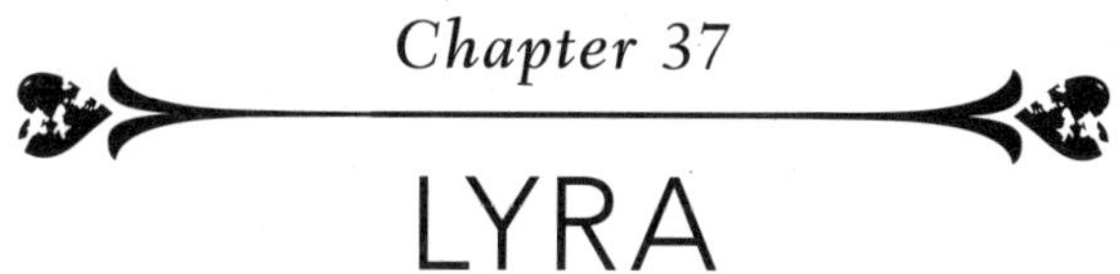

Chapter 37

LYRA

Lyra descended a hidden staircase into darkness, Grayson in front of her, Odette behind. With the sword gripped in one hand, Lyra felt her way along the wall with the other, listening for Grayson's footfalls, counting his steps.

The staircase turned, and Grayson's voice cut through the darkness. "Take my hand."

From the sound of his voice alone, she could tell he'd turned to face her, and somehow, her body's sense for his was so strong that she *knew* exactly where his hand was in the darkness.

Take my hand. Doing that would have been a mistake, so Lyra didn't. But she *wanted* to, and somehow, that was worse. "Good balance, remember?" She stepped forward, past him and down onto something... *metal*?

Behind her, Grayson addressed Odette through the darkness. "Just two more steps, Ms. Morales. I've got you."

"You *would* think so." The old woman's voice was dry. "Where are we?"

The instant that question left Odette's mouth, lights flared to life, built into the floor of the room they'd just entered. Lyra blinked, taking in her surroundings. The still-dark staircase had let out into a small room with rounded metal walls.

More chamber than room, Lyra thought. It was shaped like a cylinder, maybe seven feet in diameter, ten feet tall. *Metal walls. Metal floor. Mirrored ceiling.*

There were only two objects in the chamber: a curved monitor affixed to the wall and, beside it, a retro telephone that looked like it had been lifted straight from the nineties. The phone was see-through with a teal cord, its inner parts brightly colored—neon pink, neon blue, neon green.

Lyra walked toward the phone. Odette followed. Suddenly, there was a *whirring* sound. The floor held steady, but the metal walls shifted, whirling and closing off the stairs.

They were trapped now, just the three of them, the retro phone, and the screen, which flickered to life. Gold words appeared in elaborate script.

> ***From this point on***
> ***Three paths diverge***

Three paths? Lyra wondered at that. The words faded, and others appeared.

> ***A hint remains***
> ***But must be earned***

Lyra couldn't look away, didn't so much as blink as new lines kept replacing the old.

A riddle
A puzzle
A Hawthorne game

Once more with feeling:
They're all the same

Each team's challenge is their own
A crown, a scepter, an empty throne

Of all the words that had appeared on the screen, those stuck with Lyra the most. *A crown. A scepter. An empty throne.* That was a clue of some kind. It had to be. Lyra inched forward.

All for one
And one for all

Grayson came to stand closer to the screen—and closer to Lyra.

When you're ready
Make the call

The screen went black. Lyra's gaze locked on to the retro telephone, and then, before she or Grayson or Odette could say a word, the metal walls around them began to whir and shift again.

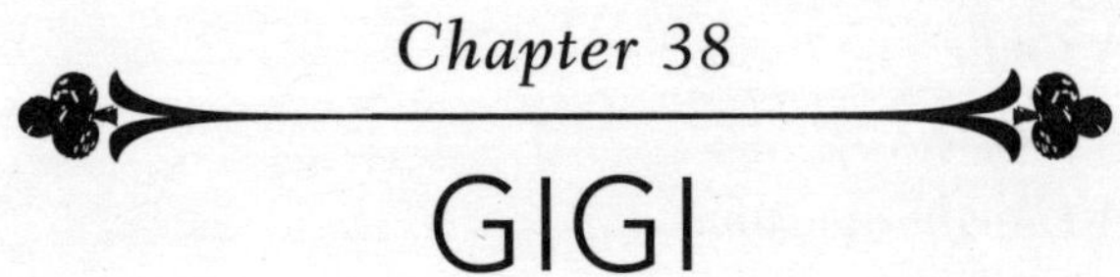

Chapter 38

GIGI

Gigi turned in a circle, the words of the poem echoing through her mind as the walls of the sci-fi-worthy chamber *whoosh-whooshed* around them. *When you're ready, make the call.* An old-fashioned red phone booth that looked like it had been lifted straight from the streets of London took up a significant portion of the room, making the remainder of the metal chamber nice and cozy—maybe *too* cozy, given the rhinoceros-sized tension between Brady and Knox.

The *whooshing* of walls stopped, and the effect was as if an invisible hand had peeled back one layer of metal for another. On the surface of the new section of wall, there were words.

I COME BEFORE FALL
AFTER THE CENTER
AND NOT BAD AT ALL

IN FRONT OF A HORSE
NAMED LILY OR ROSE
OR COOLNESS IN SHADOW
I'M ALL OF THOSE
WHAT AM I?

"A riddle." Knox's voice was terse—*terser* than usual, even. "Obviously, we're supposed to solve it."

"And then make the call," Gigi added cheerfully, "per our rhyming instructions and also that giant phone booth."

Brady considered the sword he'd claimed in the prior room, then looked up to the mirrored ceiling overhead. "Small space," he commented, his voice echoing off the metal walls, his gaze flicking toward Knox.

A muscle in Knox's jaw ticked. "Summer comes before fall."

"So does pride," Brady replied. "Give or take an article adjective."

Gigi read between the lines of that loaded exchange. *In the riddle, fall could refer to the season or a descent. And Knox really doesn't like small spaces.*

He also still didn't particularly like her. Yet.

"Okay, so summer and pride come before the fall," Gigi summarized. She looked to the next line of the riddle. "And after the center, you have what? The edge? The end? A lily and a rose are both flowers." She paused. "Summer flowers?"

"A rose is," Knox said, his voice tight. "Lilies bloom in spring."

Brady shifted his gaze from the curved wall to Knox. "So you do remember."

It took Gigi a moment of extremely tense silence to realize: a *calla* was a kind of lily.

"*Shadow* suggests the blocking of sun." Knox kept his focus pointedly on the riddle. Every muscle in his neck looked tight. "An eclipse? And *center*... the equator?"

Brady said nothing. Gigi was a babbler by nature, not at all prone to shutting up, but some moments called for giving people space—metaphorically, in this case. She stayed silent as she looped back to the beginning of the riddle. *I come before fall...*

Falling. Gigi's mind generated scattershot possibilities. *Gravity. Humpty Dumpty. All the king's horses.* Her gaze jumped to the fourth line of the poem: *In front of a horse...*

"Putting the cart before the horse?" Gigi hadn't meant to say that out loud. "Sorry."

Brady shifted his weight slightly. "Don't be."

Gigi thought back to the way he'd touched her stomach—and then she thought about something that Brady had said to Knox: *The difference is that I loved her.*

He'd used the past tense, but the feelings audible in his voice had clearly been anything but. Brady *still* loved Calla, whoever she was. And as soft a spot as Gigi had for *tragic* and as much as she didn't shy away from even the worst ideas, she also wanted to win the Grandest Game. She wanted to prove herself. She wanted to *fly* again.

So she closed her eyes, banished the memory of Brady's touch to the ether, and took a deep breath. *I am one with this metal chamber and its mirrored ceiling and whoosh-whooshing wall.* She forced herself to forget about Brady. And Knox. And Brady-and-Knox. And Calla, who was missing or dead or missing-and-dead.

I come before fall. Gigi took another steadying breath. *After the center and not bad at all. In front of a horse named Lily or Rose. Or coolness in shadow. I'm all of those...*

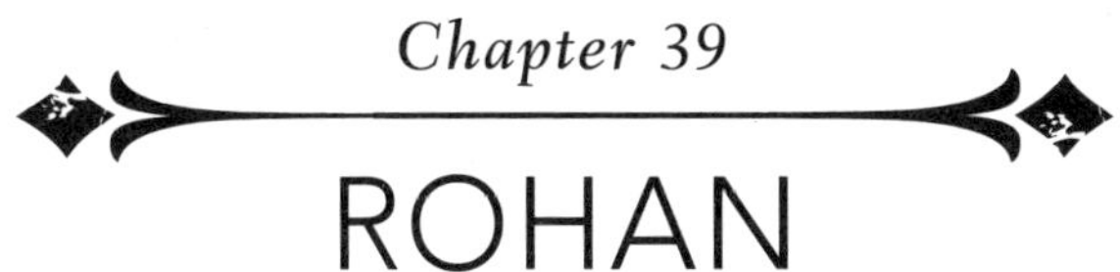

Chapter 39

ROHAN

Rohan sometimes thought of his mind as a labyrinth and himself as the creature who lived at the center. Down the different paths, there were, among other things, repositories where he kept information. There was one for details that seemed insignificant but that he committed to memory nonetheless; another for obvious leverage, waiting only for a use; and a third for information that Rohan had flagged as significant but whose significance had yet to be revealed.

It was this last corridor that Rohan found himself visiting most often. Seeing the pattern beneath the surface, sensing the hidden, making connections—that was his lifeblood. And Savannah Grayson had just given him something to work with: She *needed* this.

That was what Rohan had heard in her voice: *need* on par with his own to claim the Devil's Mercy. And that made Savannah a riddle every bit as much as the words now staring back at them from a fresh layer of metal wall.

Why would an eighteen-year-old with a multi-million-dollar trust fund *need* to win the Grandest Game?

"Eighty-eight locks." Savannah read the words on the wall aloud. *"Wait, that's not right. At least the answer is black and white."*

"This is a game of riddles now." Rohan passed the sword from his right hand to his left. *The riddle on the wall. And you.* "Riddles deliberately lead you down paths that take you further and further from the right answer. They lie with the truth and rely on the tendency of the human mind to seek confirmation of that which we already believe."

What is your Mercy, Savvy? What drives you?

"There's a twist," Savannah summarized curtly.

"More than one, I imagine." Rohan found that he could *imagine* a great deal about Savannah Grayson, but he left the desire to do so in the labyrinth, alongside his questions about her motives, and turned his attention to the matter more immediately at hand.

"A riddle, a puzzle, a Hawthorne game," he quoted. *"Once more with feeling: They're all the same."* Rohan gave Savannah a chance, albeit a minimal one, to reply, and then he continued, "I'd take the bit about three paths diverging to mean that, while this game may have started by presenting all three teams with identical puzzles, from this point on, we're on different paths. Different challenges. *A crown. A scepter. An empty throne.*"

"Three clues," Savannah said, "to who-knows-what. This riddle?"

"Time will tell." Rohan looked from her to the words on the wall. "Time always tells, Savvy."

She'd made it clear that she didn't want his empathy, which was good, given how often it was in short supply. But Savannah had his *curiosity* now instead, and most at the Devil's Mercy would have agreed: That was far, far worse.

"Can we just focus on the riddle?" Savannah said.

Rohan's smile was more wolfish than ever. "Oh, I am." *You are the riddle, Savannah Grayson.* That solving her would tell him how best to use her was a bonus. His curiosity had to be sated either way. But for now...

There was an old-fashioned rotary phone on the wall opposite the riddle, which hadn't moved at all as the underlying layers had shifted. Rohan had to admire the mechanic genius of the chamber—and the brevity of their latest challenge.

88 LOCKS
WAIT, THAT'S NOT RIGHT
AT LEAST THE ANSWER IS BLACK AND WHITE

Rohan began to loop around the chamber in a slow circle, concentrating on the middle line of the riddle: *Wait, that's not right.*

Not right could, of course, mean *wrong*. To be *right* was to be correct in a factual sense, but *right* could also mean righteous or honorable, as in a person knowing the difference between right and wrong.

Then again, *not right* could easily mean *left*.

To *righten* something was to straighten it.

If something was your *right*, you were entitled to it.

As Rohan continued his second circuit around the chamber, Savannah spoke. "What precisely is the antecedent of the word *that* in the second line?"

Wait, that's *not right*. Rohan rolled those words and her query around in his mind, a series of questions rising to the surface.

What wasn't right?

How so?

And what did a person like Savannah Grayson *need* with twenty-six million dollars?

Chapter 40

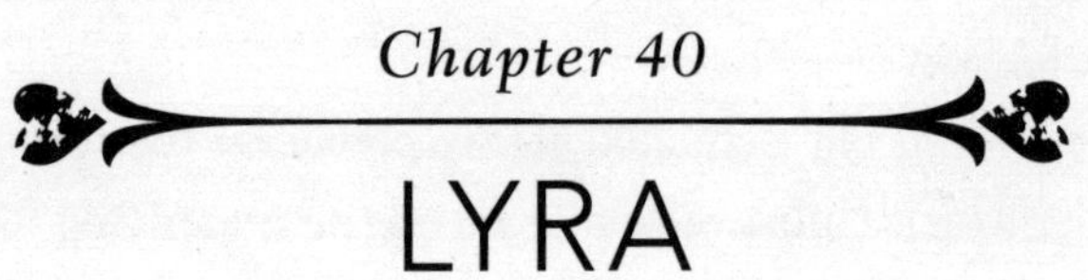

LYRA

The words on the wall stared back at Lyra, the letters evenly spaced, the grooves of the writing deep. There were six lines, twenty-six words total.

YOU MIGHT FIND ME IN A CAVE
SOMETIMES I MIGHT MISBEHAVE
WASH ME OUT
GIVE ME A KISS
DON'T SAY A WORD
BUT MAKE A WISH

"More times than I would care to admit," Grayson said behind her, "when my grandfather's games involved riddles, I lost."

Lyra felt her hand tighten around the hilt of the sword, and she told herself that it had nothing to do with the way Grayson had said the words *I lost*. His billionaire grandfather had obviously done a number on him. Lyra remembered Rohan's appraisal of the Hawthornes: *self-aggrandizing, overly angsty, and prone toward mythologizing an old man who seems like he was a right bastard.*

"Riddles are for people who enjoy playing," Odette told Grayson. "Do you consider yourself playful, Mr. Hawthorne?"

"Do I seem as though I consider myself playful?" Grayson replied.

"No." Lyra stared at the words on the wall. "But Tobias Hawthorne also didn't seem like the type to be so very fond of riddles."

The riddle rang in her mind—not the words on the wall but the ones she'd been over and over in the year and a half since Grayson Hawthorne had put it in her head that her father's final words might be a riddle. *What begins a bet? Not that.*

A bet was a wager, a gamble, a risk. An agreement, a competition with stakes, a laying of odds, a dare. An ante. Lyra had spent hours and hours lost in the weeds on that last one, because *ante* could mean *price* or *cost*, as well as *before* or *preceding*, and she hadn't been able to shake the feeling that there might be something there.

Something she couldn't quite grasp.

Something forever just out of reach.

"Your mind is not occupied with *this* riddle." Grayson's voice didn't break into Lyra's thoughts; it enveloped them. Even when he was quiet and almost gentle, there was nothing the least bit understated about Grayson Hawthorne.

A perverse part of Lyra wanted to pretend that he hadn't read her nearly as well as he had. "What can be found in a cave?" Lyra forced the tension from her body. Her gaze trailed over the words on the wall and settled on one in particular. *Kiss.*

The danger of touch, something whispered inside her, *is the cruel beauty of a moment, gone too fast and burned into skin.*

Lyra swallowed. "A frog?" That fit with the cave—and the mention of a kiss. Wasn't that the way fairy tales went? *Kiss the frog, turn him into a prince.*

"When you answer a riddle correctly," Grayson said, "everything makes perfect sense. If an answer fails to reveal the trick in the question but nonetheless seems plausible on its face, that answer is likely a decoy, meant to distract you and anchor your mind."

"I am aware of the definition of the word *decoy*," Lyra told him. "And I know all about trick questions."

"Why," Grayson murmured, "am I not surprised?"

"Close quarters getting to the two of you already?" Odette asked. The grandma-baking-cookies smile was back.

To save herself from replying, Lyra set the sword down.

"May I?" Grayson asked.

Lyra was taken back to their dance. *May I cut in?* At least he'd asked first this time. She folded her arms over her chest. "Knock yourself out, Hawthorne boy."

Grayson took the sword. Something about the lines of his body and the way he stood reminded Lyra that the correct way to hold a sword had very little to do with the hands that held the hilt.

Grayson Hawthorne held that sword like it was an exercise in whole-body control.

Think caves, Lyra told herself sharply. *Think silence. Think wishes.*

"There's writing on the blade." Grayson's voice matched his body—*utter control.*

Lyra went to see the writing for herself. "*From every trap be free,*" she read, her tone as neutral as she could make it. "*For every lock a key.*" She paused. "Sounds like another riddle."

This game was drowning them in cryptic rhymes.

"I'm starting to really hate riddles," Lyra said under her breath.

"Funny," Grayson replied, lowering the sword, his silvery-gray eyes coming to rest on hers. "I'm rather starting to like them."

Chapter 41

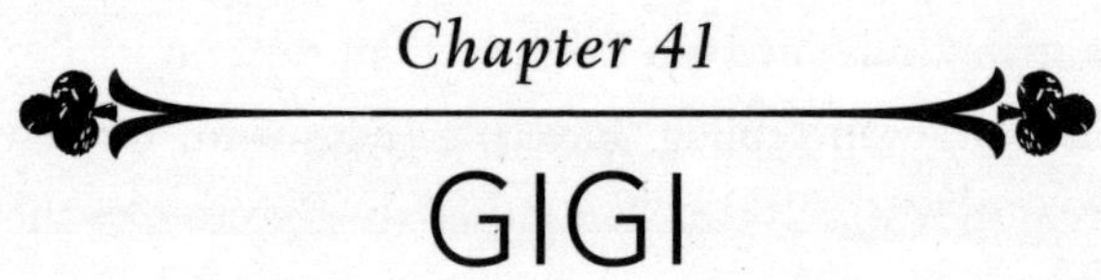

GIGI

Of all the possible solutions that had spent the last hour doing the can-can through Gigi's brain, the one that broke away to form a conga line was: *the day after the spring equinox.*

After the center. Gigi gave that element of the poem a mental checkmark. *Before fall.* Another check. *Spring is associated with sunshine—and shade.* That had to be what *coolness in shadow* referred to, right?

Or possibly a winter eclipse... Gigi could feel a mental cha-cha coming on.

"*Cart in front of the horse.*" To her left, Knox had progressed from staring at the riddle on the wall to glaring at it like it had killed his puppy or given him a wedgie or both.

"*Pride before the fall,*" Knox continued through clenched teeth. Gigi could make out beads of sweat on his temples, his neck. "*Stop and smell the roses.*"

"Common sayings?" Gigi took a subtle ballerina leap toward

him. It was notoriously difficult to rehabilitate someone in distress, and it was clear to her: Knox really, really, *really* hated small spaces.

"Clichés," Knox corrected tersely. "Take it line by line." He was starting to look kind of . . . gray.

Gigi glanced toward Brady, but he was busy searching the inside of the phone booth.

Looks like I'm on my own for Project Take Care of Knox Without Him Knowing It.

"Righto." Gigi was careful not to crowd him, but she didn't shrink back, either. "You've checked off the fall, the horse, and the flowers. Next up: *after the center* and *not bad at all.*"

"If something is not bad," Knox said, a slight rasp in his voice, "it's adequate. Fair. Okay."

"Good," Gigi suggested.

"You would say that," Knox grunted.

Gigi cheerfully one-upped herself. "Perfect!"

"*Practice makes perfect.*" That was definitely more than a *slight* rasp in Knox's voice.

Gigi wasn't as good at radiating calm as she was at vibrating with energy, but she gave it a shot. "That just leaves two lines of the riddle. *After the center. Coolness in shadow.*"

After a tortuously long moment, Knox breathed. "A center is the middle, the core."

"*Rotten to the core?*" Gigi suggested. For good measure, she breathed, too, nice and slowly.

"Works for me." Knox looked at her, really looked at her for maybe the first time since they'd met. "One left."

"I disagree." Brady emerged from the phone booth. "You're stretching. If you have to contort an answer to make it fit, it was never the right answer to begin with."

"You don't know that," Knox said lowly.

"I see patterns," Brady replied. "This isn't one."

"I swear to all that is holy," Knox gritted out, "if you tell me to *have faith*—"

"Breathe," Brady said. He came to stand directly in front of Knox. "I am telling you to breathe, Knox."

Something twinged in Gigi's chest. Some people just couldn't stop caring—even when they wanted to, even when they had reason to.

"I don't need you to tell me a damn thing, Daniels." Knox's pupils were larger than they should have been, but when he finally *looked* at Brady, they began to contract. "I'm getting out of here." There was still a noticeable rasp in Knox's voice. "We are."

There was that *we* again.

Knox stalked toward the phone booth and picked up the phone. "Clichés," he bit out. "That's my answer, and it works." A second ticked by, then two. "Sayings," Knox amended. "Adages." Another pause, and then Knox exploded. *"Son of a bitch!"*

He slammed the phone down on the receiver—and then he picked it back up and slammed it down again and again, beating the phone into metal.

Brady set down the sword and turned toward Gigi. "We're taking the hint."

Their team had only one hint to last them the entire night, but Gigi wasn't about to argue.

"We're not taking the damn hint." Knox slammed out of the booth. "We're saving it in case we need it down the line."

"No," Brady said, his tone muted, his presence anything but. For the first time, Gigi was keenly aware of just how much larger nerdy Brady was than the more intensely physical Knox. "Push the button, Gigi," Brady said quietly.

She scanned the room for the panel and found it—directly behind her on the floor.

Knox took two ominous steps forward. "Don't."

Gigi looked at Knox. She looked at Brady. And then she looked back at the panel with the buttons. She inched toward it.

Something seemed to snap in Knox. He lunged forward, but Brady was *fast*. Gigi never even saw Brady move, but suddenly, his body was a shield—or a brick wall. *Between Knox and me.*

Knox took a swing. Brady absorbed the hit without blinking, then pushed Knox back. Gigi's heart leapt into her throat. She wasn't scared of Knox—she didn't have the good sense to be—but based on his wild eyes, she also wasn't entirely sure that *Knox* was driving the bus.

He surged again, and Gigi knew suddenly: Whatever advantage Brady's size gave him, it wouldn't last.

"Push the button, Gigi. This chamber is too small. We need to get him out of here."

Before Gigi could do anything, Knox went suddenly, eerily still, assessing his opponent.

"I don't need you to *handle* me, Daniels. All you have to do is stay the hell out of my way."

"You can't do closets, Knox." Brady was implacable. "You can't do basements. You can do small rooms, but not if they don't have windows or some form of natural light."

"I can do whatever the hell I have to in order to *win*."

Gigi couldn't help hearing that as a warning.

"You think you're the only one who wants to win this?" Brady shot back.

They grappled. Brady held his own. Knox pulled back, seeming to have regained some measure of control, but there was still something leonine about the tension in his face.

"I know why you want to win this, Daniels." Knox's leg snaked out, and Brady hit the floor. Knox stood over him. "Even with twenty-six million dollars at your disposal, you're still not going to be able to find Calla. She chose to leave. She doesn't want to be found."

Brady climbed slowly to his feet. "Push the red button, Gigi."

Knox swiveled his predator's gaze toward her. "Don't you do it, little girl. You could be giving away the whole game."

I am not, Gigi thought, her voice steely in her own mind, *a little girl.* She took a step toward the panel.

"This isn't about Calla." Brady drew Knox's attention back toward him.

Knox pushed Brady back. "It's *always* Calla with you."

"This time," Brady said, shoving Knox into the side of the metal chamber hard enough for Gigi to hear the impact. "It's *cancer.*"

Time stopped then, and so did Knox. The fight drained out of him. Gigi couldn't move, either.

"My mama," Brady said, his voice hoarse. "Stage three. Ask me if there are treatments available, Knox. Then ask me if we have insurance."

Suddenly, every reason Gigi had for playing this game felt utterly insufficient.

"No." Knox stared at Brady for four or five seconds. "*No.*" Knox turned and drove his fist into the chamber wall. Hard. Gigi's heart leapt into her throat as Knox did the same thing again. And again. The sound of flesh hitting metal was horrific. The impact had to be tearing Knox's knuckles apart, but, if anything, the pain seemed to spur him onward.

Brady grabbed Knox, twisting his arms behind his back, pinning his body flat against the wall, as he looked over his shoulder and calmly met Gigi's gaze. "The button, Juliet."

Gigi hadn't even known that Brady knew her real name, but she didn't have time to dwell on that.

"If you push that button, we *will* lose, Gigi." Knox didn't call her little girl this time.

"I can't hold him much longer!"

Gigi was torn. Her mind racing, she thought about Brady's mom and the cost of losing this game. She thought about the rules, the stakes, the riddle on the wall, the fact that Knox *was not okay.*

Gigi pushed the button.

Chapter 42

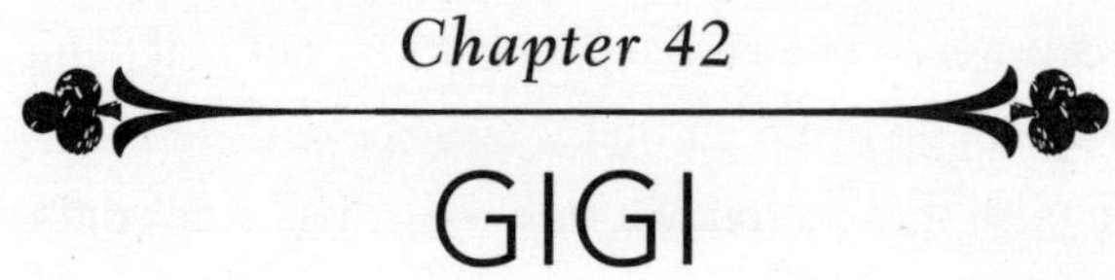

GIGI

What the hell did you just do?" Knox went still. Brady let loose of him.

Gigi took a deep breath. "I pushed the black button."

"Black," Brady repeated. "Not red."

Emergency, not hint.

"Everything okay?" A voice—Avery's—sounded from what had to be a hidden speaker.

Okay? Knox's hands were bleeding profusely. Brady had taken at least one vicious blow to the jaw. They'd both broken the rules of the game. But no one had to know that.

Since Avery was awaiting a response, Gigi improvised. "Bathroom!"

Brady's forehead knotted. Knox shot Gigi a pissed-off, incredulous, *are you insane* look to which Gigi was completely immune.

"Knox really, really has to go to the bathroom," Gigi announced. "Total urinating emergency. Very small bladder."

There was a sound that might have been a snort on the other

end of the line. Gigi was pretty sure that Avery wasn't the one snorting, but whichever Hawthorne she'd heard—*Jameson*, it was totally Jameson—didn't say a word. Avery didn't say anything else, either, as a section of the chamber wall whirled to reveal an opening to what looked to be a well-lit corridor containing exactly one door—presumably, to a bathroom.

"Thank you," Gigi called to the game makers. There was no reply. They were gone.

"Say one more word about my bladder," Knox warned Gigi, "and I will end you."

"I love you, too," Gigi replied sweetly. As he stalked off down the hall, she called after him. "You're welcome!"

As soon as the bathroom door slammed shut, Gigi turned to Brady. "Will he be okay? The bathroom probably isn't all that big, either."

"He's fine with bathrooms." Brady leaned back against the wall of the chamber and closed his eyes, just for a moment. "He'll be fine—until the next time he's not."

Gigi didn't push for any more than that. "I'm sorry about your mom," she said softly.

"Not your fault. Nothing you can do about it."

A ball of emotion rose in Gigi's throat. *Not my fault. Nothing I can do about it.* How many times in the past year and a half had she said variations of those two sentences to herself?

It wasn't Gigi's fault that her father was dead or that he'd died trying to kill Avery Grambs. It wasn't her fault that she knew and Savannah didn't or that a lifetime of being protected by her twin meant that she *had* to protect her sister, just this once. None of it was Gigi's fault, and there was nothing she could do about any of it, except keep THE SECRET and pull off the occasional, glorious act of stealthy interpersonal philanthropy.

But no matter what Gigi did, it was never enough.

"There's always *something*," Gigi told Brady. She believed that. She had to. "Brady, if I win the Grandest Game, I swear I'll make sure your mom is taken care of. Even if I lose, I have a trust fund. My access is limited, and it might require some creative quote-unquote embezzling on my part, but—"

"You need to be careful with Knox." That was Brady shutting her down and issuing a warning, all in one go. "He's done well enough the last few years. Went to college. Got a job. But no matter where he goes or what he does, the dark place is always waiting, and Knox Landry doesn't think about morality the way that you or I do. He isn't someone you can redeem, Gigi, and when I tell you that he can be dangerous, I mean it."

"For some values of the word *dangerous*," Gigi agreed amiably.

"For all of them." Brady studied her. "Do you know how the two of us met? I'd just turned six and had already skipped two grades. Knox was nine and a half and had been held back one. We were in the same class, but he never said a word to me until the day he beat up a kid who was beating on me."

"You're not really selling me on Knox's villain origin story here," Gigi warned.

"The bully was twelve, huge for his age, pretty much a playground psychopath. Knox was half his size, three times as vicious, and completely out of control. Like a scrawny, pissed-off little berserker. To this day, I have never seen anyone fight like that." Brady gave a subtle shake of his head. "Afterward, when I tried to thank my utterly unhinged, semi-feral defender, Knox told me to piss off."

Gigi wondered: If she threw herself into good listener mode with everything she had, would Brady tell her the rest of it? How he and

Knox had become like brothers? What kind of *training* they'd done? Who Severin was? Who *Calla* was?

Gigi knew better than to push for any of the answers she really wanted. "What did you do after scrawny, berserker Knox told six-year-old-kid-genius Brady to piss off?"

"Little punk decided we were going to be friends." Knox stepped back into the chamber. His hair was sopping wet, like he'd doused it—and his face—repeatedly. "Nerdy little pain in my ass just wouldn't give up. He started bringing two lunches to school each day, and it wasn't like I was going to turn down food." Knox looked away. "Eventually, I started eating dinner at his house, too. Every night."

"My mama's a good cook," Brady said, and the fact that he'd mentioned his mama at all reminded Gigi of the way the fight had gone out of Knox the moment he'd heard about Brady's mother's cancer.

Dinner at Brady's house, cooked by Brady's mama, every night. They really had been like brothers, and Gigi knew to the depths of her soul that they needed a moment. Alone. Maybe they would actually talk to each other. Maybe they'd just focus back on the riddle.

But either way, Gigi had to at least give them the chance.

Decision made, she jack-rabbited through the opening in the chamber wall. "Bathroom," she called back in explanation. "Though for the record, my bladder is actually quite large!"

Chapter 43

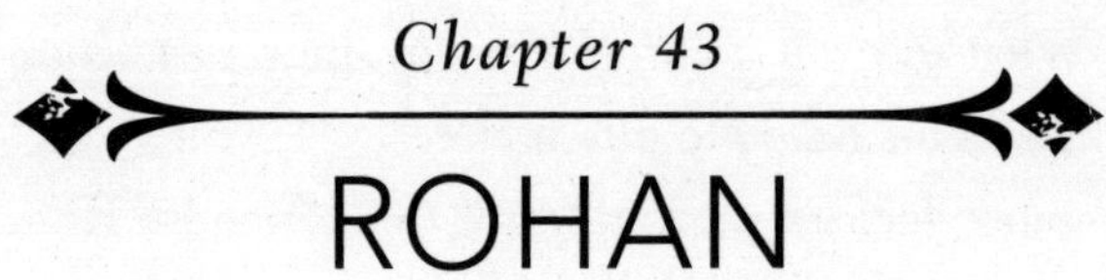

ROHAN

Time passed—too much of it for Rohan's tastes. You couldn't rush a riddle, but he saw no utility in remaining static. There were times when winning required patience, but more often, it required action.

"I'll make you a wager, Savannah Grayson."

"Will you?" Savannah's tone was coolly detached, but there was something in the set of her lips that felt more . . . aggressive.

"How many more puzzles do you think we have to solve before dawn?" Rohan was, among other things, an excellent fencer, but since the sword in his hand was made for fighting of an altogether different type, he fell back on verbal parrying. "And how long have we been staring at this riddle and getting exactly nowhere?"

No response.

"Shall I tell you what you've been thinking?" Rohan continued. "*Black and white* could mean either that the answer is clear and unambiguous or that it is literally black and white. A zebra. A newspaper. A checkerboard."

"Playing cards," Savannah countered, "in clubs or spades."

"Not bad." Rohan looked to the wall. "But not right, either." He stepped forward, running his hands over the writing, digging his fingers into the grooves of the letters. "Let's make this interesting, shall we? I'll bet that I can solve this riddle before you do. A little extra motivation never hurt anyone."

That was a lie, but Rohan was, in his heart, a liar.

Savannah didn't bite. "Either you've already solved it, and this is your poorly engineered attempt to press your advantage, or you *can't* solve it, and you're hoping in vain that this will shake something loose."

"I don't have the answer." Rohan parried once more. "I simply recognize the strategic value of changing up the game."

"You're lying." Savannah turned her back on him.

"If I win," Rohan pressed, "you have to tell me why you want to become the victor of the Grandest Game so very badly." He purposefully didn't use the word *need*. "Whereas if you solve the riddle first, I will tell you everything I know about our competition. The other players' strengths, their weaknesses, their tragedies, their secrets."

Rohan wasn't in the habit of giving other people entry to the labyrinth, but in this case, he was willing to risk a very limited exception.

"You're bluffing," Savannah said flatly, but her pupils gave her away—that and the slightest curl of her fingers toward her palms. "The players in this year's Grandest Game were never publicly announced. How could you possibly know anyone's secrets?"

Rohan gave a deadly little shrug. "Maybe I made a deal with the devil."

"I doubt you have anything he wants."

"Everyone wants something from me." Rohan found the truth useful—at times. "I know their secrets, Savvy, because knowing such things is my job."

"And what job is that?" Savannah countered.

She'd whetted his curiosity. He'd just returned the favor.

Her eyes—looking more ice-blue than gray at the moment—narrowed. "Fine. I'll accept your wager, British, but I don't want the secrets you've gathered about other people. I want yours. *When* I solve this riddle first, you have to tell me what your job is. No half answers. No prevaricating. No lies."

The Devil's Mercy was a secret establishment for a reason.

"Scared?" Savannah said.

"Terrified," Rohan replied. "You have yourself a wager."

This was good. This was *exactly* what he needed. If there was one thing that Rohan knew about himself, it was that when losing wasn't an option, he always found a way to win.

Chapter 44

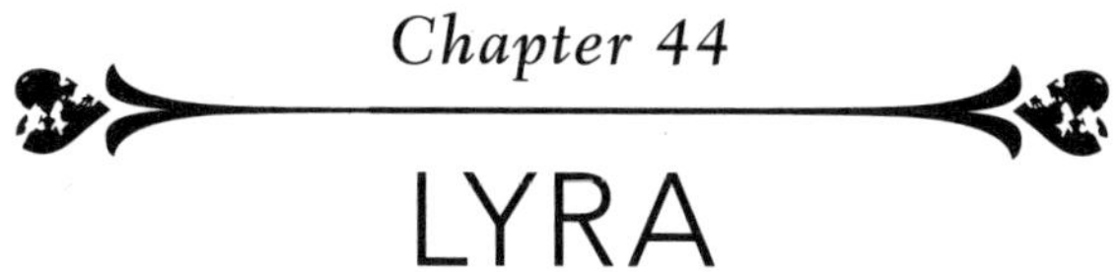

LYRA

What begins a bet? Not that. Lyra really needed to solve their current riddle so she could stop thinking about the one that haunted her memory—and so she could get out of these *tight quarters*, where Grayson Hawthorne's body was never far from hers.

"Don't say a word..." Lyra trained her eyes on the wall, reading aloud. *"But make a wish."* She paused. "Wishes. You can wish on a star. Toss a penny in a well."

"Blow out a candle," Grayson said to her left. Out of the corners of her eyes, she saw that one, stubbornly imperfect bit of his pale blond hair fall carelessly into his eyes. Again.

Why was it that nothing about Grayson Hawthorne really seemed careless?

"Blow on a dandelion." Lyra one-upped him—and kept going. "Crack a wishbone. Rub a magic lamp."

"Ill-advised," Grayson opined. "Haven't you ever heard of the difficulties of putting genies back in bottles?"

Some things were not easily undone.

Lyra bit back every single retort that wanted to come and concentrated only on the riddle. *A genie. A star. A penny. A candle.* Possible answers warred for dominance in her mind. She looked to Odette, a better option than risking even one more glance in Grayson's direction.

"Odette?" Lyra said.

The old woman stood with her right arm braced against the metal wall of the chamber, her head held at an odd angle, her chin twisted toward one shoulder. Tension was visible in her neck muscles, her face.

Not tension, Lyra realized. *Pain.* In the span of half a breath, Lyra was there, sliding a shoulder under the old woman's arm.

"I'm fine," Odette told her tartly.

"You're a lawyer," Grayson responded. He crossed the chamber in two long strides and slid under Odette's other arm. "A very expensive lawyer," he continued. "Technicalities and loopholes. So forgive me for probing your assurance further, Ms. Morales: By what definition, exactly, are you *fine*?"

Odette attempted to straighten, as much as she could, wedged between Lyra and Grayson. "Were I in need of assistance, you would know it, though I suppose, Mr. Hawthorne, that I would not turn down the use of that sword as a cane."

Lyra noticed that Odette hadn't *technically* denied that she needed help. She'd issued a conditional sentence, not a statement of fact, and she'd followed it with a distraction, trying to claim the sword.

Technicalities and loopholes. "You don't need a cane, do you?" Lyra said.

"I also do not need living crutches, and yet, here the two of you are, attempting to prop me up."

Lyra eased back. She knew what it was like to need people to think you were *fine*. Odette clearly didn't want to discuss her pain. Lyra did her the courtesy of a subject change. "You're a lawyer?"

Odette managed an eagle-sharp smile. "I didn't say that, now, did I?"

"Tell me I'm wrong, then," Grayson challenged.

"Has any good ever come of telling a Hawthorne they were wrong?" Odette retorted. She shrugged off Grayson's arm.

"Am I?" Grayson pressed. "Wrong?"

Odette snorted. "You know perfectly well that you are not."

"You told us that you spent decades cleaning other people's houses." Lyra narrowed her eyes. *"To scrape by."*

Odette had been very convincing. Just like she'd been convincing when she'd told them not to assume *facts not in evidence* about her character and her potential involvement with the notes.

Thomas, Thomas, Tommaso, Tomás.

"I'm an old woman. I've had my share of lives." Odette raised her chin. "I have lived more and loved more than your young minds could possibly imagine. And..." She took in a measured breath. "I am *fine*." Odette strode toward the wall with the riddle, her steps slow but sure. "Pain can provide clarity at times. It occurs to me: You can wash a frog, but you don't wash a frog *out*." Odette stared at the words on the wall. "Set aside the first two lines of the riddle," she murmured. "What's left?"

Wash me out, Lyra thought. *Give me a kiss. Don't say a word but make a wish.*

Thanks to Grayson, Lyra thought about blowing out candles, and the moment she did, a series of memories washed over her with the force of a tsunami: her fourth birthday—not the part of that day that haunted her in dreams, but the rest of it. She remembered her mom waking her up that morning, making her chocolate chip pancakes with cream cheese icing and rainbow sprinkles.

Happy birthday, baby!

Lyra could almost feel herself blowing out the candles her mother had put in those pancakes. *Make a wish.* And then Lyra remembered something else: a stranger picking her up from preschool that afternoon. *I'm your father, Lyra. Your real father. Come with me.*

Lie-rah.

Lie-rah.

The memory threatened to pull her under, but Lyra tooth-and-nail fought her way back to the safest part of thinking about that day: the morning and the pancakes and the candles. *Make a wish.* Her gaze held steady on the words on the wall, Lyra rounded her lips and lightly blew, and just like that, she had it.

The answer.

What did people wash out when it misbehaved? What did you use to blow out a candle and make a wish? To speak? To *kiss*?

"A mouth," Lyra said, her voice echoing off the chamber's walls.

"As in," Grayson replied, "the mouth of a cave."

Chapter 45

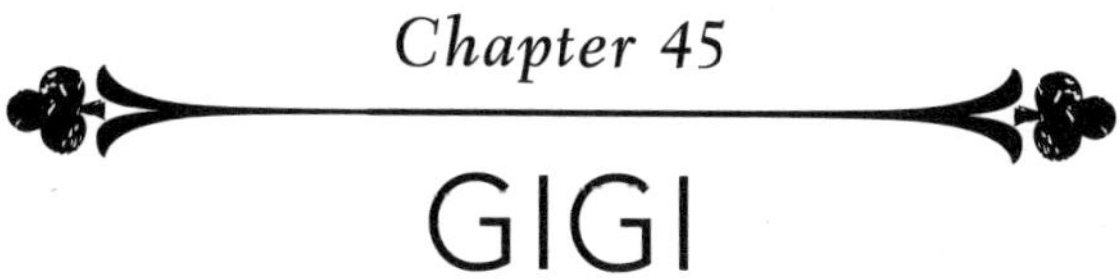

GIGI

Optimism was a choice, so Gigi *chose* to believe that the time she spent staring at herself in the bathroom mirror was productive. Best-case scenario, Knox and Brady would perform an exorcism on the ghosts of their past and hug it out, all while Gigi brilliantly and single-handedly solved their riddle. To that end, she pulled out her trusty marker, which she might or might not have had stashed in her cleavage, and hopped up to perch on the edge of the sink so she could write the words of the riddle on the surface of the mirror.

I COME BEFORE FALL
AFTER THE CENTER
AND NOT BAD AT ALL
IN FRONT OF A HORSE
NAMED LILY OR ROSE
OR COOLNESS IN SHADOW

I'M ALL OF THOSE
WHAT AM I?

Starting at the beginning hadn't gotten Gigi anywhere, so this time, she started at the end. The last line—the question—was self-explanatory. *I'm all of those* seemed to indicate that the answer somehow fit everything that had been previously described. Moving up another line got her to *coolness in shadow*, which probably, maybe, possibly, conceivably meant *shade*.

In front of a horse named Lily or Rose. In the riddle, that bit had occupied two lines, making it seem like there might be two separate answers—one for the flowers, one for the horse. But ignoring the spacing, they flowed together.

A single clue? Gigi's fingers found their way to the vibrant blue-green pendant nestled just above her collarbone. She closed her fingers around it and thought harder. *A horse named Lily or Rose.* Obviously, those were flower names, but this was a riddle. *Obvious* didn't mean *right*. So what was the *less* obvious interpretation?

What did it mean if a horse was named Lily or Rose?

"They're girls' names." Gigi's grip on the jewel tightened, as her lips worked their way into a blinding grin. A horse named Lily or Rose was *female*. "And a female horse..." Gigi could feel it: This was *something*. "A female horse is called a *mare*."

What if that was all those two lines meant? *In front of a mare.* Super-charged by the possibility, Gigi exuberantly hopped off the sink. A more coordinated or less on-the-verge-of-*something* person would have stuck the landing.

Gigi didn't.

She toppled over, and somehow, in the process of trying to catch herself, she managed to forget to let go of the pendant. She felt the delicate chain break. Her knee-jerk reaction was to open her hand.

The jewel slipped from her fingers, fell to the floor, and shattered.

No. Not shattered, Gigi told herself. *Broke.* There were only three pieces. She scrambled to collect them, and it was only after she'd picked up the second piece that she realized: The jewel hadn't *broken*, either. It had *separated*, cleanly, along the lines of the gold wiring.

Like the jeweled pendant had been cut in half before. Like the wiring had been holding it together.

Half? Gigi stared at the two pieces of the jewel in her hands—then looked to the third piece of debris on the floor, the piece to which the gold wiring was still attached. *Not the color of the ocean. Not a jewel.* Gigi made her way toward it on all fours. The third piece was tiny—and obviously electronic. A person with a less eclectic or more legal array of hobbies might not have recognized it for what it was, but Gigi did.

A listening device.

She'd been *bugged.*

Chapter 46

GIGI

Images flashed rapid-fire through Gigi's brain. *The wetsuit. The oxygen tank. The necklace. The knife.* She thought back to her altercation with Knox over the bag—and then to what Brady had said about sponsors.

They hire players, stack the deck where they can, bet on the outcome.

What if the bag Gigi had found *wasn't* a part of the game? Not a sanctioned one, anyway. Knox hadn't brought it back to the house, where Avery and the Hawthornes might have seen it.

What if that bag and its contents were Knox's so-called sponsor's way of *stacking the deck*? What if that was what he'd meant when he'd said it was *his*? What if Knox had known where the bag was stashed the whole time, and it was just his bad luck that she'd happened to stumble upon it?

You cheating cheater who cheats. Gigi stormed back to the chamber to find Brady and Knox avoiding eye contact with each other. For all she knew, they hadn't said a word while she was gone.

Brady was holding the sword again.

"Family therapy," Gigi told them. "Or, I guess, found-family therapy. Think about it."

If either of them heard the deadly tone in her voice, they gave no sign of it.

"In unrelated news: You have a lot of explaining to do, Shady Brows." Gigi held the listening device up between her middle finger and thumb. "I found this delightful little bug in my necklace—the necklace that was in the bag with the knife and all the rest of it." She jabbed the Pointy Finger of Accusation at Knox. "The bag that *you* stole and didn't bring back to this house, because you didn't want anyone to see it."

"Because I didn't want anyone to *steal* it." Knox's correction was only somewhat barbed.

Gigi turned toward Brady. "Tell me more about sponsors. About *Knox*'s sponsor."

Brady's reply and his expression were measured. "The Thorp family owns a third of the state of Louisiana—more than that if you count the illegitimate branches of the family." Brady shifted his steady gaze from Gigi to Knox. "Knox's sponsor is a man named Orion Thorp."

"This is asinine." Knox's tone wasn't measured at all. "Neither my villainous sponsor nor I had anything to do with that bag." He met Brady's gaze. "Am I telling the truth, Daniels?"

There was a long silence. "He is," Brady said finally. "Telling the truth."

Gigi wanted to argue, but she couldn't. She believed that Brady knew Knox well enough to know if Knox was lying, and she believed Brady when he said that Knox wasn't.

She couldn't *not* believe Brady.

So she changed course. "I know you're out there." She spoke directly into the bug. "I know you're listening."

It was something she'd gotten into the habit of saying a year and a half earlier—on rooftops, in parking lots, every single evening, looking out into the night. *I know you're out there.* Because if there wasn't anyone there, then no one would ever know, but if there *was* someone watching her, following her, then Gigi wanted that person to know that he couldn't hide from her, no matter how much he cloaked himself in shadow.

In her defense, she'd been followed before. By a professional.

"What are you doing?" Knox was bewildered—and pissed.

Gigi ignored him and tried again. "I know you're out there." When there was no reply—*the device probably doesn't even work both ways*—she turned to Brady. "You said there were rich families, plural, who had taken an interest in the Grandest Game."

Brady gave a little nod. "I believe most of the interested parties were contemporaries or rivals of Tobias Hawthorne."

Rivals? That felt a bit...ominous.

"What makes you so sure," Knox asked Gigi, "that the thing in your hand is a bug? And that it's not a part of the game?"

"I live a life of stealth and crime," Gigi replied pertly. "I know a bug when I see one, and I am spontaneously—but also incredibly—sure that the game makers didn't hide a bag on the island containing a whole slew of capital-O Objects."

It was so obvious now that she'd seen it. She'd thought that she'd hit the motherlode, but in a game that was meant to be competitive—and fair—why would there *be* a motherlode?

"Nash told me he liked my necklace," Gigi continued, her thoughts racing to catch up with her mouth. "I thought he was commenting on it as a kind of congratulations, you know, *well done, you tricksy*

Gigi. But what if he thought it was my necklace? That I'd worn it to the island?" Gigi's thoughts weren't just racing now. They were trying to qualify for the Indy 500. "And when Avery mentioned on the beach that some players had found hidden treasure, she looked at Odette, and she looked at Savannah, but I don't think she ever looked at me."

There was a single moment's silence. "If you're correct..." Brady's brow furrowed in what Gigi couldn't help noticing was a highly attractive way. "If the Objects you found aren't a part of the game—"

"The wetsuit inside the bag," Knox cut in abruptly. "It was damp."

"Recently used." Gigi swallowed. What did that mean?

"Maybe Knox isn't the only player in this game who has a sponsor." Brady didn't stop there. "And maybe the players and the game makers aren't the only ones on Hawthorne Island."

Chapter 47

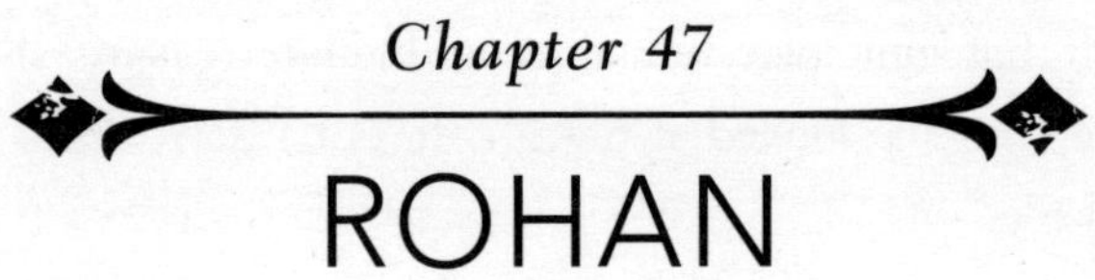

ROHAN

Rohan had no intention of losing his wager against Savannah.

88 LOCKS
WAIT, THAT'S NOT RIGHT
AT LEAST THE ANSWER IS BLACK AND WHITE

Assume the second line refers to the first, he thought. The thrum of adrenaline through his veins was as familiar to Rohan as the need to come out on top. *That would suggest that either the number or the word on that line is incorrect.*

The number eighty-eight had an obvious pattern to it—the same digit, repeated twice. Likely substitutions included ninety-nine, seventy-seven, sixty-six, and so on, all the way down to eleven. Eighty-eight could also conceivably be converted into eight squared—or sixty-four.

It's not the number. Rohan hadn't gotten this far in life by ignoring his instincts. *And that leaves only the word.*

Lock. Rohan's gaze went, of its own accord, to the platinum lock on the chain that Savannah wore around her waist. As skilled a thief as Rohan was, he deeply suspected the only way he'd be able to get that chain off Savannah Grayson was by invitation.

Not—at this point—likely.

Rohan turned his attention instead to the blade of the sword. He hadn't—and wouldn't—set it down. *From every trap be free, for every lock a key.*

Another lock. Rohan came out of himself for a moment. It was a thing that happened to him on occasion, most often when he prepared to cross a line that, in the world of decent people, should not be crossed. But this time, in the split second that Rohan felt as if he were viewing his own body from a distance, clarity washed over him.

Wait, that's not right.

Lock.

Key. Rohan snapped back to reality. *Eighty-eight keys.* The fire-hot thrill of victory would have been difficult enough to contain even if Savannah Grayson had not been looking right at him.

At the sword.

She lunged for the rotary phone, and Rohan remembered her promise in the previous room, with the sword: *This was the last time you will ever beat me to anything.*

Fortunately, in Rohan's world, promises were made to be broken.

He swept Savannah's legs out from underneath her. *No warning. No mercy.* She landed in push-up position, biceps flexed, then threw herself back up as Rohan cut past her.

Savannah went for his knees. *No hesitation.*

Rohan twisted, taking the brunt of her attack with his shinbone and staying on his feet. He locked an arm around her body, and she *bit* him, hard enough that he felt it through his tuxedo jacket—hard enough that, without that jacket, she would have drawn blood. *Vicious, winter girl.*

She damn near dislocated her own shoulder to grab him by the hair, fisting it. Rohan let loose of her body to return the favor with the long, pale braid of hers.

A stalemate of sorts.

"A piano," Savannah said, pulling Rohan's head back, just a little, and he responded by doing the same to hers, angling her face upward toward his now-raised jaw. "Eighty-eight keys," she continued as calmly as if they didn't have each other in painful holds. "Black and white."

"Indeed," Rohan said. "But it appears that you and I are at an impasse." His mind was already calculating the next move.

"What impasse?" Savannah said. "Our wager was about solving the riddle, not making the call. By those rules, by stating the answer first, I won."

Sweet hell, she was *something*. "But did you really *solve* it first?" Rohan countered. "After all, the wording of our wager said nothing about speaking the answer out loud. Is it your claim that you *didn't* see me solve it, track my gaze to the sword, and then realize what *I* had just realized?"

Savannah pulled his head back farther still, her own expression sharp as glass. "Prove it."

With a smile, Rohan threw his head back into her hand. Hard. He grabbed her arm above the elbow, forcing her body to turn, then pulling it flush with his own, and bowed his head, bringing his lips to her ear.

"I work for a secret society of sorts." Some whispers were weapons. "One that caters to the very powerful and very wealthy. My job is information, leverage, and control."

Without warning, he let go of her and made it to the phone. He picked it up.

"Xander Hawthorne's House of Riddles, Xander speaking. Answer correctly and move on. Answer incorrectly, and I can only hope that you appreciate the truly undervalued art of yodeling."

Rohan gave their answer—his and Savannah's. "A piano."

Almost immediately, the walls of the chamber began to whir. When a new opening was revealed, Rohan fully expected Savannah to stride past him and through it, but she did not.

"Perhaps you did solve the riddle first." Her voice was cool, but her eyes were hungry.

Someone liked fighting dirty.

"I pay my debts, love." Rohan allowed his gaze to lock on to hers. "Do you?"

He'd given her an answer, the one she most wanted, the one it cost him the most to give. *Tit for tat, Savvy.*

"Always." Savannah strode past him into the unknown. "And if you must know, I am doing this—playing the Hawthorne heiress's game, *winning* it at all costs—for my father."

Chapter 48

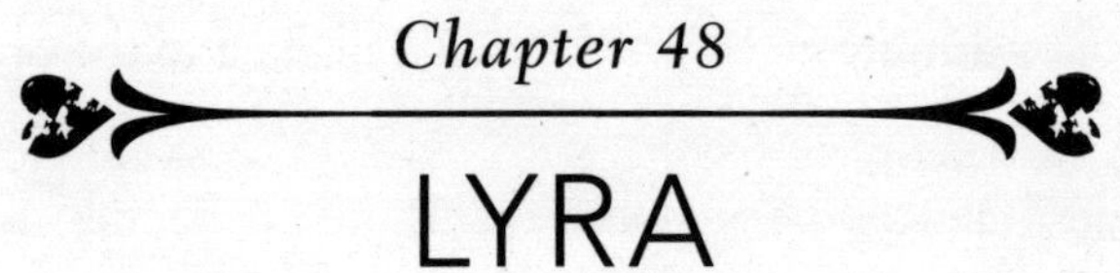

LYRA

A *correct answer. A new door.* Lyra stepped out of the metal chamber and into a darkened room. Strips of lights burst to life around the edges of the room, illuminating a windowless space with lush carpet and fabric on the walls.

A theater, Lyra realized. There was a large movie screen to her right, framed by curtains. They were a dark golden color, the velvety fabric on the walls and ceiling a deep forest green. Lyra stepped forward, then turned and stepped down. The floor was leveled—four levels, each bare of theater chairs.

The metal chamber closed, and an instant later, an old-fashioned projector whirred to life near the back of the room. A film began to play, text appearing on the screen.

PLEASE CIRCLE THE BEST ANSWER.

Lyra barely had time to decipher those words before the image changed to what looked like a multiple-choice test. There was no question listed, only answers. Each answer contained four symbols. One—choice C—had already been circled. Lyra tried to memorize the symbols in the correct answer, tracing them in the air with her index finger, committing them to memory.

A ⊛ r □

The film jumped to a scene from a black-and-white movie. A wooden rocking horse rocked back and forth in an empty room, and then the camera turned, panning to reveal—

A man sitting with his feet up on his desk. He was smoking a cigarette, his shadow stark on the wall behind him. *This isn't from the same movie*, Lyra realized. On the screen, the man took a long drag from the cigarette, and then his lips moved.

There was no sound. Whatever they were supposed to glean from this display, they were going to have to do it without the benefit of dialogue.

The man on the screen snubbed his cigarette out, and the film jumped to reveal a new scene. *Yet another movie.* This one was in color. A woman with a feminine bob said something to a man with slicked-back hair. *Still no sound.* The woman's expression was haughty. The man's was sizzling, as she plucked the martini from his hand and downed it in one go. He leaned forward and brought his lips within inches of hers.

The danger of touch... Lyra hated that she couldn't forget those words. She hated that Grayson had seen them. She looked away from the screen and flicked her gaze toward Odette. *Anywhere but at Grayson.*

Odette's hazel eyes narrowed slightly, causing Lyra to look

back at the screen as the cuts between scenes began coming more rapidly:

Four desperados sauntering away from an empty saloon.

A close-up of a woman's hand purposefully dropping a diamond earring into a sink.

A man in a white suit lifting a gun.

Lyra's stomach clenched. She hated guns. *Hated* them. And it was just her luck that the makeshift montage lingered longer on that scene. The man with the gun pulled the trigger.

It isn't real. Lyra went very still, barely even breathing. *I'm fine. There's not even sound. Everything is fine.*

And then the camera panned to a body, to pooling blood and unnatural stillness, and nothing was fine. The flashback took hold of Lyra like a shark dragging down its prey. The memory pulled her under. There was no fighting the undertow, no way to resurface.

"What begins a bet? Not that."

She hears the man, but she can't see him. There's silence, and then—a bang. She presses her hands to her ears as hard as she can. She's not going to cry. She's not. She's a big girl.

She's four years old. Today. Today is her birthday.

Another bang.

She wants to run. Can't. Her legs won't move. It's her birthday. That's why the man came. That's what he said. He told her preschool teacher that he was picking her up for her birthday. He said that he was her father.

They shouldn't have let him take her. She shouldn't have gone.

"You two look so much alike," they'd said.

She should run, but she can't. What's happening? She brings her hands away from her ears. Why is it so quiet? Is the man coming back?

The flower he gave her is on the floor now. Did she drop it? The candy necklace is still clenched in her hand, the elastic wound through her finger so tightly it hurts.

Trembling, she takes a step toward the stairs.

"Lyra." A voice washed over her, familiar in all the right and wrong ways, but even *that voice* wasn't enough to bring her back.

She's walking up the stairs. There's something at the top. She steps in something wet—and warm. She's not wearing shoes. Why isn't she wearing shoes?

What is on her feet?

It's red. It's too warm and it's red, and it's dripping down the stairs.

"Look at me, Lyra."

The walls. They're red, too. Red handprints, red smears. There's even a drawing on the wall, a shape like a horseshoe or a bridge.

You're not supposed to draw on walls. That's a rule.

It's so red. It doesn't smell right.

"Come back to me. *Now.* Look at me, Lyra."

*She's at the top of the stairs, and—the red liquid isn't coming from some*thing. *It's some*one. *Her father-not-father. It's him. She thinks it's him—except he's not moving, and he doesn't have a face.*

He blew off his own face.

She can't scream. Can't move. He doesn't have a face. And his stomach . . .

Everything is red—

Fingers worked their way through Lyra's thick hair, to her neck—skin against her skin, warmth. "You will come back to me, or I will *make you* come back to me."

Lyra gasped. The real world came into focus, starting with Grayson Hawthorne. All Lyra could see was his steady eyes, the lines of his face, sharp cheekbones, stone-cut jaw.

All she could feel was his hand on her neck.

The rest of her body was numb. She shook, her arms and torso vibrating. Grayson's hands moved down to her shoulders, his touch warm against the skin bared by her ball gown—so warm and steady and gentle and solid and *there*.

"I've got you, Lyra." There was no arguing with Grayson Hawthorne.

She let herself stare at him, breathed in and *smelled* him. *Like cedar and fallen leaves and something fainter, something sharp.* "The dream always stopped at the gunshot," she said, her voice barely even a whisper. "But just now, I flashed back and—"

"Hush now, child." That was Odette.

"I saw his body." Lyra had never realized that. Even with the dreams, her brain had still been protecting her, all this time. "I stepped in his *blood*. His face was *gone*."

She'd *seen* it in the flashback, the way she only ever saw things in her dreams.

Grayson's right hand cupped her chin.

"I'm fine," Lyra choked out.

"You don't have to be fine right now." Grayson's thumb lightly stroked her cheek. "I have spent my entire life being *fine* when I wasn't. I know the price. I know what it's like to bear that price with every cell in your body. It isn't worth it, Lyra."

He said her name *exactly right*, and Lyra's heart twisted. She wasn't supposed to understand Grayson Hawthorne, and he certainly wasn't supposed to understand her. She'd tried *so hard*—for years, she had *been* trying. To be fine. To be normal. To convince herself that it was ridiculous that one dream, one memory, could change her in such a bone-deep, life-shattering way.

You don't have to be fine right now.

"There were two gunshots." Lyra wasn't fine, but at least her voice sounded a little steadier. "He shot himself in the stomach first. He drew something on the wall with his own blood."

"Your father." Odette did not phrase that as a question. "The one who had dealings with Tobias Hawthorne."

At the name *Hawthorne*, Lyra pulled back—from Grayson's grasp on her shoulders, from his touch on her face. Odette's words were a reminder of who Grayson Hawthorne was and every reason she had *not* to touch him.

If she'd been able to run until her body gave out, she would have, but locked in this room, all Lyra could do was make her way back to the projector. *Just focus on the game.*

"What are you doing?" Grayson said, his voice softer than it had any right to be.

"I missed the end of the movie. I'm starting it over." Lyra wasn't sure how to rewind, but she saw two buttons. One had the *play* symbol painted underneath it, a recent addition to a vintage machine. The other small button wasn't labeled.

Lyra hit the unlabeled button. The wall to her left began to part, the two halves moving in opposite directions, slowly receding until they were gone. Lyra took in the sight beyond and realized that the theater room was much, much bigger than they'd realized—and the newly revealed space was nowhere near empty.

Chapter 49
GIGI

If there's someone other than the players and the game makers on this island... Gigi's mind went back to the contents of the bag she'd found. "The knife," she said urgently.

If someone had snuck a *knife* onto the island—

"I have to tell them," Gigi blurted out. "Avery. The Hawthornes." She made it two steps toward the emergency button before Brady caught her. She didn't realize at first why his hands were on her shoulders, why he'd stopped her.

"You can't tell them, Gigi."

She stared at Brady. "I have to t—"

"You're not telling anyone a damn thing, pixie dust," Knox growled.

Gigi frowned. "Pixie dust?" That probably wasn't the important thing here, but still.

"Nicknames," Knox said, sounding almost defensive. "You said mine needed work." Catching himself, he scowled. "And if you press that button, if you tell the game makers any of this, what do you think happens next? What happens to the second annual Grandest Game?"

The game was supposed to be fun. It was supposed to be mind-bending and awe-inspiring, the challenge of a lifetime. It was supposed to be *safe*.

"They wouldn't cancel it," Gigi said.

"Are you sure about that?" Knox jerked his head toward Brady. "Because his mother is the best woman I have ever known, and not all of us have trust funds to fall back on."

That hurt, but it was true. Gigi looked down. "I can help. I already told Brady—"

Shifting the sword to his left hand, Brady put his right hand under Gigi's chin and lifted her eyes to his. "The way you help," he said gently, "is by saying nothing. Knox is right. We can't run the risk that they'll cancel the game. If there is someone on this island who shouldn't be here, there's no way that person is coming anywhere near this house unless they want to be caught. Besides which..." Brady's gaze shifted to Knox. "If there is an unknown sponsor in play, that sponsor's goal is to win a bet against a bunch of other rich people with too much time and money on their hands, not to go after anyone."

"But the knife," Gigi said.

"Is in *your* possession," Brady finished, bringing his eyes back to hers. There was something about the way he looked at her, something so unexpectedly raw, that Gigi remembered that the thing that made Brady happy was his mama's dog.

And his mama. The game *had* to go on. In the morning, once their team had made it down to the dock and on to the next phase of the competition, Gigi would find a way to talk to Avery one-on-one, *really* talk to her. She'd come clean about everything, and she'd make sure that the heiress took care of Brady's mother, one way or another. But for now…

Gigi would do what she'd come here to do. She'd play. "I figured something out." Gigi stepped back from Brady's touch. "About the riddle. A horse named Lily or Rose is a *mare*."

Brady turned back to the wall. "A mare."

"Wait." Knox held out a hand. "Where's the bug?"

"The bug?" Gigi said innocently.

"What did you do with it?" Knox demanded, scanning her hands.

"I tucked it in my cleavage, next to my pen." Gigi shrugged. "I mean, I don't really have cleavage, but it is a locationally helpful term."

Knox kneaded his forehead and bared his teeth. "Someone could be listening to us *right now*."

Gigi shrugged again. "And yet, the bug is in my cleavage, and I'm betting neither of you is going to go after it, so there we are."

Brady cocked his head to the side.

"Don't," Knox warned him sharply, and then he adopted what he probably thought was a very pleasant tone. "Why would you want to stay bugged?" he asked Gigi. "Why not crush that thing and be done with it?"

Because Xander might need it whole to track its source.

"Because I don't think this necklace was meant for me." Gigi realized, after she'd said those words, that they were probably true. "And *of course* the nefarious party or parties would expect us to destroy it. I am nothing if not optimistically contrary, so I'm not going to."

Brady considered that. Crossing his arms over his chest, he studied her like a rare book and accepted whatever it was that he saw with a subtle nod.

"You have got to be kidding me," Knox muttered.

"A horse named Lily or Rose is a mare," Brady said, repeating her earlier revelation.

"Take it line by line?" Gigi suggested, turning back to the riddle on the wall. *"Before fall . . ."*

"After the center," Knox bit out grudgingly.

Brady went next. *"In front of a* mare."

"I think *coolness in shadow* probably means *shade,"* Gigi said.

"Look at the modifiers." Brady placed his palm flat on the wall beside the first line of the riddle. *"Before."* Brady moved his hand down to the next line. *"After* this . . ." he skimmed his palm over the second line, then down to the third. *"And* that."

Gigi scanned down further. *"In front of* this *or* that."

"Before, after, in front of." Knox swore under his breath. "We're looking for a *word."*

"One that can go before *fall,"* Gigi said. "In front of *mare* or *shade."*

And there it was.

"You were right, kid," Knox told Gigi. *"Not bad at all* was *good."*

"And the center," Gigi replied, grinning so hard her cheeks hurt, "is the *mid."*

Fall.

Mid.

Good.

Mare.

Shade.

Brady laid a hand on Gigi's shoulder and smiled. Not a small smile. Not a subtle one. A something-to-behold, earth-shattering, hope-you-don't-ever-want-to-breathe-again kind of smile.

"You're the one who unlocked this," Brady said. "You make the call."

A rush of energy coursed through Gigi's body like a tidal wave—or a dozen of them. Maybe it was solving the riddle. Maybe it was that smile. Either way, she practically tap-danced her way to the phone booth.

Behind her, she heard Knox, his voice low: *"What the hell are you doing, Daniels?"*

Brady's reply wasn't nearly so quiet. "Being human. You should try it."

Gigi picked up the pay phone. "The answer is *night*."

Chapter 50
ROHAN

I am doing this—playing the Hawthorne heiress's game, winning *it at all costs—for my father.* Rohan gave himself a moment or two in the labyrinth as he stepped over the threshold into darkness.

To the best of his knowledge, Savannah's father, Sheffield Grayson, had disappeared off the face of the planet nearly three years earlier, immediately after becoming the subject of FBI and IRS investigations. Rohan had pegged the man as a coward, one who had recklessly set his gilded life on fire and left his wife and daughters to face the flames alone.

And yet... Savannah was playing this game *for* her father.

You don't strike me as the forgiving type, Savvy. We have that much in common. That thought pulled Rohan from the labyrinth as the metal chamber rotated closed behind them.

Three torches burst to life in the corners of a decently sized triangular room lined with floor-to-ceiling shelves. Savannah strode forward and ran her hand through the tip of the flame of the closest torch. *Fearless.* "Real fire," she reported.

Rohan eyed the contents of the shelves surrounding them. *Board games. Hundreds of them.* In the center of the room, there was a recessed area in the floor, three feet lower than the rest of the room. Sitting in that recessed area, there was a round, mahogany table.

"No instructions." Savannah made her own appraisal of their surroundings. "No phone to make calls. No screen on which to type in answers."

All they had was the room. Rohan accessed his mental map of the house. They'd descended two flights of stairs to get to the metal chamber, which put them on the lowest level of the house—the level that had appeared to be nothing but walls.

"One of these shelves almost certainly doubles as a door." Rohan checked for obvious hinges and found none, then tested each shelf to see if any would pull inward or push out—to no effect.

As Savannah did her own inspection, Rohan leapt silently into the recessed area cut into the floor. There was an art to moving silently and quickly, to never being where other people thought you were, to cultivating the sense in your opponent, on a raw, subconscious level, that the laws of physics and man did not apply to you.

But when Savannah turned back toward the center of the room, when she registered his new location, she didn't bat an eye. She jumped down to join him. A line of tension cut across her brow as she landed.

The knee. "ACL?" Rohan said.

Savannah flicked her gaze to his. "Childhood neglect and trauma?" she returned in the exact same tone. "Or would you prefer we keep our scars to ourselves?"

"You really don't pull your punches, do you, Savvy?"

"If I were a man, would you expect me to?" Savannah ran her hand over the mahogany surface of the game table. "There's a seam, here."

Rohan crouched to look beneath the table. "No buttons or triggers," he reported, flowing back to standing position. "There may be something hidden beneath the top of that table, but we'll have to find a way to unlock it to find out. Same for the shelves. At least one of them—*that* one, I suspect—will open if we can find the right trigger."

"Solve the puzzle," Savannah said evenly. "Unlock the door."

"More puzzles," Rohan murmured, "more doors, which leaves to us the problem of finding the puzzle—or at least the first clue."

"The games on the shelves." She was already moving.

"Start with the names on the boxes?" Rohan suggested. "See if anything pops out—the proverbial needle in a haystack, if you will."

"Fine," Savannah replied. "If that yields nothing, we'll open the boxes." Her aura of intensity, Rohan noticed, was not *decreasing*. Again, he felt the call of the labyrinth, of shifting corridors and connections still to be made.

Savannah was doing this *for her father.*

"I'll start with the shelves on this wall," she said, pulling herself out of the recessed area. "You take that one."

"We'll meet in the middle," Rohan replied.

Savannah tossed a look back over her shoulder the way another person might have tossed a grenade. "If you can keep up."

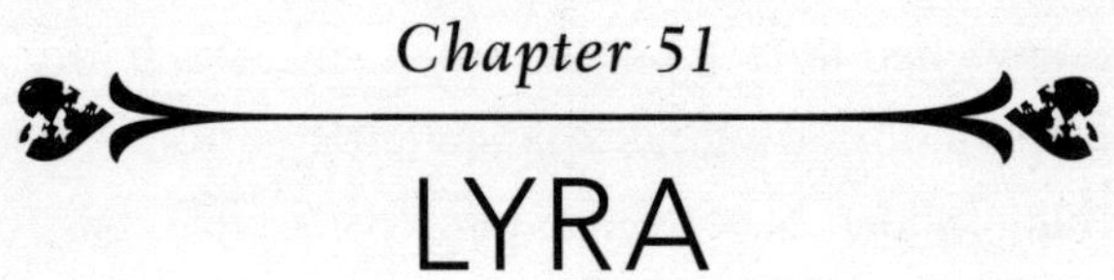

Chapter 51
LYRA

Lyra took in the now-enormous theater—and the stacks and stacks of film reels that covered the newly revealed section of the room. There were hundreds, maybe even a thousand, in metal canisters stacked six feet high in row after row after row.

With the longsword in one hand, Grayson walked the length of the room, taking stock of the sheer volume of film tins that stared back at him. Lyra pushed down the urge to follow him. She didn't need to be close to Grayson Hawthorne. She was *fine*.

You don't have to be fine right now. Lyra didn't want to admit, even to herself, the way Grayson's words had cut to her core. *I have spent my entire life being* fine *when I wasn't.*

Each time he opened a vein for her, each time he willingly showed weakness, it got harder to think of Grayson as an arrogant, cold, above-it-all, asshole Hawthorne. Each time, Lyra saw just a little more of the person she'd seen when she was sixteen years old, watching Grayson interviewed alongside Avery Grambs.

Sometimes, Lyra could practically hear the masked heiress telling her, *in the games that matter most, the only way to really play is to* live.

Her throat stinging, Lyra reached for a tin off the closest stack. There was something drawn in gold on its lid—a shape.

"You found something." Odette did not phrase that as a question.

"A triangle." Lyra thought back to the symbols at the beginning of the montage. There hadn't been a triangle—not in the circled answer. She reached for a second tin and found another triangle, and another, then she moved on to a new stack. *More of the same.* She went farther down the row and finally found a canister bearing a different symbol.

"Look." Lyra held the film tin out to Odette, her gaze cheating back toward Grayson. "There's an X on this one." Lyra jogged down the rows, grabbing two more tins from different stacks. "An E," she reported, "and . . . a different E?"

Grayson moved like a shadow, silent and swift, directly behind her. "That," he said, "is not an E. It's the Greek letter sigma." He turned his head slightly. "Which makes these three not an E, an X, and a triangle, but epsilon, chi, and delta."

Lyra chewed on that. "Anyone in this room read Greek?"

"The letters." Odette's voice was oddly subdued. "You think they spell something?"

"Not if they appear on every canister," Grayson declared. "There are too many—"

"—possible combinations," Lyra finished. It was the Scrabble letters and poetry magnets all over again.

"Yes."

Lyra hadn't been aware that Grayson Hawthorne could say *yes* the way he said *no*.

"Drawing a singular meaning from them would be an impossible task," Grayson continued, "even for someone with a certain familiarity with Greek."

"In other words," Lyra said, her voice dry, "yes, you can read Greek."

Grayson held out a hand. "May I?"

Three times he'd asked her that. *The dance. The sword. And now.* Lyra handed him the sigma tin.

Grayson opened it, examining its contents. "There's writing on the underside of the lid."

Even just the sound of his voice made Lyra remember that voice piercing the darkness. *Come back to me.*

Setting her jaw, Lyra focused on opening tins, one after another after another. Inside each, she found a reel of film, and on the underside of each lid, there was a four-digit number. *1972. 1984. 1966.* "Years?" Lyra said.

"Fair assessment." His Majesty seemed to consider that high praise. "Then again," Grayson continued, "Hawthorne games are full of bits and pieces of information designed to eat up your time and lead nowhere. I would suggest that before we spend any time decoding the writing on the tins, we first complete a rudimentary search of all of them to ensure that none contains anything... *extra.*"

"Open every canister," Odette summarized. "Then, assuming we find nothing of note in any of them, turn our minds to the letters and numbers."

"The code," Lyra said.

"The code," Grayson confirmed. "And the cipher."

Lyra caught his meaning almost instantly. "The symbols. From the film." She drew the sequence in the air from memory:

A⊛r□

"There was another set of symbols at the end," Odette told her. "You were . . . otherwise occupied when they appeared on the screen."

Otherwise occupied. Lyra refused to think about the flashback. Beside her, Grayson knelt, his black suit jacket flaring out around his thighs as he laid the sword on the ground.

"We'll rewatch the film," Lyra said, allowing herself to take in the lines of his body, anchoring herself to the here and now. "Right after we go through the tins."

"Yes." *Grayson Hawthorne and his yeses.*

They divided the room into sections, and each of them took one. Lyra fell into the rhythm of the search as time ticked by, stack after stack. *Greek letter on the outside. Year and film reel inside. Nothing else.* An hour later, Lyra had made it nearly to the end of her section of the room.

The moment she saw the symbol on the tin, she stopped breathing. *That symbol.* The Greek letter on the tin she'd just picked up was shaped like a horseshoe. *Or a bridge.*

Lyra sucked in a jagged breath, and the air burned her lungs as the roar of blood pumping in her ears drowned out everything else. Her hands went cold. Her face was on fire. Fighting the flashback was like fighting a riptide. She could feel it trying to pull her under.

Blood. She could feel it, warm and sticky on her feet.

Without warning, Grayson was *there.* "You *will* stay with me," he said quietly. "Right here, Lyra. Right now."

His hands. Her face. The past receded—only slightly.

"When I was seven," Grayson said in that same quiet, steady

voice, "I once ended up locked in a cello case for six hours alongside a longsword, a crossbow, and a very unruly kitten."

That was ridiculous enough—unexpected enough—to bring her the rest of the way back. *Here. Now.*

Him.

Grayson bent to block out the rest of the world from her view. "Give me your eyes, sweetheart."

Lyra looked at him. "A kitten?" she managed.

"A calico, I believe."

Inside Lyra, the floodgates broke. "This symbol," she bit out. Each breath she took felt like shards of glass in her lungs. "The night my biological father killed himself, he drew this symbol on the wall in his own blood."

Grayson's hands made their way from her face to the back of her neck, his touch warm and sure, as he followed her gaze to the Greek letter in question. Lyra expected him to name it, but he didn't.

"What begins a bet?" Grayson said, his voice low and humming, the kind of voice that reverberated down her spine. "*A bet*," he repeated.

"Grayson?" Lyra spoke his name like a prayer.

"It wasn't a riddle," Grayson told her. "It's wordplay. A code. What looks like two words is, in reality, only one, with the middle of the word omitted."

A bet.

"My grandfather tried this on us in a game once," Grayson continued, his voice shot through with almost palpable focus. "At the time, we were *looking* for codes, and there was more than one word that had been broken in two, so we got there eventually—or rather, Jamie did."

Intensity rolled off Grayson in waves, but Lyra barely even felt it. *Wordplay. A code. A bet.* What letters could you insert in the middle to form a single word?

"A bet." Lyra's voice rang in her own ears. "Alphabet. *What begins alphabet?*"

"*Not that,*" Grayson murmured, and if there had been space between them before, it was gone now. "Not *A*—or in the case of the Greek alphabet, not alpha."

"Not the beginning," Odette said, her voice coming to Lyra as if from across a great distance, "but the end."

The last letter. Lyra wasn't even aware that she'd reached for Grayson, but suddenly, her fingers were clamped down on his arm. With his hand still on her neck, Grayson leaned his head toward hers, bowing until their foreheads brushed.

He knew what this meant to her. He *knew,* and from the look in his eyes, she would have sworn it meant something to him, too.

Odette was the one who actually said it, her voice cutting through the air like a bullet: "Omega."

Chapter 52

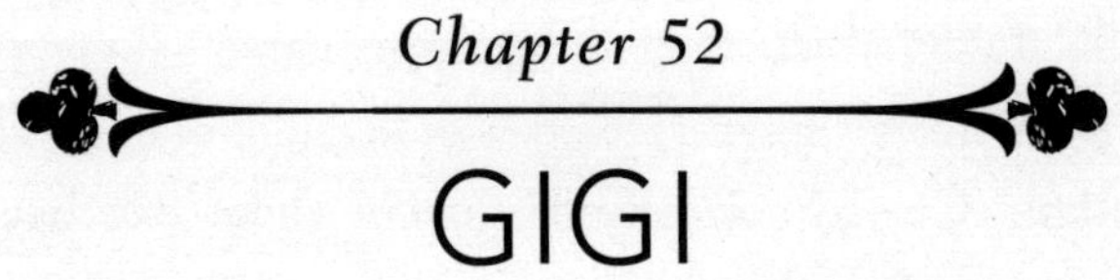

GIGI

Gigi stepped from the metal chamber onto a narrow wooden staircase that stretched up into darkness. The second she shifted her weight onto the first step, it lit up, casting a faint glow that did nothing to illuminate what awaited them at the top of the stairs. Gigi half expected Knox to push past her, but he didn't, so Gigi led the way, step after step, light after light, until she made it to the top of the stairs and a plain wooden door adorned only by four words scratched roughly into the wood.

HERE THERE BE DRAGONS.

Gigi trailed her fingers along the words, and her thoughts went to the potential *dragon* on the island—the person who'd used that wetsuit, the one who'd brought a knife and a listening device into the game.

The person who might be listening to us right now. Gigi sectioned that thought off in her mind and reached for the doorknob. It freely turned, and she pushed the door inward and stepped into…a library.

Brady and Knox stepped through the door to join her, as Gigi turned to take in the entire circular room. Brady walked to stand in front of one shelf in particular. "The spiral staircase let out *here* before."

Behind them, the *Here There Be Dragons* door swung shut. Like clockwork, a curved bookshelf descended from the ceiling, blocking off the door. The three of them were now completely encircled by fifteen-foot-tall shelves. Gigi craned her neck toward the ceiling. In the dead of night, the stained glass overhead shouldn't have cast any hint of color onto the floor, but a veritable rainbow of lights danced along the wood floorboards.

There must be a light source behind the glass. Gigi stepped through the colored lights, examining the pattern. Beside her, Knox's assessing gaze roved over the shelves and the books.

"Escape room logic?" Brady proposed, setting down the sword and crossing back to examine the section of the shelving that had just descended. "In the absence of instructions, you find your own clues."

"Search the shelves," Knox summarized.

Gigi reached for a book.

"The *shelves*, Happy." Knox's eyebrows were emphatic on that point. "Not the books. Those are a time suck waiting to happen. Search for switches or buttons built into the shelves, anything that might be a hidden trigger."

"*Happy*?" Gigi repeated. She reached over to pat Knox's shoulder. "I call that nickname progress."

"Shut up," Knox grunted. Without looking at her, he stalked toward the shelves on the far side of the room.

Brady's expression was incredulous.

"It's a gift," Gigi said.

Brady lowered his voice. "I told you—"

That Knox can be dangerous. That the dark place is always waiting for him. That he doesn't think about morality the way you and I do.

"I know what you told me," Gigi said helpfully. "I ignored it."

She ran her hands over the wood of the closest shelf, pushing her fingers into the lines of the molding, exploring the underside of each board, and then she started lifting books up to check underneath them.

After a moment, Brady began searching the next shelf over. The longer they worked, side by side, the more Gigi found herself lingering on the memory of the way he'd touched her stomach hours earlier. She thought about the fact that his brain liked *A Lot*.

She thought about his smile.

And then she thought about Knox's cutting accusation to Brady: *It's* always *Calla with you.* Brady had insisted that this time, it wasn't. And when Knox had seen the smile he'd given her, when he'd asked what the *hell* Brady was doing, Brady's reply had been *being human*.

Hyperaware of every inch of her own skin, Gigi allowed herself to disregard Knox's order to search only the shelves. She skimmed the spines of row after row of books, then snuck a look at Brady. He'd climbed up and was balanced on the edge of a shelf, five or six feet up, his arms stretched overhead, his body—arms, legs, core—making an X.

"You are incredibly well-balanced," Gigi blurted out.

"I get that a lot," Brady said solemnly. It took Gigi a second to figure out he was joking.

"Really," Brady murmured, "I've just spent a lot of time in the stacks at the university library."

"Climbing the shelves?" Gigi said, grinning. "Do they teach that in cultural anthropology PhD programs?"

"Possibly not." Amusement played around the edges of Brady's very scholarly lips.

Gigi couldn't help studying him, lips and all. *Grad school isn't where you learned balance.*

"Training," she said, keeping her voice too quiet for Knox to overhear. "All kinds. That was what you said earlier, when we were talking about Knox's A-plus in parkour—but it wasn't just Knox, was it?" Gigi thought about the way that Brady had held his own in that fight. "Training...with Severin?" That was a leap, but Gigi excelled at leaping first and looking later. For good measure, she leapt again. "And Calla."

In the worn photograph that Brady had kept in his pocket, the girl with the mismatched eyes had been holding a longbow.

Brady blinked and looked at Gigi like she'd slowly started turning into a moose, which was actually a pretty common response to Gigi leaping first and looking later.

"Brady?" Gigi wondered if she'd pushed too hard.

"You know that kid that Knox beat up on my behalf?" Brady hopped down from the shelf. "He had brothers. One day, all four of them jumped Knox and me in the woods."

"You were *six*." Gigi was horrified. Her voice was still hushed, and so was his.

"Six and a half by that time," Brady replied. "Knox was ten. And Severin was sixty-two—former black ops, very into survival. He lived off the grid out in the bayou. I never knew why he was in the woods that day, but he was." Brady paused. "Severin saw what was happening, and he put a stop to it. And then he spent the next decade teaching Knox and me how to do the same. Put a stop to things—and people—that needed stopping. *Survive.*"

"And Calla?" Gigi said.

"Calla . . ." Brady lingered on the name. "She was Severin's great-niece. His family disowned him decades ago, but Calla tracked Severin down when she was twelve. After that, she was always sneaking out to the bayou to train with Knox and me." Brady's Adam's apple moved up, then down. "No one could shoot a long-bow like Calla."

Gigi thought again about that photograph. She placed a light, hesitant hand on Brady's shoulder. "What happened to her?"

Brady reached up and squeezed her hand. Gigi squeezed back.

"She was abducted." Brady's voice was thick. "Someone took her. I was fifteen. Calla was seventeen. Knox had just turned nineteen. The two of them had been together almost a year at that point." Brady took a moment and just breathed. "Calla's family found out about their relationship, about Severin, what we were doing out in the bayou, all of it." Brady let go of Gigi's hand. "And we never saw her again."

"I'm so sorry," Gigi said.

Brady shook his head, tension clear in the lines of his jaw. "Another two weeks, and Calla would have turned eighteen. She could have left the family fold, told them all to go to hell, but the Thorps weren't about to let that happen. They played along with the police investigation, but Orion Thorp made it perfectly clear to me—they had her."

"Orion Thorp?" Dread hit Gigi like a razor-sharp icicle slicing through the pit of her stomach. "Knox's sponsor?"

Brady didn't answer that question. "Calla's name," he said, his throat tensing against the words, "is Calla Thorp. Orion is her father." Jerking his gaze away from Gigi's, Brady resumed his search of the shelves, going low.

But he didn't stop talking.

"Last year, Knox showed up at my apartment out of the blue. It had been years since we'd spent any real time together. Since... Calla. But Knox was set on playing the Grandest Game, and he wanted a partner. I guess some part of me wanted *us* back, so..."

Brady had just said *us* the way Knox had said *we*.

"Last year's game was a race," Brady continued, "clue to clue to clue. In the beginning, those clues were virtual, but eventually, they crossed over to the real world, and the race became a physical race—a global one. The game makers provided transportation, but only for the first few players or teams to reach a given clue. Knox and I were in the lead, but on the second-to-last clue, we fell behind and missed our chance at a ride. We would have been out of the competition." Brady paused. "That was when Knox was approached by Calla's father."

"Orion Thorp," Gigi said. *Knox's sponsor.*

"Knox knows what Calla's family is like. Even before she disappeared, Calla hated it there. Knox *knows* as well as I do: If Calla is still alive, they have her, and if she's not, they're the reason why." Brady's breath was audibly heavy. "And knowing that, Knox sold me out to Orion Thorp for a ride on a private jet." The muscles in Brady's jaw tensed. "He came in second in the game."

"Here." Knox's voice sliced through the air.

"Sounds like he found something." Brady's voice was still low. "You go. I'll be there in a minute."

"Are you—" Gigi started to say.

"I'm sure," Brady said.

As Gigi crossed the room, she thought about Knox's first answer when she'd asked what made him happy: *money*. He'd never tried to hide what he was.

"Here," Knox said again, his tone more impatient this time. He gestured to a wooden panel on the shelf he'd bared. Built into that panel was an ornate magnifying glass. The handle was jeweled with elaborate detailing in silver and gold. A row of tiny diamonds marked the point where the handle met the frame.

As Gigi watched, Knox pulled the magnifying glass from the wood, like the sword from the stone. There was a click, and the floorboards in the center of the room began to move. An entire section of the floor was halved, and from the depths below, something rose up—a new section of floor that clicked into place, replacing the old.

Sitting on top of that new flooring was a dollhouse.

And all Gigi could think was that Knox had never denied that Orion Thorp was *still* his sponsor.

Chapter 53

ROHAN

Rohan and Savannah met in the middle—the last shelf of games. She went high. He went low, skimming his fingers along the boxes as he registered the title of each and every game.

"Camelot," Savannah read out loud.

"Knights and a king," Rohan murmured. "Swords and a crown." Suddenly, in the place in his mind where mysteries lived to be sorted, there it was: meaning where before there had been none. "What if," he said, "we weren't given instructions for this room—this puzzle—because we'd already received them? *Each team's challenge is their own . . .*"

"*A crown, a scepter, an empty throne.*" Savannah got there in an instant.

Rohan backtracked and began pulling boxes off the shelves. "Kingdoms. Dominion."

Within a minute, Savannah had pulled five more games. Rohan

added his own stack next to hers on the ground, then they met in the middle once more. She went high. He went low.

"Mastermind," Savannah said briskly. "Appropriate, but no. Battleship, no. Risk, no. Titan?"

"Pull it," Rohan said. He went up a row.

She went down one and pulled Candy Land. "It has a king," she said.

"I can't say that I've ever played," Rohan told her. The only games one played growing up at the Devil's Mercy were games of greatest stakes—the kind played at the tables and the kind played to survive.

Rohan moved on to the final shelf. "Medici."

"Why not just call the game *dynastic power* and be done with it?" Savannah retorted.

Close enough, Rohan thought. He added the game to their stack, then continued searching. He frowned. "Here's one that involves... burritos." Savannah snorted. They fell back into silence, and then...

"Rohan." Savannah didn't say his name often, but when she did, she made it count.

He moved in a flash, coming up to stand shoulder to shoulder with her as he took in the game she held in her hands. The box was black with gold lettering.

A NEEDLE IN A HAYSTACK.

Beneath the title, there was a symbol—a diamond. Rohan thought back to their first challenge, to the scoreboard. They were the Diamonds.

"The font matches the script from the golden tickets," Savannah murmured. "This isn't a real game. They made it."

They as in the game makers, Avery and Jameson and the rest.

"Open it," Rohan said, jumping down into the recessed area that surrounded the game table. "Set it up."

Savannah landed beside him, and this time, her face didn't betray even a hint of pain, whether she felt it or not. She set the box on the table and opened it. Rohan ran his hand over the lid, then the side of the box, then flipped both lid and box over.

"Thorough," Savannah said, and something about the way she said that word made Rohan want to hear her say it again.

Dangerous, that.

He turned his attention to the contents of the box. *Two stacks of white cards*, he cataloged, *a white playing board folded in half, and eight metal game pieces.* Savannah picked up one of them: a crown—one of five, by the looks of it, each of them distinct.

"Five *crowns*." Savannah's mind worked in tandem with his own. Rohan noted the piece she'd chosen. The detailing work was exquisite. Tiny pearls lined the bottom and accented each knife-sharp point of the crown.

Rohan reached for a game piece of his own. The largest of the crowns, it looked like something out of a dark fairy tale, the metal carved in a way that called to mind antlers and thorns. The remaining three crowns in the box were simpler: one bronze, one silver, one gold. That left three other game pieces. *A spinning wheel. A bow and arrow. A heart.*

As Rohan ruminated on that, Savannah reached into the box, withdrew the game board, and unfolded it on the table. The design was simple: square spaces around the outside, rectangular outlines in the center of the board, indicating where the cards were supposed to go.

Savannah placed the cards in their spots and her game piece on the square that said *START*. Now that the box was empty,

Rohan could make out the rules written inside—or rather, the rule, singular.

All it said was *ROLL THE DICE*.

"There are no dice," Savannah observed.

"Aren't there?" Rohan replied. Beneath the table, he reached into his tuxedo jacket, then laid his fist on the table, knuckles down, and allowed his fingers to uncurl like petals on a flower.

In the center of his palm was a pair of red dice.

"I found these in my room earlier," Rohan said. "Picking them up revealed a screen, but there's little reason to think that's their only use in this game."

Savannah reached into her thick, pale braid and removed her own pair of glass dice. "Same." Her dice were white, not red, and like his, they appeared to be made of glass. "I'll go first."

Of course she would. Rohan's lips twisted as he took in her roll. "A five and a three."

"Eight." Savannah moved her pearled crown eight squares around the perimeter. The square she landed on—like almost every other square on the very simple board—was labeled *HAY*.

Rohan rolled his own dice. "A six and a two. Also eight."

He moved his game piece next to Savannah's. "Your turn, Savvy. My dice or yours?"

Savannah picked up her white dice and rolled them again. "Another five and another three."

Rohan didn't wait for her to move before he rolled. As hers had, his dice turned up the exact same numbers the second time. He tossed them again to be sure. "They're weighted to always land the same way."

That made the numbers a clue. *To this room? Or another?*

Savannah jumped her game piece forward eight spaces, then

another eight, bringing her to one of two squares on the board marked *HAYSTACK* instead of just *HAY*. The stacks of cards in the middle of the board shared that label. Savannah beat Rohan to drawing one.

"Blank." Her eyes narrowing, she kept drawing. "Blank. Blank."

Rohan took a card from the stack closest to him and used it to flip the entire stack, then reached across and did the same for Savannah's cards, scattering them out in a neat line across the board.

Among all the cards, there was only one that wasn't blank. Five words had been scrawled across that card in black marker.

THIS IS NOT YOUR CLUE.

Chapter 54

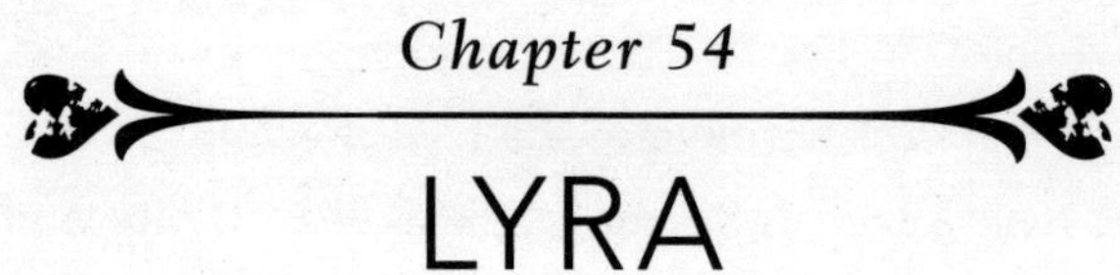

LYRA

"Omega." Lyra's voice went husky, but her body felt suddenly, unnaturally calm. Grayson's hands were still on her neck. His forehead was still touching hers. Lyra didn't have to speak up to make sure he heard her next question. "Does that mean anything to you?"

"No. It does not." Grayson pulled back from her, just enough to turn his head without letting go. His gaze settled with military precision on Odette. "Does it mean anything to *you*, Ms. Morales?"

Lyra thought suddenly about notes on trees, about her father's names, about how small the suspect pool for that act really was.

Thomas, Thomas, Tommaso, Tomás.

He'd been dead for fifteen years. Who else on this island, besides Odette, was old enough to have known anything about him?

"Omega means the end." The old woman in question lifted two fingers to her forehead and crossed herself. "'Yo soy el Alfa y la

Omega, el principio y el fin, el primero y el ultimo.' It's from the book of Revelation—Apocolipsis, in Spanish."

"You're Catholic?" Lyra said. She searched for some kind of tell in the set of Odette's features, anything that could tip off whether or not the old woman was putting on an act.

"The more pertinent question," Odette replied, "is whether or not your father was a religious man."

"I don't know." Lyra knew so very little about the shadowy figure responsible for half her DNA. *I know his blood was warm. I know I stepped in it. I know he used it to draw that symbol on the wall.*

"And that's the only meaning the word *omega* holds for you, Ms. Morales?" Grayson's hands finally dropped away from Lyra's neck as he turned and took two steps toward Odette. "The only meaning you associate with that symbol?"

"The only place I have ever seen that symbol," Odette said evenly, "is behind that altar of the church I attended as a child, and I have not stepped a foot in that church—or in Mexico, for that matter—since my seventeenth birthday, which was also, incidentally, my wedding day to a much older man who saw me and wanted me and convinced my musician father that he could make him a star."

Lyra could feel the truth in Odette's words, but even if Odette *was* telling the truth about the last time she'd seen that symbol, that wasn't what Grayson had asked.

He'd asked if it held any other meaning for her—and Odette hadn't actually answered the question.

"Ms. Morales, during your many years as a high-priced attorney"—Grayson cocked his head slightly to one side, a tiger sizing up his prey—"did you, by chance, ever happen to work for the law firm of McNamara, Ortega, and Jones?"

Odette was silent.

"And that's my answer," Grayson said. He cast a sideways glance at Lyra. "McNamara, Ortega, and Jones was my grandfather's personal law firm. He was their only client."

Odette worked for Tobias Hawthorne. Lyra stopped breathing for a second or two, then started up again. *And who knows a man's secrets better*, she thought slowly, *than his lawyers?*

A Hawthorne did this. "Please," Lyra said urgently, fiercely. "If you know something, Odette—"

"There is a game my youngest granddaughter was quite fond of as a teenager." Odette somehow managed to make that sound like it *wasn't* a sudden and absolute subject change. "*Two Truths and a Lie*. I'll do the pair of you one better and offer up three truths, the first of which is this, Lyra: I know nothing about your father." Odette shifted her gaze to Grayson. "My second truth: Your grandfather was the best and worst man I have ever known."

To Lyra's ears, that didn't sound like the declaration of Tobias Hawthorne's *lawyer*. She remembered the way Odette had said—twice—that Grayson was *very much a Hawthorne*.

Just how well did you know the billionaire, Odette?

"And my final truth for the two of you, free of charge, is this: I am here, playing the Grandest Game with every intention to win it, because I am dying." Odette's tone was matter-of-fact, if a bit annoyed, like death was a mere inconvenience, like the old woman was too proud to let it be anything else.

Again, Lyra couldn't shake the feeling: *She's telling the truth*.

"Tell, Mr. Hawthorne." Odette stared Grayson down. "Have I told a single lie?"

Grayson's gaze flicked toward Lyra. "No."

"Then allow me to remind the two of you that you already have my terms. If I am to answer the question of how I knew Tobias Hawthorne, of how I ended up on that capital-L List of his, it will happen if and only if we make it out of the Grandest Escape Room and down to the dock by dawn—which, I might point out, draws ever closer."

"Never trust a sentence with three *ifs*," Grayson told Lyra. "Particularly when spoken by a lawyer."

"You want answers," Odette told him. "I want a legacy to leave my family. To that end, we have a game to play, one that I am going to win if it's the last thing I do."

The last thing. Lyra wondered just how much time Odette had left.

Head held high, the old woman made her way—slowly, gracefully, regally—to the projector and manually rewound the film that had welcomed them to this room.

A moment later, the montage—the *cipher*—began to play from the beginning. Lyra tamped down on the deadly whirlpool of emotions churning in her gut. She'd lived with the suffocating weight of *not knowing* for years. For now, she needed to concentrate on solving this puzzle and any others that followed and getting down to the dock by dawn.

For Mile's End—and for answers.

Lyra crossed the room and paused the projector the moment the multiple-choice question appeared on-screen, studying the now-familiar symbols of the "correct" answer.

A ⊛ r □

Lyra compared that to the other three answers, all of which also contained four symbols, a mix of letters and shapes. "Odette."

Lyra's voice sounded throaty and raw to her own ears. "You said there was another set of symbols at the end of the film?"

"There is," Odette confirmed.

After the gun. Lyra felt the dread of that in the pit of her stomach and the back of her throat. *After the body. After the blood.*

"Skip to the end of the film," Grayson ordered. He was obviously trying to protect her, to spare her.

Whatever had or hadn't passed between them, Lyra wasn't about to let herself be spared anything by Grayson Hawthorne.

"No." She refused to cower—from anything, but especially from this. "We need to watch the whole thing again." In a Hawthorne game, anything could matter. "I'm not weak. I can handle it."

Grayson's pale eyes locked on hers with an odd kind of recognition, like the two of them were strangers who'd met gazes across a crowded room only to realize they'd met before.

Like they were the same.

"It has taken me a lifetime," Grayson said softly, "to learn how to be weak."

Some people can make mistakes, make amends, and move on. Lyra wanted to cut the memory of his words off there, but she couldn't. *And some of us live with each and every mistake we make carved into us, into hollow places we don't know how to fill.*

"And now?" Lyra thought about the cost of being fine, of running—and running and running and *running*—away from every person who might have realized that she wasn't, of keeping the whole damn world at arm's length. "Do you get to be weak now, Grayson?"

Look away from his eyes, Lyra told herself desperately. *Look away from him.*

She didn't. "Do you get to make mistakes now?" she said.

Silence stretched between them—living, breathing, *aching* silence.

"Only the ones," Grayson told her, "that are really worth making."

Lyra wanted to turn away from him, but all she could think about was the poem she'd destroyed, the one he'd pieced back together.

Gone too fast.

Burned into skin.

All she could think about was a masked heiress giving her advice. *Sometimes, in the games that matter most, the only way to really play is to* live.

Odette reached across Lyra and hit Play on the projector. With the moment broken—thankfully, *blessedly* broken—Lyra forced herself to catalog the scenes in the montage in purely objective terms, and she did her best to not think about Grayson Hawthorne and *mistakes*—about *weakness* and *running* and *living*—at all.

A smoking man. A stolen martini. Cowboys and a noose. A diamond earring dropped down a drain. A man with a gun. When the gun appeared on-screen, Lyra breathed through it.

She breathed, and Grayson breathed beside her. Through *the body* and *the blood*. Breaths in. Breaths out. And even though Grayson never touched her, Lyra could *feel* his hand on the back of her neck, warm and steady and there.

The montage played on.

A teenage boy in a leather jacket.

A female pilot pulling off her goggles and cap.

A long kiss good-bye.

Lyra watched that kiss with Grayson Hawthorne beside her, unable to keep herself from thinking about the kind of mistakes that were worth making.

And somewhere, in the back of her mind, the ghost of her father whispered: *A Hawthorne did this.*

A set of symbols appeared on the screen. Lyra concentrated on them. Not Grayson. Not ghosts. Not things she had no business feeling. Just the symbols.

C 2 ⊛ r

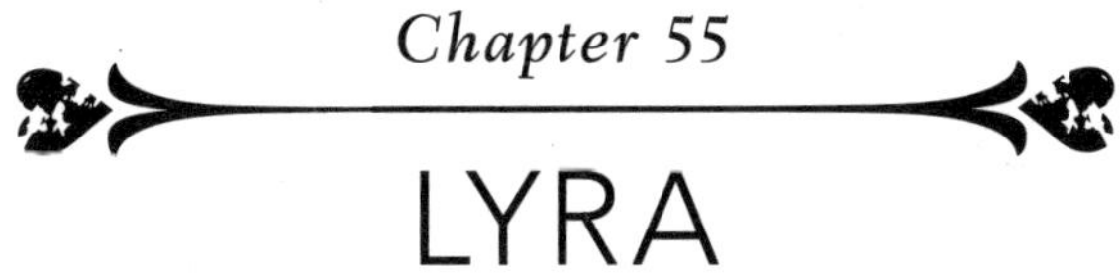

Chapter 55
LYRA

Grayson was the one who solved it in the end. "That's not a wheel, and it's not a circle. It's a *pie*. This whole thing has Xander's name written all over it."

"Pie." It took Lyra a second, and then her brain kicked into gear. "Without the *E*." She did the math—literally. "A, pi, *r*, square. *C*, two, pi, *r*. They're equations."

"The area and circumference of a circle," Grayson confirmed. "But for our purposes and doubtlessly Xander's, the important part is the Greek letter *pi*."

Greek letter. "The tins." Lyra was already on the move. "Who went through the ones marked *pi*?"

"I did." Grayson strode past her. "Here. Forty-two canisters marked *pi*. None contains anything but film reels."

"What about the years?" Lyra said. "Most of the films in the montage were older. They started black-and-white, then turned to color."

"Pull every tin from the sixties," Odette said curtly. Something about the look on the old woman's face made Lyra entirely certain that Odette knew something that they didn't.

Probably multiple somethings. "Then what?" Lyra probed.

"Watch the films," Odette said coolly. "At least a sample."

"That will eat up time," Grayson noted, but Lyra didn't see that they had any other choice.

The twenty-second pi film they tried was called *Changing Crowns*. The moment the title slide hit the screen, Odette spoke. "This is the one we're looking for."

"A crown, *a scepter, an empty throne*," Grayson quoted instantly.

"There is that," Odette agreed, as she stopped the film and peeled the long, velvet gloves off her hands. "And also: This one is one of mine."

"One of yours?" Lyra said.

Odette gave an elegant little shrug. "The man I married when I was seventeen never made my father a star," she said, an odd glint in her eyes. "I was another story."

Chapter 56

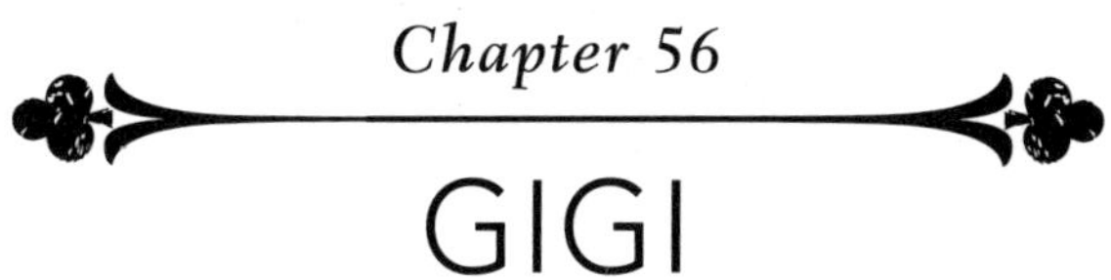

GIGI

Dollhouse was an understatement. Gigi took it all in. The entire spread was eight feet long and three deep. To one side, there was a four-story Victorian mansion, to the other, a castle that looked like it had been lifted straight from a fairy tale. In between, the streets were lined with shops—some Victorian, some medieval.

A toy shop. A dress shop. A magic shop. A forge.

The two worlds came together at the midpoint with a pair of royal carriages facing an early-model car.

The level of detail in every single piece was astounding. A single flower—of which there were at least eight dozen in the window boxes of the mansion—consisted of a stem and six detachable blooms. There were nearly a hundred dolls, each with one or more accessories.

A maid's apron. A child's teddy bear. Easily three dozen different hats.

Opposite Gigi, Knox was systematically disassembling and reassembling pieces, one by one. Brady's eyes moved, shifting from one piece to the next, but his body was perfectly still.

Gigi played to her own strengths. She made her merry way to the bookshelves and started to climb.

"What are you doing?" Knox pulled apart the forge.

"Casing the joint," Gigi replied. A bird's-eye view usually helped. She scaled higher—ten feet up, twelve.

Knox grabbed a display of teeny, tiny weaponry and stomped toward her. "For the last time," he bit out, climbing after her, "your bones *are not bendy.*"

"I think better up high." Gigi made it to the top shelf and looked down at the world in miniature below. *Take it all in, Gigi. Every detail. Every tiny window. Every little exit.*

Knox arrived at her side, and he didn't look happy about it.

"On a scale of one to ten," Gigi said, "are you going to toss someone out a window, yes or no?"

But what she was really thinking was: *Why would you work with Orion Thorp?* She *knew* Knox cared about Brady. They were a *we.* Family of choice. *Brothers.* Gigi thought about the tone in Knox's voice when he'd said that Brady knew every last damn constellation.

Why would you sell him out to Calla's family? Even if Knox did believe that Calla had left of her own volition, even if he believed there had been no foul play, he knew Brady believed her family was responsible.

You knew, and you got in bed with them anyway.

"There are no windows," Knox said gruffly. "Which, based on the view from the back of the house, suggests that there's significantly more to the fifth floor than we can currently see."

Gigi shifted her weight.

"You need to be careful," Knox said darkly.

"I'm fine," Gigi insisted.

"You're really not." Knox gave her *a look*, and Gigi noticed for the first time that his eyes were a muddy hazel, shot through with gold. "This is a competition, Happy. Brady isn't your friend. No one here is."

Knox's warning was eerily close to Savannah's. "Including you?" Gigi said.

"*Especially* me. If you're not careful, you're going to get eaten alive in this game."

Gigi thought about sponsors, about the *dragon* on the island, about the warnings, plural, that Brady had given her about Knox.

"I don't mind," Gigi said stubbornly. "Being eaten alive, I mean. If you can get them to spit you out, it's pretty much just a massage."

Knox's eyes narrowed. "You're irritating me on purpose."

Gigi shrugged and nodded down toward their puzzle below. "No dragons," she noted.

Knox's brows drew together. "The words on the door."

"*Here there be dragons*," Gigi recited. "Except there aren't any down there."

She shimmied down a couple of shelves, then leapt for the floor. Her landing wasn't exactly *graceful*, but Gigi didn't let that slow her down. Squatting next to the castle, Gigi marked the points of entry she'd seen from above. There was no staircase, no way to get from the bottom stories upward. Activity—as indexed by the dolls—was densest in the courtroom, the feast hall, and the throne room.

Throne. Fireworks detonated in Gigi's brain. Glorious fireworks!

The king doll was sitting on his throne, but the queen wasn't on hers.

Twenty minutes later, Gigi found the queen *under* one of the beds in the Victorian mansion. She wasn't exactly subtle about the way she tossed the place, so by the time she vigorously slammed the queen onto the empty throne, Knox and Brady were both staring at her.

"The poem." Brady got there first. "From the chamber. *An empty throne.* You're brilliant."

Brilliant. Gigi could get used to that.

"Nothing's happening," Knox pointed out.

Gigi turned her attention to the queen's accessories. The same *nothing* happened when she popped the crown off the queen's head, but when she grasped the tiny scepter between her forefinger and her thumb and tried to pull, she was met with resistance.

The head of the scepter was a *dragon.*

Gigi persevered. When she finally wrenched the scepter free, there was a pop.

"Quiet," Knox ordered. He lowered himself chest-down to the ground, his palms flat against the floor, his head slightly raised, just inches from the Victorian mansion. "Do that again," he told Gigi.

"I think it came from over here." Brady crouched and zeroed in on the room in the Victorian mansion that Gigi had mentally dubbed the parlor. A fancy red sofa sat opposite two blue wingback chairs. A maid pushed a tea cart. Behind her, there was a grandfather clock and a cabinet filled with books.

Gigi returned the queen's scepter and pulled it again. Another pop. Knox and Brady reached at the exact same time for the cabinet full of books. Knox let his hand drop, allowing Brady to be the one to open the cabinet. Tiny, plastic books spilled out onto the dollhouse floor.

Scrawled onto each of them, there was a number.

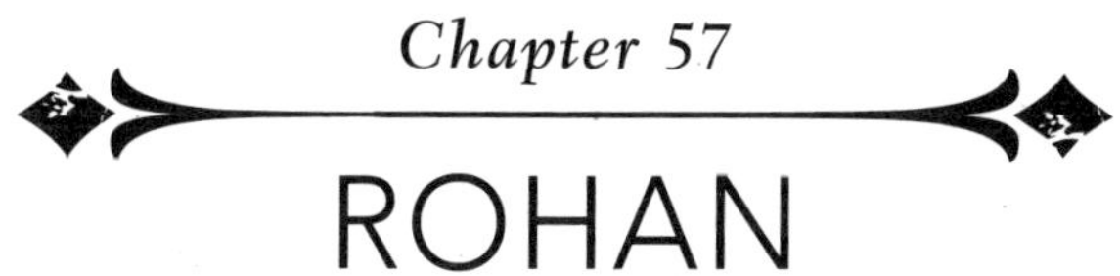

Chapter 57

ROHAN

By Rohan's estimation, they had a little over four hours left until dawn. He and Savannah had been searching for hours, and they'd made no progress.

A Needle In A Haystack wasn't their clue. It seemed, instead, to be a description of their task. They'd spent far too much time already looking for their *needle*, a clue in a room with seemingly endless *hay* to sort through. They'd gone back to the stack of boxes they'd pulled from the shelves, searching for crowns and scepters and thrones. Every applicable piece—including those from A Needle In A Haystack—had been examined.

Thoroughly.

When that had turned up nothing, Rohan and Savannah had extended their search to every other game in the room as well. They'd opened every box in search of the target items. They'd emptied the shelves and searched them, too, looking for buttons or triggers, to no avail.

And, per Rohan's mental map, this was most certainly not their final room—or puzzle.

"Savannah." Rohan didn't shorten her name. "We need to take the hint."

Savannah placed herself squarely in front of the hint button. "I wouldn't have pegged you as a person who gave up that easily."

"I'm a strategist. Some days, that's all I am: brutal, no-holds-barred *strategy*. In my line of work, you have to know when to cut your losses, when to divert."

"I suppose that's the difference between us." Savannah lifted her chin. "I don't lose, so there are no *losses* to cut."

"I could fight you for it," Rohan commented.

"Been there," Savannah replied archly. "Done that."

It was clear to him from her tone: Part of her *wanted* to spar, the same way part of him did. But strategy was never subject to *want*.

He gave her a push of a different sort. "You don't like asking for help, do you, Savvy?"

"It is less about whether I like it than whether I do it." She gave him one of those very Savannah Grayson looks, icy and sure. "I do not. People make mistakes. If you rely on others, their mistakes become yours."

Her voice was oh-so-calm, but Rohan saw the fury buried behind Savannah's silvery eyes when she said the word *mistakes*, like a fire burning inside a vault.

The labyrinth shifted. Savannah was here *for her father*, and she was angry about mistakes that were not hers.

Has Sheffield Grayson returned? Is he forcing you to do this? Or is that anger directed toward someone else? Rohan wasn't sure. Yet.

"You're angry, love." Sometimes, instead of manipulating a target's emotions, all you had to do was leverage what they already felt.

Savannah's body reacted to his voice and his words: a deeper breath, a slight curl of her fingers, tension in what he could see of her neck. "I'm not angry," she said, her voice high and clear. "Why would I be?"

"Society isn't always kind to angry women." Rohan's words hit their target.

"I don't need kindness. I just need everyone else to get out of my way."

"And I need you," Rohan replied, "to agree to take the hint. Whatever we're missing, at this point, we're just going to keep missing it. We have no direction. We have no plan. We have nothing. Do you enjoy having *nothing*, Savvy?" He paused. "Does your father?"

That was a test, an experiment. She didn't react in any visible way. Savannah's poker face was a thing to behold, and when she spoke, her tone was just as controlled. "When this part of the game is over, and you and I are no longer a team..." Finally, the real Savannah peeked through: *strength* and *endurance* and *fury*. "I am going to destroy you. And I promise, Rohan, I will *enjoy* that."

"Is that a yes?" Rohan prompted. "On the hint?"

Savannah turned toward the panel and laid her palm over the red button. "I *should* agree to take the hint, so I will." Her voice was higher now, clear and overtly feminine and pleasant. "After all," she continued, her eyes like knives, "society is kindest to women who do what they should."

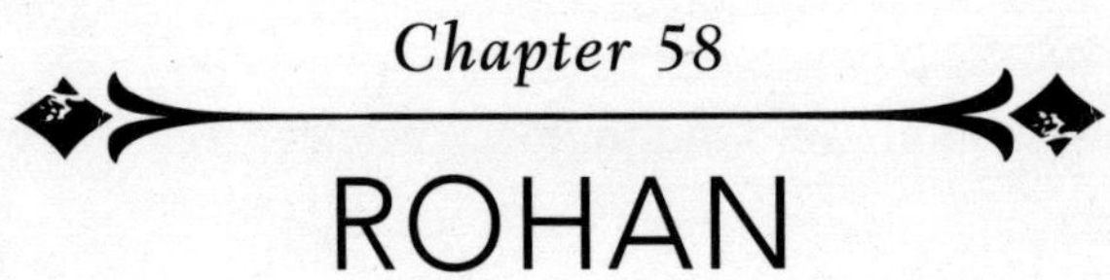

Chapter 58
ROHAN

"Diamond Team." Jameson Hawthorne's voice was all around them. "You have chosen to take your one and only hint."

Rohan wondered—briefly—where the game makers' command center was and what they had been doing to pass the time.

"But as you know," Jameson continued, "hints in this game must be earned."

Ledgers must be balanced, levies paid. Everything in Rohan's life had come at a cost.

"Door number one or door two?" Jameson Hawthorne asked. "Pick your challenge."

"Two," Savannah said immediately.

Instants later, there was a sound like the turning of gears, and the game table in the center of the room began to split at the seam they'd found earlier, the two halves of the tabletop pulled apart as if by invisible hands. A Needle In A Haystack and all of its pieces fell to the ground as the two halves of the tabletop flipped outward, rotating a hundred and eighty degrees and disappearing beneath the underside of the table. A second, formerly hidden tabletop stared back at them. *Shining hardwood, green felt.*

"A poker table," Rohan commented. Around the rim, holders had been carved into the wood for cards and for chips. The poker chips themselves—all black—were placed at equidistant intervals around the perimeter of the green felt. In the center of the table there were two small stacks of what looked to be playing cards, one set white with gold foiling, the other black with bronze and silver. Positioned next to the cards were three objects: a silver hairbrush, a pearl-handled knife, and a glass rose.

"Behind door number two," Jameson Hawthorne told them, "is a game. To earn your hint, all the two of you have to do is play it."

"Poker?" Savannah guessed. Her gaze slid to Rohan's.

"Not poker." Avery Grambs was the one who replied. "Truth or Dare—or a version of it, anyway." Something in the Hawthorne heiress's voice reminded Rohan that she had promised the players an *experience*. And then he thought about Nash's claim: *Our games have heart.*

"Working as a team—*becoming* a team—requires cooperation," Avery continued. "It requires a certain amount of openness. In some cases, it requires risk."

"Each of the chips on the table in front of you has a word written on the bottom." Jameson was clearly enjoying this far too much. "Half say *truth*. Half say *dare*. To successfully complete this challenge, you'll need to collect three from each category."

"Once you've turned over a chip"—Avery took back over—"you'll draw a card from the corresponding pile: white for truth, black for dare. The person who draws the card issues the challenge. The other person must fulfill it. If, for any reason, after drawing a truth card, you decide that you would prefer to pose your own question instead of the question written on the card, that is allowed."

"Presuming, of course," Jameson interjected, "that said question is just as *interesting* as the one we have provided."

Well, that was ominous.

"You'll notice that there are three objects on the table." Avery took back over. "The dare cards don't specify a dare. They specify an object. Coming up with an appropriate dare using that object is up to you."

Rohan wondered what kind of challenge they would have faced if they'd chosen door number one. A puzzle instead of a game? Something less . . . *personal*?

Out loud, he focused on a different question. "What's to keep us from lying?"

"I'm so glad you asked," Jameson replied. "The poker chips have a little something extra embedded in them. Place your thumb flat in the center of a truth chip as you answer or a dare chip immediately after fulfilling your dare. We'll be monitoring your heart rate, among other things. You *could* try fooling us, of course, but if we flag one of your answers as false, the challenge fails."

No hint, Rohan translated.

"What about the dares?" Savannah was using her high, clear society voice, but her body told a different story.

Her body was ready to fight.

Fight who? The labyrinth called. *And why?* Rohan resisted, staying in the moment.

"A proper dare," Jameson said, "also has an effect on one's heart rate. If you think you can trick our sensors, the two of you are most welcome to try and risk not getting your hint. *Bonne chance.*"

With that, the game's masterminds went silent.

"Good luck," Rohan translated flatly. "Jameson Hawthorne and I have a mutual acquaintance who is fond of the French version of that phrase."

The duchess. Rohan recognized the move Jameson had just made for what it was: the blighter's way of making it clear that he and Avery knew exactly what was at stake for Rohan in this game. It wouldn't have taken much for them to figure it out, given their history with the Mercy.

You two know I'm not going to try to cheat, Rohan thought shrewdly. Compared to the Proprietorship of the Devil's Mercy, what was one little game of Truth or Dare?

Chapter 59

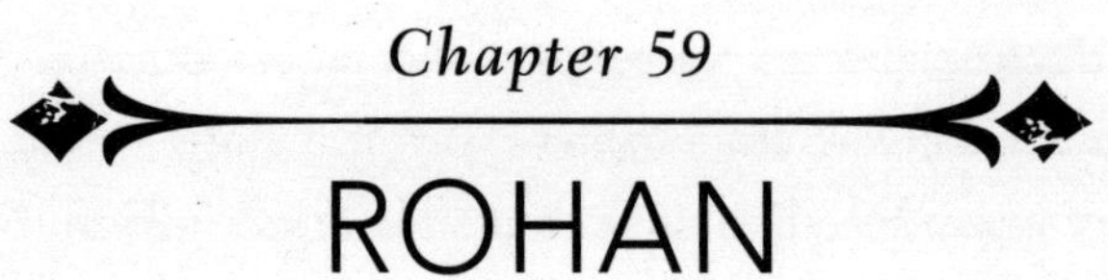

ROHAN

Savannah flipped over the first chip. "Truth." She reached for the pile of white and gold cards and withdrew one. Rohan expected her to discard the predetermined question and ask him for details about the Mercy, but she didn't—an indication that she was off her game.

Instead, Savannah Grayson read the question on the card in an almost bored tone as she placed the chip on the table and slid it across to him. "What is your earliest memory?"

Rohan placed his thumb flat on the center of the chip. "My earliest memory." Rohan's voice was unexpectedly low in pitch, even to his own ears. He was a person who kept his memories locked away in a labyrinth for a reason. Already in this game, the past had clawed its way to the surface of his mind twice, and that was two times too many.

But needs must. "I'm in my mother's arms," Rohan said, detached.

"She's humming, and then I'm in the water. We're outside. It's pitch black. The water is deep. I can't swim."

There wasn't an ounce of emotion in his tone. Detaching further, Rohan considered the origin of the phrase *needs must*, the full proverb. *Needs must when the devil drives.*

"I know *control*," Savannah said, "when I see it."

Rohan met her eyes. "It wasn't the first time." For all his *control*, Rohan could feel his heart beating harder now. "That's the most vivid part of the memory. I'm in the water. I can't swim. I can't see anything. And it's not the first time."

They'd done it to him on purpose. Rohan had no recollection of who *they* were, beyond the woman. The rest of his family, perhaps. Children didn't come to the keeping of the Devil's Mercy for *good* reasons.

The chip under Rohan's thumb lit up. He cleared his mind and set it down. *Five more to go.* He reached for a chip of his own and turned it over.

"Dare." Rohan drew a black card. The image of the hairbrush stared back at him. He looked up at Savannah, at her braid. "Take down your hair."

That wasn't strategy. Rohan could admit that, if only to himself.

He heard the breath catch in her throat. "Is that your dare?" Savannah asked. *I know* control, she'd told him, *when I see it.*

"I dare you..." Rohan banished the memory of the water and the dark. "To let me brush it."

He let himself savor the way Savannah took down her hair, as her nimble fingers made quick work of the braids on either side of her head. She was efficient.

Rohan picked up the brush.

“There,” Savannah said, clipping the word. “Done. Brush away.” There those walls were. He wondered if any part of her was thinking, as he was, of their rather tantalizing fight.

“I can come up with another dare,” Rohan told her, spinning the brush around once in his hand. “If you would like.”

Savannah gave him a look sharp enough to bisect him. “Let’s just get this over with.”

“The chip.” Rohan leaned forward to lay it on the table in front of her. She took it in her hand, and Rohan registered the way her long, pale hair danced all the way down her back with even the slightest movement.

“I won’t touch you if you don’t want me to.” Rohan walked toward her, making no effort to mask the sound of his steps. “I can come up with another dare.”

“I want,” Savannah said, “to win.”

You need to, Rohan corrected silently. The labyrinth beckoned.

“Do it.” Savannah liked giving orders.

Rohan counted her breaths and his own, and when he reached seven for each of them, he brought the brush up and began expertly working out the last remaining knots from the braids. He remembered fisting his hand in her hair, remembered her own painful hold on him, but this?

This was a different beast. *Slowly. Carefully. Gently.* This wasn’t his first time brushing hair—not even hair as long and thick and *soft* as hers. The knots were gone soon enough.

Rohan’s skill set was . . . eclectic.

He didn’t stop. He went section by section, guiding the brush through her hair and down her back, counting her breaths and his own.

One.

Two.

Three.

Her next intake of breath was a little sharper. *Do you know what that does to me, winter girl?* His thumb lightly skimmed her neck, and Savannah arched it, leaning into his touch.

His pulse. Hers. Softness and heat. Breath after breath after breath, Rohan kept brushing, kept counting.

One.

Two.

Three.

Four.

Five.

Six.

"Rohan." The way she said his name was like a knife slid between ribs.

Savannah.

Savannah.

Savannah.

The chip in her fingers lit up. "Are we done?" Her voice was lower now, low and rich and brutally, irrefutably *her.*

"Are we, Savvy?" Rohan echoed the question back to her. "Done?"

He saw and heard and *felt* her swallow. "It's over."

There was a difference, Rohan knew, between *want* and *need.* Staying on the right side of that line was an exercise of utmost control. He could *want* her to eternity and back, but he couldn't let himself *need* a damn thing.

Rohan lowered the brush. "One dare down."

"And one truth." Savannah's right hand lashed out, and an instant later, she'd turned over a third chip. *Dare.* She moved on to the card pile and drew the knife.

As the Factotum of the Devil's Mercy, Rohan had a certain level of skill with blades.

Savannah stared at the knife on the table. Rohan felt his lips curve, and then Savannah Grayson did something most unexpected: She grabbed her hair in her fist. "Cut it."

Rohan was not a person who was easily taken off guard. Schooling his features to remain neutral, he picked up the pearl-handled blade and gave it a light spin. "You want me to cut your hair with this knife."

"I *dare you* to cut my hair with that knife."

She'd felt something. Rohan thought about her sharp intake of breath, about the way she'd leaned into his touch. She'd wanted it—and him. And this was her response.

"I've done worse things with knives," Rohan warned her, "than cut hair."

"Then why," she countered, "are you stalling?"

Rohan took the knife in his hand and wondered if she was punishing herself for feeling—or him for making her feel. He placed his left hand over hers, and she pulled back, leaving him with her hair fisted in his hand, right at the base of her neck.

Before either one of them could breathe even once, Rohan brought the knife to the spot just above his hand and started to cut. It was dirty work, but he was quick about it.

Whatever measurements the chips took, when Rohan pressed his thumb to the third chip, it lit up.

Savannah stood, towering over the strands of her hair that littered the floor. "Your turn."

Vicious winter girl. Rohan flipped the next poker chip. "Truth." He drew a white card but didn't even look at the question on it. "Why did you dare me to cut your hair?"

That wasn't the question he should have asked. There was no utility to asking it. And yet...

He wanted to hear her say it.

"Why not?" Savannah moved around the table, putting it between them.

Rohan placed his palms flat on the wood and leaned forward. "That's not a real answer, Savvy. Put your thumb on the chip."

Savannah leaned forward herself, doing no such thing. "My father liked my hair long." Her voice was flat, but he could see tension in the muscles where her arm met her shoulder. "And now what he likes or wants or expects no longer matters."

"Doesn't it?" Rohan wasn't sure why talking to Savannah Grayson always felt so much like fencing, why he couldn't resist parrying every one of her moves. "You are playing this game *for your father.* One way or another, he matters very much."

Rohan reached forward, took one of the hands she'd placed flat on the table, and turned it over, placing the chip on her palm. After a moment, her jaw clenched, and she placed her thumb on the chip.

"Tell me the real reason you dared me to cut your hair, Savvy—or explain exactly what you meant when you said that you are doing this *for your father.*"

In the silence that followed, one thing became clear: Savannah Grayson would have stared him into an early grave if she could have. "I dared you to cut my hair because *you* don't get to make me feel like that."

Rohan waited for the chip to light up. Nothing happened.

"That was the truth," Savannah said. "It should have lit up."

"Maybe the chip wants you to answer my other question. The one about your father."

Savannah's most glacial stare threatened to have the opposite effect on him. "You want an explanation, Rohan? Try this one: Money isn't the only thing you get if you win the Grandest Game."

And *that* caused the chip to light up.

Savannah flipped another one. "Truth. Who is the mutual acquaintance that you and Jameson Hawthorne share who is so fond of French?"

"Her name is Zella," Rohan said, settling his thumb on the chip. "She's a duchess. One who, for whatever reason, thinks that she can take something that is mine."

That wasn't just a truth. That was *the* truth of Rohan's life. The Mercy was his, and he *was* the Mercy. Without it, he was just a five-year-old boy drowning in dark water.

No one and nothing mattered more.

Rohan waited until the chip lit up, then flipped over another one. *Dare.* He drew a card. There was only one object left on the table, so he was utterly unsurprised when the image of the glass rose stared back at him.

What do the rest of the cards hold, then? Rohan sidelined that question and locked a hand around the glass rose. And then he held it out to Savannah. "Break it."

"Excuse me?"

He leaned over to lightly place the rose down on the table, right in front of her. "I see you, Savannah. The real you. The *angry* you." Rohan let his voice go low and rough. "Fire, not ice." He nodded toward the rose. "I dare you to break it."

"I'm not angry."

It was a good thing the chip he pressed into her palm wasn't for *truth*. "Scared to let go?" Rohan asked her. "You don't want to admit how angry you are," he said, his voice low and taunting, "because if you do, someone might ask why."

There were reasons for him to ask that went beyond wanting—almost needing—to know.

It was all connected. Why she was here. That anger. Her father. *What else does the winner of the Grandest Game receive, besides money?*

"I bet," Savannah said, calmly picking up the rose, "that no stranger has ever told you to smile." She paused. "Perhaps I'm angry because women like me don't *get* to be angry."

Rohan opened his mouth, but before he could say a word, Savannah turned and threw the glass rose as hard as she could.

It shattered into pieces.

"There you are, Savvy," Rohan murmured. *I see you.*

Chapter 60

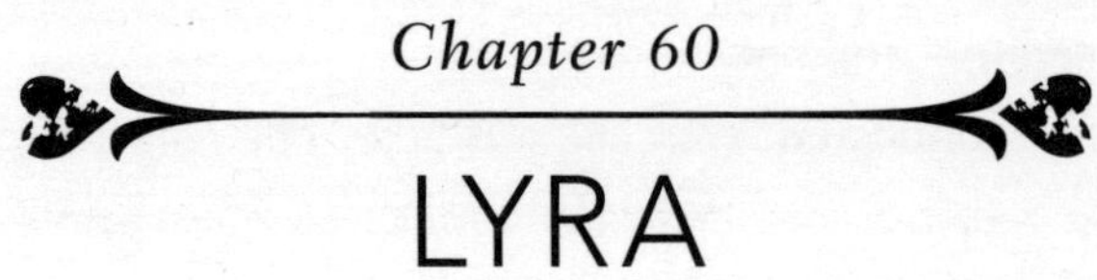

LYRA

"Oh, stop looking at me like that, you two," Odette said. "I was young."

"Let me guess," Grayson replied. "It was a lifetime ago—and how many lives?"

In lieu of responding, Odette hit a button on the projector, and the title card for *Changing Crowns* gave way to a scene—to a woman. Her hair was red. Her youth was palpable, her features both striking and *familiar.*

"You?" Lyra asked Odette.

"For a time, I was *Odette Mora*—not Morales." Odette paused the film once more. "They made me change that, just like they dyed my hair red the first time I stepped on a studio lot. I was nineteen, and I agreed to it all—the name change, the hair change, the less-than-ideal contract terms. My predator of a husband got me speaking roles in four movies before I left him. He tried to destroy me." Odette smiled that eagle-on-a-hunt, grandma-baking-cookies smile. "It didn't take. I booked a string of movies without him, a few very prominent roles, including *Changing Crowns*." She paused. "And then I stopped."

"Just like that?" Grayson said.

"I got pregnant." Odette clipped the words. "I was unmarried. I refused to *take care of the situation*, and that was the end. This was my last film."

It was on the tip of Lyra's tongue to ask Odette how she'd gone from Hollywood starlet to cleaning houses to law school—and eventually, somehow, to Tobias Hawthorne. But instead, Lyra couldn't help making an observation. "You dye the tips of your hair black now."

"Perceptive girl. I like the gray, personally—but also? Screw them for ever making me dye it red." Odette reached out and lightly touched Lyra's chin. "As a woman, I find it good for the soul to have a physical reminder of the people I've buried."

"Metaphorically buried," Grayson said. "Of course."

Odette didn't comment on that. "I was invited to play the Grandest Game," she said instead, "as one of the Hawthorne heiress's personal picks."

That makes two of us, Lyra thought. And both of them had connections to Tobias Hawthorne, to that List of his. That didn't strike Lyra as a coincidence.

"The game's architects knew that I would be playing when they designed these puzzles," Odette noted. "It appears as though they were also quite confident I would end up in *this* room. It makes one wonder, doesn't it, what else they arranged just so?"

Lyra thought about Jameson Hawthorne's wicked smile, back on the helipad. *Right after his brother heard my voice for the first time.*

"Did you ever mention me?" Lyra hadn't meant to ask Grayson

that, but she didn't back-pedal. "Or our phone calls? Did you tell your brothers or Avery—"

"No." Grayson's response was so immediate and so absolute that Lyra heard it like a slamming door.

Right, she thought. *Because what was there to mention?*

For a long moment, it seemed like Grayson might say something else, but instead, he crossed to the projector and hit Play. "I'd wager whatever we're looking for is in the first half—perhaps even the first quarter—of the film. We're on the clock, and the one universal trait of Hawthorne puzzles is that they are meant to be solved."

Lyra had no idea how much time they had left before dawn. Minutes and hours had lost all meaning. It felt like they had been locked in for days, but soon enough, one way or another, this night would end.

Soon enough, Lyra would never have to speak to or look at Grayson Hawthorne again.

Focus on the puzzle. Focus on the movie. Focus on getting out by dawn.

Within the first few scenes, it became apparent that *Changing Crowns* was a heist film, a royal romance, and one hundred percent an artifact of its time.

"You, sir, are a conman and a cad." Young Odette's voice was the same as her older counterpart's—exactly the same.

"I'm also a count," came the reply from the male lead. "And no concern of yours."

Odette is an actress. Scene after scene, Lyra considered the ramifications of that. Beside her, Grayson angled his lips downward, toward her ear.

"She's very good." His voice was just barely audible—and only to her.

Lyra kept her gaze locked on the screen and her words just as low as his. "Do you think she was lying?"

"About your father, my grandfather, or her health? No. However . . ."

However, Lyra thought, pushing down the incredible urge to look at him, *she volunteered that information right after you asked her about omega.*

The film skipped. Lyra wondered if she'd imagined it, and then it skipped again.

"Stop the movie," Lyra said, but Odette had already stopped it. The old woman expertly reeled the film back, then started manually moving it forward again, one frame at a time. Eventually, a letter popped up on the screen—a single frame inserted into the film. *O.*

"Keep going," Lyra said, the buzz of energy audible in her voice. At the next skip, there was another letter. *P.* A third frame gave them *E.*

"The next one is going to be an *N,*" Grayson predicted.

It was. Frame after frame, skip after skip, the letters kept coming. *T, H, E, D, R, A.*

Lyra's mind began filling in the blanks, but she bided her time and waited until she was sure.

W, E, R, S.

"*Open the drawers.*" Lyra's voice echoed through the theater. "What drawers?"

Like magic, a section of thick, velvety fabric fell away from the wall. Behind it, there were four drawers and an arching door with an ornate bronze knob. Inside each drawer, there was an object:

A lollipop.

A pad of sticky notes.

A light switch.

A paintbrush.

"There's writing on the knob," Grayson noted. Lyra crouched beside him to get a better look at the bronze doorknob. The metal bore only one word.

FINALE.

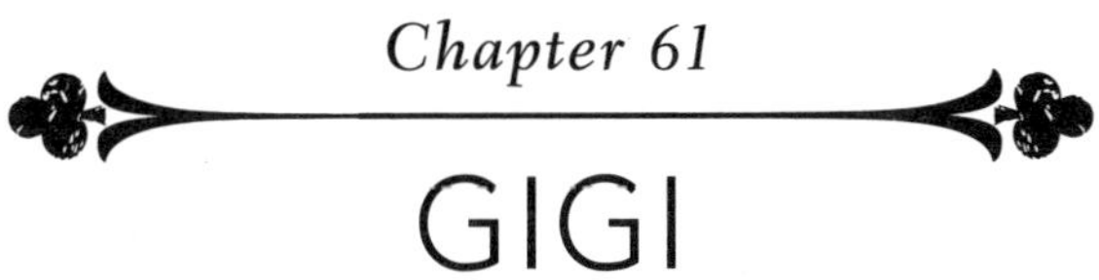

Chapter 61
GIGI

Twelve dollhouse books. Twelve numbers. A code. Gigi's brain raced like a hyperactive greyhound. *A substitution cipher? Numbers for letters?* The digits ranged from fifteen to one hundred sixty-two, with no repeats. *Coordinates? Some kind of combination?*

"Dewey decimal system?" Brady murmured beside her.

Knox crossed to the shelves and began examining row after row of books. "No numbers on the spines, no way to look them up."

Gigi picked up one of the tiny plastic dollhouse books and turned it in her hand. She spotted what *might* have been teeny tiny writing on the spine. A jolt of energy shot through her veins like eight cups of coffee—or a single mimosa.

"The magnifying glass!" Gigi ran to grab it. The ornate silver and gold handle was cool to the touch. Angling the glass toward the miniature book in her hand, Gigi was able to read the title. "*David Copperfield.*"

Brady crouched to gather the rest of the books, then joined

her, cradling all eleven of the remaining dollhouse books in his hands. Gigi took one of them from him, her fingers brushing his outstretched palm.

"*Rebecca*," Gigi read. And on it went: *Coraline*, *Anna Karenina*, *Carrie*, *Peter Pan*. *Matilda* and *Jane Eyre* and *Robinson Crusoe*.

"*King Lear*," Gigi said, and she wondered if she was imagining the way Brady's gaze lingered on her face. On her lips.

"They're all names." That was Knox. He wasn't looking at Gigi. He was looking at Brady. Hard.

Gigi focused on the books. The pattern held for the last two: *Oliver Twist* and *Emma*.

Twelve books. Twelve titles. All names. And numbers.

Gigi bounced lightly on her toes, thinking. "Why would they give us the titles?" She looked up—at the shelves overhead and all around them. "We're in the *library*." Her eyes widened. "Books and books. Little ones, big ones." She bounded for the shelf she'd searched earlier. "I think I remember seeing *Emma*."

"*Emma*," Brady murmured. "Number on the back is fifteen."

Gigi's brain took off like a rocket, and the second she found the real copy of *Emma*, she flipped to page fifteen.

And there it was.

Knox crossed the room to stand directly behind her and read over her shoulder. "Underlined words," he said. "Three of them."

"*Less*, *let*, and *looks*," Gigi read. She stated the obvious: "They all start with L." It took her five minutes to find another book from the list. "*Jane Eyre*."

"Thirty-four," Brady said without even having to look.

On page thirty-four of *Jane Eyre*, Gigi found five underlined words. "*Scarlet*, *china*, *candle*, *crib*, *scarecrow*," she reported.

"C." Brady's voice was low in volume, calm, sure.

Gigi looked back at him.

"The only letter that appears in all of those words," Brady Daniels, recognizer of patterns said, "is *C*."

"I've got *Rebecca*," Knox said from the other side of the room. "What's the page number?"

Brady answered, his voice clipped. "Seventy-two."

And so it went, book after book. The moment they decoded the last one, Gigi closed her eyes, pulling up the entire sequence in her mind.

L, C, R, E, E, T, I, H, B, P, O, M.

"Start by pulling the *T*, the *H*, and the *E*," Gigi said automatically. *The*. That left nine letters: *L, C, R, E, I, B, P, O*, and *M*.

"*Prime*?" Knox muttered. "Or *primo*?"

"*Rope*," Brady tried.

"*Rope*," Gigi repeated, opening her eyes to find his on her. "That leaves five letters." *L, C, I, B, M*. "*Climb*," she said.

Knox beat Brady to putting the phrase together. "*Climb the rope*."

The instant the words were spoken out loud, a stained-glass panel on the ceiling swung down like a trapdoor, creating an opening overhead.

And down fell a rope.

Chapter 62

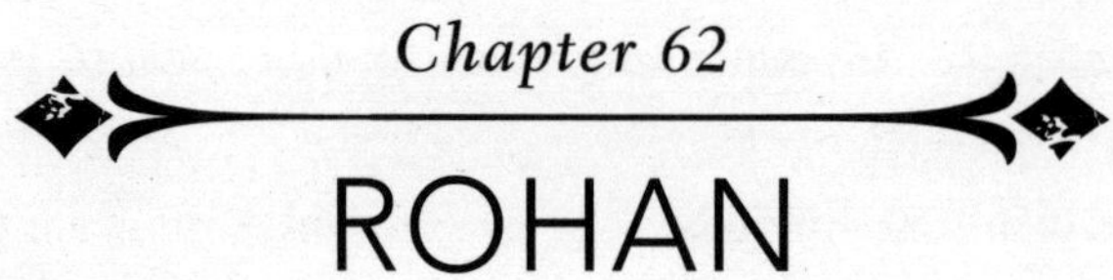

ROHAN

Rohan walked over to the panel on the wall and depressed the hint button, ensuring the game makers would hear him. "Our hint," he demanded. As far as Rohan was concerned, they'd earned it. *Three truths. The brush. The knife. Savannah's hair. The glass rose.*

"You know the card that says, 'this is not your clue'?" Avery's voice was back. "Take any of the *other* cards in the game deck for A Needle In A Haystack and hold it up to a torch."

The speakers went silent.

Savannah grabbed a blank card from the "haystack." Rohan grabbed another. They split, going to different torches, and Rohan wondered if Savannah *needed* to put space between them.

I don't get to make you feel like that? Like what, precisely, love? There were perfectly strategic reasons to want an answer to that question.

With the heat from the torch, invisible ink became visible on Rohan's card: *Say cheese.*

"A camera?" Savannah said, a sure indication that her card had borne the same message. "Or a mouse?"

Rohan tried a different tactic. "Cheese," he said.

There was a beeping sound, as the audio passcode registered, then one of the triangular room's walls began to rotate backward. It turned a full ninety degrees before clicking into place, part of a new wall in a much larger room.

More shelves. Rohan took in the room's expansion. *More games.* Fifteen feet from the poker table, there was a second recessed area cut into the floor, host to a Ping-Pong table. Rohan strode toward it and hopped down to examine the table, but in the depths of his mind, a different puzzle beckoned.

What besides money does a person get from winning the Grandest Game? Rohan ran a hand over the Ping-Pong table, searching every square inch of its surface. *Notoriety?*

At this rate, Savannah was going to need her own room in the labyrinth.

Careful, Rohan. He could still *feel* the moment the knife had cut through her hair, but there was no room in his plan—in any of his plans—for that kind of fascination. Nothing mattered more than winning.

He leapt out of the recessed area to examine the back wall, the only one in the room that wasn't covered in shelves. It was covered in Ping-Pong balls instead. Hundreds of them.

Rohan waved a hand over the wall, skimming the surface of ball after ball. "Savannah," he called. "Some of them rotate."

"Is there anything written on the balls that turn?" Savannah asked, seemingly all business as she made her way toward him and joined his search.

"Not that I can see," Rohan said. *But then, we couldn't see anything written on the cards, either.*

"Invisible ink again?" Savannah as good as read his mind. "I found one that rotates."

They continued on, rotating the loose balls until they clicked into place. Rohan half expected turning the last ball to trigger *something*—but no such luck.

"That leaves searching the games on the new shelves." Savannah gave every appearance of having shaken off the effects of Truth or Dare, every appearance of *control*. "I'll take this wall. You take—" She cut herself off and froze mid-stride. *"Rohan."*

The way she said his name killed him.

Remember who's playing who here, he cautioned himself.

"What is it?" Rohan said. As he made his way to her, he saw what Savannah saw: The shelves on the wall to the left of the Ping-Pong balls contained nothing but chess sets.

"Kings and queens," Savannah whispered. She reached for one of the boxes. Without her braid and all that hair, Rohan could make out the back of her neck, long lines, tension, and all.

He reached for a box of his own. "The crown and scepter clues are self-explanatory. As far as empty thrones go—"

Savannah cut him off. "We're looking for a set that's missing a king or a queen."

They got to work. No two chess sets were the same. There were pieces made of marble and glass, crystal and wood; boards that folded and boards that were bejeweled; simple sets and works of art; themed chess sets and children's chess sets and antiques.

And finally—*finally*—Rohan found one set that was missing a king. "Savvy." That was all he had to say, and Savannah was beside him, her long legs rendering the space that had separated them moments before obsolete.

Rohan removed the chess board from the box. The pieces were plastic, unremarkable. The board was exactly what you would expect of a cheap chess set, but that didn't stop Rohan from unfolding it and delivering pieces to their designated spots.

Savannah interjected herself into the process, and they worked in tandem—*his hands, hers, his again*—until all the pieces were on the board except for the missing king.

"There's our throne," Rohan said, nodding toward the empty square. "That, or its mirror on the other side."

Savannah reached forward and touched the square—and then she dragged a fingernail across its surface. The black on the square came off, like the surface of a scratch-and-win ticket.

Beneath, there was writing: *USE ME*.

Rohan lifted the board, sending the pieces scattering. He pushed against the square with his thumbs, and it popped out. Savannah's hand darted to catch it. She squeezed the square between her forefinger and her thumb, and it lit up with an eerie, purplish glow.

"A blacklight," Rohan murmured.

"The Ping-Pong balls," Savannah said beside him. "The ones we turned." *No hesitation.*

In an instant, they were at the back wall. "Shield them from the actual light with your hand, then try the blacklight," Rohan said.

She did. *They* did, and letters appeared one by one on the balls they'd rotated earlier, spelling out a Latin word.

"*Veritas*." Rohan said it out loud. There was a beep, and a section of the ball-covered wall separated from the rest. *A hidden compartment.* Inside there were four objects.

A lint roller.

A birthday card.

A vial of glitter.

An old-fashioned silk fan.

When they'd removed all the objects from the compartment, another, larger section of the Ping-Pong-ball wall swung outward like a door. Carved into the wooden floorboards where the wall had been a moment before, there was a single word. *FINALE*.

"One last puzzle." Savannah stepped up next to him, staring down at the word.

This stage of the game, this moment in time, was coming to an end. Soon the two of them would no longer be a team. She'd promised to destroy him. She'd promised to enjoy it. Rohan tended to believe her on both counts, which meant that if he wanted Savannah Grayson—as an asset—he would need to make his move.

"If you're about to propose another wager," Savannah said, "my answer is no." Her uneven, knife-cut hair made her look even more like a warrior wrapped in ice-blue silk. She still wore the lock and the chain around her waist, and if the weight of them was painful, she didn't seem to mind, any more than Rohan minded bloody knuckles.

"No more wagers," Rohan told her. "No more games." He'd come into this thinking of himself as a player and her as a game piece. But Rohan hadn't gotten to where he was by underestimating any opponent for long, and Savannah was far more than a queen.

She was a player, too. "I believe it's time," Rohan said, locking his eyes on to hers, "that you and I struck a deal."

Chapter 63

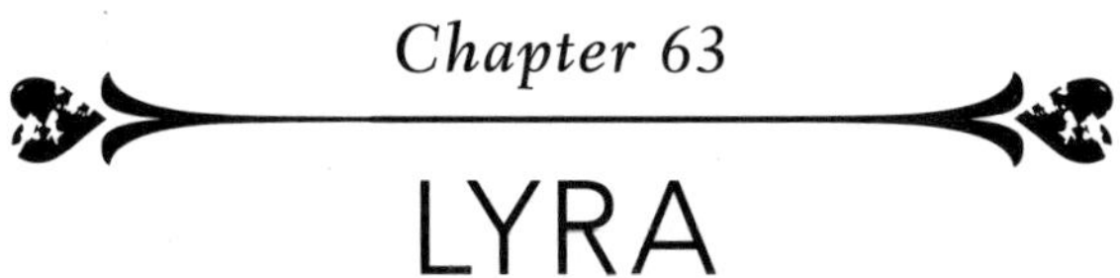

LYRA

Lyra stepped through the *FINALE* door into a massive room like none she'd ever seen. A tile mosaic covered the floor, the ceiling, the walls. A majority of the tiles were black, but every color imaginable made an appearance in the elaborate, twisting swirls of the mosaic.

"It's a ballroom," Grayson offered behind her.

Lyra made her way to the closest wall, pulled to it with almost magnetic force. She brought her hand to the surface of the mosaic, feeling each individual tile—so small, so perfectly set. How many millions of tiles had gone into making this room? *The ceiling. The floor. The walls—all except one.*

The back wall was made of glass.

Lyra stared out the wall of windows into velvety darkness. How long did they have until the first haze of soft morning light would appear? How long until the sun broke the horizon and ended this phase of the game?

Finale. This room—this puzzle—was the last.

Lyra made her way to the center of the room. The floor was smooth under her feet, the tiles laid so perfectly it felt like walking on wood. Directly overhead, there was a crystal chandelier.

Memory was a physical thing. *Back arching. His fingers, my thighs.*

"A ballroom is made for dancing," Odette commented.

Lyra banished the memory and looked down at her ball gown with its cascading blue layers. *Made for dancing.* "I don't dance anymore."

Part of her wanted to.

Part of her *ached* to.

But she put it in terms Odette would understand: "That was another life."

Lyra turned her focus to the pattern on the walls and floor: dark, mesmerizing spirals and swirls, each one unique. She paced the room, taking it all in.

"You never stopped dancing," Grayson said behind her. "Every time you move, you dance."

"I do not." Arguing with him was the easiest thing in the world.

"It's there in the way you hold your head, like there's music the rest of us can't hear." Grayson Hawthorne was a natural debater. "Every step you take, every twist, every turn, every pissed-off whirl."

He could have stopped there and won. He didn't.

"The way you stand," he continued mercilessly, "one foot slightly in front of the other. The way you lift your heels off the ground when you're deep in thought, like it's everything you can do not to rise all the way to the tips of your toes. The spread of your fingers when your hands hang loose by your side. The lines of your body when you stretch those hands overhead."

The chandelier, Lyra thought.

"Believe me, Lyra Kane." Grayson's voice was deeper now. "You never stopped dancing."

How the hell was she supposed to argue with that? How was she supposed to *exist* in a world—let alone a locked ballroom—with Grayson Hawthorne saying things like that?

You won't be locked in with him much longer. Lyra tried to take comfort in that, but it hurt—not a sharp pain, not even a new one. The idea of this night ending hurt like a once-broken bone, long-healed, that ached every time the weather turned.

The kind that might never stop aching.

Lyra laid her palm against the tiles on the wall and began to search it the way Grayson had the fireplace in the Great Room.

"There could be something to the pattern." Grayson came to join her at the wall, setting the longsword on the ground at their feet.

Lyra took a step back—from the wall, from the sword, from him. "What about the objects?" She turned abruptly toward Odette as the old woman began laying their objects out on the mosaic floor.

The lollipop.

The sticky notes.

The paintbrush.

The light switch.

"We started this game with a collection of objects," Odette noted, "and I seem to recall our Mr. Hawthorne being quite certain that one of those objects would be a clue to start us off."

"Yes, well, doubt has never been my strong suit." Grayson's gaze cheated toward Lyra's. "But if this *is* a more typical Hawthorne puzzle than the first was, we'll want to think of unconventional uses for each object." He nodded to the lollipop. "Take that."

The face of the lollipop was flat, circular, and larger in diameter than Lyra's fist. The stick was long and sturdy.

"There could be a code built into the swirling of the candy," Grayson continued, "something that identifies a specific portion of the mosaic. Or perhaps we're meant to discard the lollipop and use only the plastic wrapping that covers it."

Lyra moved to stand a little farther from him, directly over the objects, keenly aware of the way she moved and the way he watched her.

She knelt to eye the wrapping on the lollipop. "The nutritional info—"

"—could contain a hidden message or code," Grayson finished. He knelt beside her. "Or perhaps the lollipop's stick is the important part, and, at some juncture, we'll find ourselves faced with a button that needs pressing and a gap too small for our fingers to fit through."

"And these?" Lyra gestured broadly to the remaining three objects.

The light switch consisted of a panel, two screws, and a switch, all attached to a metal block with more screws. The entire thing looked like it had been plucked straight from a wall.

The sticky notes were standard size and square, the color shifting the farther down the pad you went, starting with purple and ending in red—a reverse rainbow.

"How many uses could there possibly be for sticky notes?" Lyra said.

"You'd be surprised." A person could have written a book about all the ways that Grayson Hawthorne could almost-but-not-quite smile.

"Do any of them involve a cello case, a longsword, a crossbow, and a calico kitten?" Lyra asked dryly.

Grayson *actually* smiled then, and Lyra wished that he hadn't. She really, really wished that he hadn't.

"What can I say?" Grayson told her. "I had an unconventional childhood."

A Hawthorne childhood, Lyra reminded herself. Even setting aside everything else—*blood, death, omega; a Hawthorne did this; stop calling*—the simple truth of it was that Lyra and Grayson Hawthorne were from two different worlds.

She fixed her gaze on the final object. The paintbrush looked like something from a children's watercolor set. The handle was green, the bristles black. Grayson reached forward and tested the handle, trying to unscrew it to no effect.

"We could try brushing it over the paper," Lyra said, her focus damn near close to legendary. "Or the walls."

"A worthwhile pursuit," Grayson told her. "Right after we flip that switch."

Lyra flipped it. Nothing happened. She tried the brush on the paper, then staunchly started in on the walls. Grayson fell in beside her. Behind them, Lyra heard Odette pick up one of their objects.

Probably examining it with her opera glasses. Lyra didn't turn around. She just kept at it with the brush, unable to keep her eyes from going to Grayson's hands.

His fingers were long and dexterous, his knuckles pronounced. The skin of his hands was smooth, the muscles leading to his wrists defined. There was a single scar, a subtle crescent moon beneath the nail bed on his right thumb.

Lyra focused on the brush and the wall. "I had a very conventional childhood." She stared at the mosaic so hard her vision blurred. "Ballet. Soccer. Running in the woods, splashing in the creek." Lyra pressed her lips together. "That's why I'm here."

Was she reminding herself or telling him?

"Because of your *conventional* childhood?" Grayson tapped the index and middle fingers on his right hand against a section of deep blue tiles well within his reach and almost out of hers.

Lyra rose to her toes, swiping the paintbrush over the tiles he'd indicated. *Nothing.* "My dad—my actual dad, who raised me—he owns land," Lyra said. "And a house. *Mile's End.*" She closed her eyes, just for a moment. "It's like no place else on earth, and he might have to sell."

"You're doing this for your family," Grayson said—not a question.

Lyra tightened her grip over the handle of the brush. "We're getting nowhere."

"Lyra."

She thought at first, just from his tone, that Grayson had seen something in the mosaic, but when Lyra turned her head toward him, she realized that he wasn't looking at the *mosaic*.

"I was wrong." Grayson sounded as sure of that as he did of absolutely everything else.

Lyra tried and failed to look away. "About the objects?"

"No." *Grayson Hawthorne and the word* no. "Seventeen months ago, you came to me for help."

Lyra couldn't let him say another word. If he'd never buried his hands in her hair, if he hadn't been the one to pull her from that flashback, to anchor her *here*, it might have been different. But Lyra couldn't do this.

Not now. Not on the verge of all of this ending. Not after he'd told her that every time she moved, she danced.

"Forget about it," Lyra bit out. "It doesn't matter. Just concentrate on the game."

"I excel at multitasking." Grayson sank to the place where the wall met the floor and ran his hand along the seam, looking up at her like he might never look away. "And last year, when I told you to stop calling—I didn't mean it."

Chapter 64

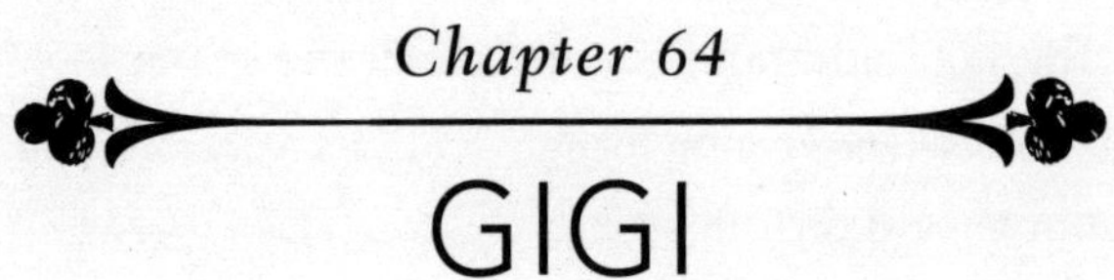

GIGI

Gigi shimmied up the rope like a person with actual biceps. It wasn't a feat of athleticism so much as an energy-fueled, near-incandescent *need* to see what came next. As her hand latched around thick, solid stained glass, she could feel someone starting to climb the rope behind her, but she didn't look back at Brady and Knox.

She pulled herself through the hole and climbed to her feet.

The attic—if you could call it that—was shaped like a pyramid, maybe eight feet tall at its highest point and lit along every edge. All four of its walls were made of glass. *The very top of the house.* Gigi pictured the roofline—and then she looked out into the night. "It's so dark outside."

"Not for long." Knox effortlessly pulled himself up and in, Brady—with the longsword somehow strapped to his back—coming next.

"We have, at most, two and a half hours until dawn," Brady commented.

Two and a half hours, Gigi thought, *until this, with the three of us, is over.*

She placed her hand on the ocean-side pane and ran her fingers over the word carved into the surface of the glass. *FINALE*.

"Here." Brady squatted. "There's a loose pane in the floor." He lifted a large stained-glass square and began pulling objects out of the compartment beneath.

A pair of sunglasses.

A roll of wrapping paper.

A ball of a yarn.

A bottle of nail polish remover.

"One of these has to contain a clue about what we're supposed to do next," Gigi said intently. The wrapping paper boasted unicorns and rainbows. The sunglasses were black with rhinestones. The yarn was multicolor—a rainbow, just like the paper.

Brady unscrewed the cap of the nail polish remover and took a whiff. "Smells like acetone," he confirmed. "Or something with a very similar chemical composition."

"This is the part where he rattles off a chemical formula," Knox said, putting on the sunglasses.

"The rhinestones really bring out your eyes," Brady deadpanned.

Gigi unrolled the wrapping paper and scoured it for some kind of clue: a unicorn that didn't fit with the rest, a rainbow missing a color, hidden letters or numbers, a variation in the pattern. When she was done with her examination, she flipped the paper over.

The back side was solid red.

Knox took off the sunglasses. "Nothing written on the inside," he reported briskly. "The lenses appear to be normal lenses."

Gigi grabbed the ball of yarn and started unraveling it on the off chance that there was something hidden at its center. *Nothing.* She turned her attention to the attic room. The floor was made of stained glass. The walls and ceiling were transparent. There was nothing in the room but the objects they'd already found.

Gigi knelt to examine the stained glass. None of the other panels were loose—but the trapdoor was still open. "Every other time we moved to a new room, we lost access to the old one," she said out loud. She made a snap decision. "Bombs away!"

Gigi dropped back down to the library. Knox cursed, but he followed her, and so did Brady.

Gigi took in the room around them. "It's gone," she whispered. *The Victorian mansion and the castle. Every last doll. Every last accessory. Every last everything.* And that wasn't all.

The bookshelves were bare.

"How is this even possible?" Brady said. "We were gone under two minutes."

"I know this one." Gigi raised a hand. "There are actually two sets of shelves positioned back-to-back, built to rotate." Gigi placed her hands together, palm against palm, to demonstrate. "We went up, they spun the bookshelves, swapping in the empty ones. And bonus—those empty shelves have a little something extra."

Symbols, carved into the wood.

The three of them spent the next hour trying to decode those symbols, looking for patterns. There were easily fifty different emblems carved into the bare shelves. Some shapes repeated. Others didn't. Gigi worked her way through each and every one.

A starburst, a heptagon, the does-not-equal sign, the letter G, the number 9, a sun…

"What's going on inside that mind of yours?" Brady came to stand shoulder to shoulder with Gigi, peering at the symbols she'd been trying to stare into submission for the past five minutes.

"Chaos," Gigi replied honestly. "Pretty much always."

Brady's lips curved. "Remind me to tell you later about chaos theory."

"Tell me something about it now." Gigi moved down the line and looked at the next symbol: zigzagging lines, stacked one on top of another. *A wave?*

"Something about chaos theory?" Brady considered that—and her. "Let's see…Initial conditions. Strange attractions. Fractal geometry."

"Give it a rest," Knox snapped on the other side of the room.

"Or what?" Brady replied. "There is no chain of command here, Knox. I'm not fifteen anymore, and we're not brothers."

That sucked the oxygen out of the room. Brady didn't so much as check Knox's reaction, but Gigi did. *Wounded eyebrows.*

"Fine." Knox's tone was bladed and unwavering. "You two keep flirting about chaos theory. I'm going back up."

Knox went for the rope. For reasons Gigi couldn't even begin to understand, she followed. By the time she pulled herself through the trapdoor and to a standing position, Knox had already claimed all four of their objects.

"What is your problem?" Gigi demanded.

"My problem?" Knox didn't even bother to turn around. "This team. Brady. *You.*"

"Growl all you want, honey badger," Gigi told him. "You don't scare me."

"Why would I want you scared?" Knox replied. "The more strategic move would be to win your trust and use that to my advantage. It's a good thing I'm so personable, isn't it, Happy?"

It was the use of the nickname that got to Gigi. "Why did you do it?" she asked.

"Do what?" Knox said tersely.

"Last year." Gigi looked down. "Why did you take a deal with Orion Thorp?" Knox didn't answer, so Gigi rephrased. "With Calla's father?"

"Brady told you . . . something."

"He told me all of it," Gigi said.

Knox looked down at the objects he'd come up here to fetch: the wrapping paper, the nail polish remover, the sunglasses, the yarn. "Calla wasn't taken. She ran away."

"Brady said—"

"Calla *left*." Knox's voice went guttural, but when he spoke again, it was in a dispassionate tone. "She wasn't abducted. Her family isn't holding her captive somewhere. She's not missing. She didn't meet with foul play. And I know that, because the night before Calla *left*, she came to me to say good-bye."

Gigi stared at him. "Why wouldn't you tell Brady that?" She paused. "Why would you tell me that?"

"Maybe I'm not just telling you." Knox turned and jerked his head toward the front of her dress. *The bug.* "The Thorps aren't the only game in town, and Orion Thorp isn't the only member of his family who likes to play. I don't know who's listening, but maybe I'll say something to spark their interest and they'll make me a more competitive offer."

Money. That was what Knox wanted her to believe this was

about, but Gigi's gut said that he'd told her because he wanted her to know that he wasn't all bad.

Knox doesn't let people in, Brady had said.

"Why wouldn't you tell Brady that Calla said good-bye?" Gigi said, quietly repeating her question. "Why would you tell me?"

"Maybe I'm telling you because I *can't* tell him." Knox shifted the objects to one hand as he lifted the other to the collar of his dress shirt. "And I have never and will never tell Brady, because Brady couldn't even begin to understand a Calla Thorp good-bye."

Knox pulled his collar roughly down, baring the skin at the base of his neck—and a white, puckered, triangular scar.

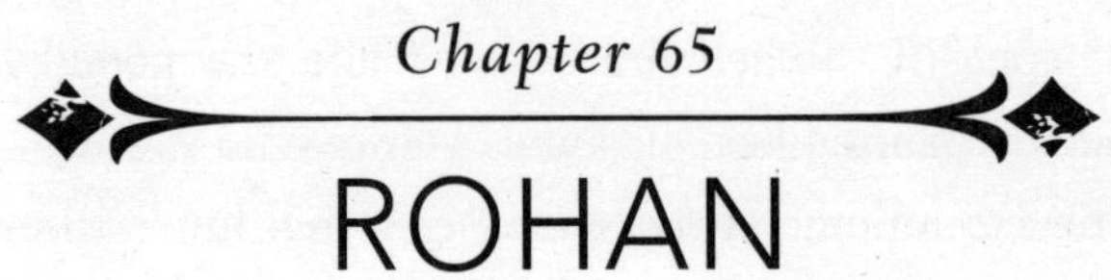

Chapter 65
ROHAN

"What kind of deal are you proposing?" Savannah asked.

A good sign, that. "You implied that you are playing this game for something other than the prize money," Rohan noted, "whereas I am interested *only* in the money."

"No deal." Savannah tried to step past him, into the next room. Their final room.

Rohan blocked her, leaving them standing very close. "You haven't heard my terms."

"Are you suggesting that you would help me win, then willingly step back and allow me to claim victory under the mere promise that I would then give the money to you?" Savannah wore her skepticism like a crown. "You don't trust me that much, Rohan—or at all."

And there was the rub. "Then perhaps the deal is this," Rohan countered. "We agree to work together on the next phase of the game—to a point." Rohan had struck his first deal with the Proprietor—with the Mercy—when he was five years old. If there was one thing he knew, it was how to bargain with the devil. "Once you and I have dispatched the competition in whatever phase or phases come next, once the Grandest Game is nearly won..." He flashed his teeth in the kind of smile that he hoped reminded Savannah of hands fisted in hair, of grips that were just a little painful. "At that point, we're free to do everything in our power to take each other down."

In the end, he would win—no matter what lines he had to cross to do it.

"You said that you would enjoy destroying me, love." Rohan smiled. "Consider the feeling mutual."

"An alliance where the end goal is betrayal." Savannah studied him for the longest time. "How novel."

"It's not betrayal," Rohan said, hyperaware of every place that her body almost touched his, "if we both go into this with open eyes."

"Believe me, British." Savannah leaned forward. "My eyes are open." Savannah pushed past him, stepping over the *FINALE* threshold. Rohan followed, turning sharply to what it soon became apparent was a hallway lined with mirrors.

He could see Savannah from every side. *Angles. Curves. Power.*

The mirrored hall let out into another room—a large one. The first thing Rohan saw was the mats on the floor, marked off just so. Propped against the closest wall were two sabers, two masks, two white jackets with metal overlay.

"Fencing," Rohan said. *How very appropriate.*

"Swordplay." Savannah looked from the sabers to the sword in Rohan's hand to his face, then strode to the far side of the room—a rock-climbing wall. She said not a single word as she began to climb, vintage silk gown and all.

Rohan noted, with some appreciation, that she hadn't parted with the three objects she'd claimed from the prior room: the silk fan, the vial of glitter, and the lint roller. She held them *and* managed to climb.

That left Rohan with the birthday card and the longsword. "That makes three swords in this game now, total," he called. "There could be something to that."

He examined the blades on the sabers. Unlike the longsword, they bore no writing. Rohan tested the weight of each of the sabers, then tried on each of the masks, before turning the jackets inside out.

"If you really wanted me to consider making a deal," Savannah called down to him, pulling herself to the top of the wall, "you'd offer me the longsword in exchange. Don't think I haven't noticed the way you guard that thing. Your body is always conveniently in between it and me."

Rohan thought he'd been subtler than that. "You're still wearing the lock and chain," he countered. "Despite the fact that it's served *a* purpose in the Grandest Game by foreshadowing the nature of the game, you cannot be sure it's served its *only* purpose. Do you blame me for hedging my bets with the sword?"

"I'm fully capable of blaming you for everything," Savannah said. "What do you make of the wall behind you?"

Is this a test, Savvy? Rohan turned. The wall in question appeared to be an enormous whiteboard. An intricate maze had been drawn upon its surface, with three end points:

A checkerboard.

A hangman's noose.

And another game, a simple one.

“*X*’s and *O*’s.” Savannah scaled down the wall and strode toward him. “Tic-Tac-Toe.”

“Also known as *Noughts And Crosses*,” Rohan murmured. He looked to the checkerboard, which was set to play, its pieces, like the *X*’s and *O*’s, magnetic.

“Games on the wall. Rock climbing. Swords.” Savannah kept her summary of their surroundings brief.

“A lint roller,” Rohan added. “A birthday card. A vial of glitter. And a silk fan.” He opened the card, and music began to play—instrumental, the song familiar.

Opposite him, Savannah opened the fan. The stiff silk fabric was a dark, midnight blue, and there was a word embroidered on it in shining, silver thread. *SURRENDER*.

Rohan read the word out loud.

Savannah looked from the fan back up to him. “Never.”

He was taken back to the base of the flagpole. Now, as then, what she’d just said sounded tantalizingly like a challenge.

“Some of us don’t find *surrender* all that sweet.” Rohan leaned forward, closer to her and then a little closer still. “Some of us prefer the fight. I am not asking you to *surrender*, Savannah Grayson. And if you think there won’t be other alliances coming out of this phase of the game . . .” Rohan played his trump card. “You clearly didn’t spend much time watching your brother and Lyra Kane.”

Half brother. Rohan anticipated the correction.

“Half brother.” And there it was.

Rohan waited. The ability to wait—in negotiation or in shadows—was one of his finest skills.

Savannah opened her mouth, but before she could say anything, darkness fell. Total, absolute darkness. *The lights in the room. The strings of fairy lights on the shore. All gone.*

There was a sound—the heater turning off.

"The plot thickens." Rohan let his voice surround her. "It appears the game makers have cut the power."

Chapter 66

LYRA

The sudden absence of light hit Lyra almost as hard as the words that refused to stop looping in her mind on gut-rending repeat. *Last year, when I told you to stop calling—I didn't mean it.*

Of course he'd meant it. He was Grayson Hawthorne, and she was nobody. What did her tragedy matter to him? What did *she* matter?

And yet.

And yet.

And yet.

"Lyra." Grayson's voice was close in the darkness. "You're okay?" He made that question sound more like a command: She *would* be okay, because he wouldn't allow her to be anything else.

"I'm not scared of the dark," Lyra told him. "I'm..." She almost said *fine*, but that word felt loaded now. "I'm just dandy."

"I'm not," Odette said, strain audible in her voice. "*Just dandy.*"

Lyra remembered the old woman's earlier pain, remembered that she was dying.

"What's going on? Tell us your symptoms," Grayson ordered.

"My symptoms include a tightness in my jaw, increased heart rate, and a desire to use foul language in particularly creative combinations."

"You're angry," Lyra realized. *Not in pain—or at least, not any more pain than you're used to.*

"We were given a certain allotment of time to complete this challenge," Odette replied, "and now, it is suddenly clear that the time we thought we had left before dawn was an illusion—a twist befitting of a Hawthorne game, is it not? Misdirection and illusions in place of truth."

Lyra thought suddenly about Odette saying that Tobias Hawthorne was the best and worst man she'd ever known.

"Had this outage been planned," Grayson said slowly, "we would have been given a hint foreshadowing its occurrence—in the metal room, perhaps, or straight from the beginning. We would have puzzled over some cryptic line or clue, and the moment the lights went out, everything would have made sudden, crystalline sense. But this? It's senseless, and I assure both of you, that is one thing that Hawthorne games are not."

Listening to Grayson, it was impossible for Lyra not to believe him—about the game and about everything else. *Last year, when I told you to stop calling—I didn't mean it.*

"The emergency and hint buttons," Lyra said, the words coming out thicker than she meant for them to. "Do they still work?"

"I'll try them," Grayson said—but Lyra beat him to it, moving through the dark like it was nothing, finding the buttons, pressing them.

There was no response.

"The radio's out," Grayson concluded. "I told you—this wasn't planned."

"Perhaps not by your brothers or Ms. Grambs," Odette said. There was something understated in her tone, something soft and deeply concerning.

"Speak plainly, Ms. Morales." Grayson ordered through the darkness.

"Layers upon layers." Odette's voice never changed—not in volume, not in pitch, not in emphasis or pacing. "In the grandest of games, there are no coincidences."

She hadn't said *the Grandest Game*. She'd said *the grandest of games*—like they were two different things.

"The house." Odette clipped the words. "This room. The locking mechanisms, the elaborate chain reactions—they aren't entirely manual, are they? They require power."

"Yes," Grayson said, and Lyra translated that Grayson Hawthorne *yes*.

This time, they really were locked in—and it *wasn't* a part of the master plan.

Chapter 67

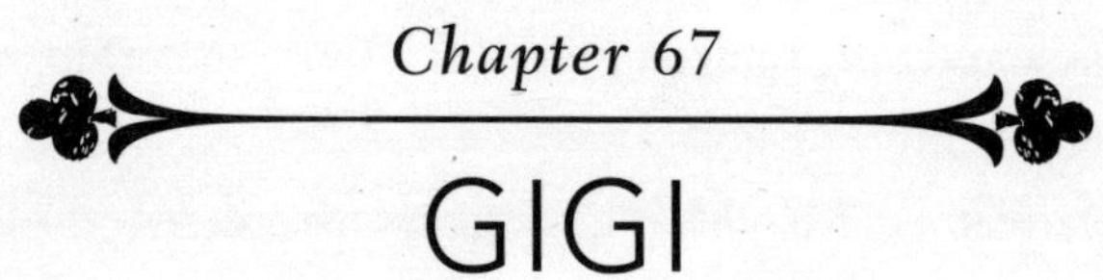

GIGI

Stay put," Knox ordered Gigi. "Stand still and try not to kill yourself."

The next thing Gigi heard through the darkness was the sound of Knox dropping down through the trapdoor. Seconds later, Gigi heard heated words being exchanged below, but she couldn't make them out. Her brain helpfully superimposed what Knox had said earlier over whatever argument he and Brady were having now.

I have never and will never tell Brady, because Brady couldn't even begin to understand a Calla Thorp good-bye. Gigi thought about the scar at the base of Knox's neck. She thought about Brady saying that no one shot a bow like Calla.

And then she thought about Brady telling Knox they weren't brothers.

Standing there—in darkness, alone—Gigi's mind went to the bug and the fact that if someone was listening, they were getting a real show. She looked out into the night.

There were no signs of a storm, nothing that would have knocked out the power. Maybe this was a part of the game. Maybe the game makers had planned this, but deep down, Gigi didn't believe that.

She believed that someone else was on the island. *The Thorps aren't the only game in town*, Knox had said, after jerking his head toward the bug. *And Orion Thorp isn't the only member of his family who likes to play.*

Gigi's hand came to rest on the outside of her thigh. Her gown was thick enough that she couldn't feel the knife underneath. *What if the power was cut?*

She fished the bug out of the front of her dress. Three breaths later, she spoke. "I know you're out there."

Silence.

"I know you're out there," she said again.

Silence, again—and then a familiar, if tinny, voice: "No, sunshine, you don't."

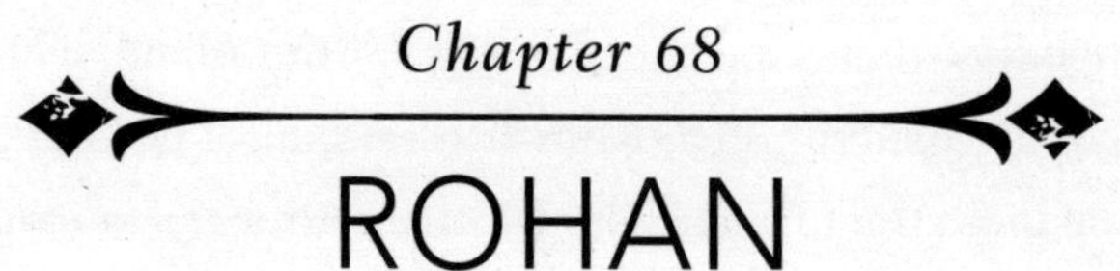

Chapter 68

ROHAN

A lack of light did little to impede Rohan's search of the room—in particular, the floorboards and walls. In a game of his design, if the lights had gone out, especially this close to the end of the game, it would have been because he'd hidden a flashlight for the players to find.

A challenge.

A twist.

A way of turning up the heat.

And yet... Savannah *wasn't* searching. Rohan listened for her movements—they were slight, targeted. She was giving their objects a thorough examination. He listened harder. The fan opened, and the fan closed.

You're not looking for a button or a switch, are you, love? You aren't looking for a light source at all.

Rohan had been taught from a young age to question every assumption, to come at problems from every angle. "You know what

I find fascinating, Savvy? Tells." He allowed her exactly one second to ponder that. "A sudden lack of motion. Too much eye contact. Too little. A tightening of the throat or shoulders. A change in pitch. The slightest flex in one specific muscle in the cheek. Even the way a person stacks their chips can tell me everything I need to know."

Rohan paused again, listening for the sound of her breathing through the darkness.

"The fact that you are not searching for a light source, or even a button or switch on those objects, is a tell."

"Of what?"

"Nicely paced reply," Rohan murmured, "just enough challenge in your tone. But the body never lies, love."

"You can't see my body. And don't call me *love*."

"That took you a quarter-second too long, Savvy. You don't believe the power outage is part of the game."

Silence.

"Tell me I'm wrong," Rohan challenged.

He could practically *hear* the arch of her brow through the dark. "If I told you every time you were wrong about something, there would hardly be time for anything else."

Rohan recognized deflection when he heard it. His brain connected the dots—one after another after another. "Are you aware," he said, testing her, "that some players in this game have sponsors?" No reply from Savannah. "Perhaps *your* sponsor calls it something different."

Silence.

"You were one of the Hawthorne heiress's personal picks for this game," Rohan continued, "so whoever approached you would have had a very narrow window of time in which to do so."

"I haven't the faintest idea what you're talking about." That she'd replied at all, let alone with a bluff that weak, he took as a sign to push a little more.

"Now, *why* would your sponsor kill the power? Surely it's not just to distract the other teams while you stay focused. To distract the game makers, perhaps? But from what, exactly? And how?"

There were few things Rohan's mind loved more than interlocking questions. Solve one, and the answers became apparent, all the way down.

Savannah was doing this *for her father.*

Rohan wasn't there—yet. But with each second that passed, he could feel himself getting a little closer. In the meantime...

"A less scrupulous individual than myself," he told Savannah, "might be considering a bit of blackmail right now, but I have no interest in gaining your *compliance.*" Rohan took a step toward her, and he made sure it was audible. "I am not looking for an obedient little piece to move around the board, Savvy."

Not anymore.

"I am looking," Rohan continued, with another, audible step, "for an alliance. A partner."

"I reject the premise that you have anything to blackmail me with." Now it was Savannah's turn to take a single, threatening step toward him. "I'm Grayson Hawthorne's sister. I will get the benefit of every doubt. And you broke Jameson's ribs. Do you really think Avery Grambs has forgotten that? That she'll listen to or believe you over me? Based on what? The fact that I didn't play this game your way in the dark?"

"Half sister," Rohan said.

"Excuse me?"

"You're Grayson Hawthorne's half sister," Rohan murmured, "as you're so very fond of pointing out." He could have pushed harder there, but he didn't. As he'd told Savannah, he had no interest in coercing her into anything.

"Since there's no need to look for a light..." Rohan took that as a given. "Perhaps we should focus on something else?" He took care of the remaining space between them and brought his hand to her left hand—and the object she held in it. *The vial of glitter.*

Wrapping his fingers lightly around hers, Rohan spoke: "The fan is in your other hand, and the lint roller is tucked into the chain around your waist, isn't it?"

"Why ask if you are already so convinced that you know everything?"

"Put the fan down for the moment."

He was fully prepared to be told to go to hell, but she must have wondered what he was up to, because a moment later, Rohan heard her slip the fan into the chain.

He reached for Savannah's free hand, then coaxed her fingers into exploring the vial as his did the same. "This vial is made of glass." In the darkness, Savannah made no attempt to shrug off his touch. "The cork at the top is made of rubber," Rohan noted. "There's a raised emblem on it."

"A star."

"The cork could function as a stamp if we could find something to use as an inkpad," Rohan murmured. "Or it could work as a key for a certain kind of lock."

"There might be something hidden inside the glitter." Savannah was not the type to let someone else take the reins for long.

"Or perhaps," Rohan countered, his voice low and heady, "what we really need is the vial. Glass can break. Shards are sharp." He thought about the glass rose and the hourglass and wondered if she was doing the same.

I see you, Savannah Grayson, even in the dark.

"The lint roller is the disposable kind with sticky sheets that tear off." Savannah's tone was remarkably even, but Rohan still knew: He almost had her.

We're better together, love. And above all, you want to win. You need *to.*

"What do you think would happen," Rohan said, "if we unrolled the sheets?"

"What did the inside of the birthday card say?" Savannah shot back.

So demanding. "Happy birthday," Rohan reported. He used his free hand to fetch the card from his tuxedo jacket and opened it, allowing the music to fill the air. "'Clair de Lune,'" Rohan told her, and then he translated the song's name: "Moonlight."

Savannah's body shifted, and Rohan felt movement in the air. *The fan.* She'd retrieved it from the chain and opened it once more. Rohan called an image of the fan up in his mind, moonlit thread against deep navy silk, and a single word: *SURRENDER*.

"Close the fan," Rohan told Savannah. "Partway. Slowly." She started to do exactly that, and he brought his hands to hers once more. "Bit by bit by bit."

Rohan wasn't a novice when it came to his own body's responses or the effect his touch could have on others. He'd done far more things—and far more creative things—in the dark than this. It defied all logic that touching Savannah Grayson's *hands* could feel like an earthquake inside of him, like he was exploring *her* bit by bit by bit.

"Stop," Rohan said. Savannah stopped. Rohan ran his fingers along the embroidered letters on the fan, some of them now obscured.

"And so," Rohan murmured, "*surrender* becomes *sunder*."

"*Sunder.* To split apart." Savannah didn't miss a beat. "To sever. To rend. To rip. That's our clue. That's where we start. We sunder the fan." She paused, and Rohan read into that—not hesitation but *consideration*.

He allowed his fingers to skim the back of her hand, knuckle to knuckle to wrist, and he told himself he had full control. Strategy and want, after all, didn't have to be mutually exclusive.

"You want an alliance." Savannah's words seemed to live in the space between them. He could feel them, feel her. "I want the longsword."

"To sunder the fan?" Rohan said immediately. "Or for later?"

"Does it matter?"

Rohan allowed himself to lean forward and whisper in her ear. "Everything matters, Savvy—until nothing does."

That was the truth. It was also a warning. And a promise. *I will betray you. You will betray me.* Winning was the only thing that would matter in the end.

"I'm keeping the sword," Rohan said. "And you're going to work with me anyway."

He counted three seconds of silence before she spoke again. "Lift the blade," Savannah said. "Now."

Another tell. Rohan pulled the sword and, with a counterclockwise turn of his wrist, brought it vertical in an instant. He felt the exact moment that Savannah pressed the silk fan into the blade. The fabric began to tear.

"Rohan?" Savannah sundered the fan. "We have a deal."

Chapter 69

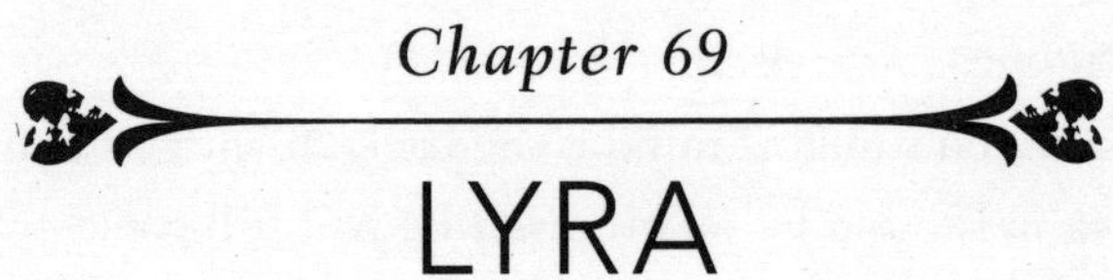

LYRA

"I don't like this," Grayson said darkly. "They should have the power back up by now."

"Thinking of breaking a window, Mr. Hawthorne?" Odette's voice was dry.

No, Lyra thought reflexively. *He's not.*

"If there's a threat out there," Grayson said, "we're safer in here. This house is highly secure."

Secure. Lyra's heart rate ticked up. *A threat.*

Odette was silent for a moment before she spoke again. "We aren't safer locked in if there's a fire."

Another fire. Lyra thought about her first impression of Hawthorne Island—the charred trees, the ghosts of the past.

"Do you have reason to believe that there is going to be a fire?" Grayson demanded.

"Perhaps old age is making me paranoid." Odette paused. "Or perhaps it's what I see when I look at the two of you. The right kind of disaster just waiting to happen. A Hawthorne and a girl who has every reason to stay away from Hawthornes."

She's talking about omega. Lyra felt that in the pit of her stomach. *About my father's death. About Tobias Hawthorne.*

"I'm sure you wouldn't mind elaborating," Grayson said, his tone pure steel.

Odette chose utter silence instead.

"*A Hawthorne did this,*" Lyra said hoarsely. "That's what she's talking about. That's what my father said, right before the riddle, right before he killed himself. That's why I have every reason to stay away from Hawthornes."

"*A Hawthorne did this,*" Odette repeated. "Lyra, your father—he said those exact words?"

"He did."

"I know," Grayson said, "that my grandfather could very easily cross the line into viewing people as cogs in a machine, as levers to be pulled, a means to his ends."

"Neither one of you knows what you think you know." Odette's voice was sharp. "The tr—" Her voice cut off mid-word. There was a thud—a loud one. *Her body, hitting the floor.*

Lyra bolted forward, heedless of the dark, but somehow, Grayson made it to Odette first. "She's having a seizure." Grayson's voice sliced through the dark. "I'm turning her on her side. I've got you, Ms. Morales."

The sound of the old woman's body jerking against the floor suddenly ceased. There was total, *awful* silence. A breath caught in Lyra's throat.

"I've got you," Grayson repeated.

"You would think so, Mr. Hawthorne." Odette's voice was hoarse. Relief shot through Lyra.

And an instant later, the lights came on.

"Sorry 'bout that, folks." Nash Hawthorne's Texas drawl sounded from hidden speakers. "Brief technical snafu on our end, but we're back. You still have sixty-three minutes until dawn. As long as at least one team makes it down to the dock by the deadline, the rules stand."

Make it out by dawn or leave the competition.

"Lyra," Grayson said. "The emergency button. We need—"

"Nothing." Odette pushed herself roughly up to a sitting position and fixed Grayson with a powerful, obstinate stare. "You heard your brother. The show goes on."

Whatever Odette had been about to say before her seizure, she gave no signs of confessing it now. She was seemingly intent on playing and winning—and nothing else—once more.

Neither one of you knows what you think you know. Lyra closed her eyes and calmed her body. *The right kind of disaster just waiting to happen.*

Lyra opened her eyes, her brain drinking in the moment and identifying the most logical way forward. *To the dock. To answers.* "I say we take our hint."

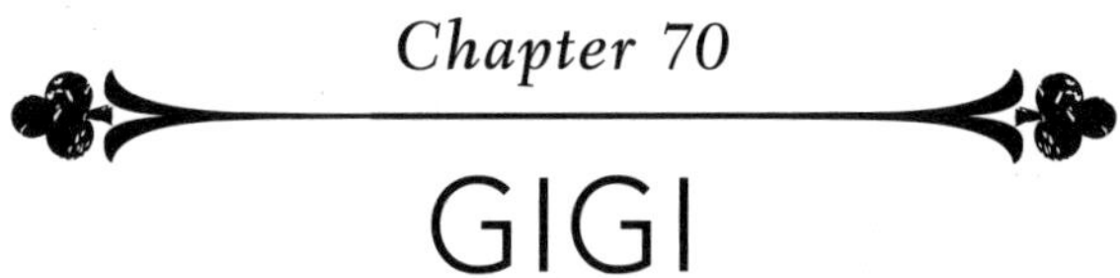

Chapter 70
GIGI

Gigi blinked against the sudden onslaught of light, unable to stop replaying the same moment in her mind that she had *been* replaying, over and over and over again.

I know you're out there.

No, sunshine, you don't.

Gigi had tried in vain to get the voice to say something else, anything else—but it hadn't worked. Only one person had ever called her sunshine, and he was bad news. *Very Bad News.* The kind of bad news that Gigi liked to think about, sitting on the roof outside her bedroom window late at night.

A sentinel. A mercenary. A spy.

He worked, she'd been told, for a very dangerous person—but that had been more than a year ago, and Gigi hadn't seen him since.

He's here. This knife is his knife. Gigi felt it, strapped to her thigh. She thought about the claw marks carved into the leather sheath, and the memory of their one and only meeting overtook her.

"You're Grayson Hawthorne's half sister." Mr. Very Bad News—Code Name: Mimosas—half glowers, half smiles at Gigi.

Should that combination of expressions even be possible? Absolutely not! Gigi approves. "And you're a total stranger in possession of family secrets I've only recently discovered myself! I love that for you!" She beams at him. "I'm Gigi, and I will be the one baffling you today. Don't worry. It's entirely normal. I baffle everybody. Are you a friend of Grayson's?"

Mr. Tall, Dark-Eyed, and Slightly Sinister stares at her. He has dark blond hair that hangs down over eyes so deep a brown they look nearly black. There's a scar through one of his eyebrows, a very harsh—yet fetching—scar.

Black tattoos mark the skin of his upper arms like claw marks.

"Yes." He speaks without emphasis or embellishment, and there is something distinctly ominous about that. "I'm a friend of Grayson's. Why don't you tell him I'm here?"

Gigi's memory skipped to another track—Grayson's reaction after she'd met Mimosas. *"No. Just no, Juliet. If you see him, you get the hell out of there, and you call me."*

"Gigi?" Brady's voice broke into the memory. "Are you okay?"

Act natural! Gigi thought. The second she heard Brady start to climb the rope, she tucked the bug back into her dress.

"Knox took it upon himself to press the hint button," Brady said, pulling himself half up to rest his elbows on the stained glass. "He chose door number one, whatever that is. No discussion."

"This is the finale," Knox called up from below. "We only have an hour left, and hints in this game have to be earned. I made an executive decision. Sue me."

"Coming?" Brady asked Gigi, and then he dropped.

Gigi wondered if Very Bad News had heard that exchange, if

he'd been listening—to her and to Brady, to Knox's big confession. And that raised another question: Who exactly did Knox *think* was listening, that he'd bared his soul like that? Because Gigi was going to go out on a limb and guess that it wasn't Code Name Mimosas.

Her mind a mess and her heart attempting to burst through her rib cage, Gigi made her way back down the rope. Her gaze caught on a square-shaped section of the floorboards that had popped up.

Knox reached into the space below it and removed what appeared to be a solid wooden box. He scowled. "What the hell is this?"

"The way we earn our hint," Brady said.

"A puzzle box." Gigi forced herself to stop thinking about anything but the game because she realized that if she could concentrate, she might actually be able to do this—win their hint, get them out of here, ensure they all made it to the next stage of the game.

She'd come clean. She'd tell Avery or maybe Xander everything. But for now, Code Name Mimosas could wait. What was one more SECRET—to her?

"If you'll recall," Gigi told her teammates and the stranger who was probably listening to all three of them, "puzzle boxes are a specialty of mine."

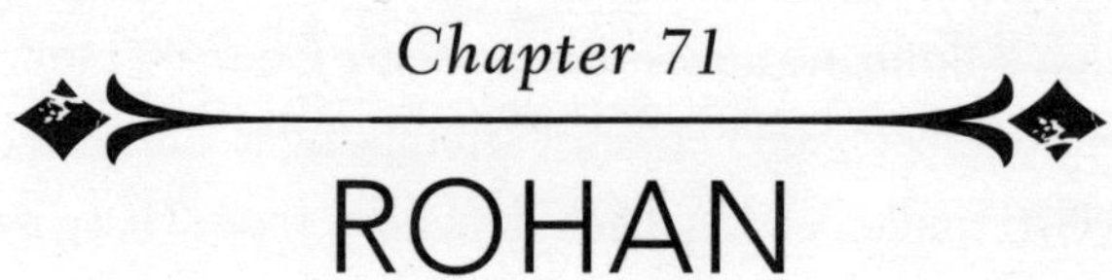

Chapter 71

ROHAN

Sundering the fan—*thoroughly* and repeatedly, first in the dark, then in light—yielded nothing.

"We're going to need that fan for something," Savannah said, "and now it's in tatters."

Rohan gave a little shrug. "Improvisation is a skill. When the moment comes, we'll improvise. Until then . . ." Rohan eyed the tatters. "I've always had a certain fascination for broken things."

"Because you like to fix them?" Savannah's tone was scathing.

"Because I like to scavenge them for parts." Rohan looked up at her. "I don't believe in fixing things or people unless I need them whole."

"I would not advise trying to fix me," Savannah told him.

"I am under no misapprehension that you need fixing." Channeling his inner pickpocket, Rohan relieved her of the glitter vial.

"What are you doing?" Savannah snapped, once she'd realized what he'd done.

Rohan uncorked the vial. "Dumping out the glitter." He upended the contents onto his palm.

"Careful," Savannah said in that mud-on-your-shoes, blood-on-your-knuckles kind of tone. "Glitter sticks to everything."

Sticks, Rohan thought. *Glitter* sticks *to everything.* "Savvy," he said. "The lint roller."

Savannah's pupils expanded, inky black against the pale, silvery blue of her irises.

"Unroll the sheets," Rohan told her.

There was always a moment in every game when Rohan saw exactly how that game was going to play out—how it was going to end.

He and Savannah Grayson were going to get out of here. They would make it to the dock well in advance of dawn. They would decimate the competition in the next phase of the game.

He would use her. She would use him.

And one of us is going to win it all.

Savannah tore sheet after sheet off the lint roller, so fast and fierce that Rohan could practically taste the adrenaline pumping through her veins.

Savannah was made for moments like this one. As was he.

"There's not enough glitter to cover all of the sheets," Rohan observed.

Savannah ran her hands over them, her fingers long and dexterous. "This one," she said, something almost brutal in her tone. "The adhesive is uneven. Parts are sticky. Parts aren't."

Rohan didn't question that—or her. He crouched and spread the glitter across the sheet. When he was finished, Savannah flipped the sheet over, dumping the excess glitter.

Rohan tried to make sense of what was left behind, but if there was a message, it was muddied.

"Glitter sticks to everything." Savannah's eyes narrowed. "The fan."

The one they'd sundered. "Time to improvise." Rohan lifted the sword. Holding it in both hands, he used the blade as a fan, his movements rapid and controlled. *Not enough.* Rohan lowered himself to the ground and began to blow.

Slowly, a message took form. *KING ME.*

"*King me,*" Savannah said above him. "Rohan." There was an urgency in the way she said his name. "*King me.* As in checkers."

As they bolted for the game on the wall, Savannah smiled—not a socialite's smile, not a wolfish or roguish one. No, her smile was ecstasy and victory and sharp around the edges, and Rohan drank it in like wine.

"Do you think we need to king a specific piece or all of them?" Intentionally or otherwise, Savannah made that sound less like a question than an invitation.

"There's also the issue of *how* we ought to king the pieces," Rohan replied in kind. "In gameplay, you can either slide a second piece beneath the first or—"

"Flip it upside down." Savannah did exactly that to one of the pieces. With no hesitation, she moved methodically down all the black pieces on the back row, flipping them over.

Rohan did the same for the red pieces. She beat him to the end of her allotted pieces, leaving Rohan to flip the very last of his. As soon as he did, the game split in two, the wall parting along the vertical axis, revealing a door. Rohan tried it. *Locked.* There was no keyhole, just a black screen next to the door.

"Enter audio code," a robotic voice declared.

The world around Rohan went still and quiet, and everything—every last damn thing—fell into place. "The birthday card," he said.

It was the only one of their four objects they hadn't used. When Rohan opened it, the gentle melody of "Clair de Lune" filled the air.

Moonlight.

The door before them opened straight to the rocky shore.

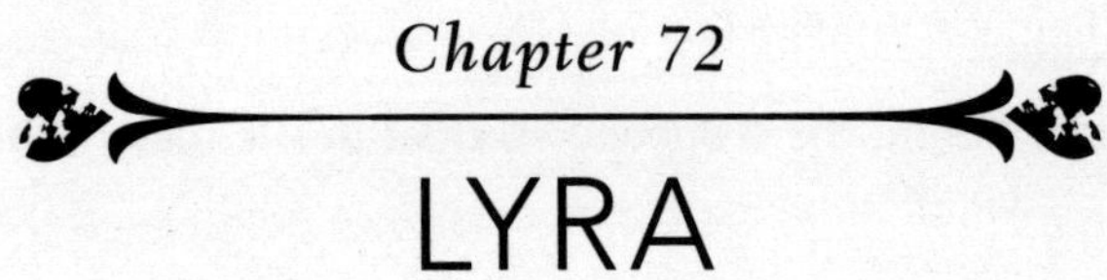

Chapter 72

LYRA

"Door number one or door number two?" Jameson Hawthorne asked.

Lyra glanced at Grayson, whose expression made it clear: He would handle this, Hawthorne versus Hawthorne.

Grayson's eyes narrowed very slightly. "Two."

"Excellent choice," Jameson replied in a tone that suggested it was anything but.

A circular section of the mosaic floor popped up and spun, revealing a compartment. Inside it, Lyra found a flatbed scanner, an empty sketchbook, and charcoal, the kind used for drawing.

"Door number one was a puzzle box, just FYI," Jameson told them over the speakers. "Door number two gets you a challenge of a different sort. What's a Hawthorne game without a little fun?"

Grayson's eyes narrowed further. "Jamie—"

"All you have to do to earn your hint," Jameson said wickedly, "is draw each other."

Draw... Lyra couldn't even finish that thought.

"They don't have to be good drawings." Avery Grambs had clearly been listening to the interplay between the brothers the entire time. "Just really look at one another and draw what you see. When you've scanned in one drawing of each person on your team, you'll get your hint."

"I know what you're doing, Avery." Grayson said the heiress's name like he'd thought it ten thousand times or more. Lyra thought again about *that kiss*—and then about the Hawthorne heiress's advice to her, going into all of this.

Live.

"Avery," Grayson said again. "Jamie?"

There was no reply. They were gone. Seconds passed, and then Grayson reached for the sketchbook and the charcoal. He angled his gaze toward Odette.

The old woman snorted. "Not me. Her."

"We're going to have a long talk very soon," Grayson promised Odette. "An informative one."

And then his silvery eyes shifted slowly to Lyra. After a long moment, he began to draw. Something about the sound of the charcoal skimming the page made it hard for Lyra to breathe. Each time Grayson looked down at the page, she got a modicum of relief.

And each time he looked up, Lyra felt his gaze as a physical thing. *Burned into skin.* She thought about dancing, about running, about being fine and not fine, about *mistakes*.

And then Grayson closed a fist around the charcoal, strode toward the scanner, and laid the sketch pad flat on the bed. He scanned his drawing, and there was a ding.

"One down," Grayson said, his voice almost hoarse. "Two to go."

Odette arched a brow at Lyra. "Your turn."

Grayson ripped the drawing he'd made out of the sketchbook, folded it in quarters, and tucked it into his tuxedo jacket. Then he held out the sketch pad to Lyra. Once she'd taken it from his grasp, his fist unfurled, the charcoal flat on his palm.

As Lyra closed her fingers around the charcoal, she knew one thing: Come hell or high water, she wasn't drawing Grayson Hawthorne. Thankfully, if Lyra *had* drawn Grayson, that would have left Odette drawing herself, so no one could argue as Lyra oriented her body toward the old woman.

Odette, the lawyer. Odette, the actress. Odette, with all her secrets.

Lyra did as Avery had bid them and really *looked* at her subject. In the lines of Odette's face, she saw the young woman from *Changing Crowns*. In Odette's eyes, Lyra saw lifetimes.

And pain.

Lyra began to draw. "What are you dying of?" She didn't beat around the bush, and Odette didn't so much as blink.

"Glioblastoma. Discovered early, for what that's worth."

"Inoperable?" Grayson pressed.

"Not necessarily." Odette raised her chin. "But I find that I am not disposed to let a doctor half my age cut into my brain in the hopes of wringing a few more months out of this life."

"It could be a year more," Grayson said. "Or two."

"The condition is fatal either way," Odette countered. "And what's a year or two, to me? I've been married three times. Divorced once. Widowed twice. And there were others, at least three of whom I would have gone to hell and back for—two of whom, I arguably did."

Lyra looked up but kept drawing. Odette's eyes locked on to hers.

"Love is a strange and wild beast," the old woman said. "It's a gift and a comfort and a curse. Remember that." She looked toward Grayson. "Both of you."

Neither one of them replied. Silence reigned as Lyra worked to complete her drawing, and by the time she was done, her entire body ached. Lyra scanned in the drawing. It wasn't a close likeness. She wasn't a good artist.

But the ding sounded nonetheless.

"One more." Lyra flipped the page and handed the sketch pad to Odette. The old woman took it and the charcoal, and then she stared at Lyra like there was a message buried somewhere behind her eyes. Finally, Odette turned to Grayson—her *actual* subject.

As Odette began to draw, Lyra's hands imagined what it would be like to draw Grayson Hawthorne. *All sharp angles, except for those lips.*

Thankfully—blessedly—Odette was done in under a minute. She held out the sketchbook to Lyra, who took it and looked down, expecting to see Grayson's face.

But Odette hadn't drawn Grayson.

The image on the page wrapped an iron fist around Lyra's heart and stole the air from her lungs.

A calla lily.

Chapter 73

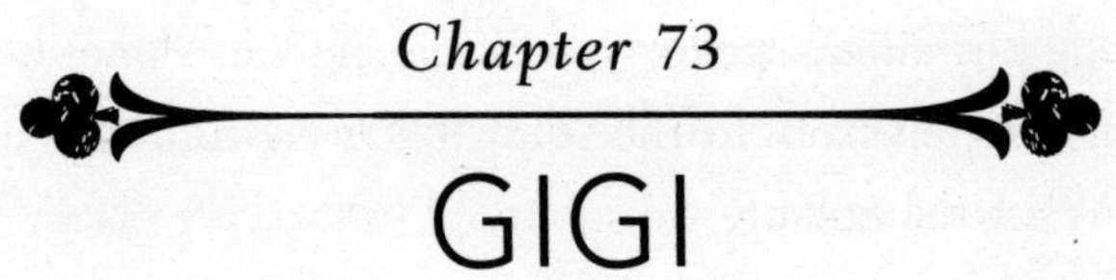

GIGI

There was a seam on the bottom of the puzzle box, circular and so fine that it couldn't be made out with the naked eye. Bracing her fingers against the wood, Gigi pushed. A disk popped out—and off.

Step one complete. A puzzle box could have five steps or fifty. For now, all Gigi had to do was focus on step two. Not on Brady, not on Knox, not on knives or scars or secrets or *sunshine*.

Step two. The wooden disk Gigi had just removed was no more than a centimeter deep. The area that had just been revealed was circular, with two metal arrows—one shorter than the other—attached at the center. The wood around the edge of the panel had been notched at even intervals. *Twelve of them.*

One of the notches was labeled with the numeral 3.

Pushing a dozen different memories out of her mind, Gigi brought a finger to the tip of one of the metal arrows. With the slightest touch, it moved, and Gigi thought back to the first time she'd worked a puzzle box.

Her father's.

Beside her, Brady spoke. "Hands on a clock."

Gigi snapped back to the present just in time to hear Knox's reply: "What the hell are we supposed to do with that?"

Gigi took a deep breath and answered. "Look for details." She flipped over the disk she'd removed from the box. On the back, with a tiny, victorious thrill, she found words etched into the wood:

Just after dawn is far too soon
The middle of a night for a raccoon
The perfect time to earn your boon
November, April, September, June

"Another riddle." Knox sounded only slightly murderous, which Gigi took as a sign of personal growth.

"Another riddle," she confirmed. "Dawn is too early. Raccoons are nocturnal."

"Soon, raccoon, boon, June." Brady's voice hummed with concentration as he brought his hand to Gigi's on the disk. "They all rhyme."

"Noon." Knox's voice was sharp as glass. "Middle of the night for a raccoon, rhyme with June. The answer is *noon*."

Gigi moved the minute and hour hands to point upward, using the 3 as an anchor. Nothing happened. "November, April, September, June," Gigi said intently. *Four months—and not just any months.* "They're the only four months with thirty days. Noon plus thirty..."

She moved the minute hand, and there was a pop. *I can do this. I really can.*

Gigi tipped the box over, and the clock fell off, hands and all. Beneath it, there was another circular section, cut into wedges like a pie. Gigi tested each wedge separately, pushing and prodding at them to no effect.

"What now?" Knox demanded.

They didn't have forever. Dawn was coming—and with it, a reckoning, one way or another.

"When you hit a dead end on a puzzle box," Gigi said, "you go back to the beginning and look for something you missed."

A trigger. A catch. A hint. In the past year and a half, she'd bought dozens of puzzle boxes and solved them all. It wasn't an obsession. Just like the Grandest Game and the reverse heists weren't obsessions. Just like she'd never obsessed over a person she'd been told was Very Bad News.

A person who worked for someone worse.

A sponsor? Gigi pushed the thought out of her head—for now—and gave the box and the wedges another once-over, then turned her attention to the discarded pieces: the wooden disk and the clock. Her gaze landed on the minute and hour hands.

They're made of metal. "What if they aren't just metal?" Gigi said. The buzz of energy building inside her, Gigi pried the hands off the clock. Gripping the minute hand by the thinner end, she ran the arrow over the pieces of the wedge. When that didn't work, she tried the hour hand.

Bingo.

"It's a magnet!" Gigi breathed. In other circumstance, she would have grinned, but she was beyond grinning now. "There must be something metallic embedded in the wood."

And so it went, step after step after step after step. Finally—*finally*—they made it to the center of the box, to a compartment and the objects inside it.

Cotton balls. Two of them. Gigi ran the tips of her fingers over the words carved into the bottom of the compartment—their hint.

USE THEM.

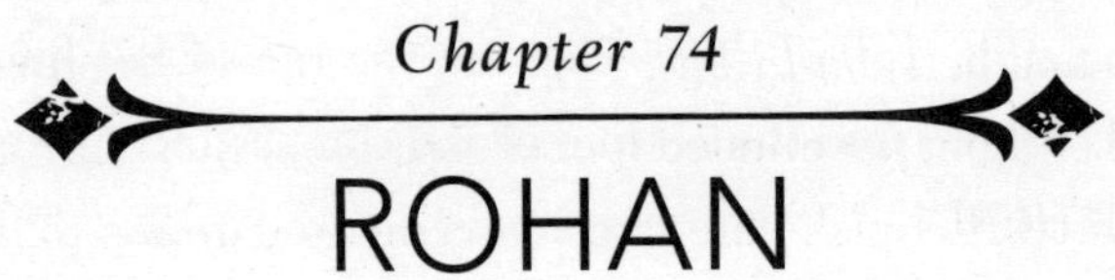

Chapter 74
ROHAN

The path down to the shore was rocky and uneven. Moonlight was in short supply. Victory was sweet, the way it always was for Rohan.

Down below, a light on the dock came on.

"There's no one there." Savannah came to a standstill. They were still closer to the house than the dock, the path lit by delicate strings of lights. "No Hawthornes. No Hawthorne heiress."

"I'd wager the game makers will make their appearance just before dawn." By Rohan's calculations, they were nearing twilight. "We'll see if either of the other teams makes it out in time. For now, it's just us."

Just Rohan and Savannah Grayson.

She stopped suddenly and turned back toward him. "Truth or dare."

Rohan had not expected that. "Pardon me?"

"Truth or dare, Rohan?"

Something in Savannah's tone reminded Rohan of the brush gliding through her hair, the slice of the knife, the shattering rose, his hands and hers, *bit by bit by bit*.

And then Rohan reminded *himself* that Savannah Grayson liked fighting dirty. "If I pick dare, are you going to dare me to give you the longsword?" *Nice try, love.*

Savannah was undeterred. "Truth or dare, British?"

"Truth." Rohan knew the game she was playing. He knew exactly what she was going to ask.

"What's the name of the organization you work for?"

"Technically, at the moment, I don't have an employer. I'm on a sabbatical of sorts." Rohan could have left it there. *The Devil's Mercy* was not a name spoken lightly—not by Rohan, not by anyone who valued their life or livelihood. Not even here, in the dead of night, alone. And yet... Rohan hadn't gotten to where he was by avoiding risk.

When he won the Grandest Game, when he took what was rightfully his, when he became the Proprietor and wore the crown... *I will* be *the Devil's Mercy.* That made its secrets his to tell or withhold.

Rohan gave Savannah Grayson her answer—a true one, a partial one. "The Mercy." Rohan felt the words on his lips as much as he felt Savannah's presence beside him in the dark—though it wasn't quite so dark anymore.

Hello, twilight. "Truth or dare, Savannah?"

She was too proud to back down now. "Truth."

Rohan wondered what she'd thought he was going to dare her to do. He took a single step toward her. "What are you after, Savvy?"

He'd asked versions of that question before, but every instinct he had said that this time, he might get the real answer, the mystery of Savannah Grayson, solved.

"If you're not playing for the money," Rohan murmured, "what are you playing for?"

Savannah stalked slowly toward him, then stopped, leaning forward, her lips so close to Rohan's that he could taste the kiss that wasn't as she gave him his due.

An answer, partial, but true. One word. "Revenge."

Chapter 75

LYRA

"I don't understand." Lyra's throat threatened to close in around that statement as she stared, dry-eyed, at Odette's drawing. *The lily.* The dream always started with the flower.

"I know you don't," Odette said softly. She held Lyra's gaze and then nodded her head toward Grayson. "You draw him, Lyra. It's time the three of us put this game to rest."

"You said you didn't know anything about my father."

"I don't." Odette was implacable. "Now draw your Hawthorne, the way I once drew mine."

The way I once drew mine. That was a confession and a proclamation and a bomb, detonated just so, and Lyra couldn't muster the ability to tell Odette that Grayson wasn't and could never be her Hawthorne.

Swallowing back the litany of questions she wanted to scream, Lyra did as Odette had instructed and began to draw. Grayson's jaw first, then brow, then cheekbones. It didn't feel anything like she'd thought drawing him would, because all she could think was *I was four years old.*

All she could think was *I was holding a calla lily and a candy necklace.*

All she could think was *There was blood* and *A Hawthorne did this* and *Omega.*

Lyra finished the drawing and scanned it, feeling like she was sleepwalking through the motion. When their challenge was deemed a success and they got their hint, Lyra barely even heard it.

"Shatter." Odette repeated the hint, but all Lyra could hear was the old woman saying other words.

Neither one of you knows what you think you know.

The right kind of disaster just waiting to happen.

A Hawthorne and a girl who has every reason to stay away from Hawthornes.

"Lyra." Grayson said her name, and when that didn't work, he said it again a second time—wrong. "Lyra."

Lie-ra.

"That's not my name," Lyra bit out.

"I know." Grayson brought his hands to her face, his palms on her cheeks as his fingertips cradled her jaw. "Shatter," he reiterated. "That's our hint. *Shatter.*"

He was always so damn impossible to ignore.

Lyra fought through the fog in her brain. "The lollipop," she whispered.

Any of their objects could be broken, but the lollipop was the only one of the four that would shatter. She tore off the plastic covering and slammed the lollipop to the ground as hard as she could, angry and desperate and needing to be right.

The lollipop shattered.

Lyra dropped the stick and fell to her knees, looking for something—anything—in the shards.

Grayson picked up the stick. "There's a cork on the end." The stick was thick—and, they soon discovered, *hollow*. Inside the stick, there was liquid.

Odette got to the paintbrush before Lyra could, but after a long moment, she handed the object in question to Lyra, who dipped the brush into the liquid inside the lollipop stick. Grayson held out the sticky notes. As Lyra painted the liquid onto the paper, an image was revealed—or part of an image, anyway.

Grayson tore off the first note, and Lyra started painting another one. And on and on it went. Grayson and Odette began fitting the images together like a puzzle. The end result was a spiral, and Lyra thought about the fact that every swirl and spiral in the ballroom mosaic was unique.

"Find it." Grayson Hawthorne and his orders.

They scoured the walls, the floor—and finally, they found the pattern that matched. Grayson laid his palms flat against the center of the spiral and pressed. Hard. Something clicked, and without warning, every tile in the spiral fell off the wall. They hit the ground like raindrops.

Like shrapnel.

In the center of the space where the tiles had been, Lyra could make out the ends of electrical wires.

"The light switch." Grayson moved quickly, and the next thing Lyra knew, he was pinching together this wire and that and screwing the light switch in with his bare hands. "Done."

Grayson looked up. Lyra flipped the switch, and just like that, a section of wall became a door.

They were out.

Chapter 76

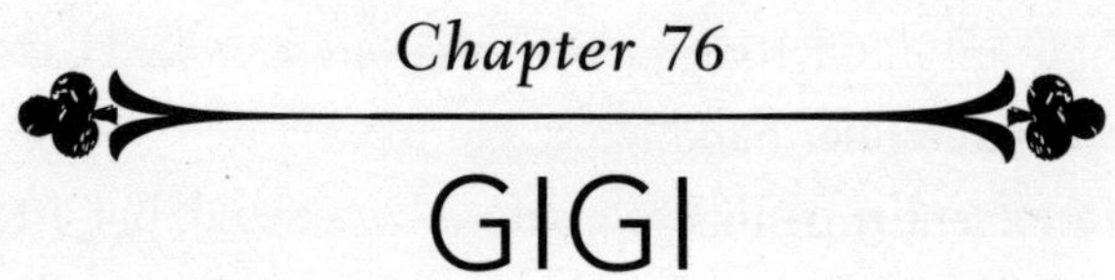

GIGI

"*Use them* how?" Brady said, staring at the words carved into the puzzle box.

Gigi's mind was whirring. She refused to blink as she cataloged and re-cataloged and re-re-cataloged the puzzle box's contents. *Cotton balls. Two of them.*

"Nail polish remover," Knox said suddenly. "You use cotton balls with nail polish remover."

Something about his voice made Gigi wonder if Knox had ever removed Calla Thorp's nail polish for her, back before she'd given him that scar.

Focus! Gigi told herself. *Focus like the wind.* "There's no nail polish to remove," Gigi said, thinking out loud. Her gaze flicked to the other objects.

The yarn.

The wrapping paper.

The sunglasses.

"The liquid might not actually be nail polish remover," Brady said. "Something with a somewhat similar chemical composition, yes, but—"

"Invisible ink?" Gigi suggested. She reached for the wrapping paper, then pulled her hand back. Something was niggling at her. It took a moment to realize what that *something* was. "There are two of them."

Two cotton balls. Gigi's gaze went back to the objects. *Two lenses.* She doused a cotton ball in the nail polish remover and grabbed the sunglasses, running the cotton ball over the lenses.

"It's working," Brady said. "Something's coming off."

Gigi had no idea what that something was—not nail polish, that was for sure, because they'd been able to look through the sunglasses. But as she poured the rest of the contents of the "nail polish remover" over the lenses, the dark layer that coated them—whatever it was—came off entirely. The lenses changed color.

Instead of black, they were red.

"The wrapping paper." Knox rolled it out and flipped it over.

The back was red. Gigi put on the modified sunglasses. The altered lenses filtered out light waves of the same color, revealing...

"Symbols! Three of them!" Gigi passed the sunglasses around so the other two could see, and then, together, the three of them searched for—and found—those symbols among the dozens carved into the shelves.

"Push them inward?" Gigi suggested.

"They wouldn't push before," Knox pointed out.

"We didn't try to press these three symbols at the same time before," Gigi told him. She was able to reach two with her own hands. Brady did the third. The symbols depressed. There was a pop, and one of the bookshelves swung inward.

A hidden door. Gigi stepped through it into a small room with a tile floor and corkboard walls.

Stuck into the walls were pushpins.

"The yarn," Gigi said. "Connect the pushpins with the yarn!" She had no idea how much time they had left before dawn, but it couldn't be much.

Get out. Get down to the dock. Then deal with the rest.

"What order do we go in?" Knox demanded.

"They're all different colors," Brady said. *"Rainbows."*

Like the wrapping paper.

Like the yarn.

"Roy G. Biv." Gigi felt like her body was a drum set, and her heart was a drummer going to town on it. "Start with red, then orange!"

How much time do we have left?

Enough to stretch the yarn between the pushpins. Enough for the light from the ceiling to cast a veritable spiderweb of shadows down onto the tile floor.

At the center of that web was a lone tile.

Knox placed his palm flat on the tile and pushed. The floor beneath them gave way—another trapdoor, which led to another staircase, which led out the back of the house and onto the rocky shore.

It was already light out, but the sun wasn't visible on the horizon—not yet. They had time—minutes, maybe, or seconds, but *time.*

Knox tore off over the rocks, toward the dock, Brady on his heels. Gigi ran, forcing herself to keep up with them, pushing as hard as she could, as fast as she could, across rocky terrain—

And then her toe caught on something.

And then Gigi fell.

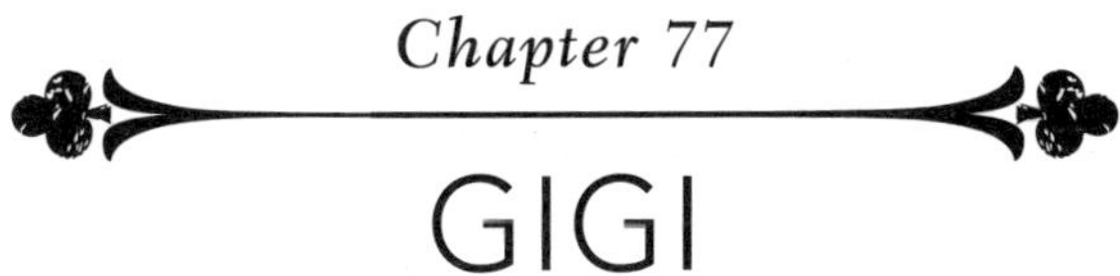

Chapter 77
GIGI

Pain. Gigi was vaguely aware of the world around her trying to go black, but she was more aware of the fact that her team hadn't made it to the dock yet. *She* hadn't. Gigi scrambled to her feet—or she tried to, anyway, but then she wobbled and went down again.

Suddenly, Knox was kneeling beside her. "You okay, Happy?"

Knox. Gigi looked for Brady, but she didn't see him. She blinked. "It was just a little boulder. It's just a little head wound. I'm fine!"

Fuzzy Knox—he was only a little bit fuzzy—did not seem to believe her. He slipped an arm under hers, and the next thing Gigi knew, Knox was carrying her and walking slowly toward the dock.

Knox. Not Brady. Brady hadn't come back for her. Gigi thought about Savannah telling her that no one in this competition was her friend, that no one could be trusted.

Knox had said the exact same thing.

And that was when Gigi belatedly realized: *Slowly?* Knox was walking *slowly* toward the dock. Toward the other teams. Toward Avery, Jameson, Xander, and Nash, who stood at the edge of the dock in a line.

Slowly. Gigi looked back to the eastern horizon and saw the sun. *Dawn.* Her throat tightened. *We didn't make it.* They'd been so close.

If she'd been faster with the puzzle box...

If she hadn't fallen...

If she was smarter and coordinated and *better,* if she was more like Savannah—

If, if, if. "I'm sorry," she told Knox.

Don't be. That was what Brady had said to her the last time she'd apologized for being herself. For being too much. *My brain likes* A Lot.

"Yeah, Happy," Knox said, stepping past the game makers and onto the dock. "Me, too."

Gigi saw Brady then. He was holding the longsword. She'd forgotten about the sword.

"Brady," Gigi said, remembering what was at stake for him, berating herself for being selfish enough to wonder why he'd run for the dock instead of coming back for *her.* "Your mom. I promise—"

"It's okay," Brady told her quietly. "My mama's fine."

Gigi went very still in Knox's arms. "Fine?" Gigi couldn't make that make sense. "She doesn't have cancer?"

He lied to us? Brady lied.

"Put her down, Knox," Brady said.

"You weren't entirely lying." Knox didn't put Gigi down. "I would have known. So who *does* have cancer?"

"Severin," Brady said after a long moment, "had cancer."

Knox stared at Brady, hard. *"Had?"*

"Pancreatic. It was quick. And, like I said, he sends his regards."

He's dead? Their mentor... Gigi tried to make sense of that, too, but the next thing she knew, Grayson was stepping right up to Knox and repeating Brady's suggestion—except coming from Grayson, it wasn't a suggestion.

"Put her down."

This time, a stone-faced Knox complied.

"You're injured, Gigi." Grayson's tone made it clear: That was unacceptable.

"Who among us is not occasionally concussed?" Gigi replied, the response—and her smile—automatic, no matter the thoughts dogging her brain.

Brady lied. Severin's dead. Knox is not okay.

"Our team is out of the game." Knox turned toward Avery Grambs. "Go ahead. Say it. We've been eliminated."

Avery ignored Knox in favor of coming to stand next to Grayson. She took Gigi's hand. "Are you okay?"

Gigi couldn't help feeling like Avery was asking about more than her head.

I'm not. I'm really, really not. Gigi couldn't beat back that thought, no matter how hard she smiled.

Avery had tried to give her a ticket to this game, but Gigi had won her own way. She'd wanted to prove something. She'd wanted to be smart and capable and *strong*.

Gigi looked past Avery and Grayson, past Brady and Knox, to Savannah. The sight of her twin's hair—jagged and shorn—took Gigi's breath away.

Savannah didn't look like Savannah anymore.

Avery squeezed Gigi's hand, then took a step back, Xander, Nash, and Jameson falling in around her. Grayson stayed right where he was, an arm wrapping protectively around Gigi's shoulders.

"Diamonds and Hearts," Avery said. "You're on to the next phase of the game. Clubs ... there's always next year."

"Once a player, always a player," Jameson said, addressing those words directly to Gigi.

She couldn't bring herself to look at Brady or Knox. Instead, Gigi looked out at the horizon. *I should tell Avery and the others about the bug. I should tell them that Code Name Mimosas is here.*

I'm going to tell them.

Right now.

There was no reason *not* to tell them anymore. But what came out of Gigi's mouth was: "Do we have to leave the island immediately?"

Gigi couldn't keep her thoughts from drifting to the thorny brush where she'd found that bag.

"You can take some time to say your good-byes," Avery told her. "Get some rest, if you need it. The boat for the mainland leaves at noon."

"I'll fix you up, kid," Nash told Gigi, an offer and an order both, as he displaced Grayson at her side, the way only Grayson's older brother could.

Gigi brought her hand to the throbbing knot on her forehead. There was only a little blood.

"What about the rest of us?" That was Savannah, her voice piercing the morning air, and Gigi couldn't help thinking that every other time she'd ever ended up probably concussed, her twin had been the one checking her over, fixing her up.

But not now.

Right now, Savannah was wearing her game face. "What's next for those of us who successfully made it to the dock by dawn?"

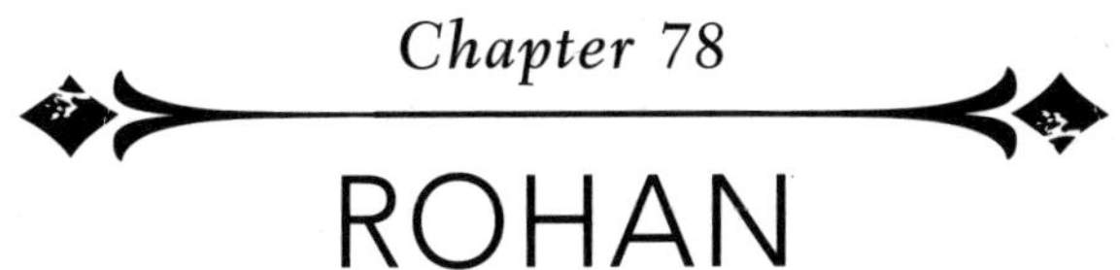

Chapter 78

ROHAN

If there was one skill—one legal and perfectly moral skill, at least—that Rohan had in spades, it was reading a room. And if there was one skill he'd honed to perfection in the past twelve hours, it was reading Savannah Grayson.

He'd heard Savannah's sharp intake of breath when her twin's head had slammed into that boulder. He'd felt Savannah's world come screeching to a halt, frozen in the seconds it had taken for Gigi to stand back up.

He'd felt the shift in Savannah once it became clear that Gigi was going to be fine.

Revenge. Rohan imagined himself in the labyrinth, placing a hand on the door to the room that contained unknowns—things that mattered, puzzles that didn't quite fit.

Grayson Hawthorne. Gigi. Their absent father. Revenge. A picture had begun to take hold. Rohan diverted just enough of his attention to the real world to look between Savannah and the game makers as Jameson Hawthorne stepped forward to answer her question.

"Those of you who remain in the game will have twelve hours to get some rest. Look for a special delivery then. In the meantime..." Jameson looked to Xander.

The youngest Hawthorne held out his right arm and dramatically pushed up his sleeve. He was wearing what appeared to be eight smartwatches. With no small amount of ceremony, Xander Hawthorne took off five of the watches and handed them out to the remaining players, one by one.

Rohan accepted his, then observed Savannah doing the same. She wasn't looking at Xander Hawthorne. She wasn't looking at her twin sister or her Hawthorne half brother, either.

Savannah was watching Avery Grambs.

Chapter 79
LYRA

Lyra looked down at the watch that Xander Hawthorne had just placed on her wrist. Words scrolled across the screen: *PLAYER NUMBER 4, LYRA KANE.*

Lyra had been number four of eight before, but she was four of five now. Her gaze went first to Grayson, who was still standing near his injured sister, then to Odette.

The three of them weren't a team anymore.

"A question," Odette said. She pinched the band of her watch between a finger and her thumb. "Are these watches transferable?"

It took Lyra's brain a second to catch up with what Odette had just asked.

"By the rules of the game," Odette elaborated, "can I give my place in phase two to another player?"

What? No. Lyra stared at Odette. *You're dying. This game—you're going to win it if it's the last thing you do.* Lyra's gaze shifted to Grayson, who looked back at her, a silent exchange that told Lyra their minds were operating in tandem.

Odette couldn't leave. Not before she'd told them what she knew.

"Why would you?" Jameson Hawthorne's expression made it clear: He was intrigued. Objectively, *intrigued* was probably a good look for Jameson Hawthorne, but Lyra barely even spared him a glance.

There was only one Hawthorne on this dock who mattered to Lyra, one Hawthorne who knew what was truly at stake here. *One and only one.*

"My health is not what I thought it was, coming into this game." Odette sold that statement like the actress she was, a proud tilt to her chin, like the admission cost her.

That's not why you're leaving. Lyra knew it. She knew that Grayson knew it, too.

This was about the omega symbol, the calla lily, the power outage. This was about Lyra and Grayson. *The right kind of disaster just waiting to happen.*

From her position on the dock, Avery Grambs silently exchanged a look with Jameson, then Xander, then Nash, before she finally looked back to Odette.

"We'll allow it," Avery said, speaking for the group.

Odette rubbed a thumb across the band of her watch, then turned toward Gigi Grayson.

"I don't want it." The sudden fierceness in Gigi's voice surprised Lyra. "I never wanted anyone to hand any part of this game to me."

Odette gave a brief nod, then her gaze shifted, sliding over Knox Landry and landing on Brady Daniels. "Care to hold out your wrist, young man?" Odette said.

Brady held out his wrist. Lyra still didn't quite believe that

Odette was going to do it, but within seconds, Brady was wearing the watch.

Odette had just given away her spot in the Grandest Game.

Why? The question pounded through Lyra.

"This is the second time I've been given a place in this game that I did not earn." Brady looked down, then up again. "Thank you, Ms. Morales."

Silence greeted that proclamation, broken only by the sound of waves lapping against the dock.

"So that's it." Knox recovered his voice first, his words intense but eerily devoid of emotion. "I'm out of the game, Daniels, and you're not. It must seem like justice to you. You couldn't have planned it better."

To Lyra's ears, that sounded like an accusation. Did Knox think that Brady *had* planned this? How was that even possible?

"Maybe," Brady said, staring out at the horizon, "I just had a little faith."

As the game makers and other players began to depart from the dock, Lyra kept her eyes locked on Odette, telegraphing a message she hoped was very, very clear: *You aren't leaving—not until you tell us what you know.*

Odette made no attempt to follow the others up to the house. Grayson stayed put, too, and soon, the three of them were the only ones left on the dock.

"You're out?" Lyra said hoarsely. Of all the questions screaming in her mind, she had no idea why she started there. "What about leaving a legacy for your children and grandchildren?"

Odette walked slowly to the edge of the dock and stared out at the ocean. "There are some legacies one does not wish to pass down."

"What the hell is that supposed to mean?" Lyra said. A chill spread down her spine.

A light wind blew in off the ocean, lifting Odette's hair off her back, punctuating the old woman's silence.

"Since it appears you are reluctant to answer Lyra's question, try mine." Grayson's air was that of a precision shooter, taking aim. "How long have you known that you were going to be leaving the Grandest Game?"

"From the moment the power was cut." Odette tilted her head toward the sky. "Or maybe it was the moment you saw my drawing, Lyra."

The lily. "How did you know?" Lyra whispered, the words clawing their way out of her. The dream always started with the flower.

"*What* do you know?" Grayson elaborated.

Silence.

"Please." Lyra wasn't above pleading.

Odette turned slowly back to face them. "*A Hawthorne did this,*" she said. The old woman closed her eyes, and when she opened them again, she repeated herself. "*A Hawthorne did this.* That is what your father told you, Lyra, prior to his final, dramatic display. *A Hawthorne,*" she repeated, emphasizing the words. "And the two of you assumed it was Tobias? *A Hawthorne,* and it never occurred to either of you that the *A* in that sentence might be an initial?"

An initial? Lyra stared at Odette, trying to make sense of that. She sorted through what she knew of the Hawthorne family tree. The billionaire, *Tobias.* His children, *Zara, Skye,* and *Tobias II.* The grandsons, *Nash, Grayson, Jameson,* and *Xander.*

Alexander. That made no sense. Xander was her age.

"Alice." Grayson went very still, his eyes finding their way to Lyra's, his body never moving. "My grandmother. *Alice Hawthorne.*

She died before I was born." Grayson's head swiveled back toward Odette. "Explain."

Odette wasn't looking at either one of them now. "There are always three." There was something eerie about the way the old woman said those words, like she wasn't the first one to say them.

Like they'd been said many times before.

"Three what?" Grayson pressed.

Lyra thought about the dream, about her father's gifts: a calla lily and a candy necklace. *With only three pieces of candy.*

"I promised you a single answer, Mr. Hawthorne," Odette said, every inch the lawyer. "The rest, if you will recall, was shrouded in *ifs*."

"You promised to tell us how you knew Tobias Hawthorne." Lyra wasn't going to give up on getting answers. She couldn't. "How you ended up on his List."

Odette stared at Lyra for a moment longer, then turned to Grayson. "As you correctly surmised, Mr. Hawthorne, I used to work at McNamara, Ortega, and Jones. That is how we met, your grandfather and I. We parted ways roughly fifteen years ago, a mere nine months into my employment."

Fifteen years. Lyra's father had died on her fourth birthday. She was nineteen and change now. *Roughly fifteen years.*

"As you have likely also surmised," Odette continued, "the nature of my relationship with Tobias was . . . complicated."

Lyra thought about everything Odette had said about living and loving. About Tobias Hawthorne being the best and worst man she'd ever known. About the loves she would have gone to hell and back for—and had.

Draw your Hawthorne, the way I once drew mine.

"Do not pretend to have had a romantic relationship with my

grandfather." Grayson's voice was like sharpened steel. "The old man was very open about the fact that there was no one after his beloved Alice. *'Men like us love only once.'* That is what my grandfather told my brother Jameson and myself, years before he died and years after you and he allegedly parted ways. I remember every word. *'All these years, your grandmother has been gone, and there hasn't been anyone else. There can't and won't be.'*" Grayson breathed, in and out. "He wasn't lying."

"One logical conclusion," Odette said in a lawyer's tone, "is that, in Tobias's eyes, I wasn't *anyone*." Her lips came together and then parted slightly. "He treated me like *no one* in the end."

Draw your Hawthorne, the way I once drew mine.

Lyra knew in the pit of her stomach and every bone in her body that Odette was telling the truth—and not as a distraction this time.

"Likewise," Odette continued evenly, "I would point out that your grandfather referred to his wife as *gone*."

Lyra's mind raced. Her mouth was dry. "Not dead. *Gone*."

"Enough." Grayson had clearly reached his limit. "My grandmother was buried. She has a gravestone. There was a funeral—a very well-attended funeral. My mother has mourned her mother's death for as long as I can remember. And you would have me believe she is alive? That she, what? Faked her death? That my grandfather knew—and *allowed it*?"

"Rest assured, he did not know—at first." Odette turned toward ocean once more. "When we met, Tobias was still grieving the love of his life. The toll of burying Alice was etched into his face and body for everyone to see. And then there was me. Us."

Fifteen years earlier, Odette would have been sixty-six, Tobias Hawthorne a few years younger.

"And then... *she* came back." Odette's voice was nearly lost to a rising wind, but Lyra heard so much more than just the words that had been spoken.

She. Alice. A Hawthorne.

"Tobias's dead wife came to him and asked him to do something for her. Like they'd never parted. Like he had not literally buried her. He did as Alice had bidden. Tobias utilized me to accomplish that favor—used me for his true love's ends—and then he discarded me and tried his level best to have me disbarred."

There it was. The answer—the only answer—they'd been promised: how Odette had known Tobias Hawthorne and why she'd been on his List.

"What was the favor he had you help with?" Lyra asked. *No reply.*

"Once that favor was accomplished, am I to believe that my long-dead grandmother disappeared once more?" Grayson's tone was impossible to read. "That my grandfather never said a word to anyone? Like mother, like son?"

Lyra was not, in that moment, capable of figuring out what that was supposed to mean.

"Here." Odette pressed something into Lyra's hands. *The opera glasses.* "They must have a use in the game still to come," Odette told Lyra. "My game no longer."

She really is leaving.

"If you are suffering from the misapprehension that we are done here, Ms. Morales," Grayson said, his tone ominous, "allow me to cure you of that notion."

Odette looked at Grayson like he was a little boy. "I've given far more than I owed, Mr. Hawthorne, and said far more than I should. The only proper answer to some riddles is *silence*."

Lyra's mind was never silent. Voices echoed through her memory—her father's, Odette's. *A Hawthorne did this.*

In the grandest of games, there are no coincidences.

There are some legacies one does not wish to pass down.

"You said that there are always three." Grayson was not wired to give up. "Three what, exactly?" No answer. "Why leave the game, Ms. Morales? Why give up your chance at twenty-six million dollars? What are you afraid of?"

Lyra thought about her father, thankful that she couldn't call to mind a single image of his body. *A Hawthorne did this.* She thought about the candy necklace, the calla lily, an omega drawn in blood.

But somehow, one question rose to the surface over all of that—the only question that Lyra had any real hope Odette would actually answer. "The notes," Lyra said. "With my father's names." Her fingers curled into her palms. "Did you write them?"

Odette let out a breath, suddenly, utterly, and unnaturally calm. "I did not."

Chapter 80

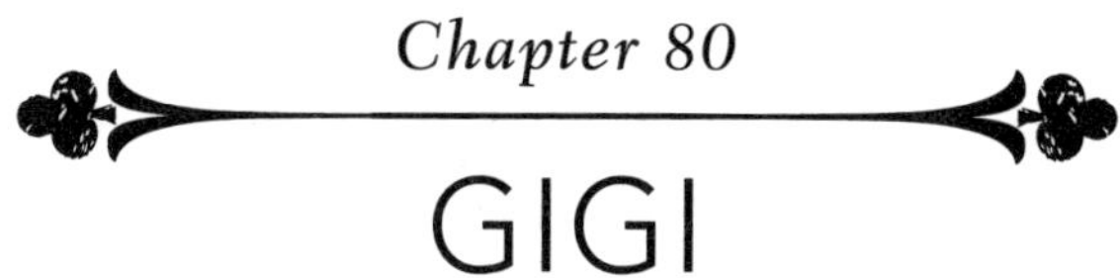

GIGI

"All patched up, darlin'."

Gigi had spent every second that had passed since she'd left the dock telling herself that she was going to come clean. Maybe not to Nash, who, like Grayson, had a protective streak a mile wide. And probably not to Jameson, who was unpredictable, but to Avery—or maybe Xander.

"Thanks," Gigi told Nash brightly. Maybe a little *too* brightly. But before he could proceed with a Southern Inquisition, there was a knock on the door to her room.

Not my room for much longer. A ball of emotion rose in Gigi's throat as Nash answered the door.

Brady stepped into the room. He'd changed back into his regular clothes, but he was still holding the sword. Looking back, Gigi realized that he'd probably been guarding it in his own, subtle Brady way the whole night. It doubtlessly had a use in the next phase of the game—if there *was* a game once Gigi spilled the beans.

I know you're out there.

No, sunshine, you don't.

"Holler if you need anything," Nash told Gigi. He palmed his cowboy hat and gave Brady a long, disturbingly neutral look, then turned and sauntered out of the room.

Alone with Brady, Gigi developed an intense fascination with her own cuticles. She felt the mattress dip as he sat down beside her on the bed.

"You're still in the game." Gigi still couldn't bring herself to look at him. She reached back to take the hair tie Brady had given her out of her hair, then handed it back to him. A muscle in her throat tightened. "Where's Knox?"

"Why," Brady said, "are you asking me about Knox?"

Gigi thought about Knox's scar—but that wasn't her story to tell. "You lied to me, Brady."

"Technically, I lied to him, and you overheard."

Gigi shook her head. *"Don't."*

"I would tell a thousand lies," Brady swore, as intense as she'd ever seen him, "to get her back."

Her. Knox had been right. It was always Calla with Brady. "Winning this game won't bring Calla Thorp back," Gigi said.

Brady was quiet for a long moment. "What if I told you it would?"

What? Gigi searched his eyes. "What do you mean?"

Brady didn't answer the question. "You could have told Nash about the bug just now, but I don't think you did. You could have had the whole game called off. You didn't."

"I haven't told anyone *yet*," Gigi corrected. Brady didn't even know the full extent of the secret she was keeping.

I know you're out there.

No, sunshine, you don't.

Brady reached over to take Gigi's hand in his. "I am asking you to let this run its course."

Gigi felt the warmth of Brady's touch. He *wanted* her to feel it.

She pulled her hand back. "Was any of it real?" she asked, her voice breaking. The way he'd touched her. The way he'd looked at her. Chaos theory.

"All kinds of things can happen," Brady said quietly, "in a closed system."

"Nothing in, nothing out," Gigi said. *A locked room. An island.*

"I wasn't lying," Brady said, his voice catching a little, "when I told you that my brain likes A Lot."

Gigi tried madly to look anywhere but at his face, and her gaze fell on the sword. "If I asked you to give that to me, would you?"

His reply was gentle. "What use would you have for it now, Gigi?"

She was out of the game, and he wasn't. "That's what I thought." Gigi summoned up her best and brightest smile, because this *hurt*. "You wanted me to feel something for you. You wanted me to trust you and like you. Maybe you thought you could use me in the next phase of the game, if our team did make it out by dawn." Gigi was still smiling. She couldn't stop. She couldn't let herself stop. "You played me, Brady."

"I'm playing like her life depends on it." Brady leaned forward, and suddenly, Gigi couldn't see anything but his face. "Juliet? I need this game to go on."

That was the second time he'd called her *Juliet*. "I never asked," Gigi realized. "How do you know my real name?"

Brady didn't reply.

Was any of it real? she'd asked him.

All kinds of things can happen in a closed system.

But that system wasn't really closed, was it? And for the first time, a possibility occurred to Gigi—not just a possibility. A *likelihood.*

"You know, it's funny." Gigi looked Brady right in the eyes. "You told me about Knox's sponsor, but you never mentioned yours."

Brady didn't deny it.

Gigi thought about Knox saying that the Thorps weren't the only game in town, saying that Orion Thorp wasn't the only member of his family who liked to play. She thought about Brady playing the Grandest Game like Calla's life depended on it. About Knox and his scar and the way he'd said that Calla had *left*.

The next thing Gigi knew, Brady was standing to go, and Xander was in the doorway.

"For what it's worth," Brady told Gigi, "in the last six years, there hasn't been anyone who could make me forget Calla. There hasn't been a single *moment*." Brady almost smiled at her. "There were moments with you."

Xander waited until Brady had left, then shut the door and turned back to Gigi with one brow raised to ridiculous heights. "I'm sensing a story."

Gigi knew that she had to tell Xander—about the bug, the knife, Code Name Mimosas, all of it. She was *going* to tell him. But somehow, what came out instead was: "I lost. No Viking epics for me."

"Says who?" Xander crossed the room and sat down beside her. "I just placed an order for a very fetching Viking helmet to don during my recitation of said epics."

"Like you don't already have a Viking helmet?" Gigi replied.

"If you want to get *technical*, I just placed an order for a backup Viking helmet for my backup Viking helmet," Xander admitted. "This one is quite large."

Gigi didn't even have to *try* to smile with Xander.

He bumped his shoulder into hers. "Just because you didn't win," Xander said, producing a scone seemingly out of nowhere and handing it to Gigi, "doesn't mean the journey was anything less than epic, and I've written Viking sagas for less."

Tell him, Gigi thought, and the words were right there on her lips: *I found a bag hidden in the brush, and inside it, there was a wetsuit, an oxygen tank, a necklace that wasn't just a necklace, and a knife.*

"I once built a Rube Goldberg machine the purpose of which was smacking my own magnificent buttocks." Xander met Gigi's gaze. "I tell you this to say that I am a man of many talents—one of which happens to be listening. I am a very good listener."

The only reasonable thing I could possibly do right now is tell him.

What did it matter that Brady had asked her not to?

What did it matter that she'd spent more nights than she could count looking out into the darkness, waiting for Very Bad News to reappear?

What did it matter that he'd called her *sunshine*?

"I have until noon, right?" Gigi said.

Xander grinned. "For the ease of my future compositions, please tell me that whatever you have planned rhymes with *Valhalla* or *cheesesteak*."

Gigi gave Xander a look. "You're not going to ask what I'm up to?"

"Like I said, I'm a man of many talents." Xander slung an arm around her. "Among them, I give excellent platonic snuggles, and I know when *not* to ask."

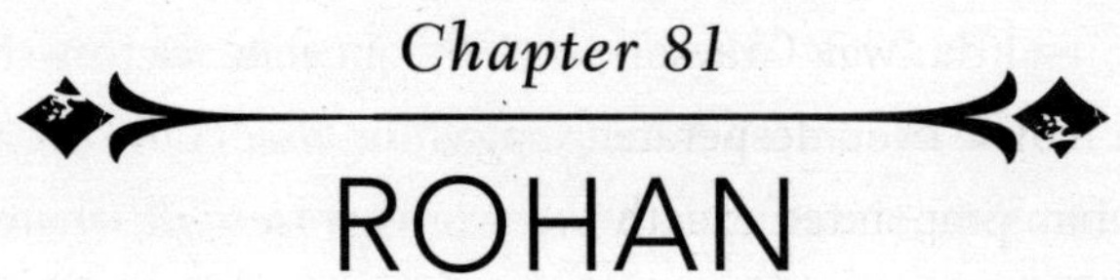

Chapter 81

ROHAN

Rohan didn't plan on spending more than four of the twelve hours between phase one and phase two of the game sleeping. He'd never needed as much sleep as other people, and years at the Mercy had honed his body and mind to operate on even less.

There were better uses for his time—such as determining his next move. *Five players left. Another challenge incoming.* With Savannah on his side, at least for the moment, Rohan could practically taste victory.

Stepping into the shower, he offered his face up to the spray, then began drawing on the steamed-up glass—with his finger this time, instead of a knife.

Knox Landry, the knight—*gone.* Same for Odette Morales, bishop, and Gigi Grayson, pawn. There was, however, a player to be added. *Grayson Hawthorne.*

Rohan's instincts said that Grayson was not a piece to be played but a player. A threat. Rohan settled on the infinity symbol to represent the Hawthorne in the game, then considered what he knew of Lyra Kane.

There was something there besides the way she looked at Grayson and the way Grayson looked right back at her, something raw and maybe even desperate. Something that could prove useful, once Rohan pinpointed exactly what it was. *Her father? Those notes she found.*

That just left Brady Daniels. *What is his game?* Rohan meditated for a moment on that. *How will he play?*

Brady Daniels.

Grayson Hawthorne.

Lyra Kane.

Eventually, Rohan's mind went to Savannah. Their alliance was, without question, his best chance of neutralizing Grayson and thereby Lyra.

There was just one matter to be settled between Savannah Grayson and Rohan first.

"I know you're there, British." Savannah spoke through the thick wooden door.

Rohan dragged a finger lightly around the ornate bronze keyhole on that door—the door to Savannah's room in this glass puzzle house. "You only know I'm here because I didn't bother masking my approach."

The door opened, and there she was, no longer wearing the ice-blue gown. Savannah's hair was wet, her body wrapped in a towel the same frosty shade as the gown.

Careful, boy. It was not often that Rohan heard the Proprietor's voice in his head, but he heard it now. *You know quite well how to recognize a trap.*

"The Hawthorne heiress." Rohan ignored the towel. "Avery Grambs."

"You think you've figured something out, do you?" Towel-clad, wet-haired Savannah could not have sounded any less impressed.

"Almost all of it," Rohan murmured.

Savannah stepped back, allowing him entry to her room. Rohan walked past her, well aware that, alliance or not, he was in enemy territory.

"I almost turned on you, down at the dock," Savannah said behind him. "It would have been easy enough." Rohan heard her lift her hand, most likely to touch the jagged ends of her hair. "*It was a dare*," Savannah said, not specifying that she was the one who'd issued that dare. "*He did it—with a knife*."

"No lies there," Rohan commented dryly.

"Grayson fancies himself my protector," Savannah said. "He would have put you down in a heartbeat."

Rohan shrugged. "He would have been welcome to try."

"The other Hawthornes would have broken up the fight—or possibly joined in—and that's when I would have pinned the power outages on you, too."

"But you didn't," Rohan noted dispassionately.

"Unlike some people, I have honor." Savannah Grayson was a woman of her word—and that *some people* hadn't been referring to him.

"It's not time to destroy me," Rohan said, his smile slow and a little jagged. "Yet."

Savannah stepped right up behind him. "Yet," she agreed.

Rohan turned, bringing them face-to-face. "Avery Grambs." Rohan said the name, then looked to her jaw. "And there's your tell, Savvy."

He brought one hand to the telltale muscle along her jawline, skimming her skin.

"It occurred to me," Rohan said calmly, "that the winner of the Grandest Game is crowned on a livestream with half the world watching."

Savannah didn't so much as blink.

Rohan leaned toward her, bringing his face even with hers. "Is that what you need for *revenge*?"

With no warning, Savannah drove her hands through his hair, curling her fingers, angling his head backward—and this time, she wasn't *attacking*. She also wasn't gentle. "What I need," she whispered, her lips very close to his, "is none of your concern."

Turnaround was fair play—his hands in *her* hair. Could she feel his breath on her neck, right below the place where her jawbone met her ear?

"Tell me, Savvy. What did the Hawthorne heiress do? What are you planning?"

She surged toward him, capturing his lips with hers. Some kisses were just kisses. Some kisses were torture. Some were necessary, the way breathing was.

Some kisses made a point.

Savannah Grayson was brutal. *And she cannot be trusted.* Rohan knew that. He relished it, pulling back, reining in the desire to devour her whole and allow himself to be devoured in return.

"Savvy. You're up to something."

"So what if I am? You'll use me. I'll use you. That's the deal." She touched him, and the power of that touch exploded through Rohan's body like fireworks, like fire, like the snapping of bone.

"Don't forget the part about destroying each other," Rohan whispered. "I'm looking forward to that."

"Do I strike you as a person who forgets anything, British?"

"Tell me," Rohan murmured into her lips. "What are you going to do if you win?"

"*When* I win," Savannah corrected.

"When you win." *You aren't going to win, love. Sooner or later, I'll be forced to flip the switch.*

Savannah stared at him and into him, like she could sense the darkness, like she wanted to see it. "*When* I win, I'm going to use the moment I claim the prize to let the world know exactly who Avery Grambs is. Exactly who *they* are."

"The Hawthornes," Rohan said.

"Without their army of lawyers to back them up. Without a PR machine. Without time to craft the perfect denial." Savannah grabbed Rohan's silk shirt in her hand. "They don't know that I know."

"Know what, Savvy?"

Savannah smiled, a tight-lipped, too-controlled smile that Rohan felt like fingernails down his back.

"Avery Grambs killed my father."

Chapter 82
LYRA

Lyra tried to sleep, and when she couldn't, she ran to tire herself out so she could get some sleep before the next phase of the game, to silence the voices in her mind.

In the grandest of games, there are no coincidences.

A Hawthorne did this.

A Hawthorne.

There are always three.

Lyra just kept running. She pushed herself past the point of all endurance, and when everything hurt, when her body threatened to quit, Lyra forced herself to keep going until she couldn't anymore.

Until she hit the ruins.

Her chest heaving, her muscles on fire, Lyra closed her eyes and paced her way through the charred and skeletal remains of the old mansion, out onto the ruined patio, right up to the edge of the cliff.

And just like that, Grayson was there. This time, Lyra felt his approach. She turned and opened her eyes.

"What we have," Grayson told her, "what Odette gave us—it's a start."

A muscle in Lyra's chest twinged. "There is no *we*, Grayson." Lyra looked down, then away—anywhere but at him. "You don't have to keep playing. We made it out. You held up your end of the deal."

"Rest assured, Lyra: I'm playing until the end." There was no arguing with that voice. No arguing with Grayson Hawthorne.

She could only *ask*. "Why?"

"I am afraid you will have to elaborate on that question."

Lyra couldn't keep herself from looking at him again, ripping him apart with her gaze, trying to see past the surface. "Why do you even care?"

About the Grandest Game.

About my father and omega.

About this.

About me.

"It's clear enough now," Grayson told her, "the mystery at hand concerns my family, too."

"Right." Lyra's lips felt painfully dry—her mouth, too, and her throat. "Of course."

What other answer had she expected? What other answer could there possibly be?

"Lyra." That was a command, a *look at me*, a plea.

She did. Look at him.

"I have always cared." Grayson's words came out rough and raw. "When you were nothing but a voice on the other end of the phone calling me an asshole. Hanging up on me. Baring your soul in a tone that made it clear you don't even know how to flinch. And *your voice*...just the sound of it, Lyra." Grayson looked away, like looking at her was almost physically painful. "I always cared."

Lyra shook her head, sending her dark hair flying. "And when you told me to stop calling," she replied, more sharpness in her tone than she felt, "you didn't mean it."

There had been a moment, back in the Grandest Escape Room, when she'd believed him. Why was it so hard to believe that now?

"That day, when you called, I was hurting." Grayson angled his eyes up toward hers. "For reasons that have nothing to do with you, I was coming undone, and I *do not do that*. As a rule, when I can no longer deny that I am hurting, I push people away. I find a way to hurt *more*."

"To prove you can," Lyra said, thinking of how many times she'd run until she hit and surpassed the point of pain. "To prove that no matter how much you hurt, you'll survive."

"Yes." This was Grayson as he'd been then, before all that practice being wrong. "I regretted telling you to stop calling. Immensely. I kept waiting for you to call again anyway. The number of hours I spent with your father's file, the number of ways I tried to find you—"

"You didn't!" Lyra didn't hold back this time. "You're Grayson Hawthorne. You don't *try* to do anything. You incline your head half an inch, and it's *done*." The words were coming faster now. "*They* found me—your brothers and Avery. They found me for the Grandest Game, so don't tell me you looked, Grayson. You're *Grayson Hawthorne*. You could have—"

"I couldn't." Grayson took a step forward. "And my brothers and Avery—they didn't."

Lyra's gaze snapped right back to his face.

"No one found you, Lyra. You came here," Grayson said, his voice low, the emphasis unmistakable. *You. Here.*

"Because I was invited!" Lyra had almost said those words once before.

Grayson didn't argue with her—not at first. He didn't have to. He was Grayson Hawthorne. His eyes did it for him.

And she just couldn't look away.

Finally, Grayson spoke, the intensity in his voice matched in every line of his stone-carved face. "I delivered Savannah's ticket myself. I offered it to Gigi first, as I'd been instructed to do, but Gigi declined. She wanted to win her own ticket—one of the four wild cards. Savannah was next in line."

"Savannah got a direct invitation to the game," Lyra said. "So?" But even as she said the word, Lyra flashed back suddenly to Brady on the dock, after Odette had given him her watch, saying that he'd been given a spot in the Grandest Game *twice*.

And Odette had also been one of Avery's picks.

"Savannah. Brady. Odette." Lyra swallowed. "Three players of Avery's choosing." She flashed back to the masquerade ball, to dancing with Grayson, to the moment when she'd been on the verge of saying *I'm here because I was invited* and ended up saying *because I deserve this* instead.

She'd been given her ticket. It had come with a note.

"After I heard your voice for the first time, I confronted Avery and my brothers." Grayson locked his eyes on hers. "I went to find out what the hell was going on, and the four of them made it very clear: You came to us."

You. Us.

"A wild card," Grayson said.

But Lyra *hadn't* come to them. She *hadn't* competed to win her ticket. Someone had sent it to her. Someone had written the words *YOU DESERVE THIS* on paper that crumbled to dust. Lyra couldn't call to mind an image of the handwriting, but she did remember one thing about it.

The ink was dark blue.

"The notes on the trees." Lyra willed Grayson to understand, even though she hadn't put her thoughts into words for him. "The ink was blue."

"Lyra?" Grayson turned her name into a question.

Someone had wanted her here.

Someone knew her father's names.

And Grayson *had* looked for her. A floodgate broke inside of Lyra. *The right kind of disaster just waiting to happen. A Hawthorne and a girl who has every reason to stay away from Hawthornes.*

Lyra reached for Grayson anyway. Her hand found its way to the back of his neck for once. "Someone sent me that ticket, Grayson. I thought it was Avery. But if it wasn't..."

"Then who the hell was it?" Grayson finished, his hand going to her cheek.

Lyra didn't pull back. He was a Hawthorne. *That* Hawthorne.

Your Hawthorne, Odette had said.

Lyra thought about the danger of touch. She thought about all the reasons she had not to do this. But as Grayson lowered his lips, Lyra rose up on her toes, tilted her head backward, moving like a dancer, needing this—and him.

Her long-held memory of *that kiss* gave way to *this kiss.* And this kiss was *everything.*

Chapter 83

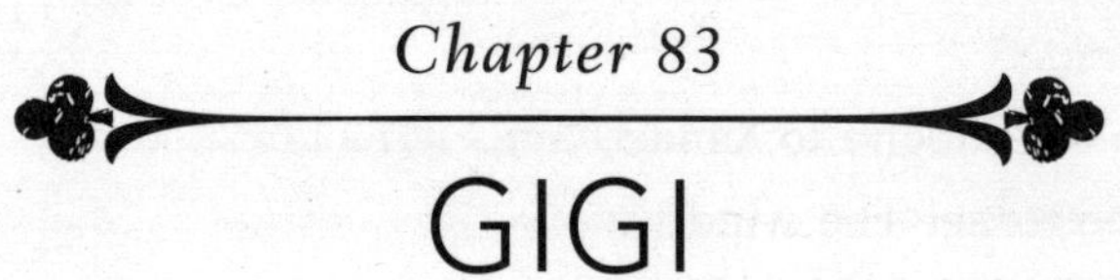

GIGI

"I know you're out there." Gigi had gone back to where she'd found the bag. No matter how many times she said the words, calling them out to the ocean, there was no reply.

"I know you can hear me. I know you're there." Time was ticking down. Her ride off the island left at noon. "I'm going to tell Grayson you're on Hawthorne Island," she warned, raising her voice. "Because if you're here, it's probably because Eve sent you, right?"

Gigi didn't even really know who Eve *was*, other than that she was young and rich and had a twisted connection to the Hawthorne family. Grayson had warned Gigi to stay away from her, too.

"If Eve sent you here, that can't be good, right? And I have a moral obligation to say something! I don't know why I haven't already. It's not like I'm even any good at keeping secrets. I *hate* secrets." Gigi swallowed. "I *hate* this."

She hadn't let herself think those words even once in the past seventeen months.

"And you!" Gigi added loudly. "I hate you very much, just for good measure." She reached into her pocket and withdrew the remains of the necklace. *All of it but the bug.* She launched it into the ocean.

"The bug I'll give to Xander," she warned.

No response. The wind whipped at Gigi's hair. She started to turn—and a hand clamped over her mouth from behind.

The hand was holding a rag. The rag smelled sweet—*sickly sweet, terribly sweet*. Gigi fought, but his other arm immobilized her.

"Easy there, sunshine."

Epilogue

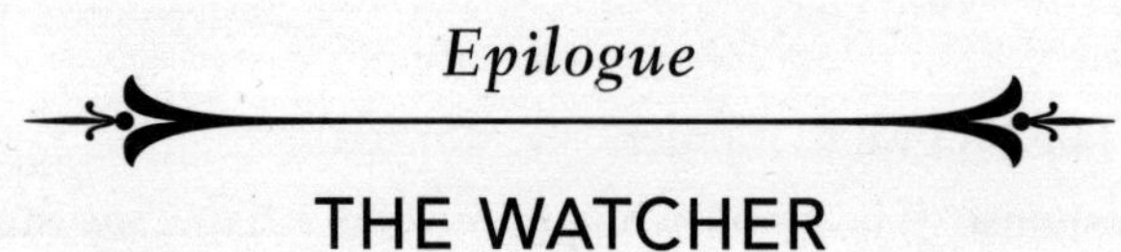

THE WATCHER

Some situations merited watching. *The Grandest Game. Jameson Hawthorne and Avery Grambs. The Kane girl, the boy from the Devil's Mercy, and all the rest.*

Perhaps watching was all the situation merited.

Perhaps there were no true problems to be solved.

Perhaps.

ACKNOWLEDGMENTS

I am so grateful to my entire publishing team at Little, Brown Books for Young Readers. I cannot imagine a more amazingly brilliant, creative, dedicated group of individuals, and I am in a continual state of awe about what this team has done for the entire Inheritance Games series.

Thank you to my editor, Lisa Yoskowitz, who saw me through three drafts of this book and two of the most major revisions of my life. There is no greater gift as an author than knowing that I can push myself and shoot for the stars because, even when I start to doubt myself, I have so much confidence in my editor's ability to help me get to where I want to be. Lisa, thank you for not batting an eye when I hand in a new draft and say "a lot of the same things happen, but almost all the words are new." Thank you for your suggestions, your help, and your support. I value our collaboration so much. Thank you also to Alex Houdeshell, for her insights into the first draft as well—Alex, I used every single piece of feedback you gave me, and it was all brilliant!

Thank you to Karina Granda for yet another amazing cover design and to artist Katt Phatt for some of my favorite cover art of all time. I am in awe of the amount of vision and artistic talent that goes into designing these covers and extremely grateful for the way these artists invite me into the process, so that we can work together to make sure each cover is its own kind of puzzle that truly reflects the book inside.

I am also incredibly grateful to the amazing sales and marketing teams who have helped get the entire Inheritance Games saga into so many hands. Savannah Kennelly, Bill Grace, and Emilie Polster, you are all so wonderfully creative and passionate, in addition to being *incredibly* fun to work with. I could sit around and brainstorm with you all day, and I am continually blown away by the way you can run with any idea and bring it to life in a far better way than I could have imagined! Thank you to marketing designers Becky Munich and Jess Mercado, for their beautiful work, and to my School & Library marketing team of Victoria Stapleton, Christie Michel, and Margaret Hansen for getting these books into the hands of young readers across the country. Similarly, I am incredibly grateful to the amazing sales team, who has done an amazing job at creating opportunities for readers of all ages to discover and invest in *The Grandest Game*: Shawn Foster, Danielle Cantarella, Claire Gamble, Katie Tucker, Leah CollinsLipsett, Cara Nesi, and John Leary.

I would also like to thank my publicist, Kelly Moran, for all her work. Kelly, I love your willingness to think big and have fun, and I also deeply appreciate the way you have protected my time and been so flexible in working with me through difficult times.

Thank you also to the production team who helped take the book from Word document to *actual book*. Thank you to production editor Marisa Finkelstein, who is always willing to go the extra mile; managing editor Andy Ball; production and manufacturing coordinator Kimberly Stella; copy editor Erin Slonaker; proofreaders Kathleen Go and Su Wu; and everyone who helped make sure that I had the schedule I needed to make this book the best I could possibly make it. I appreciate that—and you!—so much.

One of the most remarkable things to me about the entire Little, Brown team is that they are not only incredibly good at their jobs but also an absolute joy to work with, and I love how much the team clearly enjoys collaborating with both authors and one another. Thank you, Megan Tingley and Jackie Engel, for your leadership of this team and your role in sustaining that joy, as well as for your tremendous support of my books.

Thanks also go out to Janelle DeLuise and Hannah Koerner, for your work in subrights and helping to take this book to a global audience, as well as to our publishing partners at Penguin Random House UK, especially Anthea Townsend, Chloe Parkinson, and Michelle Nathan. Thank you also to my incredible publishers around the world for bringing the Inheritance Games series to readers in more than thirty countries—and more than thirty languages!—worldwide. And a special thanks goes out to all the translators who worked on *The Grandest Game*. I really appreciate the effort that goes into translating the puzzles, especially!

While we are on the topic of translated editions, I would also like to thank Sarah Perillo and Karin Schulze at Curtis Brown for their essential role in helping get this book to readers all over the world! And thank you to Jahlila Stamp and Eliza Johnson, who helped make sure all those foreign contracts actually got signed. In the past year, life has been more chaotic and I have been less organized than I ever have been, and I am truly grateful for your persistence, kindness, and patience.

I am one of the few authors I know who has been with the same agent and agency for my entire career—since I was a teenager!—and

I am so grateful to work with everyone at Curtis Brown. Elizabeth Harding, thank you for your work not just on this book but also on every book that came before it! It has been a long haul over almost two decades now, and I am so thankful both for our professional relationship and for all the support you have given me through so many seasons of my life. Holly Frederick, thank you for being such an advocate for my books, stretching way back to when I was in college! I'm so excited about so much of what we've managed to achieve these past couple of years. And thank you also to Eliza Leung, for making sure all *those* contracts get signed, and for *your* persistence, kindness, and patience, and to Manizeh Karim for your help behind the scenes.

Writing *The Grandest Game* involved all kinds of research. One of the most awesome things about having once been a professor is that my amazing friend group includes experts on all manners of random things! For this book, special thanks go out to Dr. Jessica Ruyle, radar expert extraordinaire, who made me smile so much as we talked through the science of listening devices. All mistakes in the text are mine, because Jessica is brilliant!

Finally, I want to thank my family, who have gone above and beyond in the last year to support me. Some seasons of life are more difficult than others, and I literally could not have written this book without the love and support of and sacrifices made by my parents and my husband. Thank you, thank you, thank you.

Kim Haynes Photography

JENNIFER LYNN BARNES

is the number one *New York Times* bestselling author of more than twenty acclaimed young adult novels, including the Inheritance Games series, the Debutantes series, *The Lovely and the Lost* and the Naturals series. Jen is also a Fulbright Scholar with advanced degrees in psychology, psychiatry and cognitive science. She received her PhD from Yale University in 2012 and was a professor of psychology and professional writing for many years. She invites you to visit her online at jenniferlynnbarnes.com or on Instagram @authorjenlynnbarnes.

The games continue in

GLORIOUS RIVALS

Summer 2025

DON'T MISS THE SERIES THAT STARTED IT ALL!

'IMPOSSIBLE TO PUT DOWN'
Buzzfeed

OVER 4 MILLION COPIES SOLD

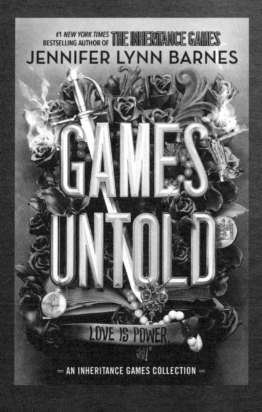